One dynasty,
passionate tales...

The Elliotts:
Bedroom Secrets

Three intense and sexy romances from three
beloved Mills & Boon authors!

The Elliotts:
Bedroom Secrets

KARA LENNOX

BARBARA DUNLOP

ROXANNE ST CLAIRE

MILLS & BOON

All the characters in this book have no existence outside the imagination of the author, and have no relation whatsoever to anyone bearing the same name or names. They are not even distantly inspired by any individual known or unknown to the author, and all the incidents are pure invention.

First published in Great Britain 2011
by Mills & Boon, an imprint of Harlequin (UK) Limited,
Eton House, 18-24 Paradise Road, Richmond, Surrey TW9 1SR

THE ELLIOTTS: BEDROOM SECRETS
© by Harlequin Enterprises II B.V./S.à.r.l 2011

Under Deepest Cover, Marriage Terms and *The Intern Affair* were first published in Great Britain by Harlequin (UK) Limited in separate, single volumes.

Under Deepest Cover © Harlequin Books SA 2006
Marriage Terms © Harlequin Books SA 2006
The Intern Affair © Harlequin Books SA 2006

Special thanks and acknowledgement are given to Kara Lennox, Barbara Dunlop & Roxanne St Claire for their contributions to THE ELLIOTTS series.

ISBN: 978 0 263 88347 3

05-0611

Printed and bound in Spain
by Blackprint CPI, Barcelona

UNDER
DEEPEST COVER

BY
KARA LENNOX

Kara Lennox, a Texas native, has been an art director, typesetter, textbook editor and reporter. She's worked in a boutique, a health club and an ad agency. She's been an antiques dealer and even a blackjack dealer. But no work has made her happier than writing romance novels.

When not writing, Kara indulges in an ever-changing array of weird hobbies. (Her latest passions are treasure hunting and creating mosaics.) She loves to hear from readers. You can visit her webpage and drop her a note at www.karalennox.com.

For Melissa Jeglinski
Thanks so much for inviting me into the Elliott world.
The story was perfect for me—you know me so well.

One

"**Y**ou have to get me *out* of this!" Lucy Miller hissed into her encrypted cell phone, the one that had been delivered to her home a few weeks ago. The phone had rung just as she'd left a staff meeting. She'd ducked into the ladies' rest room, where she'd checked every stall to make sure she was alone.

"Relax, Lucy," said the soothing voice Lucy had come to know so well. She had often fantasized about what the man who owned that deep, sexy voice might look like, but not today. Today she was too terrified to fantasize about anything but getting out of this situation with her skin intact.

"Don't you tell me to relax," she whispered back. "You aren't the one stuck in this bank trying to act normal when she knows she's about to get liquidated."

"Liquidated? You must be watching too much *Get Smart.* No one is trying to kill you."

"You didn't see the man who was following me. I know a hit man when I see one. He was wearing a coat, and it's like ninety degrees outside."

"It's also raining in D.C. today. He probably had on a raincoat."

"Casanova, you're not listening! My cover has been blown. Someone has been in my apartment. Either you get me out of here, or I'll hop the first plane I can find to South America and I'll take all my data with me!"

"No! Lucy, be reasonable—"

"I'm done being reasonable. I've done everything you asked without question. I've trusted you implicitly, though I've never met you and don't even know your name. Now it's your turn to trust me. I'm not stupid. If you don't get me out, this very expensive little cell phone is going into the nearest sewer, and you'll never hear from me again."

"All right! I'll be there by five-thirty, six at the latest. Can you hang tight till then? Can you make it home?"

Lucy took a deep breath, trying to calm herself. She'd spotted her tail three days ago, and she'd realized yesterday that someone had searched her apartment. But so far her observer was keeping his distance. Maybe she could make it a few more hours. She struggled for a reasonable tone of voice. "I'll do my best. But if anything happens, tell my parents I love them, okay?"

"You'll be fine, drama queen."

Lucy disconnected before she said something she'd regret. Drama queen? Did Casanova think she was some flaky paranoid? Hadn't she proved her worth over the past weeks? Casanova. Who'd come up with that handle, anyway, and why?

She put the cell phone back in her purse and started to exit the rest room, but then she caught a look at herself in the mirror. She looked like a mad woman, her wavy brown hair escaping from its customary bun and frizzing around her face, her cheeks flush with panic, eyes wild with fear behind her glasses. She took five minutes to neaten her hair, powder her nose and apply her pink lipstick. The shade did nothing for her, but that didn't matter. She wasn't exactly supermodel material these days. She only wore a little makeup because she was in an executive position and the other female executives did.

She'd been trying to fit in, not call attention to herself.

When she looked and felt more composed, she left the sanctuary of the rest room and headed for her office, hoping she could close the door and hole up in there for the rest of the afternoon. She was afraid that if she had to deal with anyone, she would fall apart.

Some spy you turned out to be, Lucy Miller. Disintegrating at the first sign of danger.

As luck would have it, she rounded a corner and ran right into the bank's portly CEO, the man who'd hired her.

"Oh, hello, Lucy," he said politely. "I was just looking for you."

"Sorry, I was in the ladies' room. My lunch isn't sitting well, I'm afraid." She figured he wouldn't ask too many questions about that. He was easily embarrassed, she'd discovered.

He scrutinized her face with his one good eye. The other had been destroyed in some kind of accident, though she didn't know the details. Her skin prickled with nerves. Could he see her fear?

"You don't look well," he said. "You're very pale. Are you sure you're okay?"

"I'm fine, really." Just like Mr. Vargov to be concerned. He was a kind, fatherly man, a friend of her uncle Dennis who'd given her this job when she sorely needed a safe, stable employment. She'd been underqualified for the fund auditor's job, with her piddling bachelor's degree in finance and no experience to speak of, but she felt she'd performed the job well.

Too well, in Mr. Vargov's opinion. He thought she was *too* conscientious. He hadn't taken her suspicions about embezzlement very seriously. That was why she'd gone to Homeland Security. That was how she'd gotten involved with Casanova.

"Why don't you take the rest of the afternoon off?" Mr. Vargov suggested.

"Oh, I couldn't. You said you wanted those reports—"

"The reports can wait. Your uncle would have my hide if he found out I was cracking the whip over you when you're sick."

"Thanks, Mr. Vargov. Maybe I will leave just a little early if I don't feel better."

"I think you should."

And maybe, she thought, if she left early, she could fool the man or men who'd been following her. She wouldn't mind saying goodbye to this place. She'd needed a place to recover, to heal, to get her bearings, and Alliance Trust had provided that. Her co-workers had been kind, the working conditions pleasant. Her boss hadn't required too much of her, and the salary had been much higher than someone her age and experience normally earned.

But it was time to move on. She would spend another

hour downloading as much information as she could onto her supercapacity memory stick, then leave here and never come back.

Casanova would take her to a safe house. He'd promised. And then, when all the arrests were made and the perpetrators were in jail, she could start over somewhere else. A new job, a new life.

It sounded like heaven.

At ten after three, she was ready. She stashed the memory stick in her bra. Taking only her purse and umbrella, she told Peggy Holmes, Mr. Vargov's executive secretary and the woman who knew everything, that she was going home early due to an upset stomach.

"Oh, my dear, I hope it's nothing serious. You've missed only one day of work since you started here, and that was for a root canal. On a lower-left molar, I believe." Peggy was in her sixties and had worked for Mr. Vargov for twenty-something years. With her tightly permed hair and dumpy, big-bosomed figure, she was everyone's grandmother. But Lucy knew she was highly intelligent with an astounding memory for detail and an efficiency that bordered on pathological.

"I'll be fine," Lucy said, hoping it was true.

The idea of walking into the parking garage alone held little appeal. One of the security guards would have been happy to escort her, but if a hit man was waiting for her there, she might just be dragging the guard into danger.

She shouldn't behave as expected, she decided. She would take the bus. There was a bus stop just a block from her office.

The weather was warm and humid with an insistent, light rain falling, but Lucy felt cold inside as she exited her building. She put up her umbrella, taking the opportunity to glance surreptitiously around to see if she spotted the man in the raincoat. But she saw no one suspicious.

She walked up the block, her sensible low heels tapping against the wet sidewalk. She pretended to window-shop, not wanting to stand at the bus stop too long. When she saw the bus approaching, she hurried to the stop and dashed onboard just in time. The only other people to board with her were a mom with two small children. Thank God.

When she got off at the stop near her Arlington, Virginia, town house, she still saw no one. Maybe she'd outmaneuvered him. Or maybe he'd given up on her, decided she was no one to worry about. He wouldn't have found anything incriminating in her home. She kept the memory stick with her at all times.

Her tiny town house had only one door, and this morning she'd rigged it so she would know if anyone had been inside. She checked; the tiny hair she'd caught between door and frame was still in place. She inserted her key and entered, pausing to close her wet umbrella and shake it off on the porch.

She'd lived here for two years. Her uncle had found it for her, and she'd committed to renting it without ever seeing it. It was nice but boring—like her life had been until a few weeks ago—and she'd made no effort to turn it into a real home. She wouldn't mind walking away from it.

As she closed and bolted the door, a hand clamped over her mouth and a strong arm hauled her against a rock-hard body.

Panic rising in her throat, Lucy didn't think, she just acted. The umbrella was still in her hand. She aimed it behind her and jabbed her attacker in the thigh as hard as she could.

Her attacker issued a strangled gasp and loosened his grip on her just enough that she could bend her knees and drop. As she did, she grabbed one of the man's denim-clad legs and yanked, throwing him off balance. He fell onto the marble floor with a painful-sounding thunk. Still gripping the umbrella, Lucy straightened, swiveled toward her attacker and went for his throat with the sharp tip of her impromptu weapon.

He grabbed the umbrella and deflected it. "Lucy, stop! It's me, Casanova!" He jerked the umbrella out of her hands and tossed it aside. Unfortunately, he also knocked her off balance. She fell on top of him and found herself staring into a pair of the most remarkable blue eyes she'd ever seen.

"Casanova?" But she knew it was him. She'd recognized his voice instantly.

"Jeez, woman, are you insane? You almost killed me."

"You broke into my home and attacked me, I fought back, but I'm insane?"

"You're not supposed to be home until later. I had no idea who you were. And where did you learn to fight like that?"

"I took a self-defense class. What are you doing in my house?"

"If you're under surveillance, I couldn't just come to the front door. I broke in."

"How? I have an alarm."

"Your neighbor doesn't." He grinned, and Lucy looked up and into the living room, where she saw a huge hole in her wall. "You came through the wall? You didn't frighten Mrs. Pfluger, did you? And what's my landlord going to say?"

"You won't be here to find out. We're leaving."

That was the first comforting thing he'd said. "Then you believe me?"

"Your house is riddled with more listening devices than the American Embassy in Russia. Someone's been here, all right." His expression turned grim.

Lucy dropped her voice to a whisper. "Are they listening? Right now?"

"My guess is the bugs are connected to a voice-activated recording device. They—whoever they are— probably aren't monitoring live when you're not supposed to be home. But we don't have much time. They'll catch up with you soon. I want to be long gone by the time they get here. So if you could, uh…"

Lucy was humiliated to realize she was still lying on top of him, and she hadn't made even a token effort to move. She could feel every hard-muscled inch of him pressed against her body, and she had to say the effect wasn't unpleasant. It had been a very long time since any man had touched her more intimately than with a handshake.

She scrambled off of Casanova, managing to knee him in the groin in the process, though not intentionally.

"Damn, woman, you're dangerous." He sat up and shook his head as if to clear it, and she got her first really good look at him. In all her fantasies he'd been handsome, but nothing had prepared her for the reality. He was *gorgeous*—six feet of highly toned body, thick, jet-black hair and those incredible eyes. His hair was all mussed from their impromptu romp, the way it might look if he'd just gotten out of bed.

Oh, Lucy. Knock it off.

"You've got exactly three minutes to pack anything you absolutely need. Medications, a toothbrush, change of underwear. Don't worry about clothes."

Lucy believed him. She ran into the bedroom, grabbed a couple of pairs of underwear and socks, her toothbrush and her allergy medicine. All of it could be tossed into a tiny backpack. Since she had a couple of minutes, she peeled off her skirt and sticky pantyhose and put on a pair of jeans and her running shoes. She didn't know where they would go, how they would travel or how long before they stopped, and she wanted to be comfortable.

She emerged from the bedroom with seconds to spare. Casanova was waiting for her, looking antsy, rolling up on the balls of his feet. "About time."

"You said three minutes, I took three minutes." Then she couldn't help it. She grinned.

"You're enjoying this."

"In a way," she admitted. It had been a very long time since she'd had adrenaline pumping through her veins and color in her cheeks. Years. She'd forgotten how good it felt. "And you enjoy it, too, or you wouldn't be a spy to begin with."

He nodded, conceding the point. "Let's go."

Casanova led Lucy through the hole he'd made in her sheetrock. "I'm glad Mrs. Pfluger wasn't home," she said. "You'd have probably scared her to death."

"What makes you so sure she isn't home?" And sure enough, sitting in the living room watching her TV was Lucy's neighbor, Mrs. Pfluger, who was eighty-two years old. She smiled at Casanova. "So, you're back," she said with a bright smile. Although she was nearly incapacitated with arthritis, her mind was as sharp as any twenty-year-old's. "Hello, Lucy, dear."

Lucy stared, dumbfounded. "Do you two know each other?"

"We do now," Mrs. Pfluger said. "He came to my door, and when he explained you were in danger from some terrorists, and that he needed my help so you could escape…" She shrugged helplessly, as if to say, Well, you know how these things are. Like they happened every day.

"But the wall. He ruined your wall," Lucy said.

"He handed me a wad of cash to pay for it." She turned back to Casanova. "Now, while you were busy searching Lucy's apartment, I gathered the things you would need." She gestured toward an old shopping bag. "They're clothes and other things from my fat days. I won't need them back."

Casanova inspected the contents of the shopping bag, then grinned and looked at Lucy. "Excellent. Lucy, put these things on. You're about to become Bessie Pfluger."

Bryan Elliott, aka Casanova, tried not to grin as he watched Lucy Miller wiggle into a pair of huge orange polyester stretch pants and pin them at the waist. She'd turned out to be a surprise.

He already knew a lot about her from the background information he'd obtained—where she grew up, where she'd gone to school, her employment history. He'd pegged her as the perfect mole to work inside Alliance where the embezzling was taking place—dutiful, conscientious, intelligent. And she was all those things. Over the past few weeks she had proved amazingly helpful, downloading tons of information onto the supercapacity memory stick, following his instructions without question.

In person, though, she was surprisingly feisty—and damned efficient at defending herself. With the proper training— No, he shouldn't even think about that. He'd let himself get sucked into a life of lies and shadows, and he was in so deep now he could never lead a normal life. He didn't wish that on sweet Lucy Miller, who, by all accounts, was ignorant of the uglier side of life.

But she was no longer ignorant about the ugliest clothes in the universe. She'd topped the orange pants with a tentlike housecoat with rainbows all over it. She'd tucked her hair up into a silver, curly-haired wig and donned an old pair of Mrs. Pfluger's glasses, which had red frames and were only slightly uglier than Lucy's own.

"My old walker is over there." Mrs. Pfluger gestured toward a corner of her living room.

"This will never work," Lucy said on a moan. "No one will believe I'm eighty years old."

"Eighty-two," Mrs. Pfluger said.

"Trust me, if anyone is watching the place, they won't look past the obvious at the place next door." He unfolded the portable walker and set it in front of Lucy. "Let's see you do an old-lady walk."

Lucy hunched over the walker and did a creditable imitation of an arthritic senior citizen inching along.

"Oh, heavens," Mrs. Pfluger said. "Please don't tell me I look like that when I walk."

"I'm exaggerating," Lucy said. Then she turned to her neighbor and gave her a spontaneous hug. "Oh, Mrs. Pfluger, I can't thank you enough for helping us out like this. I mean, you don't even know this guy."

"He showed me a badge," Mrs. Pfluger said innocently, having no clue the badge he'd shown her was fake and could be bought on any street corner in D.C. "Anyway, he has trustworthy eyes. He'll take care of you."

"I'm counting on it," Lucy said, giving Bryan a meaningful look. "Can we go now?"

Bryan thanked Lucy's elderly neighbor, too, then "helped" Lucy out the door and down the wheelchair ramp.

"Keep your head down. That's it," he whispered. "You're doing great. If I didn't know better, *I'd* swear you were someone's grandmother." But he did know better. The body that had been pressed against his when she'd fallen on him was not the slightest bit grandmotherly. In fact, he'd been surprised at how slim and firm she was beneath the frumpy suit she'd worn.

His Mercedes was parked at the curb. Knowing the town house might be under surveillance, he'd made no attempt to be stealthy, walking right up to the neighbor's door and ringing the bell. He'd known she would be home. He'd also known she'd been an army nurse in Korea and her husband had been a World War II veteran. He'd been counting on her patriotism to make her willing to help him out, and he'd been right.

As he usually was. He liked to cover all the bases.

As soon as the motor started and the car was underway, he relaxed slightly. If anyone had been watching, Lucy's old-lady act had fooled them. No one was following.

Bryan drove to a mall parking lot and pulled the Mercedes into a spot fairly close to where he'd found it.

"Why are we stopping here?" Lucy asked.

"Switching cars." He turned off the engine and pulled his Multi-Key from the ignition.

"What is that?" Lucy asked, pointing to the strange-looking device. Then she gasped. "Oh my God, you stole this car!"

"Just borrowed it. The owner is blissfully shopping at Marshall Fields. She'll never know."

"That is really scary," Lucy said. "That such a device even exists, and that our government employees steal cars."

"Government employees do a lot worse than steal cars, I'm afraid," he said as they exited the Mercedes. Unfortunately, he'd just found out the hard way what certain government employees were capable of.

Lucy grabbed the walker from the back seat, but she didn't use it. She walked beside him with a spring in her step, lithe and graceful. He led her to the car he'd arrived in, a silver Jaguar XJE. Since he'd been driving his personal wheels and not a "company car," he hadn't wanted to risk it being identified. Thus the switcheroo.

"Hmm, I liked this even better than the Mercedes," she commented as she put the walker in the trunk. "Is this one stolen, too?"

"No, this one's mine."

"I hadn't realized government employees earned enough money to afford a Jag."

"We don't. My government salary isn't my only source of income." He'd never imagined his cover business, the one he set up to satisfy friends and family, would turn so lucrative. He opened the passenger door for her. "You can ditch the disguise, now. We're safe."

"Thank God." She pulled off the wig. Her real hair pulled loose from its bun in the process, spilling over her shoulders in a rich chestnut cascade. He'd never found brown hair all that exciting before, but Lucy's was thick and luscious.

By the time he'd made it around to the driver's side, Lucy was out of her housecoat, which she'd thrown on over her white tailored blouse. Then she cursed. "I forgot my jeans."

"No, I put them in—" Then he stopped. He'd been so fascinated watching Lucy shimmy out of them, revealing a glimpse of her sensible white panties, that he *had* forgotten to bring the jeans along. "We'll get you some clothes, don't worry."

He had no business thinking about Lucy's panties, sensible or otherwise. He had a helluva problem here.

Finding the listening devices was disturbing enough. He'd been sure Lucy was exaggerating, that no one was following her or sneaking into her home. But she hadn't installed those listening devices herself.

In fact, once he'd examined the bug in her telephone, the list of suspects who could have planted it had shrunk to a handful. That bug was the latest technology, purchased from Russia. So new, in fact, that only his agency had access to it. Besides the Russians, of course. And he didn't think the Russians were involved in this.

Someone in his own organization had betrayed him, which meant his life and Lucy's weren't worth a used teabag unless he found out which agent was the Benedict Arnold—and neutralized him or her, fast.

Two

They drove in silence for a few minutes. Bryan took a circuitous route out of the city, darting on and off the freeway to be absolutely certain they weren't being followed. Then he headed north on Interstate 95 as a plan slowly formed.

"Are you okay?" he asked Lucy. She was awfully quiet. He'd expected her to be peppering him with questions about where they were going and what would happen next, questions to which he didn't have all the answers.

"I'm fine."

"I'm sorry I put you in danger."

"I knew what I was getting into when I signed on for this gig. You told me there would be some risk."

She didn't know the half of it. He'd never expected the risk to come from his own people. "You did great. I wish we could have finished the job, though."

"I did."

"Pardon me?"

"After I talked to you, I knew I wouldn't be returning to Alliance Trust. So I threw caution out the window. Before, I was careful to cover my tracks when I downloaded information. I figured that didn't matter anymore. So I just downloaded everything in sight. Practically the whole computer system. I can't believe how much that little memory stick holds."

"You downloaded everything?" he asked, hardly able to believe it.

"Everything I'll need. It will take some time to go through it all. Whoever was embezzling from the retirement funds was very sneaky. But I've got calendars, phone lists, log-on and log-off times, passwords, who attended what meeting when. Using a process of elimination, I can figure out who made the illicit withdrawals—I know I can."

"You won't have to. The agency has some of the best minds in the country—" He stopped. Until he knew who had betrayed him, he didn't dare turn this information over to anyone. One keystroke, and all of the evidence Lucy had risked her life for could be erased.

"I could do it," Lucy said. "I'm very good at puzzles. Maybe your organization has experts and high-tech equipment, but I know the people involved. I know how everything worked at that bank. No one is more qualified than me to analyze this data."

She might just be right. "What will you need?"

"A computer powerful enough to handle the amount of data involved. A quiet place to work. That's it."

The plan he'd been working on earlier became a bit firmer in his mind. It was kind of crazy. But he didn't know any other way to keep Lucy safe. He had access to any number of safe houses, but safe from whom? Everyone who was part of this mission knew those houses, too—Tarantula, Stungun, Orchid and his immediate supervisor, Siberia. His list of suspects. Four people whom, until an hour ago, he would have trusted with his life.

"I think I can accommodate you," he said.

"Okay, then." She settled back into her seat, looking satisfied. "Where are we going?"

Finally. He'd wondered when she would get around to asking that. "New York."

"Your home turf."

Bryan felt a prickle of apprehension. How did she know that?

"Your accent," she said before he had a chance to ask. "I went to school with a guy from New York. Long Island. You sound just like him."

Observant little thing, wasn't she? During his training, he'd learned to erase every trace of accent from his voice. His safety, and that of his wealthy family, depended on keeping every detail of his personal life separate from his life at the agency. It was like that for all the agents he worked with. They all used their code names, and they never revealed any personal information for any reason.

How had he let his guard down long enough that Lucy had figured out where he was from? Maybe he was slipping. Because of the intense pressure, a lot of agents didn't last long in the field.

"You work for the CIA?" she asked.

He used to. They'd recruited him in college, when he'd been studying business management with every intention of joining the family business, Elliott Publication Holdings. They said it was because of his straight As and his uncommon athleticism. He'd worked a lot of undercover.

Then a nameless, faceless person had recruited him to a newly formed investigative arm of Homeland Security, an agency so secret it didn't have a name. The agency had no central office, and it wasn't mentioned in the national budget. Basically it didn't exist.

Lying usually came easily to him. But for some reason he didn't want to lie straight-out to Lucy. He settled for a partial truth. "I work for Homeland Security."

"I didn't know Homeland Security had its own spies."

"Things are still evolving there."

"How does one become a spy?"

"Why, are you interested in joining up?"

"Maybe. Anything's better than what I was doing."

He'd only been kidding, but she was serious. "So why did you work at a bank if you didn't like it?"

She shrugged. "It was expected of me. And the money was pretty good. I'd been thinking about doing something else, though."

"Like what?"

"I dunno. Running away and joining the circus, maybe. I'd make a good lion tamer."

"You?" he blurted out, then wished he hadn't, given Lucy's reaction. He'd insulted her.

"Why couldn't I tame lions?"

"I'm sure you could. You could poke them with umbrellas."

"I think you're making fun of me. But you didn't think it was so funny when I had you on the floor. I almost gave you an impromptu tracheotomy with my trusty umbrella." She looked around the car. "Oh, we left it behind. I liked that umbrella."

"I'll buy you a new one," he said, feeling a bit sorry for her. Her life had been disrupted, and it would never be the same. He didn't think that fact had sunk into her head yet.

"We won't be going back, then," she said.

"Not in the foreseeable future."

"Good. If I'd had to spend one more night in that boring town house with its boring white walls, wearing those boring suits, I'd have slit my wrists."

She'd surprised him again. He'd done a considerable amount of research on Miss Lucy Miller. She came from a solid Kansas farming family, had attended the state university, got good grades. She'd been working at a job for which she was underqualified, but her employee reviews had come up glowing.

The only mystery about Lucy Miller was a period of about two years shortly after her college graduation, for which Bryan could not unearth much information. Her passport indicated she'd done some traveling abroad. The best he could figure, she'd been soaking up some culture before tying herself down to a serious career. She had an older brother who lived in Holland, so she might have been staying with him.

"My family will be worried," she said.

"You won't be able to contact them."

"Ever?" she asked in a small voice. "Am I going into the witness protection program?"

"Is that what you want?"

She sighed. "I could stand a new identity. I've always hated the name Lucy. But I want to pick the name."

"What would you pick?"

"Certainly not something as silly as Casanova—though I guess given the way you schmoozed Mrs. Pfluger, it fits. She's always been mean as a snake to me."

"Casanova wasn't my idea. You can call me Bryan." She would have learned his real name soon enough.

"And you can call me…Lindsay. Lindsay Morgan."

"Sounds very sophisticated. Does it have any significance? Do you know anyone named Lindsay? Or Morgan?"

"No. I've always liked the actress Lindsay Wagner. You know, the Bionic Woman. I catch it on late-night TV. And Morgan—I don't know. I pulled it out of thin air."

Exactly what Bryan wanted to hear. "Then Lindsay Morgan it is. Get used to it."

Oh, God, she thought, he was serious. She was really getting a new identity. A new life. A new job, a new home, maybe somewhere exciting like New York. She knew she should be terrified. Ruthless criminals with ties to international terrorism had broken into her home and planted bugs. They might even now be searching for her, intending to kill her.

But she could feel nothing but anticipation.

She wished her parents didn't have to worry, though. She wanted to ask Bryan if she would ever see them again. But she had a feeling he really didn't know the answer to that question. Something was troubling him. She got the feeling he was on shaky ground, that the turn this investigation had taken had thrown him for a loop.

He hadn't believed her when she'd told him she was being followed. He'd only come to her town house because she'd threatened to disappear with all the data.

He'd been very surprised to discover she was right, that the operation was blown to bits.

Did he suspect she was the one who'd blown it?

"I didn't give myself away," she said abruptly, wanting to clear this up right now. "I was extremely careful. Until today I did the downloading only five or ten minutes at a time, always when I was alone in my office, the door closed. I never said anything to anyone. Ever. And no one had access to the memory stick. I kept it in my bra."

He looked over at her. "Really? Is it there now?"

"Yes."

The car swerved slightly, and not for any apparent reason. Lucy wondered if something as innocent as mentioning her bra had startled Bryan. But how could it? The guy was a spy—he'd probably seen things unimaginable to normal people. Surely the mention of women's underwear wouldn't faze him.

Especially *her* underwear, which was about as boring as underwear could get.

It had been a very long time since anything she said or did had any effect on the opposite sex. She had buried that flirtatious, reckless girl under a frumpy suit, thick glasses and mousy hair, and she'd done it for a reason, she reminded herself.

So Bryan had probably been avoiding a bump in the road.

They drove for almost five hours, but the days were long in July, so it was still daylight when they hit New York. Lucy had been to the city many times, but it had been a while, and she'd forgotten how much she loved it. New York had an energy unlike any other city in the universe. Even if she'd had her eyes closed, she'd have known she was here. The traffic noise and exhaust fumes were peculiar only to this place.

"Are we staying in Manhattan?" she asked.

"Yes."

"Are you putting me up in a hotel?"

"No. I don't want to go anyplace where ID is required until we get your new name officially established."

"A safe house, then?"

"The safest."

He flashed her a brief smile, and it was the first time she'd seen him looking anything but grim since they'd met. That smile did things to her insides. No wonder cranky Mrs. Pfluger had become so cooperative. If Bryan had taken ten more minutes, the older woman probably would have dropped her own pants. Jeez, Lucy couldn't believe she'd taken off her jeans in front of a strange man. But she'd been just panicked enough not to care.

They'd crossed over to Manhattan via the Lincoln Tunnel, and in midtown they were surrounded by skyscrapers, buses, cars, taxis and pedestrians. People were everywhere. And such interesting people! All colors, shapes and sizes. Some were elegantly dressed—theatergoers on their way to catch the curtain perhaps. Some in bedraggled business attire, waving down taxis, looked like they were just getting off from a long day at the office. And of course there were the ubiquitous colorful characters—hot-dog vendors, shady men selling designer-watch knock-offs and bootleg DVDs, and your garden-variety vagrants.

She'd forgotten how much she loved this city, though it held some painful reminders, as well. Normally she didn't allow herself to think about her last time here, when she'd made a headlong dash home, crying the entire way. But now she did, and she found the pain wasn't so sharp anymore. She felt more sad and wistful than anything.

She'd healed during the past two years. She'd needed the downtime, the safe haven her job at the bank had provided. But she was ready to move on now—older and wiser. She was actually grateful to the embezzler, whoever he or she was, for shaking her out of her boring, complacent life, or she might have remained there indefinitely, afraid to live again.

She was living now, that was for sure. Riding up Tenth Avenue in a Jaguar with a spy. Not your everyday occurrence.

Lucy cracked open her window, and the wonderful city smells assailed her. She got a whiff of some exotic food—garlic, tarragon, curry—and her stomach rumbled. It occurred to her she hadn't eaten since breakfast, and even then she'd barely managed to choke down some yogurt. She'd been too nervous about her situation.

"I'm starving," she said. "Any chance this safe house will have food in the fridge? Or maybe we can order in Chinese?" she asked hopefully.

"Don't worry, I'll feed you."

They were driving through the Upper West Side now, the street lined with posh shops, trendy restaurants and bodegas, and residential high-rises where the beautiful people lived. Most of her time in New York had been spent around here, near Cruz's apartment.

They passed a restaurant called Une Nuit—"One Night" in French. Though it was early by Manhattan standards, a line of trendily dressed hopefuls was already forming at the door.

"I read about that place," she said, nodding toward it. "In *People* magazine, I think. Or maybe *The Buzz*. Some movie star had a birthday party there or something."

"It was one of the Hilton sisters."

"Oh, so you keep up with the gossip? How does a spy have time to read *The Buzz*?"

"Actually, I didn't read about it. I was there."

"No kidding? You know the Hilton sisters?" Lucy had always been starstruck. She'd been addicted to celebrity magazines since junior high and had fantasized about someday being one of the beautiful people—or at least hanging out with them.

She'd learned the hard way that the celebrity scene wasn't all parties and glamour. In fact, beneath all the glitz, it could get pretty rotten. But even after her unhappy brush with that life, she hadn't lost her fascination with it.

Bryan didn't answer, but he pulled his car around a corner and into an underground garage, inserting a pass card to gain entrance.

"Um, we're not actually stopping to eat, are we?" Lucy asked, looking down at her orange polyester pants. "I mean, I'd love to go to that restaurant someday, but they wouldn't let me in the door dressed like this."

He grinned. "I could get you in. But, no, we're not going there right now. This is actually your safe house." He pulled into a reserved parking space and cut the engine.

"Seems a funny place for a safe house," she commented. "I thought we'd be a little more…isolated."

"A safe house can be anywhere, so long as no one

knows about it." He led her through a door that was marked Entrance Une Nuit. But once inside a small, featureless foyer, they didn't follow the signs to the restaurant. They boarded a rickety-looking elevator. Bryan pushed a button that had no floor number on it.

"Password, please," came a computerized voice.

"Enchilada coffee," Bryan replied. The elevator started up.

The amazement on Lucy's expressive face gave Bryan a rush of pleasure, and he had to admit that, despite the gravity of his situation, he was enjoying Lucy's reactions. He'd expected her to be a basket case, a perpetually panicked paranoid. But she'd risen to the occasion, showing a presence of mind few civilians possessed.

"How James Bond," Lucy said. "The elevator is password protected?"

"With the latest voice-recognition software. No one gets into this loft but me—and my guests, of course."

"So this is where you *live?*"

"Yeah. You have a problem with that?"

"No, but it seems a little odd, that's all. I didn't think spies normally brought witnesses in protective custody to their homes."

"They don't. This is a special occasion."

"Why? Surely this case isn't a particularly big or significant one. You must have dozens, *hundreds* of people attempting to funnel funds to terrorists."

He debated how much to tell her. But he decided she could handle the truth. He wanted her to understand she could trust no one but him. "I have strong reason to believe I've been betrayed by my own people—which means there's not a safe house in our system that's truly safe. This is the one place I could think of where no one could possibly find you."

"You mean, the people you work with—the other spies—don't know where you live?"

"They don't even know my name. To the others in my cell, and even to my boss, I'm Casanova."

"Wow."

The elevator doors opened, and Bryan led Lucy into his private living space. A couple of years ago, he'd bought the entire building where Une Nuit was located. He'd renovated and expanded the dining area, used the second floor for offices and storage, and had the top two floors converted to living space.

He'd spared no expense—he hadn't had to. Though he had some family money, and he was well paid as a top-echelon government agent, this was the home that Une Nuit had built. The restaurant, which he'd originally opened as a cover so that not even his closest friends and family would know of his true vocation, had become unexpectedly popular—and lucrative.

The apartment's floor plan wasn't completely open, but a few interior walls had been placed at odd angles so the place didn't feel like a box. The foyer opened up on one side to an enormous, modern kitchen he'd designed himself, with the latest in brushed-steel appliances. The kitchen was open to the living room, which faced a row of tall windows looking out onto Columbus Avenue. The floor was the original warehouse planking, sanded and polished to a high sheen. Some walls he had left as natural brick, while he'd had others plastered and painted a pristine white.

The furnishings were ultramodern, comfortable but sparse. He did his entertaining in the restaurant, so he didn't need lots of chairs or sofas. Original art adorned the space, but again, not too much—a small abstract painting here, a funky sculpture there. Things he'd seen, wanted, picked up. Mostly from starving artists getting their starts, although a few pieces might be worth some serious money by now.

"I love this place!" Lucy whirled around, trying to take it all in. "You live here? You actually live here?"

"When I'm home, which lately hasn't been all that often."

"How long will I be staying here? Not that I'm complaining, just trying to prepare myself. Will you want me to testify at a trial? Will I have to stay indoors all the time, or can I go out?"

He smiled at her exuberance, which radiated from her every pore. He'd thought her plain when he first saw her, but he could see that wasn't true, even in those horrible orange pants. She had an infectious smile and bright, lively eyes in a shade of pale blue he'd seldom seen.

"I won't keep you locked up like a prisoner," he said. "We'll be able to venture out some. I don't imagine you'll run into anyone you know this far from home." As for his family, there was no way to avoid them. He would have to find a way to explain her sudden presence in his life.

"Um, actually, that's not true," she said. "I lived here for a while."

"What?" This was news to him. The exhaustive background check he'd done on her hadn't mentioned any residences in New York. "That's impossible." But then he remembered those two years when she'd disappeared from the system.

"Have you ever heard of a band called In Tight?" she asked.

"Sure. They're hot right now. In fact, didn't they play the Super Bowl half-time this year?"

She nodded. "I used to work for them."

Now it was Bryan's turn to be shocked. "You? Working for a rock band?"

"I answered an ad on the Internet, and I got a job working on In Tight's finances—you know, helping to manage the money when they did concert tours, stuff like that."

Bryan had a hard time picturing Lucy Miller hanging out with wild-haired musicians. Was it possible she was pulling his leg? Was Lucy Miller a pathological liar?

"I did a background check on you," he said. "There was nothing about—"

"They paid me off the books. They weren't as famous then. They gave me a place to live, too, so you wouldn't have found an apartment under my name. I'm just telling you this so you'll know that I might run into people who would recognize me."

"We'll just have to make sure that doesn't happen." He studied her from head to toe, thinking how she could be made to look different—different hair, different eyes. "How would you feel about a makeover?"

He was worried that he'd insulted her, but instead she brightened. "Oh, I'd love one. Can I be a blonde? I think Lindsay Morgan would be a blonde."

"If you like. My cousin Scarlet is the assistant fashion editor at *Charisma* magazine. She can bring over a truckload of clothes and cosmetics, hair stuff. Do you need the glasses?"

"Only if I don't want to run into walls."

"We'll get you some contacts. Maybe green ones, though it's a shame to cover up those pretty blue eyes."

She looked away, embarrassed. "Don't tease me. My eyes are a very ordinary shade of blue—almost gray. Boring."

"I don't find them boring at all."

She peeked up at him. "You're serious."

Maybe he shouldn't have said anything. He didn't want Lucy feeling threatened, since she was forced to shack up with him. "Don't worry, I'm not going to hit on you. But you do have pretty eyes."

"Hit on me. Right. So when is the magical transformation going to take place?"

"How about after dinner?"

Bryan showed Lucy to the guest room, which had a private bath. "Where do you sleep?" she asked.

"My room's upstairs, along with a study. I'll show you later. My computer's up there, and if you're serious about deciphering the data you brought from the bank, you'll be spending a lot of time at the keyboard."

"Absolutely."

"I'll leave you to freshen up, then, while I do something about dinner."

"Okay. Do you have a robe or something I can wear until your cousin brings me some clothes? I don't really want to put Mrs. Pfluger's polyester pants back on after my shower. In fact, I'd like to burn them."

"I'll bring you something."

Bryan didn't actually have a robe, but he found her a pair of pajamas still in the package, a gift from his gram. Every year she gave him pajamas, and he'd never had the nerve to tell her he didn't wear them.

When he returned to Lucy's room, the shower was

running, the bathroom door open a crack. He felt a less-than-admirable urge to peek inside the bath and see what she looked like without clothes. Ever since she'd fallen on top of him, his imagination had been running wild.

He didn't, then wondered why he was being so noble. He was a spy, used to peering at other people's secrets. He set the pajamas on the bed and then went to see about dinner. A quick call downstairs to the restaurant took care of that. Then he had to deal with Scarlet.

"You know I love a makeover challenge," Scarlet said, warming to the idea right away. "John's away on business, so my evening's free. I'll stop by the office, grab everything I need and be there in an hour or so."

"Are you guys getting married?"

"The wedding's not till next year, and if you didn't travel so much for the restaurant, you would know these things. Honestly, don't they grow decent spices in America?"

Hmm. Maybe his standard excuse for his frequent absences—that he was seeking exotic spices—was growing a little thin. "I have to keep up with the latest," he said blandly.

"So where'd you find this girl, anyway? What's the story? Normally the girls I've seen you with don't need any help in the clothes or cosmetics department."

"Oh, she's not my—" He stopped. How was he going to explain Lucy's presence to Scarlet, and to the rest of his family? She could be under his protection for months. He couldn't keep her under wraps all that time. "She's not my usual type, true," he continued smoothly. "But Lindsay's special. Frankly, I think she's perfect just the way she is. She's a country girl, you know, the all-natural look. But she's the one who wants a makeover. She wants to fit in better in New York."

"I'll be happy to help Lindsay any way I can," Scarlet said, and Bryan read between the lines. She was going to pump Lucy for every shred of information she could get about Bryan's new romance. He'd better go warn Lucy that she'd just become his girlfriend.

Three

Lucy couldn't believe what she'd just overheard. She hadn't meant to eavesdrop. But as she wandered into the kitchen fresh from her shower, she couldn't help but hear Bryan talking to his cousin. And he'd passed her off as his new girlfriend.

Bryan turned, saw her and realized she'd heard. "Uh, yeah. Guess we need to talk about this. I'm sorry, but I don't know any other way to explain what you're doing here. My family doesn't know I'm a government agent. No one knows. And they can't know. I have to keep those two parts of my life completely separate, for the welfare of everyone concerned. You understand that, right?"

"Yes. But—"

"You've already proved you can be cool under pressure. When Scarlet gets here, just follow my lead. You're okay with this, right?"

Oh, she was more than okay. The idea excited her. But there was a big problem. "Sure, I can deal with it, but who on earth is going to believe I'm your girlfriend?"

"Why wouldn't they?"

"Because I'm just a mousy little banker from D.C. and you're a…a…"

"I own a restaurant. That's all anyone knows." The phone rang and he picked it up. It didn't escape Lucy's attention that he didn't argue about her self-assessment. Apparently he agreed with her description of "mousy."

"Okay, thanks." He hung up and turned back to Lucy. "That's our dinner. I'll be right back."

While he was gone, Lucy tried to wrap her mind around the idea that she was going to be posing as Bryan's girlfriend. Once upon a time she'd thought of herself as quite the hot chick. After all, she'd caught the eye of Cruz Tabor, drummer for In Tight, one of the hottest men in the country if the tabloids could be believed. She'd told herself when she took the job with In Tight that she wouldn't behave like a groupie, that just being around the band was excitement enough for her.

Then Cruz had started flirting with her, and she was a goner. She'd believed every lie the bastard had told her. He'd said she was gorgeous, sexy, hot. He'd taken her on tour, letting her travel in first class with the band, buying her expensive presents.

But then she'd discovered he said all those things, did all those things, with every woman he slept with. And there were lots and lots of them. She'd been so naive, such a dumb bunny, to think she was anything special.

This was way different, though, she reminded herself. She *wasn't* a hot chick, and she wasn't deluding herself into believing she was. So how would anyone else believe she'd caught Bryan's eye? Bryan was pretty hot himself. He could have any woman he wanted.

He knew the Hilton sisters. His trendy restaurant drew celebrities all the time. Did he sleep with any of them? How was she supposed to compete with that?

She found some dishes in the cabinets and set two place settings at the polished-granite bar. A few minutes later, the most wonderful aroma invaded her nose, followed by Bryan stepping off the elevator with two huge white bags.

Lucy's stomach rumbled again. "What *is* that?"

"Shrimp and vegetable stir-fry Polonnaise. It's not too spicy, and you can pick out anything you don't like."

"Stir-fry with a French sauce?"

"Right. That's what Une Nuit is all about—Asian and French fusion dishes." He set the bags on the counter, then gave her a quick once-over. She was wearing his pajama top with nothing on underneath. It was modest enough, covering all the important bits and hanging almost to her knees, so in deference to the fact it was summer in New York, she hadn't bothered with the bottoms.

Now she wished she had. She felt suddenly vulnerable with her bare legs and a breeze from the air conditioner stirring around her private parts.

"Nice look," he said with a wink. Then he turned and started unpacking the bags, stacking a mound of food on each plate and not even noticing that the hair on her forearms stood on end and her skin was flushed with awareness.

Oh, grow up, she scolded herself. He'd probably seen

a hundred women wearing a lot less than a shapeless pajama top adorned with—yes, scenes from France.

He selected a bottle of chilled white wine from a climate-controlled wine safe as big as a refrigerator. "You like wine?"

"I don't— Why, yes, I do." She'd been about to say she didn't drink. Alcohol was one of the things she'd given up when she'd made the decision to change her life, grow up, live like a conscientious adult instead of a wild, irresponsible teenager.

But after the day she'd had, a nice glass of Chardonnay sounded really nice. And it wasn't as if she'd ever been an excessive drinker. But copious alcohol consumption by the people around her had been a big part of the life she'd left behind.

Bryan filled two crystal glasses and handed her one. "A toast. To your new life as Lindsay Morgan."

"To Lindsay." She clinked her glass with his and took a sip of the crisp, dry wine. This whole thing was so surreal.

She hopped up on a bar stool and dived into the food, which was absolutely the most incredible meal she'd ever eaten. "Oh, my God, this is so good. No wonder your restaurant is so successful. Did you start it, or buy it as an ongoing concern?"

"It was a moderately profitable French bistro when I bought it. Merging French with Asian started out as a joke, really, one night when the manager, the chef and I had a little too much to drink. Then I thought, why not? We all started experimenting in the kitchen, adding one thing and then another to the menu, and it just exploded in popularity."

"I can see why." Her taste buds were cheering over

the subtle blend of exotic spices and the delicate textures, while the beautiful blend of colors and shapes and aromas engaged her other senses. She ate it all and didn't regret it a bit, even when she was stuffed. If Bryan was going to feed her like this every day, she was going to have to use the home gym she'd seen tucked away in another bedroom.

When they finished, Lucy hand washed the dishes and put them away—no sense running the dishwasher for two people. A buzzer alerted them to Scarlet's arrival, and Bryan went down to greet her and help her carry up her things.

Lucy was nervous about meeting Bryan's cousin. She hadn't had to deal with a boyfriend's family since high school. She tried to tell herself it didn't matter whether Scarlet liked her. Bryan wasn't her real boyfriend, and this situation was temporary. When they caught the embezzler, she would start a new life away from here and she'd probably never lay eyes on Bryan or Scarlet again.

But it did matter. She still wanted Scarlet to like her. But she figured she would be found sadly lacking. The woman was an assistant fashion editor for one of the hottest women's magazines in the country, after all. Scarlet was used to dressing supermodels and movie stars, not frumpy little bankers wearing oversize men's pajamas.

The elevator opened, and Bryan returned carrying an enormous armload of clothing. Following him was one of the most beautiful, exotic creatures Lucy had ever seen. She was almost as tall as Bryan, reed slim, with a gorgeous head of light-auburn hair that fell in abundant, bright waves around her shoulders and down her back. She wore a bright-green, gauzy off-the-shoulder shirt and snug pants in a coordinating print, all of which set off her pale-green eyes—eyes that zeroed in on Lucy and missed nothing.

"So you're my victim," she said cheerfully, dropping her own armload of clothing, a shopping bag and a cosmetic case the size of an industrial tool chest. She came forward, hand outstretched. "Hi, I'm Scarlet. You must be Lindsay."

Lucy uttered some pleasantry, but inside she was trembling. What had she gotten herself into? She was living a lie, starting right now. What if she couldn't pull this off? Bryan had been very clear about how important it was to keep his secret agent life separate from his family, and she wouldn't be able to live with herself if she messed that up for him.

"Stand up," Scarlet said. "Let's see what we have to work with."

Bryan leaned one elbow on the bar and watched, obviously interested in the proceedings, and Lucy felt her face heating again. This was going to be embarrassing enough without *him* watching, seeing her every physical flaw pointed out.

Scarlet apparently sensed Lucy's unease, because she turned to her cousin. "Don't you have something to do? A restaurant to run? Stash was complaining to me that you're piling too much work on him with all your gallivanting around Europe and Asia."

"I want to see what you're going to do with her."

"No," she said firmly. "Lindsay's makeover is about her, not your fantasies of the perfect woman. Now go away. And stay gone at least until midnight."

Bryan grumbled, but he turned and headed for the elevator. Then he abruptly changed direction and walked up to Lucy. "Have fun, okay? I'll see you in a while." And then he touched her cheek, gently angling her face toward him, and kissed her lightly on the mouth.

The kiss lasted maybe half a second, but it electrified everything inside Lucy from her toes to her scalp, and she had to grip the back of the bar stool she'd just vacated to keep from keeling over.

Oh, Lord, she was in trouble. She knew deep down that it was all an act, that Bryan had been working undercover for years and that the ruse of a girlfriend came as easily as breathing to him. But it was all new to her. The casual possessiveness he'd treated her to had felt awfully damn real.

Scarlet, apparently oblivious to the tidal wave of feelings coursing through Lucy, was testing the weight and texture of Lucy's still-damp hair.

"You've got great hair," she said. "Thick and healthy. It'll do just about anything you want. I assume you'll want to keep most of the length, but we can do some layers—"

"No. I want it short. I want it to look as different as possible. And blond."

"You want highlights?"

"Oh, no. I want to be radically blond."

Scarlet grinned. "I'm so glad you said that. I was prepared to be cautious, but if you'll trust me—let me go crazy on you—you'll be ready for a *Charisma* cover shoot when I'm done."

Lucy laughed self-consciously. "Well, I hardly think that."

"Why not? You've got excellent bone structure, regular features, good teeth. The glasses, though, have got to go."

"I want contacts," she said, remembering Bryan's instructions. "I want green eyes. Bright green. But I'm afraid there's not much you can do about my figure."

"Hey, most of our models have even less in the chest department than you do. You'd be surprised what good foundation garments can do. You're slender, which means the clothes will fit you. Help me carry all this stuff into the bedroom and we can get started."

"I'm staying—" Lucy almost blew it in the first five minutes. If she was Bryan's girlfriend, she wouldn't be in the guest room; she would be sharing the master bedroom with him. "I'll be staying here for quite awhile, I guess, and I don't have any clothes at all. I'll need everything." There. She congratulated herself on a skillful recovery.

"What happened to your clothes?" Scarlet wanted to know, obviously sensing a juicy story. "And don't worry, nothing you could say would shock me. My twin sister is marrying a rock star."

"Really? Which one?" Please, dear God, don't let it be anyone she knew, anyone with In Tight.

"Zeke Woodlow."

Lucy was infinitely relieved—until she put it all together. She'd read about Zeke's engagement in *The Buzz.* "Your sister is Summer Elliott. You're the Elliott family, the ones who *own* all those magazines." One of the richest families on the Eastern Seaboard.

Scarlet looked startled. "You didn't know that?"

Maybe she'd just better shut up. "I didn't know Bryan was one of *the* Elliotts. I'm a little slow—just putting it together now. We haven't been dating for long," she added, hoping that would explain away her cluelessness. "As for my clothes, I, uh, burned them. I need a fresh start."

"Burned them? Where?"

Belatedly Lucy remembered you couldn't burn anything in New York—it was against the law.

"Back home."

"Where's home?"

"Kansas. On a farm." That much, at least, was true. She'd grown up in a small, conservative Kansas farming town, and her parents were still there.

"What was Bryan doing in Kansas? I thought he was in Europe."

"Oh, he was. We met in Paris."

"Then you went home to the farm, burned your clothes and came back here? Naked?"

Lucy smiled as if this wasn't the most ridiculous story anyone had ever tried to pass off as the truth. "Right."

"Girlfriend, I like your style."

Bryan was still trying to recover his equilibrium as he headed down to the restaurant. He'd realized he was going to have to make it look good if his family was ever going to believe Lucy was his girlfriend. He'd never had a serious relationship before. Well, he'd tried once, but he'd quickly found out that women didn't like it when he disappeared for weeks at a time. He'd decided that as long as he was in the spy business, it wasn't fair to any woman to try to have a relationship. Not only would they have to put up with frequent absences, but there was always the chance he wouldn't come home.

If that ever happened, the poor woman would probably never find out his fate.

So he dated casually. He occasionally slept with a woman if she was hot, willing and understood the ground rules. He'd seldom brought a woman into his loft, and he'd certainly never installed one as a live-in mistress. For his family to buy "Lindsay's" sudden presence in his life, he was going to have to claim he was utterly smitten. And that meant acting the adoring boyfriend, with public displays of affection, longing glances, the whole nine yards.

He probably should have prepared Lucy better for the role she was playing. They hadn't even gone over a cover story—where Lucy was from, where they'd met.

Oh, well, Lucy was smart enough to wing it. As long as she reported back to him any details she'd given Scarlet, so they could keep the story consistent, it would be okay.

As for that kiss, Lucy had looked like the proverbial deer in the headlights when he'd swooped in for the light smooch. But he was the one who'd been surprised. Her lips had been soft and warm, and her vulnerability had somehow transmitted itself straight from her soul to his, all in the half second of contact between their mouths.

It had been the merest brushing of lips, so innocent, yet it had shaken him to his shoes. No kiss had ever done that.

He'd mostly composed himself by the time he entered the restaurant kitchen, but the memory of the kiss remained in the back of his mind.

"Hey, boss, you're back!" one of the sous-chefs greeted him.

"*Monsieur* Bryan!" called out another. "Hey, those Florentine eggrolls are going like hotcakes."

The head chef, Kim Chin, who ran the kitchen like a marine bootcamp, looked up from his sauté pan and grunted a greeting. "'Bout time."

All right, so he'd been neglecting his business lately. No one said it was easy working two jobs, and the

Alliance Trust case had been occupying every waking hour these days. While Lucy had worked it from her end, Bryan had been tracking down the people receiving the embezzled funds, working with two French agents to prevent any of the illicit funds from reaching terrorists in Iraq while not tipping off the bad guys on the American side. Not until he had them all rounded up could he assemble the evidence needed to put them away for a good long time.

"Where's Stash?" he asked Kim.

"Out schmoozing the beautiful people, of course, the worthless Frenchie." Which was pretty funny, since Stash practically lived at the restaurant, keeping everything running, paying the bills, meeting payroll, handling all the hundreds of details that kept Une Nuit at the top of everyone's list.

"Bryan, you're back!" Stash greeted him with a hearty hug and a double air-kiss. Stash Martin was an energetic Frenchman in his thirties. With equal parts stubbornness and optimism, he was the perfect manager for an often absent owner. "What keeps you away for so long, eh?" he asked with a French accent. "The place could have been turned into a hot-dog stand while you were gone."

Bryan had prepared a long, shaggy-dog story about his exploits in Europe. Instead he said, "I met someone." He had to set up Lucy's cover story, he reasoned. Lying came easily to him, given the number of years he'd worked undercover. But the scary thing was, he didn't have to manufacture the edge in his voice when he talked about Lucy. What had started as a fairly routine job had turned into something exciting and challenging—and for all the wrong reasons.

* * *

Lucy stared at herself in the mirror, then stared some more. Scarlet hadn't allowed her to watch the transformation, so her own image was a complete surprise. No, a shock. Her mother wouldn't recognize her—which was the point, of course.

Her brown hair lay in piles on the floor. Scarlet had cut it to chin length, dyed it to a pale blond, then blow-dried it straight so that it fell in a shimmering fringe that bounced with her every move. Her eyebrows had been plucked and reshaped, and the artfully applied cosmetics had sculpted her face and redefined the shape of her mouth. She now had cheekbones.

Then there were the clothes. After sorting through the piles and piles of glamorous outfits, Scarlet had decided that Lucy needed a look, and had chosen an array of clingy knits in a palette of soft colors—mossy green, plum, cantaloupe, tawny gold. The outfit she wore now was a pair of green low-rider pants and a cropped tank top that clung to all her curves. A second shirt in a paler green, with a front zipper and short sleeves, went over the tank. Wedge-heeled sandals and bold jewelry completed the look.

The most amazing thing, though, was the fact that she had cleavage. Scarlet had found her a really clever push-up bra that made her A cups look like Cs.

Lucy kept putting her glasses on to look at herself from far away, then taking them off and peering at her face from close up. She just couldn't believe it. She *did* look like someone who could be Bryan Elliott's girlfriend. Someone who belonged in New York. When she'd lived here before, she'd never felt quite at home, never really shed her Kansas persona.

"This is just amazing," she said for about the third time.

"The models you see in magazines don't have anything we don't have," Scarlet said. "Hairstylists, makeup artists, good lighting and a skilled photographer can turn the plainest-looking woman into a knockout."

Lucy was convinced. But she wasn't sure the Lucy Miller on the inside matched the one on the outside. Beautiful women—like Scarlet—had an inner confidence, a way of moving and talking that Lucy lacked.

"What if I can't carry it off?" she asked in a small voice.

"You'll manage. Listen, I can't imagine Bryan hooking up with a woman who isn't really, really special. He saw something in you, something inside. Just remember that, and you'll be fine."

Oh, yeah. What Scarlet didn't know was that Bryan didn't pick her at all. She'd dropped into his lap, and now he was stuck with her.

"So are you close to Bryan?" Lucy asked, figuring this was a golden opportunity to find out more about her supposed boyfriend.

"All the Elliott cousins are close. Here, stand up on the bed and let me shorten those pants. You're as slim as a model, but not quite as tall as one."

"Do most of you work for the magazines?" Lucy asked, trying not to think about the fact she was standing on Bryan's bed, trying not to think of him sleeping there. Or doing something else.

"We all work for Elliott Publication Holdings in one capacity or another. Except Bryan. He's the only one to escape that fate."

"Why is that, do you think?"

"Oh, he had other ideas from the time he was young. His heart problem kept him somewhat separated from the rest of us, I think. Until he had his operation, he couldn't run and play with us, and we were an extremely active bunch. Turn."

Lucy obediently turned, but her mind was reeling. Heart problem? Bryan?

"By the time they fixed his heart, his interest in food and cooking had already developed. Then he got into sports, bigtime—had to outdo his brother and all his cousins, as if he was making up for lost time. The magazines just didn't hold any appeal for him, I guess. Oh, he studied finance in school with some vague notion of going to work for the company, but that didn't last long. He wanted to do his own thing. He may have been the smartest one in the bunch."

"Why would you say that? Working for *Charisma* must be like a dream."

"Ordinarily, yes. But with the competition going on— Oh, Bryan probably didn't tell you about that, and why would he?"

Lucy was intrigued. "What competition? Tell me."

"My grandfather has decided to retire and make one of his children the CEO of the corporation. Each is currently head of one of the magazines—*Pulse, Snap, The Buzz* and *Charisma*. So the one whose magazine shows the biggest profit growth by the end of the year wins the top spot. Needless to say, everyone is at each other's throats. My boss, Aunt Fin, practically lives at the magazine, she's so obsessed with winning. And Uncle Michael— Well, his wife, my Aunt Karen, is recovering from breast cancer and he should be focusing on that, not worrying about a stupid contest."

Scarlet had gotten a bit worked up, and she stopped suddenly. "I'm sorry. Bryan would skewer me like a shish-kebab if he knew I was airing family laundry to his new girl."

"I won't say anything," Lucy assured her.

Lucy glanced at her new watch—a big, copper-colored bracelet thing—and was surprised to see it was after 1 a.m. Bryan wasn't home yet. What was he doing, she wondered. He obviously wasn't anxious to get back to her. It was probably a relief to be free of her for a while.

"Well, I hate to undo your hard work, but I think I'll take off all this makeup and turn in," Lucy said. "It's been a long day. Thank you so much, Scarlet. It was really nice of you to spend your evening this way."

"My pleasure, believe me. It was nice to get away from family and work pressure for a while." The two women embraced, and Lucy felt a rush of warmth and gratitude to Scarlet. She hadn't had any close girlfriends the last couple of years since moving to D.C. A few women at work had invited her occasionally to join them for dinner or drinks or a movie, but she'd kept her distance. She'd told herself it was because she wanted to keep her focus on work and not get distracted until her career was better established. But she could see now she'd been punishing herself. Having fun had gotten her into a lot of trouble. Therefore, fun was bad and it had to be eliminated from her life.

She imagined Scarlet already had a full complement of friends, though. Anyway, Lucy probably wouldn't have time for socializing. She had to go through all the data she'd downloaded from the bank and figure out who the embezzler was.

She helped Scarlet pack up her things and walked her

to the elevator. "I'd walk you down and help you carry all this, but I don't know how to get back in."

Scarlet rolled her eyes. "Bryan's silly elevator. He does have some pretty valuable artwork he doesn't want stolen, but he so overdid it with the security."

Maybe, but Lucy was grateful for it. They said goodbye. Then Lucy headed back up to the loft's upper level, which housed the master suite and Bryan's study. She wanted to move all of her things back down to her own bedroom before Bryan returned.

No such luck. She heard the elevator as she was heading down the stairs with an armload of clothing, her new wardrobe.

"Lucy?" he called out as he strode into the living room. "Oh, there you are. It took longer than I thought to go through the—" He stopped midstride and stared at her. "What have you done to your hair?"

"You…you don't like it?" Lucy squeaked. Scarlet had pointed out that men liked long hair, and Bryan might not be too keen on the short 'do. Her hair barely skimmed her jawline. Lucy had hesitated only briefly. The point was to look different, not to please Bryan.

But now she realized how badly she wanted him to like the new Lucy. Or rather, Lindsay.

"You just look so— Come down here. Put those clothes down and let me have a look at you."

Lucy did as asked, laying the beautiful new clothes on a chair and standing there, feeling enormously self-conscious as Bryan looked her up and down, then walked behind her and all around her, his expression unreadable.

He came closer and reached toward her face. She tried not to react as he removed her glasses and studied her features.

"Scarlet gave me the name of an optometrist who can fit me with green contacts. I can do that tomorrow."

"Okay." He didn't give her back the glasses. Instead, he stuck them in his shirt pocket.

"Well?" she said impatiently. "Will I do? Or do I just look ridiculous?" Maybe she was a sow's ear that couldn't pass muster as a silk purse.

A smile spread slowly across Bryan's face, which was a bit blurry to her. "Oh, you'll do, all right. Lucy, you look like a movie star." His gaze on her was like a heat lamp. Or maybe the heat was coming from inside her. She couldn't see him all that well, after all. She was probably imagining the blatant interest in the way he looked at her.

Suddenly, all she could think about was the way he'd kissed her earlier, so casually, and how she'd almost melted on the spot. It was all a game to him, but she wasn't used to being deceptive.

"Don't you think you should start calling me Lindsay all the time?" she said, sounding testy even to her own ears. "And if you're going to kiss me like you did, at least give me a little warning."

"We're supposed to be besotted with each other, so you can expect me to kiss you just about any time."

"O-okay."

"You don't sound too sure." He grasped her upper arms with both hands and looked deeply into her eyes. "Do you think you can pull this off? If not, we'll have to think of something else. My family can't suspect the truth. That would be a disaster."

Lucy was disturbed by the idea that he might change his mind, take her somewhere else, dump her in some hotel or something. In a very short time, she'd accustomed herself to the idea that she would be posing as Bryan's live-in lover.

"I can pull it off," she said. "But if we could rehearse—I mean, get our stories worked out, so I could, you know, know what to expect—"

He was watching her mouth. She stopped self-consciously. "Have I smeared my lipstick?"

"No, sweetheart, you look perfect. I was just thinking that we can't have you looking like a startled cat every time I touch you or kiss you. So you're right, of course. We need to rehearse." And with that, he slanted his mouth against hers and kissed her as if he meant it.

Four

Lucy tasted like wild cherries. Maybe it was her lipstick, or maybe it was just how Lucy Miller tasted, but what Bryan had intended as a friendly, you-don't-have-to-be-afraid-of-me kiss had turned into something much more.

Before he knew what was happening, Lucy's arms had snaked around his neck, and she was kissing him back in a way that told him *fear* wasn't in her vocabulary. She kissed as though she was born to it. Clearly she wasn't the inexperienced virginal miss he'd pegged her for.

Or maybe he'd awakened some innate talent she had. He liked that idea better. He didn't want to think about Lucy kissing other men, sleeping with other men.

Not that he would be sleeping with her. That would be taking their ruse a bit far. But kissing—for the sake of her cover story—was okay.

It was more than okay. He groaned as he buried his

hands in her newly shortened locks. Her hair felt like the softest silk, and he found he didn't really miss all that long, heavy hair. He liked the way the short ends tickled his hands and arms.

He stopped just short of pulling her hips against his and letting her know just exactly how okay her kiss was. But he did invade her mouth with his tongue, deepening the kiss, breathing in the heady scent of cosmetics and shampoo and new clothes that clung to her.

He'd never known new clothes could smell so sexy.

She pulled away suddenly, staring at him with wide, startled eyes. "What are you doing?"

That was a very good question. He casually pulled his hands out of her hair. "I thought we were rehearsing. Getting comfortable with each other."

"Well…okay, I got it. That's enough practice."

He couldn't help grinning. "You sure?"

"Yes, quite sure."

She ran nervous fingers through her hair, mussing it worse than he'd done, and straightened her clothes. She was breathing hard, her breasts rising and falling so dramatically that he was sure she was going to pop out of her teeny tank top.

Where had those plump breasts come from? He hadn't seen them earlier. Since he doubted Scarlet had given Lucy silicone implants, the breasts must have been there all along, hidden under the frumpy outfits.

"I really need to go to bed," she muttered, turning away. "I'm sure everything will make more sense in the morning. Oh, tomorrow remind me to bring you up to date on everything I told Scarlet. She was curious about me, and I'm afraid I just blathered the first thing that came into my mind."

"Like what?"

"Well, you and I met in Paris. I returned to my home in Kansas, burned all my clothes and traveled to New York, naked."

"*What?*"

"We'll talk about this tomorrow, okay? I really have to go to bed. G'night, Bryan, and thank you for everything." She grabbed her pile of clothes and fled, her sandals thunk-thunking against his wood floor as she headed for the guest room.

Traveled to New York, naked? What had possessed Lucy to say something like that? But since she'd said it, he couldn't get the picture out of his mind—Lucy boarding a plane, naked. Walking through the airport without a stitch on. Climbing into a cab—

No, he'd better not even go there. He was turned on enough already.

The woman was a siren, a witch. His groin ached with wanting her. Pretending to be besotted in front of others would be no problem—he was rapidly becoming obsessed. It was how to behave in private that would prove the problem.

He'd better just hold himself in check. Lucy was a key witness in what could ultimately prove to be a case of terrorism. He had no business kissing her or thinking about sleeping with her.

She'd said she was okay, that she could fake it. That had to be good enough. So, no more rehearsals. Professional, he had to be professional. He couldn't take advantage of a woman whose life had been turned upside down. She'd done the right thing for her country, and for her trouble she'd been spied on, lost her job and her home and couldn't contact anyone she knew. He was her anchor in a storm, and it would be easy for her to develop feelings all out of proportion.

He'd seen it happen before. He couldn't take advantage of her vulnerability. She didn't seem the casual-fling type, and that was all he could offer.

Lucy couldn't sleep, despite the fact she was exhausted. Her mind raced, reliving that kiss over and over, recalling every nuance of the pressure of his mouth on hers, the intoxicating warmth, the possessiveness, the feel of his hands in her hair and all over her.

She'd come alive like never before—not just her body or her hormones, but her whole being. The kiss had been…transcendental. She couldn't think of any other word to describe it.

Yet she knew that for him it was just another kiss. Rehearsal. Part of his business, his job. Keep the witness safe, make sure she knows her stuff, keep his family in the dark so they're safe, too.

She couldn't really blame him just because *she* reacted so profoundly to a simple kiss.

Her body still vibrated with the aftereffects, which only highlighted a sad fact about her life: for the past two years she'd been all but dead. A dull brain inside a dead shell, going through the motions, performing her job, staying out of trouble.

Only trouble had found her.

She might have been better off if none of this had happened. Maybe she'd have snapped out of her fugue on her own. Still, she couldn't say she was sorry to leave that life behind.

But she had to manage herself better. Not like when

she'd gone to work for the band. If she'd stuck to her guns back then, being satisfied simply to be on the fringes of that exciting world, she'd have been okay. Instead she'd deluded herself into thinking a millionaire rock star was going to marry her.

Her current situation wasn't so dissimilar. She'd again found herself on the fringes of an exciting world. This time it wasn't sex, drugs and rock 'n' roll, but spies, embezzlers and terrorists. Neither was a world she belonged in.

She had to remember that and not let herself get deluded into believing she was in any way special to Bryan, no matter what motions he went through.

Lucy eventually drifted off. When she awoke, daylight poured through her bedroom window, and a delicious smell tickled her nose. Whatever it was, it drew her out of bed like a black hole draws antimatter. She jumped in the shower, then stepped into a pair of white silk panties. Scarlet had given her about a dozen pair of the most delicious panties, all still in their packages. Apparently designers and clothing manufacturers sent freebies to the magazine all the time, hoping models or celebrities would wear them for photo shoots.

Lucy only had two of the magical push-up bras, though. When she'd seen the price tags on them, she'd nearly fainted. Who paid $80 for a bra? She would, she realized, now that she'd seen the miracle it performed.

Ordinarily, if she wasn't going to work, she'd put on a pair of jeans and a T-shirt. But Scarlet told her those clothes were out—they didn't go with "Lindsay's" new look. She would have to get used to wearing clingy knit pants and miniskirts, tiny crop-tops and blouses that revealed lots of skin.

She picked an outfit at random—a fawn-colored miniskirt and a fitted, sleeveless blouse with a subtle gold stripe. She didn't worry about makeup or jewelry— she would put them on only if she was appearing in public. She certainly didn't want Bryan to think she was trying too hard.

When she emerged from her bedroom and entered the kitchen, she found out what smelled so good. Bryan was making Belgian waffles, with fresh strawberries and real whipped cream.

"I'm going to be big as a house if you keep feeding me this way."

"Good morning to you, too." Bryan kept his attention on his cooking, never even glancing her way. "Sleep okay?"

No. I lay awake thinking about your blasted kiss. "Fine, thanks." She tried not to look at him, because if she did, she would think about kissing him. She couldn't help herself. He looked absolutely mouthwatering with his dark hair mussed, his face unshaven. He wore running shorts and a well-worn T-shirt with a Boca Royce Country Club logo on it. She recognized the name as an exclusive Manhattan club patronized by the very, very wealthy.

She was so in over her head.

He didn't look at her. He was busy filling mugs from a coffeemaker that looked like it belonged at NASA. The fragrance blended with the smell of waffles and strawberries, and her stomach growled.

"I've been out for a run—I do that most mornings," he said. "You can come with me. I also have a home gym."

Lucy had never been much of a jock before. "Maybe I should try running."

"If you like eating, it's a necessity."

She'd never been all that interested in food—maybe because she'd always had plenty. Growing up on a farm, the dinner table was loaded with meat, potatoes and fresh vegetables. But her mother had always urged her to eat more, claiming she was finicky as a cat.

When she'd hung out with In Tight, everyone had been more interested in drinking than eating, though there had always been something available—pizza or burgers. She'd eaten just enough to maintain her weight, so she hadn't ever felt the urge to work out.

Now she was ravenous. She dived into her waffle, savoring the pure maple syrup and the crunchy-out-side, tender-inside texture. "Yeah, I'm going to have to do something, or all those pretty clothes Scarlet gave me won't look too hot."

"You can run with me tomorrow."

"I don't have any running shoes. Or gym clothes."

"You can buy some when we go out for your contact lenses."

She wondered how much money she had in her purse. Sixty dollars maybe, if she was lucky. "I can't use my credit cards, right?"

"No. No transactions involving your real name, for any reason. No telephone calls, either—not to anyone, even someone you think the bad guys would never be watching. I don't know the extent of their reach, but these guys are connected. Really connected."

That reminder brought Lucy back to earth in a hurry. She shivered as she thought about those "bad guys" in her apartment, searching through her things, listening to her on the phone.

When Bryan finished the last waffle, he popped it

onto a plate and finally spared a glance for Lucy. He did a double take.

"You can't expect me to be glamorous twenty-four hours a day," she groused. "Scarlet might have changed some of the trappings, but I'm still Lucy Miller."

"Did I complain?"

"No. But you were looking at me."

"I was looking because the clothes and hair color are still so different. I have to get used to them."

"Me, too. I hadn't realized how positively frumpy I'd become. But even in my wilder days, I still looked like me."

"You still look like you." He came and sat next to her at the bar, then leaned close enough that she could smell the faint scent brought on by his morning exertions. Not expensive cologne, but soap and sweat. A healthy, male scent. "Your smile is the same. You have a very pretty smile, only you don't use it enough."

"I don't have much to smile about." But that really wasn't true. Yes, she'd become the target of some unsavory people, and yes, she'd lost her job and her home and her very identity. But she just didn't care that much about those things. She was hanging out with a dangerously sexy spy and she was going to help him solve a crime. She had a wardrobe to die for and a personal-style consultant any woman in the world would give up her acrylic nails for.

"That's better," Bryan said, and Lucy realized she'd given him the requested smile.

Four hours later Lucy was in Victoria's Secret, feeling a bit like Julia Roberts in *Pretty Woman*. Bryan had taken her first to get the contacts. She'd been fitted on the spot with a pair of bright-green lenses, and she'd walked out of the optometrist's office feeling unburdened without the heavy glasses. She could see better, too. She'd forgotten how superior vision with contacts could be.

Next, Bryan had taken her shopping for all the things Scarlet hadn't provided—mostly athletic clothes. He'd bought her a pair of first-class Nike running shoes and a couple of color-coordinated designer outfits. She'd never worn designer clothing before yesterday, thinking it was silly to pay so much for a label. But she'd found out the clothes really were superior in quality. The fit and feel were fantastic.

She'd mentioned that she didn't have any sleepwear, so Bryan led her into the pricey lingerie store.

"We don't have to do anything this fancy," she protested. "You've already spent so much—"

"I can afford it. I want you comfortable, and you can't be comfortable in some cheap polyester pajamas."

"I can't be comfortable in a peek-a-boo nightie, either," she pointed out. But as she looked around, she realized the sleepwear here was gorgeous—not the least bit sleazy. She saw beautiful silk nightgowns in the most delicious pastels, but she also saw some pretty cotton nightshirts, and she knew that was what she should choose. Something supercomfortable.

"Uh-oh," Bryan muttered as she tried to find her size in a peach nightshirt.

Lucy's skin prickled with nerves. "What?" Had the bad guys tracked her down already? She glanced around, wondering if there was anyplace she could duck for cover if bullets started to fly.

"It's my stepmother. Of all people." He sounded disgusted. "Put down that nightshirt. I wouldn't buy a girlfriend anything like that. Here." He grabbed three skimpy nightgowns from a rack and thrust them at her. "Go try these on. Maybe you won't have to meet her. Oh, cripes, she's seen us. Too late."

The woman in question was petite and very thin, with unnaturally platinum hair in an expensive cut. She wore a pair of snug, low-rise jeans and a clingy shirt that looked pretty good on her surgically enhanced figure.

She might have been pretty but for the superior sneer on her face, which Lucy guessed was perpetual.

"Bryan, what on earth are you doing in a lingerie store?"

"Hi, Sharon," he said without much enthusiasm. The two didn't touch. "I'm buying a gift. This is Lindsay Morgan. Lindsay, my stepmother, Sharon Elliott."

Sharon nodded her acknowledgment while giving Lucy a thorough once-over. "Soon to be Sharon Styles again, thank God."

"It's nice to meet you," Lucy said politely. "Bryan, I'll just go try these on and give you two a chance to visit." And she scurried toward the dressing room, anxious to escape the obvious tension between Bryan and his stepmother. Her absence would also give Bryan a chance to explain her presence however he chose, without worrying she would say something to mess up his story. She was so new at this undercover thing, and she figured it was better if she got used to it in small doses. She hadn't forgotten the crazy story she'd blurted out to Scarlet, which they now had to live with.

When she got to the dressing room, she quickly undressed and tried on one of the silk nightgowns. Though Bryan had chosen the clothing at random, he'd gotten her size right, and the gown was absolutely gorgeous.

Without meaning to, she pictured herself wearing it in Bryan's loft. With Bryan looking on approvingly.

Though there was no one present to know her thoughts, her face flamed. She decided right then she would choose this gown—and a couple more just as sexy. She was done being frumpy, even if Bryan would never see the lovely scraps of silk on her.

"*Who* is *she?*" Sharon asked the moment she and Bryan were alone.

"I met her in Paris, but she's from Kansas," Bryan said, sticking to the story Lucy had told Scarlet. Although Sharon didn't have much contact with the family since the divorce proceedings had begun, she did talk to Bryan's father from time to time as they wrangled over the settlement details.

"And you're buying her lingerie?"

He shrugged. "Something wrong with a man buying his girlfriend lingerie?"

Sharon's eyebrows flew up. "Oh, so she's your girlfriend. I don't recall that you've had a girlfriend in a number of years." As if that made him suspect.

Bryan chose to let that comment pass. "Lindsay is pretty special."

"She seems very…sweet," Sharon said. "Well, I must get on with this. I've been invited to a wedding shower, and though I hate those things, it's at the Carlyle, and I heard there might be a couple of celebrities present."

That figured. Sharon had always been a social climber extraordinaire. She came from a wealthy family—Patrick had handpicked her for his son Daniel, after all. But her parents weren't famous-rich, like the Elliotts, and she'd reveled in her society-wife role, snubbing her old friends and collecting a new, richer batch. Now she was trying to elevate her status even higher.

He didn't dislike Sharon, for she'd been tolerant enough to him and his brother, Cullen, two boisterous stepsons. But she didn't give him any warm fuzzies, and she'd been pretty obstinate about the divorce.

She drifted away to shop, and Bryan found himself alone, staring at the wide array of sexy lingerie. Each thing he looked at—each bra and panty set, each nightie, each thong—he couldn't help but picture on Lucy.

He'd been hoping last night was just a fluke, that he'd merely been turned on by the glamorous trappings Lucy had displayed. But when he'd seen her this morning, he'd known it was something far deeper than clothes or hair color that attracted him to Lucy Miller.

Lucy had an inner core of goodness that radiated from her. He'd never met anyone like her. He, on the other hand, was part of an ugly, shadowy world. Their two worlds were colliding, but that contact could only be temporary. She didn't belong in his, nor he in hers. He had to remember that.

Lucy reappeared a few minutes later. "Is she gone?"

He nodded. Sharon had grabbed a slinky black nightgown, paid for it and left without a backward glance. He wondered if she would find an excuse to call his dad and report what she'd seen. Despite the pending divorce, Sharon loved to gossip. "I'll put those up for you," he said to Lucy, holding out his arms. "You can go back to the nightshirts."

"No, thanks. I want these."

He looked again at the slinky, transparent fabrics

and daring, skin-revealing styles of the nightgowns she held, and his jeans grew noticeably tighter in the crotch. He did *not* need to think about Lucy wearing those!

Five

Lucy wore her ice-blue nightgown to bed that night. She felt sexy in it, which made her think of things she probably shouldn't. But she couldn't make herself clamp down on her fantasies. She'd spent two years seeing herself as a nonsexual being, and she didn't want to return to that. It was wonderful being able to *feel* again, even if some of those feelings were painful.

In the morning she dressed in a pair of pink exercise shorts, a sports bra, a pink tank top with the word Diva across the chest, and her new running shoes. She wore a terry sweatband to keep her hair out of her face.

Bryan was waiting for her when she emerged, grinding beans in his futuristic coffeepot.

"Ready?" he asked, looking pointedly at her bare legs. At least he wasn't focusing on her chest, or lack thereof. She'd gotten used to the cleavage her fancy push-up bras produced, but those bras weren't practical for running.

"I'm ready, but I warn you, I'm out of shape."

"We'll take it easy."

Five minutes later Lucy was thinking, If this is easy, I'd hate to see rigorous. She was huffing and puffing like a leaky accordion, her every muscle protesting. She'd had no idea she was in such bad condition.

To his credit, Bryan said nothing, just loped along beside her, breathing normally.

After a few minutes Lucy got into a rhythm and she felt a little better. She started to pay attention to the sights around her, the people hurrying to catch a bus or taxi, the bagel vendors, the honking horns and flocks of pigeons.

Oh, how she loved this city. She hadn't, however, often seen it at this hour of the morning. The In Tight crew was accustomed to starting the day around noon. Mornings, she discovered, had the same energy, but also a feeling of anticipation, of possibilities.

"You doing okay?" Bryan asked.

She nodded.

They veered into Central Park where they joined dozens of other morning joggers. Lucy dropped back a little so she could run behind Bryan and enjoy the view. He had the most gorgeous, tanned, muscular legs she'd ever seen, and a tight butt she wanted more than anything to grab. She giggled and almost choked to death because she didn't have the spare oxygen for laughter.

She stopped and coughed a few times, and Bryan, looking concerned, tapped her on the back until she was better.

"Maybe we should head back," he said.

She nodded, unable to speak.

"That was really good for a first time out."

She smiled at him, and he smiled back, and her heart did a little *plonk*. She wished he wouldn't be so nice to her. She wished she wasn't just a job to him, a responsibility to be taken care of. She wished they'd met some other way, and maybe they could go out on a date like normal people.

Her life was pretty far from normal.

She was sweating like an ox by the time they made it back to Bryan's building. Instead of going straight up, they swung into Une Nuit. Bryan introduced her to his manager, Stash, a charming man with a French accent who eyed her speculatively as Bryan put together a plate of pastries.

"This the one, eh?" he said.

"This is the one," Bryan confirmed, flashing a slightly embarrassed smile.

The one? What the heck did that mean?

Lucy looked around the huge commercial kitchen, which appeared to her like a forest of stainless steel, everything impeccably clean and sparkly. Three men and one woman wearing tall chef's hats bustled around preparing the day's menu, all joking and laughing in good-natured camaraderie.

This would be a fun place to work, she caught herself thinking. Not like Alliance Trust, where no one cracked a smile or spoke above a whisper, and the only smells were of new carpet and money. Honestly, that place was like a mausoleum.

"You want to see the rest of it?" Bryan asked, apparently noting her interest.

"Oh, yes, please."

He led her through a wide, swinging, double door into the main dining room, flipping on a couple of light switches as they went. The decor was nothing short of seductive. Low red lighting illuminated the copper-topped tables, which were surrounded by black suede banquettes and armchairs. Tables and booths were tucked away at odd angles in little corners, and she imagined the famous people who ate here enjoyed the sense of privacy.

The floor was black-and-red stone—marble, or maybe something else. Contemporary wrought-iron chandeliers hung here and there, each one different, each one a work of art.

"Wow, this is beautiful. Did you decorate it yourself?"

"No, I hired a design firm. They did my loft, too. I can't take credit for that. Except some of the artwork."

"It's wonderful. Can we eat here some time?" She nearly swooned at the idea of an intimate dinner with Bryan. Since they would be in public, they would have to act like a couple in love. It wouldn't be too difficult for her.

"You can eat here anytime you like. Stash will take care of you."

That wasn't really what she wanted to hear. She wanted Bryan to be the one taking care of her. They could share a plate of crepes stuffed with stir-fry—or whatever exotic thing was on the menu—and feed each other with chopsticks.

Bryan showed her the bar area, which featured smaller tables and less-cushy chairs, for those waiting for a table or just stopping in for a cocktail.

"Downstairs there's a private dining room, for parties and such. Do you want to see it?"

She glanced at her watch. "I suppose we better get going. I have a lot of work to do on the computer today."

They went upstairs, showered, then met again in the kitchen to gobble down the French pastries and coffee. Yes, she was going to have to make running a habit.

Hours later Lucy was firmly ensconced in Bryan's private study, which was upstairs off the master suite. The door had been locked the night Scarlet came over— Lucy had checked the door out of curiosity. But this morning he'd let her in, fired up his computer and put her to work. She had not only the memory stick she'd taken with her when she fled from D.C., but all of the data she'd provided Brian with over the past few weeks. He had been going over it himself, along with some of Homeland Security's top computer experts, but none of them had been able to figure out who was siphoning money out of the pension funds. The embezzling had been disguised to look like ordinary transactions. Fund managers bought and sold stock and securities all the time. Only by comparing the transactions with the various fund managers' portfolio profiles could the bogus stock sales be ferreted out.

For the past three hours, Lucy had been going over personal e-mails. She felt terrible for invading her co-workers' privacy, but Bryan had assured her it was both legal and necessary. The embezzler wasn't operating in a vacuum. Maybe he wasn't stupid enough to leave incriminating evidence in an e-mail—but maybe he was.

Bryan had left her alone to attend to his own business. He was checking in with the other agents on his team to see if any progress had been made from their ends. When she heard footsteps coming up the stairs,

Lucy was almost giddy at the prospect of seeing him again. She told herself it was only because she was anxious to report what she'd found. But deep down she knew it was more than that. She was forming an unhealthy attachment to her superspy, which was only going to lead to pain and disappointment.

But what could she do? She couldn't order her emotions to behave. And her hormones were completely out of her control.

Bryan entered the study, and Lucy's smile died. The strain on his face was obvious. "Bad news?"

"One of the agents on my team is MIA."

"Oh, no, that's awful!"

"No one has heard from him in three days."

"What do you think happened? Where was he the last time you knew?"

"He's been in France. He infiltrated the bogus charity your embezzler has been funneling money to, and was tracing down wire transfers that matched the amounts we know were stolen from Alliance at certain times. But now he's vanished. Either he's blown his cover…or he's the traitor. But I find that impossible to believe. I've worked closely with Stungun on two other missions. I'd have trusted him with my life anyday."

"Stungun?"

Bryan rolled his eyes. "We all have code names. We don't know each other's real names. Not even my superior knows who I am."

"What are the other agents' code names?"

"My team consists of me, Stungun, Tarantula and Orchid. Siberia is our control—our boss."

"It's okay for you to tell me that?"

He smiled briefly. "We change the code names all the

time. I'm Casanova right now, but I've been Jackknife, Hustler and Hopper."

"Hopper?"

He shrugged. "'Cause I'm quick like a rabbit, I guess. I didn't come up with it." He sat wearily in a leather office chair. "Have you found anything?"

"You wouldn't believe what I've found out. John Pelton, one of our loan officers, has been downloading porn. Really raunchy stuff. I *never* would have guessed. Then there's Cassie Hall and Peter Glass. They've apparently been carrying on a torrid affair—and they're both married to other people! I feel like a pervert, reading their e-mails."

"Anything pertinent to the case?"

"I've been comparing log-ins to the times various illegal transactions were made. It's painstakingly slow, but I think I might be able to figure out who the culprit is by process of elimination."

"Any front runners?"

"I've been able to eliminate a couple of people. But there are still dozens of candidates. Most people stay logged in all day when they're at work. Still, it's a start."

"Good. Keep at it. There are cold cuts and fruit in the fridge if you're hungry."

She glanced at her watch and was surprised to see it was almost two. She'd been so engrossed in solving the puzzle, she'd been oblivious to the passage of time.

"I'm afraid I have more bad news," he said, his tone positively funereal.

"What? It's not my family, is it? They haven't reported me missing or anything, I hope." She wasn't in close contact with her parents—she talked to them every couple of weeks. They wouldn't be worried about her yet.

When he didn't answer at once, she felt panic creeping over her. "Bryan? What is it?"

"It's my grandparents. They're holding a dinner tonight at their house on Long Island. It's a command performance. We have to be there."

"Oh." Word had apparently gotten out about Bryan's new girlfriend, and she was being summoned for inspection.

"The good news is," he continued, "my cousins and aunts and uncles will be there, and they're all at each other's throats these days, so there'll be lots of drama to keep everyone distracted. The focus won't be solely on you—though you'll receive your share. Are you up to it?"

"Sure. As long as no one asks me how I got from Kansas to New York with no clothes."

Bryan waited nervously in the living room while Lucy got ready for dinner at The Tides, the home where he'd spent a lot of his growing-up years. She'd been very nervous about what to wear when he'd told her the Elliotts dressed for dinner.

His grandparents could be a bit pretentious, no two ways about it. And controlling? They gave new meaning to the word. The competition Patrick Elliott had set up among his children and grandchildren was a perfect example. He liked to make them jump through hoops.

Still, they were good people, and they wanted what they thought was best for their loved ones.

When Bryan heard Lucy's bedroom door open and shut, his gaze went immediately to the corner around which he knew she would soon appear, and he caught himself holding his breath. Having seen some of the clothing Scarlet had picked out for his "girlfriend," he couldn't wait to see how Lucy had tricked herself out tonight.

He wasn't disappointed. When she came around the corner, she wore a clingy halter dress in a muted, burnt-orange color. It came almost to her knees, the hem ending in a flirty little ruffle, but that didn't make it conservative. It showed every delicious curve of her body. She'd draped a silk fringed shawl over her bare shoulders, the color ranging from pale peach to a dark orange. A bold silver necklace called attention to her long neck and the enticing curve of her breasts.

"Too slutty?" she asked. "I don't want your family to think I'm easy, although if I've moved in with you after knowing you only a couple of weeks, I guess I must be."

"You look terrific, not slutty at all." He wanted to touch her. He wanted to untie the little bow at the back of her neck and peel that dress right down to her waist. He wanted to kiss the shiny gloss off her lips and tease her breasts until her nipples were hard against his palms—

"Bryan?"

"What?"

"Shouldn't we go? I don't want to be late."

Bryan forced himself to think about the time he'd crash-landed a plane in a Greenland blizzard and had survived for two days on four granola bars. Cold, very, very cold. He'd gotten frostbite and had almost lost his little toe.

Better. "Yes, let's go." He offered her his arm in a courtly gesture, and she took it, smiling uncertainly. "You look like a goddess, you know."

"Oh, stop."

"You do. And it's not just the designer clothes and trendy hair. Since your makeover, you carry yourself differently."

"It's my inner Lindsay," she quipped, though he could tell she was pleased with the compliment.

On the drive out to Long Island, Lucy worked at memorizing their story. They'd met at a Paris café where Bryan was swapping recipes with a chef. She'd gone there thinking she would write a novel but had found out she couldn't write. Now she was trying to find herself. She'd inherited a bit of money and so was in no hurry to get a job.

They invented fake names for her parents and a fake Kansas town as her home.

"You can say you worked at a bank, since you know that world, but make it somewhere besides D.C."

"What about my education? I have a finance degree."

"Keep it, but say you went to…I don't know. Loyola. None of my family has ever been near Chicago."

"I'll just try to steer conversation away from me. I'll ask questions about you instead. That worked pretty well with Scarlet."

"Oh, really? And what did Scarlet say about me?"

Lucy put on her most innocent face. "She said when you were a kid you liked to pull the wings off flies and burn things."

"What?" The look on his face was priceless.

"I'm kidding. She said you were the only one who didn't go into the magazine business. Why is that?"

"I'd planned to. I actually studied finance, with some vague idea of working in the EPH home office. But the government recruited me before I graduated. I knew I couldn't tell my family I was training to be a spy— they'd have gone through the roof. So I bought a restaurant instead."

"Why a restaurant?"

"I met Stash when I was still in school. It was his dream, and I knew I liked food. So I bought the café and hired him to run it. I had no idea I would enjoy it so much. I'd planned on being more of a silent owner, but it hasn't worked out that way."

"Tell me more about your family. Who will be there tonight, besides your grandparents?"

"No telling. Most of the family comes when Granddad calls, unless they're testifying before the Supreme Court or vacationing in Sri Lanka. But with everyone so tense these days, I'm not sure."

"Will either of your parents be there?"

"Not Mom. She doesn't set foot at The Tides. Dad will probably be there, though."

"Your parents don't get along, then?" Lucy was saddened at the thought of Bryan and his brother growing up with two feuding parents. Scarlet had let it slip that Bryan's parents had split when he was about twelve.

"Oh, no, actually they get along fine. It's Patrick my mom can't stand."

"Your grandfather?"

He nodded. "I don't think she's spoken to him since I was a kid. She's kept in touch with my aunt Karen, but no one else in the family."

"Why the feud?" Lucy wanted to know.

Bryan shrugged. "She never said, but I think she blames Granddad for the divorce somehow. Like I said, he is controlling. And when I was— Well, you don't want to hear all that."

"I do, really. Unless you'd rather not."

He continued only reluctantly. "When I was a kid, I had to have an operation—the kind our insurance wouldn't pay for because it was considered experimental. Granddad paid for it—and I'll be forever grateful to him, because it saved my life, literally. But I think he felt my parents owed him after that, and he used that debt to keep them under his thumb. Ultimately, I think that's what caused the divorce."

Bryan looked so sad, almost shattered, that Lucy reached over and laid her hand on his arm. "Surely you don't blame yourself. You were just a little boy. You had no control over a health problem."

"I know. But the fact remains, if I hadn't gotten sick, our lives would have been a lot different."

"And maybe you wouldn't have pushed yourself to become a super athlete, and you wouldn't have been recruited by the CIA, and you wouldn't have been assigned to my case, and whoever was watching me would have killed me. You can't play the what-if game. It's silly."

He looked over at her and smiled. "You're an amazing woman, Lucy Miller." He took her hand and squeezed it, then didn't let it go.

"Lindsay Morgan." She felt the warmth of his touch all the way to her heart. If it felt this fantastic when he touched her hand, what would it be like if he touched her other places?

Don't go there.

He only released her hand when he had to shift gears, downshifting as he reached their destination.

The Elliott home was in the Hamptons, where else? Lucy had been to the Hamptons a few times for some wild parties, so she thought she knew what to expect. But The Tides, as it was called, shocked her nonetheless. The turn-of-the-century mansion—no other word for it—was perched on a cliff above the shore. To get to it, Bryan turned his Jaguar down a private drive, where a guard waved him through.

"A gated community," Lucy said. "Nice."

"Not a community. Just one house."

"You mean that security guard sits there all the time to guard just one house?"

"That's right."

Lucy thought she'd seen wealth and opulence, but she was afraid her preconceived notions hadn't prepared her for the Elliott estate. As the perfectly manicured grounds passed by outside the car window, she wondered how she would measure up. Designer clothes and a chic haircut didn't change the fact she was a farm girl from Kansas.

The house up close was even more impressive than from a distance. The rusty sandstone monolith came into view as they rounded the last corner and drove onto the circular drive, and it literally took Lucy's breath away. The high, peaked roof was gray slate, and there were so many gables and turrets and cupolas and multipaned windows that Lucy's head spun.

"Wow."

Bryan laughed. "I loved this place growing up. Always so full of activity, laughing, fighting. Granddad has talked about downsizing now that it's just the two of them most of the time, but I doubt they'll ever do it. Gram loves this place too much. She says the grounds remind her of Ireland."

Other cars had already arrived. Bryan parked and came around to open Lucy's door, but she was already out of the car by the time he arrived. Again he offered her his arm. "Remember, we're smitten."

As if she had to struggle too hard. They walked up the brick stairs to the porch. Not standing on ceremony, Bryan opened the door and ushered her inside a marble foyer with a crystal chandelier twenty people could have swung from. Straight ahead was a formal living room; to the right, Lucy glimpsed a dining room with a massive table already set with linens, china, crystal.

Despite the luxury, the house exuded a welcoming warmth. Elegant and understated, the decor didn't scream professional decorator. Instead Lucy was willing to bet the lady of the house had decorated it herself. There were family photos and knickknacks everywhere, arranged in attractive groupings. The furniture, while upholstered in stylish colors, appeared to have been chosen for comfort and sturdiness.

A group was already seated in the living room, and the murmured conversation stopped the moment Bryan and Lucy entered. They all looked expectantly at the newcomers.

"Bryan." A handsome man in his forties bounded up and approached Bryan with a hearty handshake. He looked too young to be Bryan's father, but with the physical likeness between the two men, they couldn't be anything but father and son.

He focused on Lucy. "And you must be Lindsay. I'm Daniel Elliott, Bryan's father."

They shook hands. "I guessed as much."

"Everyone," Bryan said, "this is Lindsay Morgan. I would appreciate it if you didn't scare her to death.

Remember, the Elliotts en masse can be a trifle intimidating."

Lucy was introduced to each Elliott in turn. His brother, Cullen, was easy to remember, because he looked enough like Bryan to be a twin. Cullen's wife, Misty, was also memorable, mostly because she was close to six feet tall, pregnant and amazingly gorgeous.

Scarlet she knew, of course, but now she met her fiancé, John Harlan, an ad exec. And Scarlet's twin sister, Summer, who was a carbon copy, if a tad less flamboyant. Summer's fiancé, Zeke Woodlow, made a definite impression. Who could forget him? He was a rock star, and a golden god of a man even when he wasn't assuming his stage persona. He and Summer were on a break from touring, Summer explained, while she and her twin planned their double wedding.

But after a while, the names and faces began to blur. Trying to remember her cover story *and* commit names to memory proved too much for Lucy's little brain. It wouldn't matter in the long run, she told herself. In a matter of weeks she would be gone, hardly a blip on the collective memory of the Elliott clan.

But it did matter. She wanted the Elliotts to like her. She wanted to be a positive reflection on Bryan.

Finally Bryan's grandparents appeared. Lucy had never met a more intimidating man than Patrick Elliott. Though well into his seventies, he was still strong and vital, and it was clear his word was law around here.

"So you're the new girlfriend," he said, giving her a once-over as if she were a horse he'd bought at auction.

Bryan made polite introductions, but Patrick didn't do anything so modern as shake Lucy's hand. He nodded brusquely.

"Don't mind him," said Maeve, Bryan's grand-mother. She was a petite woman and still a beauty. Her mostly white hair, piled up on her head in an elegant upsweep, carried traces of auburn, and her nose bore a sprinkling of pale freckles. Her green eyes were sharp as a bird's and missed nothing. "He's a gruff old goat, but deep down he's a charmer. Welcome to The Tides, Lindsay."

Maeve grasped both Lucy's hands and squeezed them, and Lucy instantly fell in love with the woman. She was just adorable.

Though Lucy quickly ceased to be the center of attention, she could sense the Elliotts watching her at various times. When others arrived—Bryan's uncle Shane and his cousin Teagan and Teagan's fiancée, Renee—conversations broke into small groups, and the talk focused on the magazines. Which was only natural, since almost all of them worked for EPH.

Even an outsider could see the tensions. Those who worked for the same magazine flocked together, some-times with heads bent low. Sometimes voices were raised, then boisterous laughter would break out, a spontaneous hug here and there.

Lucy wasn't used to any family showing their feelings so freely. In the home where she'd grown up, she'd been taught to keep emotions in check. Voices were never raised, laughter seldom heard. And hugging? Forget it.

No wonder Lucy had rebelled so far in the other direction, allowing her life to get about as messy as one could get.

"Let me refill that wine, Lindsay," Daniel said. "Which one were you drinking?"

"Uh, red?"

"Burgundy? Or was it the pinot noir?"

Lucy felt sure she should know the difference, but she didn't. Her parents hadn't allowed alcohol in their house, and In Tight had leaned toward beer and the hard stuff.

At her clueless expression, Daniel took her elbow and led her to the bar, where several bottles were lined up. "This is the burgundy," he said, "a particularly nice one from Australia. The pinot noir is a Chilean variety. Dry, but with a hint of floral and oak." He smiled at her. "Pretend you're interested in my boring dissertation on wine, okay? Make me look good."

Lucy laughed. "I am interested. I just don't know much about wine. I think I drank from the bottle with the green label."

He picked up the bottle and refilled her glass. "Actually, I have an ulterior motive in cutting you out from the herd. I wanted to have a private word with you."

Uh-oh, here it comes, Lucy thought, tamping down her panic. Bryan's father had picked up on something out of kilter. She'd blown it.

"I'm very worried about Bryan. He's been traveling so much lately. And when he showed up for his brother's wedding here in May, he had a split lip and a limp. He claimed he was in a car accident, but his car didn't have a scratch on it."

This was all news to Lucy. She looked up at him blankly.

"You mean, you don't know?"

"We haven't been dating for long," she said, her voice shaking with nerves. "It's been a real whirlwind. I still have so much to learn about Bryan. He hasn't mentioned any car accident." All of which was true.

"I feel like he's hiding something. And I'm not just being a paranoid dad. His mother is worried, too. And Cullen. We all feel like he's not being honest with us. Maybe trying to protect us."

Oh, dear. How was she supposed to respond to that?

She wanted to tell Daniel not to worry, but in good conscience, she couldn't. Bryan was in danger almost all the time. She wanted to reassure Daniel that Bryan wasn't involved in something nefarious, that he wasn't embroiled in trouble. She couldn't do that, either.

"Bryan is a very private person," she finally said.

"But what was he doing in France? Surely it couldn't take weeks and weeks to swap recipes."

Bryan had told her to stick to the truth as much as possible. But she knew nothing about what he did in France. She shrugged helplessly. "He was meeting with all kinds of people."

"You mean like chefs and restaurant managers and spice dealers?"

And terrorists and spies. She nodded.

"Well, maybe there's more to running a restaurant than I thought. Maybe now that he has a girlfriend, he'll stay home more. You'll take good care of him, won't you?"

"More like he's taking good care of me."

Six

Dinner was the typical five-course extravaganza. Though the Elliotts had a chef come in even for their family dinners, Maeve was a fine cook in her own right and couldn't resist dabbling in the kitchen. The meal tonight was vichyssoise, followed by a field-green salad, braised salmon, beef tips with fresh asparagus, and fudge-caramel mousse.

"What do you think, Bryan, love?" Maeve asked. "Up to your standards?"

"Gram, you know even Une Nuit can't compete with the dinners you serve here," he said diplomatically. He'd enjoyed the dinner but he'd spent most of his time watching Lucy, who was so nervous she could hardly swallow. She was doing a spectacular job posing as Lindsay. She'd often shot him nervous but affectionate looks throughout the evening, and a couple of times she'd sought him out and taken his hand.

He had to admit, the feel of her smooth little hand in his had stirred something inside him until it was becoming increasingly difficult to separate fact from fiction. But that was the general idea when working a cover story. Live it, believe it, and you could be convincing.

But was he living it a little too much? He certainly had no problem doting on "Lindsay." He even stole the cherry from the top of the mousse and presented it to her, which started a boisterous argument among the cousins. When they'd been kids, they'd always fought over the cherry until Maeve had been forced to go to the kitchen and bring out the jar of maraschinos, giving each of her grandkids one.

"So," Patrick said, "where is your twin sister this evening, Shane?"

"Why are you asking me?" said Shane, who was editor in chief of *The Buzz.* "You know Fin. She's eating and sleeping at *Charisma* these days, she's so obsessed with this competition."

The others at the table agreed. This was one of those times Bryan was truly grateful not to be in the magazine business. He didn't like this competition among his aunt, uncles and cousins for control of EPH. He had no idea what his grandfather's goal had been in setting up the contest, but surely it wasn't to put them all at each other's throats.

"No need to criticize," said Scarlet, sticking up for her boss. "Aunt Finny is devoted, that's all. She truly cares about *Charisma.*"

"Oh, and I don't care about *The Buzz?*" Shane shot back.

"I didn't say that."

More arguments broke out after that. Bryan leaned back and folded his arms, rather enjoying the melee. The things some people thought were important.

Lucy interrupted his amusement. "Excuse me," she said quietly to him. "I'll be back."

He thought she'd just gone to the powder room, but when she hadn't returned in ten minutes, he started to worry. Maeve had brought out the dessert, and Lucy's sat untouched.

Realistically, Bryan knew nothing could happen to Lucy while she was at The Tides. The place was safe as Fort Knox. But her absence made him uneasy, and he excused himself to go look for her.

The downstairs guest bath door was open, the light off. If she'd ever been there, she wasn't there now.

He wandered all around the first floor, thinking maybe she'd gotten distracted by his grandparents' artwork or knickknacks, some of which were museum quality. But she was nowhere.

Surely she hadn't gone upstairs. Unless she'd felt ill and wanted to lie down. But wouldn't she have said something to him?

He checked upstairs and still didn't find her. Now he was truly worried.

He returned to the dining room. Her chair remained empty.

"Bryan?" his grandmother inquired. "Something wrong?"

"I seem to have lost my girlfriend."

"We probably upset her with all our arguing," Scarlet said. "Bryan was right when he said we could be scary."

Scary, maybe, but his family stuck together in a crisis. And though this didn't exactly qualify as a crisis yet, the others didn't hesitate to put down their dessert spoons, push back from the table and go in search of Bryan's lost date.

He found her a couple of minutes later. Theorizing that she might have stepped outside for a breath of fresh air, he went out to the patio, then to the steps that had been carved out of the cliff leading down to the private beach. He spotted a solitary figure, standing on the sand below looking out to sea, and his whole body relaxed with relief.

He stepped back inside to let the others know he'd found her. Then he went down to the beach.

She didn't hear him over the waves until he was almost upon her. She turned, startled, and her cheeks were wet with tears.

"Lucy, what on earth is wrong?"

She swiped at one cheek with the back of her hand and laughed self-consciously. "I'm sorry. I didn't mean to worry you. I only intended to step outside for a minute. My head was spinning. I shouldn't have had that third glass of wine."

"It's us who should be apologizing, arguing like that when we have guests. I'm sorry if we upset you."

She laid a hand on his arm. "I didn't mind the arguing. That's not it."

"Then what is it?" he asked, bewildered. But then again, most women bewildered him. They were such complex creatures.

"I was just thinking how fun it would be to belong to a big, boisterous family like the Elliotts. And that got me to thinking about my family. We don't fight, true, but that's because we hardly ever talk. And of all stupid things, I sort of started to miss my parents. And I started thinking, if I don't make it through this—"

"Make it through?" He couldn't help it, he had to interrupt. "Lucy, you'll make it through. It may take time, but look at the progress we've made already."

"I told you I was being silly."

"I know this thing has turned your life upside down. I admire the fact you were brave enough to take on embezzlers and terrorists. Not everyone would do that."

She shrugged.

"I'll get you back home to your normal life as soon as possible," he said, though he didn't look forward to pushing her out of his life. But that was inevitable. Tempted though he was, he couldn't allow Lucy or any woman to get close to him. It wasn't fair and it wasn't safe.

"It certainly hasn't been all bad," she said with a sniff. The ocean breeze had all but dried her tears. "At home I don't get to dress like this or have dinner at a gazillion-dollar mansion or meet publishing luminaries."

"Publishing luminaries with bad manners," Bryan added with a rueful laugh. "Ah, Lucy, you're a good sport."

He gave her a spontaneous hug, which he'd intended to be brief and brotherly. Instead, Lucy put her arms around him and hugged him back, hard, pressing her luscious body against his.

Almost of its own accord, his hand slid down to her slender waist, then lower, flirting with the curve of her bottom.

When he realized what he was doing he froze. He'd been about to grab Lucy's butt! He forced himself to ease his grip on her, to gradually pull away.

She looked up at him with those vibrant green eyes

still dewy with tears, her pink mouth slightly parted. And the expression in her eyes, one of such utter trust, did him in completely.

No one had ever looked at him that way. Before he knew what was happening, he bent his head and closed the few inches between them, capturing those moist, pink lips with his.

Her lips were rose-petal soft, and as open and giving as a rose in full bloom, too. Bryan's energy collided and melded with Lucy's as their vibrations became one, breathing and heartbeats in sync, until he wasn't sure where he ended and she began.

His body, which had been tuned to Lucy's station almost from the moment they met, leaped to life with a craving so keen it was painful.

She tasted faintly of the wine she'd been drinking, and he tasted more deeply, coaxing her with his tongue to open even more. She did without hesitation. Again the utter trust she showed blew him away.

It was that trust that finally dragged him to his senses. He could not take advantage of this situation. He'd gotten Lucy into her current position and had promised to protect her. She was depending on him for every-thing—food, clothing, shelter. To abuse his position was unconscionable.

He pulled back again, and this time he put his hands on her bare arms and gently pushed her away as he broke the kiss.

"We shouldn't do this."

She blinked a couple of times, and he wondered if he imagined the hurt look in her eyes. But in the span of another heartbeat, she smiled mischievously. "Why not? We're supposed to be smitten. I was just playing the part."

"Honey, if that was acting, you deserve an Academy Award."

"I'm very talented," she agreed, leaving him to wonder what exactly she meant by that. A talented actress? Or talented in other ways?

As they turned toward the staircase, Lucy boldly put her hand on his butt and squeezed. "Very talented."

So, no ambiguity there. She'd practically issued an engraved invitation that she was open to making love.

Regrettably, it was one invitation he was going to have to decline. But that didn't mean he couldn't think about it—which he did, through the remainder of dessert and after-dinner coffee, through the farewell hugs and promises to drive carefully, and throughout the drive home.

He was as primed as a sixteen-year-old on his first car date—and unfortunately about as likely to get lucky. Every time he glanced over at her, her blond hair swirling about her face from the breeze coming through the moon roof, her eyes drowsy from good food and wine and pure exhaustion, he wanted to come out of his skin.

He escorted her to the elevator in his building, careful not to touch her. "I'll be up in a few minutes," he said. "I need to check on things at the restaurant."

She glanced at her watch. "Isn't the restaurant closed?"

"Uh, right. I need to be sure things are ready for to-morrow." Which was a silly reply, because Lucy knew Stash took care of the day-to-day concerns. But it was the best he could come up with. He couldn't possibly go up to his apartment with her until he had his libido under control. In his current state, she had only to hint at seduction and he would be at her mercy. Seeing as how he didn't know what she had in mind, he thought it would be safer to keep his distance.

"All right. Well, I guess I'll see you tomorrow, then."

"Tomorrow. Oh, and Lucy, you did great tonight. Posing as Lindsay, I mean. I don't think anyone in my family suspects a thing."

"I'm not so sure about that, but thanks."

He gave the verbal command that would send the elevator up to his loft, then stepped out and let the doors close between them.

He used his key to get into the darkened restaurant. What he needed was to burn off excess energy, and whipping something up in the kitchen ought to do the trick, he thought. Something decadent, something with chocolate and bourbon, the best substitutes for sex he could think of.

Maeve had given him his love for fine food. When his brother and cousins were outside playing and he couldn't join in because of his heart ailment, Maeve would take him into the kitchen. He would pick out a recipe from her many boxes and cookbooks, and together they would cook. He learned to associate the heady smells of yeast and chocolate and toasted almonds with happy times, and to this day puttering in the kitchen could take the edge off when he was tense, or when he had to figure something out.

His plan was to dream up a new dessert and play around with the ingredients while he put some serious thought to how to track down Stungun—and either rescue him, find out who killed him—or bring him to justice if he was the traitor.

Instead, his thoughts turned again and again to Lucy—how she'd looked on the beach with the wind in her hair and her clothes molded against her body, the strength in her stance and the vulnerability in her face, her intelligence and bravery.

Soon he had three different sauces on the stove and he was going to work on some heavy cream with the KitchenAid mixer. An orange cake was in the oven— not one of these fluffy, melt-in-your-mouth cakes, but something with some substance. He didn't yet know what the end product would be, but he planned to eat the whole thing himself, until his appetites were subdued—or he was too sick to even think about making love to Lucy. Only then could he return to his apartment.

Lucy lay in her bed in one of her slinky new nighties, trying her best to find sleep. But she couldn't help thinking about the kiss on the beach.

That kiss had been no acting job, on her part or Bryan's. She'd tasted the naked desire in the kiss, sharp as a knife and strong as a tidal wave. She'd felt the answering call in herself, a yearning so strong she couldn't deny it. She'd floated on air the rest of the long evening at The Tides, unbothered now by the Elliotts' noisy bickering, not nervous about carrying off her role as Lindsay Morgan. She'd played her part well—really well, apparently, given what was happening between herself and Bryan.

The only question left was, would they act on the waves of desire coursing between them?

She knew she wanted to, and she'd let Bryan know her feelings in no uncertain terms. But she still wasn't sure what he wanted. He hadn't said a word about it during the silent drive home.

Now, as the minutes clicked by on her bedside clock,

it became more and more evident that he wouldn't come to her. He was staying away on purpose, trying to avoid any awkward good-night scenes.

She knew that for him to make love to her would cross an ethical boundary, and she respected Bryan's wish not to mix his professional life with his personal.

But how often did two people resonate the way she and Bryan did? How did one simply turn one's back on those feelings?

She couldn't do it.

When more than an hour had passed, Lucy's frustrations turned to worry. What was keeping him? What could he possibly have to check on at the restaurant that would take this long? Had something happened to him?

When she couldn't stand not knowing any longer, Lucy got out of bed and threw on a pair of warmup pants and a T-shirt. Hardly clothing designed for seduction, but seduction was far from her mind now. She put on her glasses—a new, more stylish pair with lightweight lenses Bryan had insisted on when they'd ordered her contacts—and headed for the elevator.

She could get out of Bryan's apartment, but unless she found him, she couldn't get back in. So she took a few dollars with her and Scarlet's phone number, in case she got locked out. Then she got in the elevator and headed down to the restaurant level.

The restaurant had been dark when they'd arrived home, but she could see a light coming from somewhere now. She tried the door. It was locked, so she banged loudly.

At first no one came, and Lucy envisioned the worst—Bryan lying on the floor in a pool of blood, helpless to answer her knock. But finally she saw a shadowy figure approaching. Apprehension seized her, followed quickly by a rush of relief when the figure resolved into Bryan's familiar form.

He turned the dead bolt and opened the door. "Lucy, what are you doing here?"

"I couldn't sleep. I was worried about you when you didn't come back." She realized how stupid that sounded. She was worried about a superspy, so she was coming downstairs to rescue him?

He smiled indulgently at her. "Thank you for worrying. And I'm sorry, but I got caught up—"

"What is that smell?" she demanded, cutting him off. She yanked the door open wide enough that she could slide inside past Bryan. The smell coming from the kitchen drew her like the pied piper's music.

"It's just a…dessert."

"After all the food we ate at your grandparents' house, you were hungry?" But even as she said that, her own stomach growled, reacting to the commingled scents. Whatever was cooking, she wanted some of it.

"Cooking helps me think," he said.

She zeroed in on the tall cake sitting on a cooling rack. "Orange, that's what I smell."

"Right. It's an orange pound cake."

"And chocolate. And…bourbon?"

"You have a good nose."

"What is this dessert?" she asked, intrigued.

"I don't know yet. I'm making it up as I go along."

Lucy inspected the sauces slowly simmering on the stove, taking a good whiff of each one. Her mouth watered. Unable to resist, she dipped a finger in the warm chocolate sauce and took a taste.

"Mmmm."

"Lucy! This is a restaurant. You can't do that."

"You're not actually going to serve that cake to patrons, are you?"

"I can't now." But he grinned. "Actually, I was planning to eat the whole thing myself."

"Not without my help, you don't. What comes next?"

She watched as Bryan used a very sharp knife to cut the cake into four layers, all perfectly uniform. "You're good with a knife," she said.

"I'm good with all my tools," he replied, paying her back for her saucy comments on the beach earlier.

"I'll bet you are."

He gave her a warning look, then returned his attention to the cake. He spread fresh whipped cream on the bottom layer, then spooned on some of the chocolate sauce and set the second layer on top. Then came more whipped cream and the bourbon sauce, and another layer. Yet more whipped cream, more chocolate sauce, and some toasted almonds, and the final layer.

"I want to drizzle a glaze on top, but I'm not sure what to flavor it with. Lemon?"

Lucy shook her head. "Too much citrus. I don't know what I'm talking about, but how about crème de menthe? When I was little, I used to mix orange sherbet with mint-chocolate-chip ice cream."

"You innovator, you." He grinned. "Okay, what the hell." He quickly mixed up a glaze, adding a dash of spearmint extract rather than crème de menthe, which he thought might compete with the bourbon. He garnished the cake with orange slices and sprigs of fresh mint.

"It's the most beautiful cake I've ever seen," she said reverently.

"You're not laying it on a little thick, are you?"

"No. It's a work of art. Shame to cut into it. But you are going to cut into it, aren't you?" she asked anxiously.

In answer he got out two plates, then wielded his knife and spatula to cut two perfectly uniform slices, which he laid on the plates sideways. He topped each with another small dollop of whipped cream and a mint leaf.

"Presentation is everything."

Lucy knew she should be admiring the dessert. But she'd eyed a small spot of whipped cream on Bryan's cheek, and she became fixated on it.

"What?" he asked.

"You have whipped cream on your face."

"Oh." He rubbed one side of his face with the dishcloth he kept over one shoulder, missing the spot completely.

"Here, let me." She took the dishcloth from him. But instead of wiping his face, she stood on her tiptoes and licked off the whipped cream.

Bryan's pupil dilated. "Oh, Lucy." His voice was hoarse with suppressed passion. They were standing near the stove, and Lucy reached over to the pan of chocolate sauce, dipped her finger in again, and wiped a little on his other cheek before sucking the end of her finger.

"You do get dirty when you cook, don't you?" She again stretched up on tiptoe so she could dart her tongue out and lick off the chocolate.

"You are a very wicked girl." He dipped a finger into the bowl of whipped cream and spread a smear across her lips. "Oh, dear, look, I've made another mess."

Lucy reflexively licked at the whipped cream, but Bryan shook his head. "No, no, you've missed most of it." He leaned down and claimed her lips with his.

The kiss started out light and teasing, but it didn't

stay that way. His mouth went hard, demanding, his breathing harsh and rapid, and Lucy drank it in, his passion elevating hers.

She hadn't meant to come in here and seduce him. Not exactly, anyway, but clearly that was what she'd done. And this time they were not in a public place, there was no family nearby. They were in a deserted restaurant with just the heady scents of chocolate and orange surrounding them.

Bryan's kisses moved from her mouth to her jaw and down her neck to her collarbone. He caressed her breast through the thin warmup. "You're not wearing a bra."

"I dressed in a hurry." She pulled his hand against her breast again, hungry for the feel of him. She wanted his touch everywhere on her body.

He slid the zipper on her shirt down, following with a trail of kisses that ended between her breasts. Then he insinuated his hand inside the shirt and eased the fabric aside, bringing her breast out into the light.

He pushed her up against the Sub-Zero fridge and kissed her breast, first with reverence, then with an increasing hunger. As he suckled, flames of hot desire shot from her breast through her body to the very core of her, and the heat made her whimper with need.

He peeled off her shirt and then his, fumbling with the buttons in his haste, getting his hand caught in the cuff, tugging until buttons flew off. He pressed his bare chest against hers and groaned.

"Oh, yes." The hair on his chest abraded her sensitive nipples, sending more of those white-hot flames licking through her, making her squirm.

"Lucy, we have to stop."

"Oh, no. No, no, no, don't do this to me."

"We don't have any birth control."

"We don't need it. I have the implant."

"Seriously?"

She went to work on his linen suit pants. "I wouldn't joke about something like that. Now, make love to me, Bryan Elliott, or that pot of chocolate sauce is going over your head."

Seven

Bryan had always been a man who used his good judgment in all decisions, but he was beyond judgment now. Lucy Miller had just removed the last barrier to their making love. No unforeseen consequences could result from their intimacy.

He kissed her again, inhaling her. She smelled even better than the chocolate, which would have been a poor substitute for indulging in Lucy.

"I should take you up to bed," he whispered.

"No. You'll change your mind if I give you even half a chance."

"Or you will." He slid both hands inside the stretchy waist of her warmup pants. She wore only the briefest of thongs under them, which meant her cheeks were bare. He filled his hands with her rounded bottom while he continued kissing her, rubbing up against her small but perfect breasts. Her nipples were hard as glass beads against his chest, and they burned him like a brand.

She managed to get his pants unfastened and her own hands were as busy as his. She thrust them inside his boxers, groaning as one hand found his arousal.

"Whoa, Lucy." He had to distract her or he was going to go off like a defective bottle rocket. He couldn't recall the last time he was this turned on, possibly never. But he felt as if the foreplay had been going on all evening. Every look she gave him, every innocent or not-so-innocent touch, had led to this.

He pulled her pants and thong down past her knees in one fluid movement. She gasped in surprise, but she was about to get an even bigger surprise. He leaned down, placed a shoulder against her waist, wrapped his arms around her thighs, and picked her up in a fireman's carry.

She squealed in protest. "Bryan, what are you doing? Put me down." She reached out and slapped at his rear, but it was hardly more than a tap.

He retaliated with a slightly smarter smack to her bare bottom. "Behave."

"Ow!" She laughed. "What are you doing?"

He carried her only as far as the large counter where the chefs assembled the plates of food just before the wait staff whisked them out to their patrons. "You think you're the only one who's allowed to do something outrageous? You think you're the only one who can seduce?"

"Oh, Bryan, I didn't set out to seduce you. Not really." She wrapped her hands around his head, pressing his face against her breasts, and he didn't protest. He was in heaven.

"I was worried about you. You'd been gone so long.

If you hadn't had the whipped cream on your face, this never would have happened."

"Well, it did, missy. You started it and I'm going to finish it." He leaned against her, pushing her until she lay with her back on the counter. Then he stripped her pants and underwear all the way off her feet, pulling off her running shoes in the process. They dropped with a clunk to the floor, and he pulled her knees apart and stepped between her thighs.

She quivered with anticipation, and he had to admit it would have been easy just to drop his own pants and bury himself in her. He tested her readiness with one finger and felt that she was slick.

She gasped at his featherlight touch.

"Please," she said. "Do it now."

Not before he'd tasted her. With his own stomach knotted in anticipation, he leaned down and, using his fingers to open her, lightly grazed her with a flick of his tongue.

She wiggled and moaned again. "Oh, no, please, no more…"

"Maybe you'll think twice before you do that trick with the chocolate sauce again," he said with a low growl before tasting her once more. He held her hips firmly so she couldn't wiggle right out of his reach, and he tasted her yet again, drinking more deeply this time, letting his tongue explore.

Lucy reached out and grabbed a handful of his hair. "Bryan!"

He did not take pity on her. He waited until he sensed she was verging on the peak of pleasure. Then he raised up, shed his own garments, slid her hips to the edge of the counter and plunged himself into her warmth.

"Oh!" Lucy cried out. "I can't— Oh, my—"

Bryan thrust again, more deeply this time, and again until he was buried to the hilt. She was tight and warm and slick and he was going to lose control of himself. It was too much.

He felt Lucy's spasms of ecstasy just before she cried out one last time. Three more hard thrusts, and it was over for him, too, but he'd known he wouldn't last long inside Lucy. Not with the buildup he'd had over the past hours—hell, the past days.

Lucy sat up suddenly and, still joined to him, threw her arms around him and kissed him. She clung sweetly to him and rubbed her face against his hair.

"Please don't leave me, don't ever leave me," she said. "I want to be together like this forever."

He thought about telling her how awkward it would be for the chefs to work around them when they came to work tomorrow, but he held his tongue. This wasn't a moment for humor.

Lucy might seem strong, but in many ways she was fragile, and he had to remember that. She might have been a bit brazen tonight, but he knew she didn't take this sort of thing casually.

He tried not to take her plea about never leaving too seriously. People said all kinds of strange things during a sexual climax. Refined ladies cursed like sailors, and sailors wept like children.

He hoped she didn't mean anything by it. Because he would leave her eventually. No matter how much he didn't want to.

He gently separated himself from her, wrapped his arms around her and slid her off the counter and onto legs that wobbled slightly before she found her balance.

"You okay?" He smoothed her hair out of her face.

"I think I'll live."

"Ready to put your clothes on and go upstairs?"

"You aren't seriously asking me to go upstairs without eating some of that cake, are you?"

Funny, he'd forgotten all about the cake. "Let's take it with us. We can eat it in bed."

She grinned, pushed him farther away from her and retrieved her discarded clothes. "Last one dressed has to spread whipped cream all over the other one and lick it off."

That was one contest Bryan wouldn't mind losing— though winning sounded pretty good, too.

Lucy had sobered by the time they got upstairs, fully dressed and carrying two plates of cake plus the rest of the dessert, which Bryan had sealed into a Tupperware cake plate.

Her face grew warm as she recalled how wanton she'd been—and then how she'd clung to Bryan, pleading with him not to leave.

She hadn't meant to do that last part. She'd still been in the throes of the most intense orgasm of her life, and the words had just poured out of her right past her brain.

She knew she still had some issues about Cruz Tabor. The In Tight drummer had ended the relationship without warning, in the cruelest of fashions, and now she had a sort of phobia about being abandoned.

But such pleas would be useless where Bryan was concerned. Their relationship could not be anything but temporary. He'd given her fair warning—unlike that bastard Cruz, who'd led her to believe he was crazy in love with her and that he would marry her someday.

She would just make things worse if she clung to Bryan. She had to adopt the mindset that every day they had together was a gift, and that when they inevitably parted ways, she would have some incredible memories and, hopefully, no hard feelings.

Hell, she wasn't even sure Bryan wanted to have a relationship, temporary or otherwise. She'd pushed him into sex, and men were pretty helpless to say no when sex was offered.

She chanced a glance at him as the elevator reached his loft. He was staring at her.

"What?" she said with a nervous giggle.

"You're just so absolutely gorgeous I can't stop looking at you."

"Oh, yeah, right. In these really sexy clothes, no makeup, glasses, my hair's a wreck—"

"Stop that. You are beautiful, with or without designer clothes and cosmetics. I don't know who told you you weren't, but he was an idiot."

The door opened, and he ushered her ahead of him.

"It wasn't a he. It was my mother. She thought I was going straight to hell when I died anyway, for being willful and lazy and disrespectful. But she said that at least she didn't have to worry about me doing bad things with boys, because God hadn't gifted me in a way that would make any boy take notice."

Lucy had always made light of her mother's criticism, but saying the words aloud after all these years still produced a tightness in her chest.

"That's criminal," Bryan said, his jaw pulsating. "No wonder you don't miss your parents so much."

"Oh, she meant well. She was always so afraid for me—afraid for my soul. She just knew I was headed down the path straight to hell. The sad thing was, I proved her right."

"You?"

"I lived up to her worst fears." And that was all Lucy would say on that subject. "Can we really eat cake in bed?"

"Your mother wouldn't approve."

"My mother would be on her knees for a week, praying for my salvation, if she knew I'd colored my hair. Eating cake in bed with a man would be beyond her comprehension."

"Then I guess we won't worry about what Mom would think."

Lucy took a deep breath and realized, for the first time in a long time, that she didn't feel guilty for enjoying herself, for having fun. Maybe she was making progress.

She nodded toward the stairs. The last of Bryan's anger left his face. He grinned, left the cake in the kitchen, took one of Lucy's plates and her hand and led her upstairs.

"Here's the thing about eating cake in bed, though," he said with mock gravity. "There are rules."

"Such as?"

"You have to do it naked."

"I can do that." She smiled wickedly, set the plates down on the king-size bed and took off her clothes. In less than a minute they were both naked and in bed, feeding each other the decadent dessert without benefit of forks, which they'd forgotten.

"This cake is fabulous. You just made this up to-night?"

Bryan made a production of licking whipped cream

off her fingers. "You inspired me. I needed something so decadent it would distract me from you. I'm going to put it on the menu, and I'm going to call it Lucy's Cake."

"Don't you mean Lindsay's Cake? Everyone would wonder who the heck Lucy was."

"Once we catch our embezzler—and find Stungun—you can go back to using your real name."

"Right." Lucy didn't add that once that happened, there would be no more need for his girlfriend ruse. No more need for her to remain in New York.

Bryan set the two empty plates on the nightstand and slid more deeply under the covers, pulling her with him. "We need to work off a few calories, you know," he said.

"I'm all sticky. Maybe I should take a shower."

"I like you all sticky." To prove his point, he kissed all around her mouth and started doing crazy things with his hands, rubbing her belly and thighs, petting her as if she were a cat.

Lucy wondered if he'd noticed that her belly wasn't quite as flat and firm as it ought to be. Also, anyone who looked closely would see her faint stretch marks.

She reached over and turned off the lamp. Maybe someday she would tell Bryan the truth about her past. But not tonight.

Bryan woke before dawn, and it took him a few seconds to reason why there was a warm female body snuggled up to him. When he remembered, he smiled. He and Lucy had gone completely crazy last night. He'd never have guessed that a mild-mannered little bank employee in a shapeless suit would be such a wildcat in bed. She wasn't just responsive, she was imaginative. He'd believed himself to be fairly experienced and uninhibited, but she'd shown him a few things that had driven him completely wild.

He should have felt guilty for taking Lucy into his bed. She was a witness, a civilian cooperating to bring down a terrorist sympathizer. She'd done everything he'd asked of her, and he'd promised his protection.

But he couldn't muster much guilt. He didn't feel as if he'd taken advantage of her. Though he'd been the one to initiate their first kiss two days before, she'd been the aggressor last night. He'd gone out of his way *not* to seduce her. She'd come to him with her eyes wide open, knowing he was not cut out for a committed relationship.

As for compromising her ability to be a good witness, he didn't see it. As far as anyone would know, she was posing as his girlfriend so he could protect her. No one ever needed to know that the fiction had become reality. He could keep a secret—and apparently Lucy could, too. There were definitely parts of her past she hadn't revealed.

She was entitled to her privacy. Whatever her secrets, he didn't imagine they had any bearing on the case. But he wanted her to trust him.

"You awake?" she whispered.

"Mmm-hmm."

She snuggled closer. "Why? It's not even light out."

"Just thinking. Lucy, you don't have to answer if you don't want, but I'm just curious. I dug around in your past pretty thoroughly, and I didn't find any boyfriends in the past couple of years."

"No, I didn't date anyone after I moved to Virginia."

"Why do you have the implant, then?"

"I'm optimistic?"

"You weren't acting like a woman on the hunt for a lover."

"But I found one. By accident. And isn't it a good thing I'm protected?"

"Yes, of course." He wasn't quite sure why he was so bothered by this scenario. He supposed it was because he was trained to notice inconsistencies. And women with no immediate prospects for sex didn't usually worry about birth control.

"All right, I'll explain it to you," she said. "It's not a pretty episode in my past, and you'll probably be repulsed, but I want to be honest. Your background check missed a few relevant facts about me."

"Those two missing years?"

"Yeah. I wasn't just working for In Tight. I was sort of a…well, a groupie."

"You?"

"I started out just wanting to do my job. I was content to be a very small part of In Tight. I was starstruck, and being close to a rock band was like heaven, especially after my conservative upbringing. Most of the guys knew my name, and they actually talked to me occasionally—usually when they wanted to get paid—and that was fine with me. Then came Cruz Tabor."

"He's in the group, isn't he?"

"The drummer. He started coming on to me—big-time. I was just this nerdy accountant from Kansas, and he made me feel special. We started…well, I guess you wouldn't call it dating. We started sleeping together."

That bastard! Then Bryan tempered his first thought. After all, wasn't he guilty of the same thing? That Tabor guy had fallen victim to Lucy's winsome charms, and who could blame him?

"He treated me pretty well at first," Lucy continued. "We were a couple. I even got my picture in a tabloid once, though I wasn't identified. When the band went on tour, he let me ride with him in first class—they didn't have their own private jet back then."

Bryan wondered how he could have missed all this when he'd dug into Lucy's past. But it sounded as if her activities with In Tight wouldn't have left a paper trail, and he hadn't gone so far as to interview her family or friends. The check had been more routine than that. He'd mostly been concerned with whether she had a criminal record or mental illness.

He lightly rubbed her arm, urging her to continue.

"Things were pretty good, until I got pregnant."

Bryan grew very still. Lucy had been pregnant?

"Cruz had said he loved me, that he wanted to marry me as soon as the band got better established. I thought he'd be happy about the baby. Instead he was horrified. No, that's not the right word. Disgusted. He blamed me for not being more careful, and he told me to…to g-get rid of it." Her voice cracked, and Bryan pulled her more closely against him.

He felt a rage against the insensitive bastard. "If I ever meet this man, I'll yank out his esophagus," Bryan said. "You didn't…" But maybe she had. Clearly she had no child now.

"No, I didn't terminate the pregnancy. I told Cruz I thought he was horrid and that I was having the baby. He said he would deny it was his and claim I was a slut and I slept around with everyone."

Bryan's anger escalated toward boiling. "DNA could have proved—"

"I didn't want that man acknowledged as my child's

father. Not after the way he acted. He knew I could prove he was the father, and he offered me money to just go away. But I didn't take it. I just left."

"So, what happened?" Bryan asked, though he was afraid he knew.

"I went home to the farm. My parents were scandalized, of course. They dragged me to church a lot and prayed for me. But I was their daughter, and eventually they forgave me. Then I lost the baby."

"Oh, Lucy, I'm sorry."

"The strange thing was, I really wanted her. Everyone said losing her was a blessing, but I didn't agree, and I felt so guilty, like I was being punished. I should have listened to my parents. I shouldn't have been so wild. Taking risks for myself was one thing, but my foolhardy behavior had created a human being. It sobered me. To make amends, I swore I would never, ever take any kind of risk, ever again. I would work at the job my uncle found for me, I wouldn't call attention to myself, I would be humble."

"And the implant?"

"I'm weak," she said. "I wouldn't go looking for trouble, but what if trouble found me? I wanted to be ready, just in case. I wouldn't, couldn't, take a chance on another unplanned pregnancy. And was I right? Yes. Trouble found me. And I have no ability to resist temptation, as I've so amply illustrated tonight."

"You're not weak," he said. "You're one of the strongest women I've ever met. You made a mistake—you fell in love with the wrong man, that's all. It happens every day."

"But who's to say it won't happen again? To me?"

He understood exactly what she was saying. He was

the wrong man for her. Another bad choice. "I would never turn my back on my own child," he said.

"I know. You're not anything like Cruz. He was a self-absorbed, spoiled child. You're responsible and mature."

"You can say that with a straight face after everything we did last night?" He almost blushed thinking about what they'd done in the restaurant kitchen.

"Yes, I can. I know you would put my life before yours in a heartbeat. But I also know that you would not choose to have a baby. Fortunately, that's not something you have to worry about."

He shifted his weight on top of her and kissed her, filled with a rush of affection for her. She'd made some difficult decisions. She'd taken responsibility for her actions.

He wished he could be the right man for her. She deserved someone who would love her unconditionally. Someone who would be there for her, always, not running off on dangerous missions, staying gone for weeks at a time. Someone who would welcome her babies.

Yes, she was right about him. He would not choose to bring a child into the world—for all the same reasons he chose not to marry or let his professional and personal lives become enmeshed. He refused to put his loved ones in danger or make them worry about him.

"I guess I didn't repulse you?" she asked.

"Nothing you could do would repulse me." On the contrary, everything she said and did turned him on more. She was like an addictive drug.

"Good. Because I was rather enjoying all this." She reached down, running her hand along his ribs, then across his chest. Her fingers paused to explore the raised scar that ran along his sternum.

"You'll find lots more of those on me if you look," he said. "I've got a dandy one on my leg, another across my back. I'm not very pretty."

She huffed at that, then skittered across his belly with her hand, arriving at his growing arousal. "This is all the pretty I need." She took it possessively into her hand.

He groaned.

"I know it's temporary," she said.

"It'll last long enough."

She giggled. "No. I meant you and me. I know we can't be together long-term. But I'm okay with that. I don't want you to feel bad."

"I don't feel bad. I feel very, very good, and I'm going to feel better in a moment or two." He moved on top of her. He did not want to talk about, or even think about, the day they would say goodbye.

Lucy stood under the spray in Bryan's enormous shower, feeling cleansed both inside and out. She was glad she'd unburdened herself last night. Maybe her confession was a bit more elaborate than Bryan had been prepared for, but she'd needed to say it. She hadn't talked about Cruz or her pregnancy to anyone since her miscarriage. Her parents had wanted her to bury the past, forget it had ever happened. But as awful as it was, Cruz and the pregnancy were a part of her now. She felt she had a new perspective on it. Yes, she'd been naive, and she'd made a mistake. But she wasn't evil.

Thanks to Bryan, she wasn't stuck anymore. She could move on, live normally, leave the sackcloth and ashes behind.

Bryan tapped on the bathroom door. "You're going to use up all the hot water."

He was back from cleaning up the restaurant. "Then join me." She'd been fantasizing about herself and Bryan in this decadent shower, with its acres of red glass tile and twin shower sprays, since she'd first seen it the day Scarlet came over for her makeover.

"Hey. You don't have to ask me twice."

Just when she thought she couldn't possibly make love again, for she ached in places she hadn't known existed, they did.

Eight

Lucy had mixed feelings about her computer work now. Yes, she wanted to solve the puzzle of who the embezzler was at Alliance Trust. But the sooner that person was arrested and all parties brought to justice, the sooner she and Bryan would part.

Duty won out, and she worked hard on her latest project, which was matching up log-in times with the times the illicit funds transfers had occurred.

By lunch, she'd eliminated several more candidates. She was closing in. Only five suspects. One of them was Omar Kalif, a loan officer of Iranian descent. She'd always liked Omar. He was funny and hardworking, and he would turn himself inside out to find a way to get a client qualified for a loan. He had a darling wife, two kids…

Well, she would let Bryan worry about that. Her job was to solve the puzzle.

Bryan had told her he would be tied up today and probably wouldn't be home until late. He'd been vague about what he would be doing. She didn't know if he was in the city or had jetted off some place, risking life and limb.

She tried not to think about it. She tried not to worry, to keep herself busy. But she had a vivid imagination. If anything ever happened to Bryan, would she be notified? What about his family? Would anyone explain to them that he was a spy, that he'd died defending their country? Or would he just disappear, leaving the family to wonder?

She couldn't live like that long-term. Even if Bryan were willing to change his policy and make a commitment, she didn't think she could. Yes, it was exciting working with and living with a spy. But it wasn't a forever kind of arrangement.

Bryan had told her to go downstairs to the restaurant when she got hungry, that Stash would take care of her. He'd fixed the elevator so it would recognize her voice and had instructed her on passwords and "panic passwords"—in case she was ever in the elevator under duress. She'd laughed at the cloak-and-dagger antics, but he'd been serious.

She went down to Une Nuit to rustle up some lunch. She entered through the kitchen, and her face grew warm as she was reminded of what had gone on there the previous night.

"Lindsay!" Stash Martin greeted her with a double air-kiss. "Bryan said you'd be down for lunch. Scarlet's in the Elliott booth if you want to sit with her."

"I don't want to intrude—"

"Nonsense. I am sure she would welcome your

charming company." Refusing to acknowledge any further protests, Stash led her into the dining room, where Scarlet, dressed in the most gorgeous teal dress with feathers all around the neck, shared a booth with another woman who had her back to Lucy.

Scarlet looked both surprised and pleased when she saw Lucy. "Oh, please join us," she said. "We haven't even ordered yet. This is Jessie. I don't think you've met her."

The other woman smiled warmly and shook Lucy's hand. "Nice to meet you, Lindsay."

"Same here. Scarlet, I didn't realize you had another sister."

"What?" both women said at the same time.

Lindsay looked at Scarlet, then Jessie, then Scarlet again. Though they weren't as similar as Scarlet and Summer, the family resemblance was unmistakable.

"You're sisters, right?"

Scarlet laughed, and Jessie just looked horrified.

"What in the world would make you think that?" Jessie said, a little more strongly than Lucy thought was called for.

"Sorry, I thought I saw a family resemblance," Lucy said, trying to smooth over the awkward moment. "My mistake."

Scarlet explained, "This is Jessie Clayton. She's my intern at *Charisma*."

"You know," Jessie said, "I've really got an awful lot of work to do. I think I'll skip lunch." She tried to slide out of the booth, but Scarlet leaned over and put a hand on her arm to stop her.

"Oh, come on, Jessie, I'm not a slave driver. You can take time for lunch."

"No, really, I have to go." She stood and made good her escape despite both Lucy's and Scarlet's protests.

Lucy sat on the recently vacated leather banquette. "Sorry. I didn't mean to scare her off."

Scarlet looked perplexed. "That was strange. I wonder what got into her? Maybe she was distressed at the idea that she looks like me."

"Oh, yes, you're such an ogre," Lucy said. "No one wants to look like you."

"Do you really think there's a resemblance? Because I thought so, too, when I first hired her, but then I decided I was imagining things."

"Well, lots of people look similar," Lucy said, down-playing the uncanny resemblance. "She's probably got Irish in her, like you."

Scarlet ordered mineral water and her favorite salad Niçoise, which came adorned with tiny eggrolls. Lucy, who continued to be delighted by the French/Asian blended menu, ordered an egg-drop soup Florentine.

"That's all you're having?" Scarlet asked.

"After that huge dinner last night, I haven't been very hungry." Not to mention the orange-chocolate-mint cake.

"So where's Bryan today?"

"Out and about. I'm not sure."

"So he doesn't tell you any more about his business than he tells anyone else?"

"I don't want to be nosy."

"Well, I am. Honestly, the whole family is a little fed up with him. He's been so secretive lately. We all thought maybe you were the secret, but apparently not, since he's still doing his disappearing act."

"He'll be back tonight," Lucy said, trying to mask her reaction. She wondered if Bryan knew just how worried his family had become about him. That was something he'd tried to avoid at all costs.

Scarlet asked about Lucy's clothes, how everything was working out and whether she needed anything else. "We're doing a shoot tomorrow with the most gorgeous Givenchy eveningwear. One of the dresses would look perfect on you. Hey, maybe you could model it. We pay well."

Lucy laughed. That was all she needed, her picture in a national magazine. She might as well send a map to the embezzler with a dotted line leading straight to her.

"No, I don't think so. I have work to do."

"Oh, your novel! I'm so glad you decided to give it another try. How's it going? I know an agent at William Morris. I could probably get you a read."

"I'm a long way from having anything to show." And, boy, wasn't that the truth. "But thank you. You're awfully nice to me."

"That's because I want you to stick around. Bryan clearly needs you in his life. I don't think I've ever seen him quite as happy as he was last night. He couldn't stop staring at you."

Lucy blushed. She wanted to reassure Scarlet that she would stick around. But, of course, she wouldn't.

"Scarlet, hi!" A striking woman with the brightest red hair Lucy had ever seen stopped at their table. Scarlet stood to give the other woman a hug. The redhead towered over Scarlet, no easy feat. She had to be well over six feet tall. Then Lucy realized her face was familiar. She was a supermodel. She went by Redd.

"Redd," Scarlet said, "this is Lindsay Morgan, Bryan's girlfriend."

Lucy had never quite gotten over her awe of celebrities, even after the Cruz disaster. She babbled something to Redd, who eventually left to find her own table.

"It must be fun, seeing celebrities all the time," she said.

"You'll get used to it."

Lucy only wished she would have the opportunity to get used to it.

Bryan didn't get home until close to nine that night. Lucy couldn't help herself. She launched herself into his arms the moment he got off the elevator.

"Hey, hey," he said, returning her hug, rubbing her back. "Is something wrong?"

"I was just worried about you."

"Why? I told you I'd be late."

"I know. But I didn't know what you were doing, and I have a vivid imagination. I saw you getting shot, stabbed, poisoned—"

"Oh, Lucy." He kissed her tenderly. "I wasn't doing anything dangerous. Just boring legwork. Checking in with snitches, trying to get a lead on Stungun. I met with Siberia."

"Does he know Stungun's true identity?"

"No. Only the head of the agency knows. But he's going to find out. He's making a case to the director tomorrow. We've got to find him."

"I've made some progress on my end."

"Really?"

"Do you want something to eat? Stash delivered a huge dinner. I didn't eat a third of it."

He didn't let her go. "I'm starved, but not for food."

"Hmm. I think you tend to confuse your appetites." She slid out of his grasp. "Sit. I'll warm up a plate and explain what I've found."

As she heated up the coq au vin tempura, she told him what her research had led her to that afternoon. And she didn't like it one bit.

"I've eliminated everybody but one person. I've double- and triple-checked, and she is the only one who has been logged in every single time there was an illegal withdrawal."

"She?"

"Peggy Holmes, Mr. Vargov's personal secretary. She's a mild-mannered grandmother who's been working at the bank for more than twenty years. I don't really see how she could be a terrorist sympathizer."

"You'd be surprised. One of her children is married to a man who travels frequently to the Middle East with his business. Nothing wrong with that in itself—"

"You already know that?"

"I've done background checks on everyone at that bank. Now that you've identified Peggy as a viable suspect, I'll zero in on the son-in-law."

"But Peggy Holmes? I just don't see it. Of course, she does enjoy helping others and being of service. She lives to please Mr. Vargov. So maybe if someone approached her, made it sound like she'd be doing a great service…"

"What about Mr. Vargov? As the bank president, he'd be in a position of authority and power. You haven't said much about him. He has relatives in former Soviet republics—"

She shook her head. "It couldn't be him. I was able to eliminate him as a suspect first thing. He was in a meeting during every single transaction."

"Every single one?"

"Well, the first few that I looked at. I stopped checking after I was able to eliminate him." When

Bryan still looked skeptical, she added, "Mr. Vargov does attend a lot of meetings."

"Just for fun, let's see where he was during all of the transactions."

"All of them? There are dozens."

"All of them."

Three hours later Bryan had the answer he was looking for. Mr. Vargov had been in some type of meeting on the bank premises during every single illicit transaction. During the two weeks he was on vacation, not a single withdrawal took place.

"But he wasn't even logged onto the computer during most of the transactions," Lucy objected. "He couldn't have performed those withdrawals without logging in and using a password."

"And how hard do you think it would be to figure out his trusty secretary's password? She probably has it written down someplace."

"But how could he have—"

"On his PDA. Your conference room has wireless capability. He could carry on a conversation, casually tapping on his Palm Pilot as if recording lunch plans, log on to the bank's system using Peggy's password, and move money around. Easy as pie."

"I can't believe I didn't see it. It's so obvious! Oh, but Mr. Vargov is so nice. He's like a father to me. He's always been kind, gave me a job when he didn't know me at all, paid me more than I was worth, gave me a really nice office."

"Think about it. If you were going to raid pension funds, who would you want doing the audits?"

Now Lucy got it. "Someone inexperienced. Underqualified. Stupid."

"You would want to pay that person handsomely, keep them happy. A happy employee is much less likely to rock the boat than a dissatisfied one. But you were too smart for him. And too conscientious to forget what you saw just to hold on to your cushy job."

"It all makes sense now." She swiveled in her chair to face Bryan, who'd been sitting behind her looking over her shoulder. "That has to be the answer."

"We are a good team, you and I," Bryan said with a broad grin. "I never could have figured this out without you." He pulled her into his lap and nuzzled her neck. "What do you say we celebrate?"

She kissed him hungrily. After her long day at the computer, and all her worrying about Bryan, she craved release—and she knew just how to get it.

"You'll never guess who I met today," Lucy said later as they lay in bed. "Redd, the supermodel."

"She comes in a lot. She likes the wasabi pate."

"Don't you love owning a restaurant? I think it would be so fun, like entertaining every day. Making up special dishes for special customers, recommending wine—Well, okay, I'd have to learn about wine. But you must enjoy it."

"I do. I wish I could devote more time to it."

Lucy hesitated, then decided she owed it to Bryan to be honest with him about what she'd heard from his relatives. "Your whole family is worried about you, you know. They've noticed your long absences—and your injuries at your brother's wedding. What was that all about?"

"Car accident."

"That's what your father said, but he didn't believe it."

Bryan sighed. "It was actually a car bomb. In France.

I realized something was wrong and got out just before the explosion. No one was seriously hurt, thank God."

Lucy was horrified. The car bomb in Paris? "I read about that in the news. It was blamed on terrorists."

"I was with Stungun, investigating the charity, the one our embezzler is sending his funds to. I must have gotten close to them—but not close enough."

"You're not ever allowed to go back to France, do you understand?" Lucy said fiercely. "My God, someone there tried to kill you!"

He shrugged. "It happens a lot."

"Don't tell me any more. I can't stand it."

"I won't. But you have to reassure my family that everything's fine. Can you do that?"

"No, Bryan, I can't. I can't tell them not to worry when you could get blown up at any time."

"I'm not going to get blown up."

"Someday, some bad guy is going to catch up with you," she said in a small voice.

He kissed her cheek in an achingly tender gesture. "I'm not going anywhere. I promised I wouldn't leave you, didn't I?"

"You'll be gone again tomorrow."

"For a few hours only. I'll be back. We're having a big party at the restaurant. The half-year profit margins have been calculated at EPH, and the company has broken all previous records. Apparently Granddad's little game has produced the desired results."

"Which magazine is winning?"

"*Charisma*. No one's too surprised, the way Aunt Fin's been working her tail off. But there are still six months to go."

"Have you talked to your dad?"

"He doesn't seem to care that *Snap* is in last place. I think he's a little more broken up about his divorce than anyone suspected."

"Well, the breakup of any marriage is traumatic, even a bad marriage," Lucy said pragmatically. "He's got another six months to pull things together. Do you want him to get the CEO spot?"

Bryan shrugged. "I just want him to be happy. He hasn't been happy in a long time."

Lucy was bored out of her mind. Bryan had been gone longer than the "few hours" he'd promised, but she didn't hold it against him. He was working hard to catch the embezzler, which was his job.

But she missed him, and she had no more computer puzzles to distract her. She'd gone about as far as she could with the data she'd downloaded from Alliance Trust. Now it was up to Bryan to confirm the theory they'd come up with.

He didn't give her many details, but she gathered that he was having Mr. Vargov put under surveillance. Such operations were tricky, involving other arms of Homeland Security besides his own. And given that he had to protect his anonymity, even from other operatives, arrangements had to be made through intermediaries and other secure communications, all of which could take time.

Three hours before the EPH party, Bryan's phone rang. Lucy checked the Caller ID and saw the call came from Une Nuit, so she answered happily, thinking Bryan must be back.

Instead, she found Stash Martin on the other end of the line. "Lindsay, I am glad I caught you at home."

Like, where else would she be? "Bryan just called and said he would be delayed. He wants you to finalize the menu for the party tonight."

"Me? Why?"

"He said you have good taste."

"Good taste in men, maybe," she said, which made Stash laugh. "All right, I'll be down in a minute." She was grateful for any distraction, provided her magic key still worked on the elevator. She hadn't asked Bryan about that.

Fifteen minutes later she and Stash were bent over an array of menus, some printed, some handwritten, that had been assembled for various parties over the years. Apparently, the regular menu didn't include even a fraction of what the kitchen could do. Bryan regularly rotated dishes on and off, which kept things interesting for the clientele.

"Stash, you have to help me choose," she said, overwhelmed by the exotic-sounding dishes. "Is there anything that's a particular favorite of the Elliotts? Anything they hate? Do any of them have food allergies?"

"No allergies. One or more of the ladies are always watching their carbs, so you should choose at least one dish with that in mind."

"All right, how about this grilled chicken with the cashew and water chestnut stuffing?"

"Excellent choice. Now, something with a bit more oomph for the adventurous palettes."

"Quiche Cantonese?"

Stash nodded his approval. They went on in this fashion, with Stash giving her hints. Obviously, he could have put together the menu by himself, but Bryan had wanted to let her make the choices, which warmed her heart. He was being very thoughtful. Her choice of wine was strictly a guessing game, but she trusted Stash not to allow her to make a really dumb mistake.

As she showered and began to dress a little while later, she realized she was looking forward to her dinner. She'd enjoyed planning it and couldn't wait to see how the Elliotts reacted to it.

She'd meant it when she told Bryan she thought owning a restaurant would be fun. She'd always enjoyed good food and had been ecstatic to discover dishes beyond the plain meat and potatoes she'd been raised on. She could hold her own in a kitchen. Her mother had taught her the basics, and she'd done some experimenting during her In Tight days, before Cruz had begun taking up all her time and attention. During the past couple of years she hadn't cooked anything too exciting—that would have fallen under the category of indulging herself and having fun, things that had been off her list. But she'd bought cookbooks and read them.

She loved Une Nuit—the whole package. She loved the bustle in the kitchen, the various chefs yelling at each other, sometimes in languages she didn't understand. She loved the smells and sounds, the well-heeled patrons in the dining room, blissfully unaware of the contained panic going on behind closed doors as Chef Chin demanded perfection. She loved the soft jazz music that played in the background, the muffled din of forks and chopsticks and ice tinkling in glasses, the easy laughter as diners reveled in their own senses.

She sighed. It wasn't her world, but she enjoyed being a part of it. This was much better than being on the fringes of the music business, which was glamorous but painfully sordid.

The bedroom door opened, and Lucy gasped and held her skirt in front of her until she realized the intruder was Bryan. He grinned at finding her in her panties and bra.

"You scared me half to death. The least you could do is stomp when you come up the stairs, so I'll have some warning."

"I'd much rather catch you unaware," he said with a devilish glint in his eyes. "Aren't you fetching. C'mere."

She did, and he wrapped his arms around her and kissed her as if he'd been away for weeks instead of hours. Her knees got all wobbly and her chest ached from shortness of breath.

"Sorry I took so long. Did you get everything sorted out with Stash?"

"You didn't ask?"

"I came straight upstairs. Couldn't wait another moment to see you, and thank goodness I didn't delay." He slid one hand inside her panties.

"We don't…uh…really have time to…uh…" She couldn't come up with a more energetic objection. In truth, they could have had an appointment with the Queen of England, and she'd have made the monarch wait.

"We'll just have to be fashionably late."

Bryan had his clothes off in seconds. Rather than take her to the bed, he sat in a cushy chair that was intended for reading, and pulled Lucy into his lap. She didn't need much coaxing; the moment she'd seen him, her body had started preparing itself for him. She was flushed, her nipples hard and aching for his touch, and she was warm deep inside and already tingling between her legs though he'd not yet touched her there.

She wiggled out of her panties, threw her bra aside, all the while making certain to brush against Bryan's arousal as much as possible. When she turned to face him again, she straddled him in the big chair, torturing him unmercifully by brushing her soft curls against him.

"You're teasing me."

"Are you suggesting we rush?" she asked innocently.

From behind, he reached between her legs and slipped a finger inside her. She gasped and whimpered, no longer in a teasing mood. "Okay, let's rush."

"That's my girl," he said as he poised his shaft at her entrance. She lowered herself onto him, letting him slowly fill her, enjoying every inch of him.

Once they were joined, he did manage to take his time, grasping her by her bottom and controlling the depth of his strokes. She braced her hands on his shoulders and, as always, let him have his way with her. Any control she had over him was a myth in her own mind.

She let her body take over, her mind just along for the ride, until the exquisite pressure released in an explosion of tingly heat and tremors that reverberated all the way to her fingers, toes and eyelashes.

Bryan let go as the last of her cries of passion echoed across the bedroom. She fell on top of him, too weak to sit up straight, and felt his body convulse as he emptied himself inside her.

They didn't move for a couple of minutes until Bryan finally broke the silence. "I love watching you come."

"Ditto."

"You don't hold back anything. It's all in your face to see—every emotion is all right there."

She sincerely hoped not—because she feared she

was falling in love with Bryan Elliott, and there wasn't a damn thing she could do to stop it except walk away.

And that cure was worse than the disease.

Nine

They were ten minutes late for the party in the private dining room on the floor below the restaurant, but no one seemed to notice or care. The first appetizers were being passed around, wine was flowing and conversation hummed.

Bryan noticed that someone had put place cards on the table. "Was this your idea?" he said, picking up his own and showing it to Lucy.

She nodded. "I thought it might be better if everyone from the same magazine didn't sit together. So we don't have conversational cliques."

And Lucy had done something else rather bold: instead of putting together two long tables, she'd arranged the copper-top tables into a big square.

"Is it okay?" she asked uncertainly. "I thought everyone would be able to see and talk to everyone else this way."

"You think my family needs to talk more?"

"They talk a lot. Just sometimes not in the most productive ways. And some of them could do with more listening."

Bryan laughed. "I hope you're not fantasizing you can be a peacemaker. The bitching and moaning and yelling isn't going to stop until someone is named CEO."

"I can try."

Stash appeared to take drink orders, but everyone seemed content with the wine.

"Do you want to check the menu?" he whispered to Bryan.

"I'm sure it's fine. But I don't see any garlic butter."

"I'll send someone down."

"I'll come up and get it. I want to make the rounds in the dining room."

Upstairs, he did some glad-handing. He sent a bottle of wine to a man he recognized as a competing restaurateur, comped a plate of hors d'oeuvres to several cast members from a soap, paid his respects to an opera diva.

Then he spotted someone he hadn't seen in his rounds, a woman dining alone at a small table, nursing a glass of red wine. Her eyes darted around the dining room until finally her gaze found him, and she smiled uncertainly.

He walked briskly to her table, and she stood to greet him.

"Mom. Why didn't you tell me you were coming? How come no one told me you were here?"

Amanda Elliott hugged her son, then straightened her neat suit jacket. "I'm not sure your new hostess recognized me. And if you're busy, it's okay."

"Never too busy for you. Mom, there's someone I'd like you to meet. She's downstairs." He hesitated, knowing his mother was no longer comfortable around the Elliott clan. "We're having a party to celebrate EPH profits."

"Then you're busy. I'll come back—"

"No, Mom, I think you should join us. Karen's here." His aunt Karen was the one Elliott Amanda had remained close to, other than her sons.

"Is Patrick here?" she asked warily.

"He meant to be, so he could whip everyone into a frenzy of competition. But he canceled. Gram's not feeling well, and he didn't want to leave her home alone."

Amanda immediately showed her concern. "Maeve's all right, isn't she?"

"Just her arthritis acting up. Come on, bring your wineglass. Everyone will be happy to see you."

"Everyone? Then your father's not here?"

"Everyone, and he is here. His divorce from Sharon is final, you know."

"I heard. I also heard about your new girlfriend, and I am curious."

Bryan took his mother's arm, giving her no chance to protest further. He forgot about the garlic butter that had sent him upstairs in the first place.

"Everyone, look who I found."

Amanda looked embarrassed, but Bryan wasn't disappointed in his family. Several of his cousins popped out of their chairs to greet Amanda with a hug. They were all fond of her, and her absence at family gatherings was always commented on, except by Patrick.

Then there was Daniel, Bryan's father, who never said anything about Amanda. But Bryan knew his parents still had lingering feelings for each other.

"Mom," Bryan said, "I want you to meet Lindsay Morgan."

"Lindsay." Amanda took both of Lucy's hands in hers. Bryan was alarmed by the sheen of tears in his mother's eyes. What was that about? Surely the mere sight of Lucy didn't fill Amanda with despair. She'd never been like some moms, thinking no girl was good enough for her boys.

They exchanged a few pleasantries, and Lucy said, "Oh, Mrs. Elliott, won't you join us?" Without even realizing it, Lucy had slipped into the role of hostess. It seemed a natural for her. What was more, it felt somehow…right.

"Call me Amanda, please. And I can see you all are in the middle of something. Bryan insisted I come down and say hi, but I'll be on my way now." But her turndown lacked conviction. Bryan could tell she wanted to stay. Though she often claimed she'd been much happier away from the big, noisy Elliott clan, Bryan knew she sometimes missed being a part of something larger than herself.

"Oh, nonsense," said Karen, and Bryan could have kissed his aunt. "You come join us."

"You can take Finola's chair," said Bryan's uncle Shane. "Obviously she can't tear herself away from work, not even to gloat that she's in first place."

This comment started a round of arguments, as it had been intended to do. Amanda shrugged and took the last empty chair where Finola's place card sat. Bryan watched his father's face to gauge his reaction. Daniel's gaze hadn't left Amanda since she'd entered the room, and any fool could tell he was anything but indifferent. But he was guarded enough that Bryan, even with all his training in body language, couldn't tell whether

Daniel was pleased or angry to have his ex-wife—his first ex-wife—thrust into his company. They sat only two chairs away from each other, with a table corner between them, so they could easily converse if they wanted.

More appetizers appeared, followed by the soup and salad choices Lucy had made. It would have been hard for her to go wrong—everything on the Une Nuit menu was designed to be mixed and matched. But Bryan was nonetheless pleased with and, yes, proud of the menu Lucy had put together. He told himself it was because he wanted her to appear to be a good match for him, as befitted their cover. But he knew it went deeper than that, which troubled him. He had no business getting so attached to her. Given the progress they were making on the Alliance Trust case, she wouldn't be with him for long.

As various members of his family got up to stretch their legs between courses, a certain amount of musical chairs took place at the table. Bryan found himself seated next to his cousin Liam, one of Uncle Michael and Aunt Karen's sons. Liam was the chief financial officer at EPH, and just before the main course, he'd made a brief speech detailing the profits at each of the four EPH magazines. He'd also read a prepared speech from Patrick congratulating all of his children and grandchildren for rising to the occasion and making the competition a real horse race.

That had produced a few snide comments about what, exactly, Patrick had intended besides increasing profits, but Lucy, of all people, managed to smooth over the outbursts of acrimony and keep the evening on a pleasant note.

"So, Liam, how close is the race?" Bryan asked his

cousin confidentially. "You gave us the raw numbers, but I understand the winner is the magazine that grows the most, percentagewise."

"It's closer than you can imagine," Liam said in a low voice. "But I chose to underplay that. Other than to say that *Charisma* is in first place, I don't want the other editors to know just how close they are. It'll only make them crazier."

"Things are kind of tense, huh?"

"You have no idea. Everyone's on their best behavior tonight, maybe out of consideration for you and Lindsay and some of the others here who aren't directly involved with the magazines. But I'm afraid—really afraid— that this crazy competition of Granddad's is going to create rifts in the family that can never be healed."

"You're talking about Finola?"

"She was already on shaky ground with Granddad. Frankly I was relieved she didn't show tonight. I'm not sure she could have buried the hatchet, even for one evening."

"In one of her brothers' heads, maybe. Well, she's always had something to prove."

Stash and three waiters chose that moment to appear with several of Une Nuit's famously decadent desserts as well as some pistachio sorbet for those with more modest appetites. When serving was completed, he leaned down to whisper something to Bryan.

"Oh. I'll be right up."

He excused himself from the table, but before he went upstairs, he stopped by Lucy's chair. "Any interest in meeting Britney Spears?"

"Really?" Lucy squeaked. "She's here?"

"Having drinks."

Lucy didn't have to be asked twice. He thought it was charming that she was so starstruck, that her unfortunate experience with Cruz Tabor hadn't made her bitter.

Upstairs the bar was packed, but the crowd seemed to part for Bryan. Many of the regulars knew him and nodded, giving curious glances to Lucy, but he didn't want to take time for introductions now.

He found the Britney Spears party at the very epicenter of the crowd. The star stopped midconversation to greet him. He welcomed her warmly to Une Nuit, introduced her to Lucy, who managed to squeak out a nervous greeting. He ordered a bottle of Cristal on the house, handed Britney a card and told her to call him or Stash if she ever needed anything. He was about to leave when the flash of a camera caught his attention.

The first thing Bryan did was step between Lucy and the camera, which he couldn't see, but he knew the direction it had come from. He didn't relish having his own picture taken and usually managed to avoid it, since celebrity wasn't exactly good for the anonymity required of an undercover operative. But better his face in a tabloid's than Lucy's.

With the second flash, he saw the perpetrator, a tall, skinny kid with frizzy hair and a pocket camera.

Bryan reached him in an instant, grabbed his arm and prevented him from taking another shot. "That's not allowed in here." He walked the kid to the front door.

"You're throwing me out?" he said in a loud enough voice to garner attention.

"No. You give your camera to our hostess for safekeeping. She'll give it back when you're ready to leave."

"Forget it, man," the guy said, jerking his arm out of Bryan's grasp and huffing out the door.

Bryan made a quick apology to Britney, who was gracious about it, and he and Lucy returned to the private party downstairs.

"That was cool," Lucy said. "Thanks. You must think I'm silly."

"No," he said, but he was too preoccupied to say more. Should he have followed that kid, taken the camera away? He wasn't one of the known paparazzi. Probably just a Britney fan. Still, fans sometimes sold their pictures to the tabloids.

Well, nothing he could do about it now.

The next morning, on the way home from their morning run, Bryan stopped at a newsstand and bought the latest issue of *Global News Roundup,* one of the tackiest tabloids on the market. Rather than celebrity news, the *Roundup* sported doctored photos of the president with his supposed alien baby, a giant squid the size of the Queen Mary, and stories about how the government was practicing mind control through chlorinated tap water.

"Not your usual reading material," Lucy commented as Bryan paid the vendor a couple of bucks.

"I have my reasons."

"Surely no paparazzi would stoop to publishing Britney's picture in that rag."

Bryan laughed. "No, I'm not worried about that."

He didn't explain further until they were home, showered, and had shared a breakfast of yogurt and whole-wheat bagels. She'd been pleased to discover Bryan didn't always indulge in the high-fat fare from Une Nuit.

When the dishes were washed and put away, Bryan opened the briefcase he'd taken with him yesterday and produced a thick stack of *Global News Roundup,* to which he added the current issue.

"I have to leave again today."

Lucy groaned. "I know your work is important, but I'm getting a little stir-crazy, stuck in your apartment all day by myself."

"Our surveillance of Vargov has produced some results. He made contact yesterday with a known terrorist sympathizer. Their conversation was encrypted, but the lab is working on it. We think it might lead us to Stungun. If it does, we'll have all the evidence we need to make arrests."

Lucy knew she should be excited to hear that news. She would be out of danger; she could resume her normal life—whatever that was. She could call her parents, who by now might have started to wonder where she was, if they'd tried to call her.

But Bryan's news brought her no joy. "So is this supposed to keep me entertained while you're away?" she asked, ruffling the stack of tabloids. If he thought stories of mutant three-headed dogs and monkey colonies on Mars would be her choice of entertainment, he didn't know her very well.

"In a way, yes. You're good at puzzles, and I've got one for you."

Lucy's interest ratcheted up a notch. "Yeah?"

"The publisher of this rag is a suspected spy. We believe he's supplying information to—oh, let's just say governments unfriendly to the United States— through secret drop sites. And the locations for those drop sites are encoded and published somewhere in his magazine. Our code breakers are working on it and I thought you might like to take a crack."

Lucy was unabashedly thrilled at the idea. "How could I possibly do better than professional code breakers?"

"They're good at encryption, but their training puts limits on them, too. Because you aren't trained, you can think outside the box. Just have a go."

"Okay. But I'll still miss you."

"I'll try and get back soon." He gave her a kiss that ensured she would think of him often during the day, and then he was gone.

Lucy spread the tabloids out on the living room floor—there were eight weeks' worth. She had to figure out what was common to all the issues. For instance, could the encoded information always be hidden in an alien story? Or a story by a certain reporter?

None of her initial ideas worked out, but she kept trying, reading every story, hoping something would jump out at her.

Bryan couldn't have chosen a better way to distract her. She really did love puzzles. She'd invented her own secret code in sixth grade, which she and some of her friends used as the basis for an exclusive club.

She filled legal pads with scribbles, combining and recombining words and phrases. She'd briefly thought maybe the Lucky Lotto numbers were the key, making references to page numbers, column numbers, column inches, but nothing panned out.

Finally she got the idea to look at the ads. There was one ad for a weight-loss product that caught her attention. It ran in all eight issues, and though the graphics looked similar each time, the text in each one was radically different. The advertising copy seemed odd to her— and not totally persuasive. No pseudoscientific jargon, no claims of pounds melting away while you sleep.

She did a web search for the product. She found a badly designed Web site and some discussions on a dieting listserve in which people were puzzled because the product was always out of stock. Yet the ads kept running….

Positive she was onto something, Lucy kept at it. When Bryan returned later that afternoon, she had covered every surface of his living room with yellow paper and sticky notes.

"Bryan!" She jumped to her feet, then almost fell over as her legs cramped from too many hours of sitting on the floor. She realized she was starving too, and was shocked to see the time. She'd forgotten to eat.

"Did you make any arrests?" she asked, not too sure she wanted to hear the answer.

"Not yet. Vargov knows we've got him, though. He went on the run."

"Oh, no."

"We know where he is, but he thinks he's slipped the noose. We're just waiting to see where he goes for help, who he contacts. It shouldn't be much longer." He took his first good look at his living room. "What in the world have you been doing?"

"Breaking a code."

"Any progress?"

"I know this sounds crazy, but I think I've figured it out."

"Ha! I knew you could do it."

Unable to contain her excitement, she showed Bryan how the coded copy referred to a URL connected to the product Web site. On a page of customer testimonials, a matrix of numbers and letters specified streets and block numbers in and around New York.

"You take my breath away," Bryan said. "This is brilliant."

But suddenly all Lucy could think about was taking Bryan's breath away by another method, one that involved a lot less clothing.

Bryan obviously had the same idea, and they didn't even make it to the bedroom. They didn't make it past the living room floor. They rolled naked on the soft, lamb's wool rug, and when their fevered lovemaking was concluded, they both had multicolored Post-it notes stuck to their bodies and in their hair.

A few days later Bryan came home in a foul mood from another of his mysterious errands. It was the first time Lucy had seen him anything but perfectly controlled—well, except for when they were making love—and her heart just about stopped when he rebuffed her normally affectionate greeting.

He was getting tired of her already, she realized. They'd spent too much time together.

He did not volunteer any information about his day, and she didn't ask. She wasn't entitled to the details of his investigation, after all, and she was frankly surprised he'd told her as much as he had over the past few days.

"Scarlet has tickets to a play," she ventured, thinking he might need a diversion. "She invited us to come along with her and John."

"You go ahead if you want. I'm waiting for phone calls."

Lucy knew perfectly well he could receive phone calls anywhere. He didn't need to stay home for that. But she let it pass.

"Then I won't go, either," she declared. "It wouldn't be any fun without— Bryan, what's wrong? Has something happened?"

"Stungun's dead. They found him in the Potomac River."

"That's terrible. I'm so sorry."

"He's been dead for at least a week."

"Which means he didn't disappear because he was on the run. He was murdered."

"Someone killed him, yes. His body wasn't meant to be found. They wanted me to believe he was the betrayer. Now I have no idea who it is. But the list of suspects is shrinking."

He didn't seem to want comforting, so Lucy didn't try to touch him. "I'm so sorry," she said again. "Were you close to him?"

"We don't make friends at the agency. But he was a good man. I didn't want to believe he was dirty. Part of me is relieved that he probably wasn't. But that doesn't do him much good in his condition."

"His family will know he died a hero. Does he have a family?"

"I have no idea. We never exchange personal information."

Lucy wondered whether poor Stungun had a mother, a wife, kids who would mourn him or maybe think he'd run out on them. Would they ever know what happened? Or would he just never come home?

"What if something happened to you?" Lucy asked in a quiet voice. "Would your family know?"

"I have a safety deposit box that will be opened in the event I disappear or die, explaining everything to my family. Well, as much as I can explain."

"I'm not sure I want to talk about this anymore. It's too depressing." A few days ago she'd been so excited about solving the code in the tabloid. She'd been giddy at the idea that her information might help catch a spy and prevent sensitive information from getting into the wrong hands. Now the whole spy thing left her sick to her stomach. It wasn't glamorous. It was dangerous and ultimately tragic.

"There's more bad news," Bryan said. "Vargov got away. He went into a crowd and lost his tail."

Lucy hadn't believed she could feel any lower, but now she did. Even the realization that she wouldn't be leaving Bryan's protective custody anytime soon didn't cheer her. This was no way to live, scared to go out in public, feeling powerless, no job, no home of her own.

They had to catch Vargov and his accomplice. "Do you have a plan?"

"I'm working on it." He took a deep breath, then looked at Lucy and managed a smile. "I'm sorry. I feel like I've really messed things up for you."

"I don't know what you could have done. Who was tailing Vargov?"

"What?"

"Isn't it possible someone let him go on purpose?"

He shook his head. "We recruited some FBI agents on that detail. They couldn't possibly be involved."

Lucy didn't know what else to say on the subject. "Are you hungry?" she asked.

He seemed to have to think about that. "Yeah. I don't think I've eaten all day. Let's go downstairs. The restaurant is quiet this time of day."

Lucy wasn't hungry, but she wanted to keep him company.

Stash put them in the booth reserved for the Elliotts, the most private spot in the whole restaurant. Bryan requested a bowl of Irish stew, though it was hot as blazes outside.

"Surely that's not on the menu," she said, since Irish stew was neither French nor Asian.

"Comfort food. Chef Chin can make anything. Gram used to make that for me."

Poor Bryan. She'd never seen him in such a state. She wanted to make it better, but she couldn't. So she remained silent, sipping on a cup of coffee. She'd be there for him if he wanted to talk.

He ate his meal in silence, too. She doubted he even tasted it—his thoughts seemed to be far, far away.

Stash wandered by and, seeing that Bryan's bowl was empty, asked, "You want some dessert? Chef Chin was experimenting with some lemon-butter fortune cookies this afternoon. I thought they were *magnifique*."

"Sure," Bryan said absently. Stash headed for the kitchen, but his cell phone rang and he stopped midstride to answer. Bryan watched him, and the ghost of a smile crossed his face. "Ah, I know that look. Stash has a new girlfriend. Those cookies are long forgotten."

"I'll get them," Lucy said, scooting out of the booth.

"Lucy, you don't have to wait on me."

"I don't mind. Sit tight."

Lucy wandered into the kitchen, which was strangely deserted. Now, she thought, where would Chef Chin have stored those cookies? There was a hallway lined with custom shelving where staples were stored in clear plastic storage bins of various sizes. She found something that looked like fortune cookies, opened the container and took a whiff. Lemon. These had to be the ones.

She picked up the container, turned and ran into the chest of a young man wearing the apron of a busboy.

"Oh, excuse—" A hand over her mouth cut off her apology, and the plastic container fell to the floor, cookies spilling and breaking everywhere.

"Shut up," came the urgent voice of the man behind her. "Cooperate, and you won't be hurt."

Oh, right! He wrenched her arms behind her, attempting to handcuff her. Lucy screamed and kicked out viciously at the busboy in front of her. She got in one good blow to the guy's stomach before he captured her legs and quickly wrapped duct tape around her ankles. He performed this task with amazing efficiency, giving the impression that Lucy wasn't his first kidnapping. In seconds flat she was immobilized, gagged and being carried toward the back door.

Ten

Bryan couldn't say exactly what it was that made him follow Lucy to the kitchen. But he felt suddenly uneasy at the idea of Lucy alone and unprotected in a public place. A busboy who had been vacuuming nearby during the lull in business had abruptly abandoned his chore when Lucy passed and had headed too casually in her direction. Bryan followed. He tried to talk himself out of his paranoia. There was no way Vargov or anyone else could know where Lucy was staying. Even his fellow agents had no way of knowing.

Still, he went after her.

When he reached the kitchen, it was oddly deserted. Then he heard a scuffle coming from the pantry hallway, and he didn't think, he just went into action. The gun he kept in an ankle holster somehow made it to his hand as he peered around the corner into the hallway just in time to see two men dressed as busboys heading for the delivery door with Lucy trussed up between them.

"Freeze!" Bryan yelled. They dropped Lucy with a bone-crunching thud. One of them reached into his apron. Bryan wasn't going to give him a chance to show him what was in the pocket. He aimed and shot. The busboy swiveled in time to avoid a fatal shot; he took a bullet in the shoulder and was gone, the other man ahead of him.

Bryan gave chase as far as the alley, but they'd disappeared by the time he cleared the door. He longed to chase them, run them down, demand to know who'd sent them—and how they'd known where to find Lucy. But his concern right now had to be for Lucy. He didn't know whether she was injured or how seriously. She'd been clearly conscious, and he'd seen no visible blood, but other injuries were possible. He returned to her at once. "Don't try to move, Lindsay," he said, amazed he could keep her cover even in the midst of this mess. "You might be injured." He gently pulled off the tape that had been slapped over her mouth.

She struggled to breathe, and Bryan feared the worst. Spinal injury? Broken ribs, punctured lung? But then she managed to gasp in a bit of air.

"I'm…okay."

"You don't look okay." He gave her a smile and brushed the hair back from her face. "Don't try to move, okay?"

Stash appeared in the hallway looking frantic. "What the hell just happened? I found Kim and two of the sous chefs locked in the freezer!"

"Attempted robbery gone bad, I think," Bryan said innocently.

"I…wouldn't cooperate," Lucy said. "They wanted

to kidnap me. My father has money." She pushed up on her elbows despite Bryan's attempt to get her to lie still. "I'm okay, just got the wind knocked out of me."

Bryan was amazed she'd come up with a cover story so quickly.

"Did I hear a shot?" Stash asked. Chef Chin, the other chefs and a couple of waiters had gathered to stare, mouths open in amazement.

"That was just the door slamming," Bryan fibbed. He had reholstered his gun before anyone saw it.

"We should call the police," one of the chefs said.

Bryan supposed there was no way around it. It would look odd if he didn't want to bring in the cops. They'd all gotten a good look at the "busboys," who apparently were new hires just the day before. That in itself wasn't unusual; restaurant staff came and went quickly.

Bryan could have easily picked the handcuff lock and freed Lucy's hands, but that might have invited speculation, too. So he waited for the cops to arrive, and one of them had a handcuff key. An evidence technician collected the duct tape, hoping to find prints.

Blessedly, none of the restaurant patrons ever knew anything was wrong. Only a few tables were occupied, it being way too early for the dinner crowd. The cops conducted their interviews in Bryan's office even as the kitchen was being restored to normal.

The man Bryan had shot managed to leave no blood behind him, and Bryan wondered if he'd been wearing a bulletproof vest.

It was all over in a couple of hours. Lucy was banged up, but that was all.

"What do we do now?" Lucy asked forlornly the

moment she and Bryan were alone. "That wasn't a random act of violence, was it?"

"No way. Pack a bag. We're getting out of here."

"And going where?"

"I don't know. We can't use any of the agency safe houses. I'll figure something out, though."

Lucy did as she was asked without question, disappearing into her bedroom to pack up her few belongings. When she reappeared, pale but looking determined, Bryan thought his heart would break for her. He'd almost lost her. If Vargov had gotten his hands on her, Bryan was a hundred percent sure he'd have killed her. He probably knew she'd stolen data. He had no way of knowing she'd already analyzed the data and implicated him, though he must suspect it.

"We're taking Stash's car," he said. "I told Stash you were upset and I was taking you away for a couple of days, and that my car was in the shop." Stash, always the loyal friend, hadn't even questioned Bryan's story. He'd give Bryan the shirt off his back if Bryan asked.

Minutes later they were on the road in Stash's Peugeot. Rush hour was in full flower, and the stop-and-go traffic was making Bryan crazy. It was impossible to tell whether anyone was following under these circumstances.

"How did they find me?" Lucy asked.

"You haven't called anyone, have you? E-mailed?"

"No, I promise, I haven't contacted anyone. I would tell you if I had. What about that picture from the restaurant?" she asked.

"I monitored all the tabloids, any paper that might publish bad celebrity photos. Nothing."

"What about Web sites? There are a number of fan

sites where amateur photos are welcome. I'm ashamed to admit I used to cruise them all the time."

"Hell, I never even thought of that. But what are the chances that some terrorist would be cruising celebrity fan sites?"

"You'd be surprised. Millions of people search for Britney on the Web every day. Just picture it. Some underling has the tedious job of surveilling my town house in Arlington, waiting for me to come home. He's bored, he's cruising the Web on his cell phone looking for dirty pictures, and there I am."

Bryan agreed that was how it could have happened. "If I ever see that little punk with the camera, I'm going to rip out his esophagus."

"That seems to be a favorite fantasy of yours."

"Oh, that's nowhere near my favorite." He reached over and squeezed her hand. "I know I've said it before, Lucy, but you absolutely amaze me. You held it together really well, protecting my cover even when you'd barely escaped with your life."

"You've kept your superhero identity a secret from your family for a long time. Who am I to ruin it?"

"It's gotten a lot harder, keeping it a secret," he said. "But every time I think about telling them, I imagine my mother's reaction. Or Gram's. They would completely freak out, and I'd have to quit. I'm not ready to quit."

"When you find work you love, I imagine it's hard to give it up."

"You imagine?"

"I haven't found mine yet. Clearly it's not auditing pension funds or managing a rock group's money."

"You'd be good at restaurant management," he said impulsively.

"Oh, I don't know anything about that," she said with a laugh. "I've never even been a waitress."

He didn't argue with her. But he was starting to entertain this fantasy of Lucy working at Une Nuit. She'd be there for him whenever he returned from a mission. Someone he could talk to about his work—at least in general terms. Someone who understood that his work was important and who wouldn't begrudge him the traveling.

But that was a selfish fantasy. He couldn't expect Lucy just to sit at home waiting patiently for him to return, never knowing where he was or what he was doing or whether he was in danger. All of the reasons he'd had for staying unattached still applied.

Once they got away from the city, it was easier for Bryan to determine that no one was following them. He did some basic evasive driving, taking exits at the last minute, pulling U-turns, zig-zagging through residential streets. But no one was tailing them. He stopped to buy gas, casually sweeping the car for tracking devices while the tank filled. Of course he didn't find any; his unseen enemy would have had to anticipate Bryan borrowing Stash's car. But at this point, there was no such thing as paranoia. The bad guys could figure out at any time what car Bryan was driving; by then he wanted to be well away from New York City.

He could take Lucy to a hotel, but hotels required credit cards, of which he had dozens in different names—none of them safe to use. And any hotel that operated on a cash-only basis wasn't some place he wanted Lucy to stay.

Bryan's satellite phone rang. His nerves already on edge, he jumped at the sound of it. He'd always been told that his location could not be traced using this phone, but he suddenly didn't trust anything he'd ever been told by anyone.

"You aren't going to get that?" Lucy asked.

"No." The Caller ID screen was blank—not a good sign.

"So we're totally on our own?"

Bryan didn't know how to answer that. He had the might of the United States Government behind him. But he had to use a certain chain of command, and if he trusted the wrong link in the chain, they were likely both dead.

He decided, though, that he had to trust someone. And if he had to pick only one person, it would be the man currently calling himself Siberia—the man who'd trained him when he'd first moved over to Homeland Security, the man who'd been his mentor. Siberia was not a particularly likable man—his nickname wasn't random. He was cold. But he was smart and capable, and right now, he was the only choice Bryan had.

He dialed the number. "Casanova?" the familiar voice answered on the other end of the line.

"Did you try to call me just now?"

"No. Why?"

"There've been some new developments." He explained to his superior about the photograph, likely published on the Internet, and the kidnapping attempt. "I have to take her someplace safe. But the safe houses that are available aren't safe from our own people—and unfortunately I'm more sure than ever that's where the threat lies."

Siberia was silent for a long time, so long that Bryan feared they'd lost their connection. Finally he spoke again. "There is a place, a new safe house that's just come available. No one in the agency knows of it but me."

"Where is it?"

"In the Catskills. Very isolated. Put Lucy there. Then you and I will put an end to this thing. I have some new intelligence. I believe I know now who our turncoat is. And I know how to catch her *and* Vargov. But it will require us working together."

Her. So Siberia believed the traitor was Orchid. He didn't know what to say. He'd always thought Orchid was solid. She was middle-aged, plain, unremarkable—all the things that made for a forgettable person, which was good for an agent.

"I think someone got to her with romance," Siberia said. "She probably never had a lot of boyfriends. Women are vulnerable that way."

Privately Bryan didn't think women were any more vulnerable than men, whose brains started to misfire the moment a beautiful women entered the room. But he didn't want to argue about it. Presumably Siberia had more to go on than Orchid's gender.

He had a hard time believing Orchid would fall prey to some Romeo terrorist sympathizer. But by the nature of their work, he didn't know her that well, so he couldn't say for sure.

"So where is this little safe house in the woods?" He didn't like it, but he felt he had no choice. He would have to leave Lucy alone, unprotected. But if they could end this thing once and for all, Lucy would finally be safe. And maybe his stomach, which had been twisted in knots for days, could return to normal.

Siberia gave him directions to the cabin in the Catskills, which he memorized. One of his strengths as an agent was his perfect recall. He seldom had to write anything down.

He told Lucy the plan. She didn't seem easy with it, either, but she didn't object. She probably thought he knew best. He wished he thought that was true.

"It'll take two or three hours to get there," he said. He wanted to avoid the toll roads, because often there were cameras at toll plazas. There wasn't much chance their enemy would know what direction they'd gone, but he wasn't taking *any* chances.

The countryside was beautiful, lush and green and dotted with small lakes that shimmered in the setting sun, but Bryan hardly saw it. He kept thinking of the confrontation ahead, and wondering if he would have to kill one of his comrades. And whether he would return to Lucy—or someone else would come for her, breaking the news of his demise.

Now that the shock of Lucy's almost-kidnapping had worn off, she looked tired. A bruise had formed on her cheekbone, and he noticed her reaching up to touch it, to test the soreness. She probably hadn't even known she had the injury until the adrenaline had worn off.

They stopped long before they neared their destination to buy provisions, choosing a crowded chain grocery store in the town of Monticello, where they weren't likely to be noticed or remembered. Bryan included a deli sandwich Lucy could eat in the car. He wasn't hungry, but he'd had the stew earlier. She hadn't eaten since God knew when.

She claimed not to be hungry, either, but she did nibble at the sandwich and sip at a bottle of juice to make him happy.

It was almost nightfall by the time they reached the cabin. Bryan was glad he hadn't had to find it in total darkness. It was up a twisty, narrow mountain road where one false turn could land a car in a ditch—or worse. He'd been relieved to see the cabin when it finally appeared around a bend. It was larger than he expected, well maintained, but old. Probably no air-conditioning or heat.

"It looks nice," Lucy said optimistically. "I've never stayed in a mountain cabin. It'll be like a vacation."

"You should be working on your book."

She grimaced. "Ah, yes. Scarlet offered to put me in touch with a literary agent. What are they going to think when I never write anything? Then again, I won't be here to explain. You'll have to tell them we broke up."

Bryan was sad to say he hadn't even thought that far ahead. "I dread telling the family *that* almost as much as telling them I'm a spy."

"Why's that? I'm sure women have come and gone from your life before."

He shook his head. "My family is absolutely nuts about you. Gram is already planning the wedding. And Cullen— Ever since he found love, he thinks everyone should be matched up, married and having kids."

"Unfortunately, not everyone has a happy ending. C'mon, let's check this place out," she said brightly, clearly wanting to drop the subject.

The cabin was quaint, and it had been aired and cleaned recently. They carried the groceries into the kitchen, which was small with outdated appliances.

"I think you'll be comfortable enough here for a few days."

"You aren't going to stay with me." It was a state-ment, not a question.

"I have work to do."

"Couldn't Siberia do it?"

"This is my case. I owe it to Stungun to see it through. It's my fault the man is dead."

"Don't say that. Of course it's not your fault. You're doing the best you can. We all are." She slid her arms around him and pressed her face into his neck. "For that matter, it's my fault, too. I obviously did something that gave me away to Mr. Vargov."

"No. He was already suspicious of you. You'd come to him with the problem first, remember."

"Well, there's no sense in rehashing. Let's move forward."

"To move forward, I have to catch the person responsible."

She sighed. "I know. I just wish we could have more time…" She sounded as if she wanted to say more, but she censored herself.

"More time for what?"

"For this." She kissed his neck, then opened two buttons on his shirt and kissed his chest.

"Ah, Lucy. What you do to me." He needed to leave. The sooner he took care of business, the sooner he could get back to her—and maybe figure out a way to be with her. But he couldn't bear just dumping her here and taking off.

He wanted—no, he *needed*—to be with her one last time, like he needed air to breathe.

Lucy thrilled at the way he responded to her touch. She'd never known she could have such a profound effect on a man, but his smooth skin quivered as she raked her palm down the muscles of his back, and his breathing came in ragged gasps as she touched her tongue to first one of his nipples, then the other.

There was no playful banter, no teasing. Bryan took her hand and led her up a flight of stairs, where she presumed bedrooms could be found. They entered one randomly. It was tucked up under the eaves with a window facing a breathtaking sunset. The old-fashioned iron bed had an antique quilt and half a dozen pillows covered in crisp, white cases.

Bryan undressed her slowly, paying special attention to each part of her he bared. Nothing escaped his attention—not her collarbone or the inside of her elbow or her ankle. Every place he touched her or kissed became an erogenous zone. Her senses were magnified so that she discerned the texture of his lips, the warmth of his breath against her skin, the sound of her own blood pounding in her ears.

She couldn't remember undressing him—maybe she was too engrossed in her own sensations to do it. But he ended up naked somehow, and he gently urged her onto the soft, much-washed cotton sheets, which smelled fresh, as if they'd just been pulled from the line, dried by wind and sunshine and put on the bed awaiting their arrival.

It was like making love on a cloud. The pillows were feather, and as they maneuvered on the bed, rolling this way and that, first Bryan on top, then Lucy, the pillows ended up surrounding them.

When he finally parted her legs and entered her, Lucy wanted to weep, she was so overwhelmed with the joyous sense of completion, the sense of rightness that this was where she belonged, with Bryan, in some dimension apart from embezzlers, terrorists and murderers. She wanted that more than she wanted her next breath. And as Bryan's strokes grew faster and harder, and warm rivers of sensation coursed through her limbs, coalescing into a cyclone deep in her center, she did cry.

Because this was goodbye.

He hadn't said it, but he didn't need to. He was leaving. And whatever happened, they wouldn't be together again. If he caught the traitors, they would no longer be a threat to her. She would return to her normal identity, get another job. She would cease to be Lindsay Morgan, Bryan's hot new girlfriend. And if the unthinkable happened, if he wasn't successful with his mission…

That alternative was too horrible to think about.

"Are you crying?" he asked a few minutes later, when their breathing had returned to something close to normal.

"No." But the tears were evident in her voice.

"Lucy, what's wrong?"

"Nothing. Oh, I'm just being silly. I know you're leaving. I know you have to. And I'm just scared of the future, that's all."

"Don't be scared. Siberia said he had a lead. We'll catch these guys, and I'll be fine, and I'll come back to get you and you'll be safe."

"Of course everything will work out," she said, feeling braver now that she heard the confidence in his voice. "I told you it was silly."

"I do have to go, though." His voice was tinged with regret.

"I know. But could you…could you just hold me until I fall asleep? And then slip away? I don't want to watch you leave."

"You are in a state, aren't you?" He laughed, but it was a soft, gentle laugh, filled with fondness. He slipped his arms around her and pulled her tight against him, drawing the sheet up over their naked bodies.

Lucy willed herself to relax, knowing if she didn't, Bryan would be waiting all night for her to fall asleep. As her muscles softened, one by one, tension turned to fatigue and she managed to drop off.

When next she woke, it was dark outside, the room slightly chilly. And she was alone, the space beside her cold. She turned on a lamp and checked her watch. It was after midnight. She saw then that Bryan had taken her little superspy phone from her purse and left it on a pillow with a note. The note instructed her to keep the phone with her, and what number to call if she had an emergency.

She shivered at the thought of that. Surely no one could find her all the way up here. All that was left for her to do was wait.

She thought she remembered Bryan leaving, putting on his clothes, lightly kissing her cheek. But maybe she'd only dreamed it. Because she also remembered him saying in a hoarse whisper, "I love you, Lucy."

Eleven

It was one of the few face-to-face meetings Bryan had had with Siberia. They met at a sidewalk café in D.C. the morning after he'd left Lucy. Each time his mind tried to wander to thoughts of her, to the way she looked when she slept, like a sexy fallen angel, he had to herd his attention back to the current time and place. If he and Siberia could solve this case, then he could think about Lucy all he wanted. Be with her, hold her, make love to her.

That was all the motivation he needed to stay focused.

"Vargov left a paper trail," Siberia said. He was an overweight man in his fifties who hadn't worked in the field in years due to an accident that had left him blind in one eye. His function was solely to coordinate intelligence. He wore a full, bushy beard, aviator sunglasses and a French beret, looking today more like an eccentric movie producer than a spy.

"He's in France," Siberia continued. "Tarantula is there now, coordinating with French intelligence agents. There's a very good chance Vargov will be apprehended. If you want to go there as insurance, it might be a good idea."

Bryan hesitated. He wanted to be where the action was. But the idea of going so far from Lucy made him uneasy. "I feel it's more important to protect our witness," he said.

"I could send a man—"

"No," Bryan said immediately. "I don't want another soul to know the location of that house. These guys— these terrorists, whoever they are—they're connected. The fact that they found Lucy the first time is nothing short of amazing. I still don't know where the picture was published."

"It was on a Britney fan site," Siberia said with a grimace. "I found it. Good disguise, by the way, but Ms. Miller's face was clear."

"So what's left?"

"Orchid."

Bryan was sick, thinking about his fellow agent-gone-bad. "I still can't believe it."

"I pray we're wrong. We won't know until we find her. I'm coordinating with the homicide investigators here. They think I'm CIA. I'll know more about the time and cause of Stungun's death soon."

"Who was he?" Bryan asked suddenly. "Surely it doesn't matter now." He couldn't stand the anonymity. He needed to put a real name to the man he'd known, a hometown, a family.

"I honestly don't know," Siberia said. "He was using one of the identities provided by the agency. I'm working through the chain of command to get more information. I'd like to be able to tell his family that he died defending his country—provided that's true. We still don't know. If he was dealing with terrorists, they've been known to turn on their own kind."

The thought sickened Bryan. Was this what he had to look forward to the rest of his life? Dealing every day with the scum of the earth, perhaps the worst of the scum his own supposed allies? Unable to trust anyone, not even his fellow agents?

Bryan knew then that he wanted out of this game. What had seemed exciting years ago was less than appealing now—the lying, the danger, the betrayals, the paranoia.

This was all Lucy's fault, he thought with a faint smile. She'd made him realize what was missing from his life—and what he very much wanted.

Lucy hadn't yet been at the cabin twenty-four hours and she was going stir-crazy. She'd explored every nook and cranny of the old house. There was a porch out back with a hammock, and she'd already had one nap. There was no TV, no radio, no way to keep in touch with the outside world. The highlights of her day so far had been a bowl of cereal for breakfast and a ham sandwich for lunch.

The scenery was breathtaking, and at any other time she'd have delighted in the views and the cool mountain breezes, a welcome respite from the heat of the city in the dead of summer. But she couldn't enjoy anything until she saw Bryan again, safe and sound. What had seemed an exciting lark when it started was now wearing on her nerves; she wanted it to be over. Now.

Mostly she wanted everyone out of danger. What if Vargov went after her family? But she also needed to know if what she and Bryan had shared was real, or merely a product of enforced proximity and too much adrenaline running through their veins.

Her feelings for Bryan felt very real to her, and he seemed to care for her beyond his responsibility of keeping her safe. But what did she know? She'd gotten it wrong before.

Whatever the results, she didn't want to live any longer in the fictional world of Lindsay Morgan. She needed to know if little Lucy Miller from Kansas had a chance with a superspy.

The idea seemed ridiculous, but she still hoped.

There was nothing to read in the house, not even a deck of cards to play with. How was she supposed to occupy herself? She finally decided to go for a run. Bryan had told her to stay put, but she would be no safer inside the house than out. The people who were after her weren't amateurs. Locked doors and windows would be no impediment if they really wanted her. At least if she was away from the house, she couldn't be cornered.

Besides, she'd gotten used to having a daily run with Bryan.

She donned her stylish shorts and matching tank top, thinking what a waste it was to sweat in such chic clothes when there was not a soul out here to see her. Thinking of Scarlet and her ban on T-shirts made her smile. Scarlet had been so good to her, and Lucy had started to think of her as a friend. Too bad she couldn't continue that friendship after Lucy and Bryan parted ways.

Taking the phone with her, Lucy stepped outside, locked the door, pocketed the key and set out at a brisk walk, continuing up the mountain road. She wondered how close to the top her cabin was, and if there was anyone else living up this way. She sure didn't see any signs of habitation, nor had she seen or heard a single car since she'd arrived. She'd thought the Catskills were more populated.

The uphill grade and uneven road surface made Lucy's run a challenge, but she pushed herself, figuring if she wore herself out, a shower and a nap might eat up the rest of the afternoon and it would be dinnertime. Finally, after about thirty minutes, she turned and headed back. The downhill trip was faster, and soon her cabin came into view.

She heard a car engine, and her heart beat faster. Bryan! Was it possible he'd resolved things so quickly? But she realized the car engine didn't sound like Stash's Peugeot, nor like Bryan's Jaguar. In fact, it sounded like a diesel car.

Reacting on pure instinct, she plunged into the heavy woods that surrounded the cabin, finding a vantage point where she could watch the road from behind a huge fallen tree.

She was probably being silly. It was no doubt some family on vacation, out for a drive. But soon the dark-blue Mercedes came into view, and she recognized it instantly.

Her heart beat double time and her skin, already flushed from her run, broke out in sweat. What was *he* doing here? How had he found her?

She pulled the phone from her pocket and carefully pushed the series of buttons that would put her in contact with Bryan. If Bryan was able to answer. Her imagination went into overdrive. What if Vargov had captured Bryan and tortured him into revealing Lucy's whereabouts?

The phone gave a series of beeps but nothing else. No ringing. No dial tone. No nothing. She tried again. Same beeps. Same nothing.

She whispered a curse. What was wrong with the phone? She was sure she was using it correctly. The battery was fine. But no calls would go through. Not even a call to 911.

What if Bryan was on his way back to the cabin this very minute? He would pull into the driveway, blissfully unaware that anything was wrong, and Vargov would kill him! She had to get down the mountain to the last little town they'd passed through—was it called Icy Creek?—where she could notify someone. And she had to make sure she met Bryan if he was headed this way. But to get past the cabin, she would have to go out in the open—or circle through the dense woods, way around.

As she dithered about what to do, the cabin's front door opened, and Vargov came out. He looked left, then right, scanning the woods. Her heart pounded. He was looking for her. He climbed into his car, and Lucy crossed her fingers. If he drove up the road looking for her, it would be her chance to get past the house. Sure enough, he headed up the mountain.

Just as she was about to make her move, she heard something, a loud something coming toward her, breaking branches and crunching leaves. Was it Vargov? Panic zinged through her. How had he found her so quickly? Did he have heat-seeking scanners? A tracking dog?

Then she realized it was not Vargov, and she didn't know whether to be relieved or not.

Because it was a black bear.

Okay, it would probably run if it saw her. Still, she

zipped up the nearest tree like a monkey, grateful for her rural upbringing. Her family had owned a small peach orchard, so she'd climbed her share of trees.

Wait a minute. Didn't bears climb trees?

It came closer. She was twenty feet up, well out of its reach, but it seemed to be very interested in her. It reared up on its hind legs and leaned up against the tree trunk, sniffing madly.

Oh, God, what if it started climbing? She considered screaming, but that would bring Vargov straight to her. Did she prefer to be shot, or eaten?

Just then there was another noise. The bear turned, wary of a threat. This time it was Vargov. He was quieter than a big man should be, hardly even crunching leaves, but she could hear his breathing. He'd probably parked the car up the road some place where it wouldn't be spotted so when she returned, she would assume all was well. Then, returning to the cabin on foot, Vargov had heard the bear and thought it was her.

Vargov and the bear saw each other at about the same time. The big man cursed and raised his gun, shooting at the hapless bear. He missed. The startled bear lumbered off at a gallop.

"Christ," Vargov muttered, still breathing hard and rubbing his neck. He was sweaty and pasty. "I'm too old for this."

He looked around, but he didn't look up. Lucy clung to her tree branch, the rough bark scraping her skin, the mosquitoes chomping on her, and prayed.

He holstered his gun and headed back toward the cabin.

Lucy waited until he'd gone inside, then clambered down. The business with the bear had wasted precious time. She'd lost her chance to get past the cabin. She would have to circle far around through the woods. But there was no other choice. She plunged into the thick undergrowth, getting slapped by twigs and branches, trying to be quiet in case Vargov had some listening device.

When she judged she was a good distance from the cabin, she headed downhill roughly parallel to the road, wondering how far she would have to hike before she reached Icy Creek.

Then she heard another car engine.

This time, to her horror, she recognized the distinctive rumble of Stash's Peugeot. She was still too far from the road to get there in time to head Bryan off. She broke into a run, heedless of the branches whipping at her face, hair and clothes. For a moment she thought she might beat him...but she was too slow. She broke cover just as the Peugeot turned into the cabin's driveway. The engine switched off and the driver's door opened.

"Bryan!" she called out. He froze, turned. "It's a trap!" She motioned frantically for him to get back in the car.

Her warning came too late. Shots rang out from the house. Bryan dived behind the car.

Lucy knew she should make for the safety of the woods. But all she could think about was being with Bryan again, facing the danger together. She made a headlong dash across the road toward the cabin. More shots came from the house, churning up the asphalt road inches from her feet. She expected one to rip through her flesh any moment. But by some miracle she made it to the car in one piece.

Bryan dragged her down beside him, then behind

him, placing his body between her and the shooter. "Lucy, are you crazy? You almost got killed."

"Yell…at me…later." She sucked in great gulps of air, feeling like she might pass out. "What do we do now?"

"Who's in the house?"

"Mr. Vargov."

"That's impossible. Vargov is in France."

"Don't you think I know my own boss?" she said impatiently. "It's definitely him. I took off into the woods, and a bear chased me, and then Vargov showed up and he shot at the bear—"

"Lucy, slow down. You're not making a lot of sense."

"Maybe we can outrun him," she said suddenly. "He's thirty pounds overweight and blind in one eye, so he has lousy depth perception."

"Maybe so, but he almost got— Did you say Vargov is blind in one eye? And overweight?"

"Yes. Didn't you know that?" She'd assumed he knew everything.

"Siberia is blind in one eye. And overweight. It's why he's not in the field anymore. Christ, Lucy, they're the same person."

Lucy let the implications sink in. No wonder Bryan had been having such a hard time with this case. His boss had been providing him with misinformation.

Bryan swore again and pulled his cell phone from his pants pocket. Almost instantly he realized it wouldn't work.

"Mine doesn't work, either," Lucy said. "I wanted to call you and warn you, but I couldn't."

"Vargov must have put a scrambler device in the cabin. It's why he lured us here—so we couldn't call for help."

"Then what do we do?"

Bryan silently reviewed their options. "We hold out until dark. We might stand a chance of making a break for it if Vargov can't see us."

But Vargov had no intention of allowing them to wait him out. Another flurry of shots rang out from the house. Bryan returned fire, breaking all of the upstairs windows. He practically sat on Lucy to keep her down and out of the line of fire.

When the shooting stopped, it was eerily quiet. Even the birds had stopped chirping, and the breeze had died to nothing.

"Maybe you got him," Lucy whispered.

"Doubtful." Bryan's voice had a strange, strangled sound to it. The hand he'd placed on her shoulder to keep her low to the ground lost its grip, and his gun rattled to the pavement.

"Bryan?"

He slumped against her, bleeding from a wound to the shoulder, dangerously close to his chest.

"Bryan!" In her panic, she forgot about the man shooting at them. Her only thought was that she would have to get Bryan some medical attention or he would die—and that meant getting him into the car and driving down the mountain.

He was conscious, though barely. "What—what are you doing?" he asked when she tried to hook her hands under his arms and lift him.

"You have to get into the car."

"Lucy, get down!" That was when she realized she'd been standing almost upright, and no one had shot at her.

Maybe Bryan had hit Vargov after all. Maybe he was reloading, or out of bullets altogether. She didn't have time to speculate. Bryan was bleeding at an alarming rate. The front of his shirt was soaked in red.

"You have to help me, Bry," she said. "You're too heavy. I can't lift you into the car myself."

Somehow, he managed to summon the strength to rise, casting a wary glance toward the house. But there was no more shooting. Lucy retrieved his gun, just in case, and together they hobbled to the Peugeot's passenger door. Lucy opened it, and Bryan fell inside.

The keys were in the ignition, thank God. She ran around, jumped behind the wheel, cranked up the car, backed out of the drive and screeched off. It was only when the cabin was half a mile behind them that Lucy dared to breathe a sign of relief. "We did it," she said, feeling only a mild sense of elation. One hurdle crossed, lots more to go. "Bryan?"

He was slumped in his seat, unconscious.

Twelve

The moment Lucy had reached Icy Creek, she tried her phone again, and it worked perfectly. She dialed 911, and in an astonishingly short time, tons of people came to her rescue. Two off-duty paramedics were summoned to administer emergency care to Bryan while arrangements were made to airlift him to the closest trauma center, Saint Francis Hospital in Poughkeepsie.

Someone had given her a map to Poughkeepsie, and Lucy had made it there in one piece only by the grace of God, because her mind wasn't on her driving. When she arrived, she could learn nothing about Bryan's condition other than that he'd still been alive when he'd arrived, and he'd gone almost immediately into surgery.

During the drive, which had seemed to take hours, Lucy had made a decision. Bryan was close to death, and she did not want him to die alone, with his family blissfully unaware of his condition. So she'd called first Daniel Elliott, then Amanda, then Scarlet. Bryan might not approve; explanations would have to be made, explanations Bryan would have just as soon skipped. But he would just have to be mad at her.

When his mother and father arrived, at virtually the same time, he was still in surgery.

"We couldn't wait," the young E.R. intern told them as they stood together, gripping each other's hands. It was the first time Lucy had seen Bryan's parents touch, or even acknowledge each other. "We'll let you know as soon as he comes out of surgery."

After the doctor walked away, Amanda's face crumpled. "I never thought we'd be facing this again," she said to Daniel.

Again? Lucy thought. Then she remembered about Bryan's childhood illness. He'd had high-risk surgery to correct his heart defect. His parents had probably spent more time than anyone should in hospital waiting rooms.

They both turned to her. "Lindsay, can you tell us more about what happened?"

"We were in a cabin in the Catskills," she said, choosing her words carefully. She didn't want to lie, not anymore. But she revealed only as much as she had to. "There was an intruder. He shot Bryan."

"How did you escape?" Amanda asked. "Did the intruder get away? Did you call the police?"

"I honestly don't know how or why I was spared," Lucy said, tears pressing hot and insistent behind her eyes. "All I remember is that I got Bryan into the car and got out of there. I contacted the authorities, but I don't know what happened to the man with the gun."

She hoped Vargov was alive. She wanted to testify and put him in jail for the rest of his life.

"I don't understand," Daniel said, giving Lucy a hard look. "First someone tried to kidnap you, then you had some kind of home invasion. Are you involved with criminals?"

"Not intentionally. I'm a material witness in a criminal case."

"But how does that involve Bryan?" Daniel wanted to know.

Amanda laid a quieting hand on her ex-husband's arm. "I should think that would be obvious, Daniel. Our Bryan is a spy."

Lucy gave a little gasp of surprise, but other than that she didn't confirm or deny.

"A what?"

"I should have put it together earlier," Amanda said. "The frequent absences, the injuries, the security measures at his apartment. And that phone of his— that's not an ordinary cell phone."

Daniel stared at Amanda in amazement. "You're telling me our son is a spy? How could you know that?"

"A mother knows these things," she said mysteriously.

Scarlet arrived with John, and then other Elliotts began trickling in. Some of them Lucy had met, some she hadn't. But apparently, when one of their own was threatened, they banded together, because she heard none of the bickering that had characterized previous family gatherings. There were lots of hugs and tears. Even the mysterious "Aunty Fin" showed up.

Lucy sat in a corner, feeling like the outsider she was, as Daniel and Amanda filled in family members as they arrived.

When two men in suits showed up, the mere sight of them filled Lucy with dread. They came straight for her, as she'd known they would.

"Ms. Miller?" one of them said.

Lucy rose and walked with them into a hallway, where the Elliotts couldn't hear the conversation.

They gave their names, claiming they were with the CIA.

"Listen, whoever you are, I don't care if you were sent by the president himself. I know you want me to go with you. I know you want me to tell you what happened. But frankly, I don't trust anyone right now. In the last forty-eight hours I've been almost kidnapped, shot at, and very nearly eaten by a bear. A United States agent tried to kill me—and he shot the man I love, who is in surgery right now fighting for his life. I'm not leaving here unless you remove me bodily from this hospital. I will report to the closest FBI field office tomorrow morning and give you and anyone who'll listen a full report. But not tonight. Is that clear?"

The two men looked at each other as they inched away from her. "Yes, ma'am." And, amazingly, they left. She wouldn't have believed that little Lucy Miller from Kansas, dressed in shorts and a tank top, could intimidate two federal agents, but apparently she had.

She returned to the waiting room to resume her vigil. Scarlet sidled up to her, giving her torn, filthy outfit, her messy hair and her scratched and scraped skin a disapproving look. "If fashion is a religion," she said solemnly, "you've broken virtually every commandment."

Bryan's first conscious feeling was one of panic. Shots fired. Pinned down. Pain, blood—then nothing.

Lucy! Oh, God, what had happened to Lucy? Was she dead or alive?

"Lucy," he mumbled.

Gradually sensation returned. Someone was holding his hand, but he couldn't quite summon the strength to open his eyes.

Next he became aware of sounds and smells. Alcohol. Betadine. Sterile sheets and beeping machines.

Suddenly he was ten years old again, coming out of surgery to repair his heart.

"Bryan? Are you awake?"

It was his mother squeezing his hand. Except he wasn't ten years old anymore. "Lucy," he said again. "Is Lucy okay?" He pried his eyes open to see both of his parents. "What are you doing here?" he asked, his voice sounding wispy and weak.

"Lindsay called us. How do you feel?"

Like his head was full of cotton and his chest full of knives. But he remembered how his mother felt every little pain right along with him, so he didn't tell her the truth. "I'm good," he said. And he was alive, at least, which was something. Then it sank in, what his mother had just said. "Lindsay" had called them. Lucy had at least made it off the mountain. "Is Lindsay okay?"

"She's got a few scrapes and bruises, but she's fine," Amanda assured him.

"What about me?" His body didn't feel normal, but he knew the surgical anesthesia always made him feel not quite connected to his body.

"You lost a lot of blood," Daniel answered. "The bullet nicked an artery, but it didn't hit any major organs. You'll be fine."

"And when you're fully recovered," his mother said

sweetly, "I'm going to kill you. Why didn't you tell us you were a secret agent?"

Uh-oh. His secret was out. Bryan supposed he should be surprised his perceptive mother hadn't put it together earlier. "'Cause you'd have grounded me."

Amanda's eyes filled with tears. "Oh, Bryan. We didn't go to all the trouble to get you heart surgery and save your life so you could throw it away chasing down terrorists and whatnot."

"Lucy—I mean Lindsay—told you everything?"

"She hardly told us anything," Amanda replied. "She said something about an intruder, that's all. But I put it all together. Bryan, I'm so angry with you." She sniffed back tears, and Daniel put his arm around her. "But I'm so proud, too."

It occurred to Bryan that this was the first time he'd seen his parents together like this since their divorce more than a dozen years ago.

"Where's Lucy?" he asked. "Hell. Lindsay—"

"We get the picture," Daniel said. "Lindsay is Lucy. She's in the waiting room. Two goons who looked like they could have been from the cast of *Men in Black* showed up wanting to take her away, but she got rid of them."

Bryan summoned a smile. That sounded like his Lucy. "Could you bring her here? I need to see her. I have to tell her—" Hell. He didn't know what he wanted to tell her. But if he could just see that she was okay, then he could handle the aftermath of this fiasco. And there was going to be a hell of an aftermath.

"I'll go get her," Amanda said. She patted Bryan's leg, then slipped out the door, leaving the two men alone.

"She's really special, this Lucy?" Daniel asked.

"More than you can know." Bryan shifted, trying to find a more comfortable position. The painkiller was wearing off, and the ache in his shoulder and chest were getting worse. "I don't know that we can— I mean, the only reason we were together—"

"If she's special, don't let her go," Daniel said solemnly. "No matter what anyone says. I'll let you rest now."

Bryan wanted to protest that he didn't need rest. He wanted to see Lucy. But he did nod off.

The next time he opened his eyes, she was there, sitting in a chair next to his bed. Someone had given her an old college sweatshirt to put on over her tank top. She was scraped and bruised, no makeup, her hair looking as if it hadn't seen a comb in some time. And she was the most beautiful woman he'd ever seen.

"Lucy?"

"I'm here."

"Sorry I'm not at my best."

"You're alive, which makes you exactly perfect in my book. And now you'll have a new scar to go with the others." She blinked back tears, proving she wasn't as cavalier as she was trying to be.

"You saved my life," he said. "There's no way to thank you."

She shrugged. "What else was I supposed to do? Anyway, there wasn't that much risk. Mr. Vargov is dead—that's why he stopped shooting at us. He apparently had a massive heart attack in the middle of trying to kill us."

"That was decent of him." At her stricken look, he immediately said, "Sorry. In my business, sometimes black humor gets us through tough times."

"I know he was a criminal and a traitor and a terrorist sympathizer, but I have a hard time equating that with the man I knew who was so kind to me. I shouldn't be sorry he's dead."

"You're allowed. Not everything is black-and-white, good and bad. Most criminals have some good in them. Who told you he was dead?"

"Orchid got in touch with me—she seems to be running things for the moment—but she didn't tell me much else. She said I should go home. Since Vargov's dead, she says I'm out of danger."

That was something Bryan would want to verify himself. "So you want to go home, then?"

She shrugged again. "Maybe I'll still have a job. The bank will need someone to help them restore those pension funds. I could get my umbrella back. I liked that umbrella."

Bryan thought for a long time before he responded to that. He thought about his longstanding rule to avoid commitments. He thought about how close he'd come to dying and how much he wanted to live to a ripe old age.

And he remembered what his father had said to him so recently, about not letting Lucy slip away. That was just what was going to happen if he didn't take a stand.

"What if I offered you another type of job?"

"What?"

"You have an uncanny talent for solving puzzles and finding patterns. Such skills are invaluable in intelligence work."

She looked at him like he was crazy. "You think I should become a spy?" she whispered.

"I was thinking more of a freelance consultant.

Working behind the scenes. I'll bet our government would even send you to code-breaking school."

Her eyes widened. "Really? I'd love that."

"And when you aren't working a case, you could help me with the restaurant. The place needs a female presence. People respond to you—you're a terrific hostess, you have good instincts when it comes to food…" He trailed off when he saw that he was not getting the response he'd hoped for. He'd been so sure she would love the idea. "You don't seem too enthusiastic."

"Oh, I would love the work, I'm sure. It's just—"

"You don't love me."

"Of course I love you. Oh, shoot, I wasn't going to say that. How pathetic is it, an accountant from Kansas falling for a millionaire superspy?"

Bryan couldn't breathe for a moment. This was better than he'd dared hope for. He thought maybe, if given more time, Lucy might be persuaded to fall in love with him. He'd never dreamed…

"If you're in love, why do you look so miserable? Haven't you figured it out yet? I want you to stay in New York because I'm head-over-heels crazy for you."

She brightened, but only for a moment. Then her eyes filled with tears. "I couldn't stand it, Bryan. I couldn't stand having you disappear with no explanation, not having any idea when you'd be back—or even *if* you'd be back. When I realized you'd been shot, I thought I was going to die myself. I'm not cut out to be a spy's girlfriend."

Bryan's heart swelled. He held out his hand. "Lucy, come here, please."

She did, though reluctantly, and he took her hand and squeezed it.

"If I was a little bit stronger, I'd pull you right into this bed with me, put my arms around you and never let you go."

"But—"

"No, no, hear me out. As of right now, I'm retiring. No more fieldwork. No more danger, no more unexplained trips abroad. No more lying to my family."

"But you…you love your work. You told me that yourself."

"It's exciting, yes. But staying alive is even more exciting. Particularly now that I have you to stay alive for. There are lots of other jobs I can do for the agency, or some other branch of the government. Intelligence gathering, sifting through data, coordinating efforts, debriefing agents, interviewing suspects—I'm trained to do all of that stuff. But I also want to spend more time at the restaurant. So we have lots of choices. If you stay in New York."

"Can I keep the clothes?" she asked, and he suspected she was trying to distract herself from actually having to answer him.

"I'll buy you all the clothes you want. Whoever that designer is who makes all those slinky dresses and whatnot, we'll go talk to him. Maybe he makes wedding dresses." He held tightly to her hand so she couldn't escape.

She used her other hand to muffle a shriek. "Bryan. Don't say things like that unless you mean it, it's cruel."

"You think I don't mean it? I want you to be my wife, Lucy. And frankly, if I don't marry you, my family is going to disown me. So, what do you say?"

"I think you're crazy." She tugged at her hand, but he refused to let her go. "This isn't how it's supposed to be!"

"I'll do the candlelight and violins as soon as they let me out of here. Put me out of my misery, Lucy."

In answer she leaned over the bed and kissed him, until one of the machines monitoring his vital signs started beeping out an alarm.

A nurse rushed into the cubicle. "What are you doing?" She angled a severe look at Lucy. "You, out."

Bryan kept hold of her hand. "Was that a yes?"

She nodded, her eyes filled with tears.

Two weeks later, on a hot day near the end of July, Lucy and Bryan were married at The Tides. Scarlet found her the perfect wedding dress, left over from a recent bridal spread *Charisma* had done. It was simple, with clean lines and unadorned silk. She paired it with an elegant pearl tiara.

Bryan sent Lucy's parents two round-trip, first-class tickets to New York, and though they'd never been out of Kansas in their lives, they came. They'd never even realized their daughter had gone missing. They'd called once, got her answering machine, figured she was traveling on some lark and put it out of their minds. Since they didn't know of her escapade, she didn't fill them in.

She didn't want them to spend the rest of their lives in church praying for her.

"You're not pregnant, are you?" her mother had whispered almost the moment she got off the plane.

Lucy laughed, amazed that she could. "No, Mom. I'm just in love."

"Well, I think you picked a good one this time. Have you ever traveled first class? Oh, my."

All of the Elliotts came for the wedding, even a few

more Lucy hadn't met. She still hadn't learned all their names.

Bryan closed down Une Nuit for the day and invited all the employees out to The Tides, except for the new busboys, who were now in jail.

Stash came, of course, driving his Peugeot, which now sported a few bullet holes. Bryan's employer had offered to repair the damage, but Stash enjoyed showing off the holes and bragging, to anyone who would listen, about his small part in the takedown of international terrorists. Lucy tried to steer her parents clear of him.

Bryan looked dashing as ever. The bandages on his shoulder hardly showed through his tuxedo, and he dispensed with his sling for the ceremony and the photos, but put it back on shortly after. He wasn't supposed to use his right arm while the tissues healed, but he claimed he wasn't in any pain.

The ceremony itself was short and sweet. Then there was the feasting, the way only restaurant people and Elliotts could feast. Chef Chin took over Maeve's kitchen like a general conquering a town. Maeve was more than happy to just get out of the way and enjoy the day.

The crowning glory of the reception feast was a four-layer cake, Bryan's little surprise for Lucy. She hadn't realized exactly what kind of cake it was until he fed her a piece of it for the photos.

Orange cake, garnished with chocolate and mint glaze. Not exactly traditional. But at the first taste, Lucy could feel her face heating—and other parts of her as well.

"Lucy, something wrong?" Bryan asked solicitously.

"I'm just having a Pavlovian response," she said, never imagining that orange cake could make her feel…amorous.

"I'm putting this cake on the menu, you know. Bryan and Lucy's Orange Wedding Cake."

She stood on her toes and whispered in his ear. "It would have been more appropriate as Bryan and Lucy's Honeymoon Cake."

"Don't worry, we'll take some with us."

Amanda, Bryan's mother, had arrived seconds before the ceremony, breathless and tense. Now he hugged her. "I was afraid you might not come, Mom."

"I wasn't about to miss my son's wedding—even if I do have to be under the same roof with *him*." She nodded toward Patrick, Bryan's grandfather.

This family had more drama and intrigue than a soap opera. But all families had their little issues, and Lucy vowed to accept them all as they came along. She reveled in the laughter, the smells and tastes of the day. She even enjoyed the family bickering, which they simply were not able to refrain from. She loved that she was now part of this crazy clan.

"You happy?" Bryan asked Lucy quietly as they posed for yet more pictures.

"Deliriously."

"You should be afraid. Very afraid."

"Because…?"

"You fit in perfectly. You've become an Elliott."

Lucy could think of nothing more wonderful.

* * * * *

MARRIAGE TERMS

BY
BARBARA DUNLOP

Barbara Dunlop writes romantic stories while curled up in a log cabin in Canada's far north, where bears outnumber people and it snows six months of the year. Fortunately, she has a brawny husband and two teenage children to haul firewood and clear the driveway while she sips cocoa and muses about her upcoming chapters. Barbara loves to hear from readers. You can contact her through her website at www.barbaradunlop.com.

For my sisters.
Denise, Karen and Melinda

One

If Amanda Elliott had her way, New York would have a law against ex-husbands. She took a deep breath, curled her toes over the pool deck at Boca Royce Health Club and dived headfirst into the fast lane.

A law against ex-husbands who invaded a woman's life. She stretched her arms out, surging her body forward until she sliced back up through the surface.

A law against ex-husbands who stayed fit and sexy for over fifteen years. Her right arm pulled into a freestyle arc as she kicked into her rhythm, letting the cool water block out the world.

And a law against ex-husbands who held a woman tight, whispered words of comfort and made her insane world tip right again.

She scrunched her eyes shut against the illicit memory, stroking hard until her fingertips brushed the smooth pool wall at the opposite end. Then she twisted her body to kick into the next lap.

While the politicians were at it, they should write a law against sons who were wounded in shoot-outs, sons who were secretly government agents and sons who went to spy school *without* their mother's permission.

It wouldn't take much. A simple amendment to the admissions disclaimer, and no woman would ever again have to wake up and discover she'd given birth to James Bond.

Amanda pulled past the blue halfway floats.

Her son Bryan was James Bond.

She laughed a little desperately at that one, nearly sucking in a lungful of water.

Try as she might, she couldn't imagine Bryan with a forged passport, driving exotic cars through foreign countries and pressing little remote control devices to blow things up. Her Bryan loved puppies and finger painting, he lived for those sweet little cream-filled coconut puffs you could only get at Wong's on the corner.

She was grateful he was getting out of the spy game. He'd vowed as much to his new bride. Amanda had heard it with her own ears. So had Daniel.

Her stroke faltered. This time her ex-husband's image refused to disappear.

Daniel had comforted her through the long night of Bryan's surgery. He'd been her pillar of strength, holding her up when she swore the sheer weight of terror would topple her. At times, he'd squeezed her so tight that over a decade and a half of anger and mistrust melted between them.

Détente?

She made another turn, pushing off the pool wall with her feet and knifing back to the surface. She swam harder, and her jaw tightened as she concentrated on her strokes.

Détente wasn't even a possibility.

It would never be a possibility.

Because Daniel was a true-blue Elliott. And Amanda…wasn't. East-West relations were a cakewalk compared to that.

The truce was over. Bryan was well on the road to recovery. Daniel was back on his own side of Manhattan. And Amanda had opening arguments in front of Judge Mercer tomorrow morning.

Her knuckles hit the wall at the end of another lap. *Five,* she counted off in her mind.

"Hello, Amanda." Daniel's familiar voice came out of nowhere.

She scrambled to bring her body to vertical, scrubbing the chlorinated water out of her eyes and blinking at her ex-husband's fuzzy image. What was he doing here? "Is it Bryan?"

Daniel flinched, quickly shaking his head. "No. No. Sorry. Bryan's fine." He crouched on the concrete deck, putting them closer to eye level.

Amanda whooshed out a breath of relief, clinging to the trough at the edge of the pool. "Thank goodness."

"Cullen told me I'd find you here," he said.

Her anxiety rushed back at the mention of her second son. "Is it Misty?"

Another shake of Daniel's head. "Misty's good. The baby's kicking up a storm."

Amanda studied his expression. His face was calm and impassive. Whatever had dragged him out of the office in the middle of the day wasn't life threatening.

He straightened back to full height, and her gaze strayed to his muscular chest, then to his navy trunks. His feet were bare, and he sported a six-pack of a stomach that would be the envy of a man half his age.

Her mouth went dry, and she suddenly realized she hadn't seen Daniel in anything but a designer suit for sixteen years. The man who had hugged her goodbye had a body to die for.

She bicycled her legs, trying to restore her equilibrium in the deep water. "Then what are you doing here?"

"I'm looking for you."

She blinked again, trying to make sense out of his words. Unless she'd missed something, they'd said their goodbyes at Bryan's wedding and had gone back to their respective lives.

Daniel should be perched behind his mahogany desk at *Snap* magazine right now, fighting tooth and nail with his siblings over profits and market share. As he was locked in a battle for the CEO position at Elliott Publication Holdings, it should have taken a catastrophe of biblical proportions to get him out of the office during work hours.

"I wanted to talk to you," he said casually.

"Excuse me?" She shook the water out of her ears.

"Talk. You know, when people use words to exchange information and ideas."

Clearing her ears hadn't helped. Daniel had tracked her down to *chat?*

He smiled, bending at the waist to reach out his hand. "Why don't we get a drink?"

She pushed away from the pool edge and began treading water. "I don't think so."

"Come out of the pool, Amanda."

"Uh-uh." She wasn't chatting, and she sure wasn't hopping out in front of him in a tight one-piece.

He might look like an advertisement for *Muscle Mass Monthly,* but the earth's gravitational pull was winning the war with her body.

"I've got forty-five laps to go," she said.

Fifty laps was a stretch, but she was upping her workout— starting here and now. Whether Daniel ever saw her in a bathing suit or not, a woman had her pride.

Daniel crossed his arms over his broad chest. "Since when do *you* stick to a plan?"

He wanted to start in on their weaknesses?

"Since when do *you* finish work before eight at night?" she asked.

"I'm taking a coffee break."

"Right," she drawled, with a skeptical nod.

He frowned, looking imperious despite the swimming trunks. "What's that supposed to mean?"

"It means you don't take coffee breaks."

"We've barely seen each other in over fifteen years. How would you know whether or not I take coffee breaks?"

"When was the last time you took one?"

His cobalt eyes darkened. "Today."

"Before that?"

He was silent for a moment, until one corner of his mouth quirked in a grin.

She splashed at him. "Knew it."

He ducked. "Do I have to come in there after you?"

"Go away." She had a workout to finish and a head to get clear. It was all well and good to lean on Daniel when their son was in mortal danger. But the truce was over. It was time to return to their respective trenches.

"I want to talk to you," he called.

She kicked farther into the lane. "We have nothing to say to each other."

"Amanda."

"If Bryan's not back in the hospital, and if Misty's not in labor, then you and I are leading separate lives."

"Amanda," he repeated a little bit louder.

"It says so on our divorce papers." She swam away.

He paced along the edge of the pool, his voice muffled by the water covering her ears. "I thought…then you…making progress…"

She gave up and turned into a sidestroke, gazing at his long, lean body while a shriek sounded from the diving pool. It was followed by the thump, thump, thump of the board's recoil.

"Progress toward what?"

His eyes narrowed. "I hate it when you play dumb."

"And I hate it when you insult me."

"How am I insulting you?"

"You called me dumb."

He spread his hands in frustration. "I said you were *playing* dumb."

"Then you called me scheming."

"Do we have to do this?"

Apparently, they did. Every single time they got within fifty feet of each other.

"I was there for you, Amanda."

She stilled, and the water lapped lightly against her neck. He was using it against her already?

He raised his palms in a gesture of surrender. "And you were there for me. I know. I know."

"And it's over," she said. "Bryan's alive..." Her voice cracked over her son's name, and she drew a bracing breath. "And Cullen is happily married."

Daniel crouched again, lowering his voice. "What about you, Amanda?" His blue irises flickered with the reflection of the water.

Nope. She wasn't doing this to herself. She wasn't getting into a conversation with Daniel about her emotional or mental state.

"I'm definitely alive," she informed him tartly, then did a surface dive and resumed her swim.

He continued walking along the deck, keeping pace, watching her strokes.

Soon, all she could think about was how far her butt was

sticking out of the water and whether or not her suit was riding up.

She paused at the opposite end, swiping her hair away from her eyes.

"Will you be leaving now?" she asked. She wasn't about to attempt forty-four laps with him sizing up her thighs.

"I want to talk to you about a legal matter," he said.

"Call my office."

"We're family."

She whooshed away from the edge, creating an eddy around her body. "We're *not* family." Not anymore.

He glanced around. "Do we have to do this here?"

"Hey, you can be wherever you want. I was swimming away, minding my own business."

He nodded toward the mezzanine floor that overlooked the pool. "Come up and have a drink."

"Go away."

"I need your legal advice."

"You have lawyers on retainer."

"But this is confidential."

"I've got laps left to swim."

His eyes focused on her blurred shape beneath the water. "You don't need them."

Her heart tripped over a beat. But then she remembered the way glib compliments rolled off his tongue. She turned and stretched into freestyle again.

He followed her to the other end and was standing there when she came up for air.

She sighed in frustration. "You can be a real jerk, you know that?"

"Go ahead and finish. I'll wait."

She gritted her teeth. "I don't think so."

He grinned and reached out his hand.

* * *

Daniel was worried she wouldn't fall for his ruse. Then he'd have to find another way to lure her into conversation. Because he definitely had a few things left to say.

Over the past few weeks, he'd seen her frantic schedule. He'd overheard the late-night calls. And he'd watched the way her clients took advantage of her.

Her dark eyes narrowed warily, and he moved his hand a little closer, wiggling his fingers in encouragement. He just needed her attention for a few days, maybe a couple of weeks. Then she'd be back on track, and he'd get out of her life for good.

Finally, she grimaced and tucked her small, slick hand in his palm. He tried not to be too obvious about his sigh of relief as he gently lifted her from the water.

She straightened on the deck, and he took in her toned limbs and the way her apricot suit clung to her ripe curves. Because she favored casual clothes now—clothes that tended toward loose and baggy—he'd thought maybe she'd gained weight over the years. Not so.

She had a ton of fashion potential. Her figure was gorgeous. Her waist was indented, her stomach smooth and tight, her full breasts rounded against the wet Lycra.

A long-dormant jolt of desire hit his system. He clenched his jaw to tamp it down.

If he alienated her now, she'd bolt. Then she'd spend the rest of her life swimming away her office hours and wandering around midtown Manhattan in khakis, gauzy blouses and clunky sandals.

He cringed at the image.

She might not admit it, but she needed to broaden her professional circles, cultivate prosperous clients and, for the love of God, dress for success.

She extracted her hand from his.

"One drink," she warned, giving him a don't-mess-with-me look as she whisked water droplets from her suit.

"One drink," he agreed gruffly, dragging his gaze from her luscious figure.

She took in his dry trunks, wrinkling her nose. "You didn't even get wet."

He cupped her elbow and turned her toward the locker rooms. "That's because I wasn't here to swim."

Her skin was slick and cool, like the tile under his feet. She stopped at the head of the corridor and turned to face him. He could almost see her mind ticking through the situation, formulating arguments.

He scrambled for a distraction. "Don't suppose you'd consider a family changing room for old times' sake?"

That put a flash in her mocha eyes, but it also shut her up. Which was what he'd had in mind.

He didn't really have a legal matter to discuss. It was a spur-of-the-moment excuse to get her out of the pool, and it was going to take a few minutes to put the finer points on the lie.

He gave her what he hoped was a nostalgic smile. "The boys sure loved it here."

"What is wrong with you?" she asked.

"I'm just saying—"

"Fine. Okay. The boys loved it here."

She was silent for a moment, then her eyes softened. He felt himself sinking into his own memories.

The shouts of children faded, and he suddenly saw two small, dark-haired boys whizzing down the slide and doing flips off the diving board. Boca Royce was the only recreation he and Amanda could afford during their lean years—thanks to the Elliott family lifetime membership. And Bryan and Cullen used to swim their little hearts out.

His memory moved on to the end of the swim day, when the boys were ready to drop. He and Amanda would bundle them home for frozen pizza and a cartoon movie. Then they'd tuck them in and curl up in their own bed for a leisurely evening of love.

His voice turned husky. "We had some good times, didn't we?"

She didn't engage, didn't meet his eyes. Without a word, she turned on her heel and marched down the corridor.

Just as well.

He was here to offer her a few basic pointers, to get her professional life on track.

Anything else was off-limits.

Way off-limits.

Amanda felt considerably less vulnerable in faded jeans and a powder-blue tank top. In the ladies' change room, she finger-combed her damp hair and smeared some clear lip gloss across her mouth. She never used much makeup during the day, and she wasn't about to put any on for Daniel. She wasn't blow-drying her hair, either.

Throwing her bright yellow athletic bag over one shoulder, she exited the change room and trotted up the wide stairs to the mezzanine.

One quick drink. She'd hear him out, refer him to somebody much higher priced than she was then maybe go see a good therapist.

At the top of the stairs, a set of arched, oak doors led to the pool lounge. A receptionist at the marble counter stopped her and asked to see her membership card. Before she could retrieve it from the depths of the bag, Daniel appeared, impeccably dressed in an Armani suit.

He took her arm and gave the receptionist a curt nod. "That won't be necessary. She's my guest."

"Technically, I'm not your guest," Amanda pointed out as he pushed on the oversize door. "I'm a member, too."

"I hate it when they card you," said Daniel, gesturing to a small, round table near the glass wall overlooking the pool. "It's so tacky."

"They don't recognize me," she said. The receptionist was only doing her job.

Daniel pulled out one of the curved-back chairs, and Amanda sat down on the leather cushion, plunking her bag on the hardwood floor.

"Maybe if you were to—"

She glanced at him over her shoulder.

He snapped his jaw shut and rounded the table.

As he sat down, a waiter in a dark suit appeared. "Can I get you a beverage, sir?"

Daniel raised his eyebrows in Amanda's direction. "Fruit juice," she requested.

"We have an orange-mango blend," said the waiter.

"Sounds good."

"And for you, sir?"

"Glen Saanich on the rocks. Yellow label."

"Very good." The waiter gave a sharp nod and left.

"Let me guess," she said, not in the mood to let the cut off insult slide by. "You were going to say that if I wore a power suit nobody would check my ID."

He didn't even bother to disagree. "The clothes do make the woman," he said.

"The *woman* makes the woman," she replied.

"A business suit and a nice pair of heels would give you a lot of credibility."

"I dress like that for the courtroom, not to get into exclusive clubs."

Daniel scooped the fanned, linen napkin from his water goblet and plunked it on the table. His study of her became more intense. "What *do* you plan your wardrobe around?"

"My life. My job. Just like everybody else."

"You're a lawyer."

"I'm aware of that."

"Amanda, lawyers usually—"

"Daniel," she warned. Whatever it was they were here to discuss, it wasn't going to include her clothing.

"All I'm saying is drop by a boutique. Get a standing appointment at a salon—"

"My hair?"

He paused and something flickered in his expression. "You're a beautiful woman, Amanda."

"Right," she huffed. Too bad she had ugly clothes and bad hair.

"I'm talking a couple of blazers and a bit of a trim."

"So I won't get carded at Boca Royce?"

"It's not just the ID card, and you know it."

She stiffened her spine. Maybe not. But it was also none of his business. "Back off, Daniel."

Unexpectedly, he held up his hands in surrender. A few beats later he offered an apologetic grin.

Somehow his easy capitulation felt unsatisfying. Which was silly.

He reached across the table and snagged her napkin, dropping it beside her glass so their view of each other was unobstructed. Her gaze caught on his strong, tanned fingers, and she had a split-second flashback to his hand against her skin. She swallowed.

Their waiter appeared, setting their drinks down on coasters and leaving an appetizer menu behind.

"Hungry?" asked Daniel, letting the menu fall open.

As if she was going to drag this out over phyllo or sushi. "No."

"We could get some canapés."

She shook her head.

"Okay. Then I'm good with the scotch."

She focused on the expensive amber liquid, ruthlessly reminding herself of who he'd become. It had been a long time since she'd served him Bud in a can.

"Thirty-dollar scotch?" she asked.

He closed the menu and set it aside. "What's wrong with the scotch?"

"You ever drink beer anymore?"

He shrugged. "Sometimes."

"I mean domestic."

He lifted his glass and the ice cubes clinked against the fine crystal. "You're a reverse snob, you know that?"

"And you're a straight-up snob."

He stared at her for a long moment, those knowing eyes sending a shiver up her spine.

Out of self-preservation, she dropped her gaze to the tabletop. She wouldn't let Daniel's opinion get the better of her. Forget the haircut. Forget the designer clothes.

His opinion of her meant nothing, nothing at all.

"Why do you suppose…?" he asked softly, and she glanced up. He started again. "Why do you suppose we argue so much?" The question was undeniably intimate.

She refused to match his tone. "Because we cling to the hope that one day we might change each other's minds."

He was silent for a long moment. And then a genuine grin grew on his face. "Well, I'm open to improvement if you are."

Uh-oh. She didn't know where he was going with this disarming act, but it couldn't be good. "Can we cut to the chase?"

"There's a chase?"

"The confidential legal matter? The thing you brought me up here to discuss?"

A fleeting expression tightened his features, and he shifted in his chair. "Oh, that. It's a matter of some, uh, delicacy."

That got her attention. *"Really?"*

"Yes."

She leaned forward. Was there a veiled message in those words? Was Daniel in some kind of trouble?

"You telling me you *did* something?" she asked.

He blinked. "Did something?"

"You actually broke the law?"

His brows knit together. "Don't be absurd. Jeez, Amanda."

"Well, then, what's with this secret meeting in the middle of the day? And why with me?"

"This isn't a secret meeting."

"We're not at your office."

"Would you come to my office?"

"No."

"There you go."

"Daniel."

"What?"

"Get to the point."

Their waiter appeared. "Anything from the menu, sir?"

Daniel barely turned his head. "The canapé tray will be fine."

"Very good, sir."

As the waiter left, Amanda raised her eyebrows in a question.

"You never know," said Daniel. "We might be here awhile."

"At the rate you're talking, we sure will."

He took a sip of his scotch. "Fine. I'll cut to the chase. I'm looking into an interpretation of our employee manual."

"The employee manual?"

How on earth was that a delicate matter? Here she thought the conversation, his life, was about to get interesting.

He nodded.

She shook her head in disappointment and reached for her athletic bag. "Daniel, I don't practice corporate law."

He trapped her hand on the table, and her entire arm buzzed with the sensation.

"What do you mean?" he asked.

She tried to ignore his touch. "I mean it's not my specialty."

"Well, maybe not labor relations…"

She shifted in her chair. She couldn't yank her hand from his. That would be too obvious. "I practice criminal law."

He stared at her in silence, the pulse in his thumb synchronizing with hers.

"Crime," she offered helpfully, tugging her hand ever so slightly.

He blinked in confusion.

"Surely you've read the newspapers, seen the dramas on television…"

"But… Private lawyers don't prosecute criminals."

"Who says I prosecute them?"

His hand tightened convulsively. "You *defend* them?"

"Yes, I do." She made no bones about trying to free herself this time.

He let her go. He glanced away. Then he stared at her again. "What kind of criminals?"

"The kind that get caught."

"Don't be facetious."

"I'm dead serious. The ones that get away with it don't need me."

"Like thieves, prostitutes, murderers?"

"Yes."

"Do the boys know about this?"

"Of course."

He hardened his jaw. "I don't like the sound of that."

"Really?" As if his opinion had any bearing on her career decisions.

"Really, Amanda." He reached for her hand with both of his this time. "I thought…" He shook his head. "But this is dangerous."

His touch might be disturbing, but his words were even more so.

She fought him on both fronts. "This is none of your business, Daniel."

He stared at her intently. "But it *is* my business."

"No."

"You're the mother of my children."

"No."

"I can't let anything—"

"Daniel!"

His hands tightened, and he got a familiar look in his eyes. That look said he had a plan. That look said he had a mission. That look said he was going to save her from herself.

TWO

Daniel needed to talk to his sons. Well, one son, to start off with. He supposed he'd have to wait until the bandages came off to confront Bryan. But Cullen was getting a piece of his mind right away.

He tossed his credit card on the counter at the Atlantic Golf Course pro shop.

Amanda a criminal defense attorney? Of all the lunatic ideas. After their divorce she'd pursued her B.A., then a graduate degree in English literature, then three years of law school, and she was throwing it all away on lost causes?

The pro shop clerk bagged a royal-blue golf shirt, while Daniel signed the receipt.

Her clients probably paid her off in stolen stereos.

Maybe the bank robbers had cash—small, unmarked bills. And then only as long as they'd pulled a few successful jobs before they got caught.

His ex-wife was defending bank robbers. His sons had

known she was in danger. All these years, and they hadn't bothered saying anything. Was it not a salient point to bring up in conversation?

"By the way, Dad. You might be interested to know that Mom's consorting with thieves and murderers."

Sure, he and Amanda had agreed not to bad-mouth each other in front of their kids. And, for the most part, that meant not talking about each other in the early years of the divorce. But Bryan and Cullen were grown men now. And they were perfectly capable of seeing danger when it hovered in front of their eyes.

Daniel exited the pro shop and headed for the locker room. Misty had said Cullen's tee time was six-thirty. That meant he'd be coming up on the ninth hole about now.

At his locker, Daniel hung up his suit jacket, his tie and his dress shirt. Then he tugged the new golf shirt over his head and straightened the collar. He left the clubhouse through the terrace café.

Normally he'd check out the dining room, maybe exchange an informal word with some of his business associates. But not today. Today he marched straight down the shade-patterned pathway.

Cullen had some explaining to do.

Five minutes down the path, he spotted Cullen on the ninth green, lining up for a putt. He turned and angled toward him, not caring in the least about etiquette.

"Hey, Dad." A hushed voice to his left stopped him in his tracks.

He turned to see his older son. "Bryan?"

Standing at the edge of the green, Bryan sported a sling to protect his injured shoulder.

He nodded to Daniel.

"What the hell are you doing here?" Daniel hissed.

"I'm golfing," said Bryan.

"You're injured."

Cullen looked up from the putt. "Will you two shut up?"

Daniel clamped his jaw until Cullen's ball had disappeared into the hole.

"Hey, Dad," said Cullen, sliding the handle of his putter through his fist as he paced toward them. He handed the club to his caddy.

"You just got out of the hospital," Daniel said to Bryan.

Bryan headed for his own golf bag. "It was a superficial wound."

"It was a bullet hole."

"In my shoulder."

"You were in surgery for three hours."

Bryan shrugged his good shoulder and accepted a putter. "You know those doctors. They eke out every billable minute."

Daniel rounded on Cullen. "You actually brought him golfing?"

"I'm taking the drives," said Cullen easily. "He's only putting."

"And he's cheating," said Bryan, lining up his one-handed shot.

"Like I need to cheat to beat a cripple," Cullen called.

"I can't believe Lucy let you out of the house," said Daniel. Bryan had always been the daredevil of the family, but this was ridiculous.

"You kidding?" asked Cullen. "Lucy paid me to get him out of the house."

"Apparently I'm not a good patient," Bryan said, swinging at the ball and missing the hole.

"That's five," said Cullen.

"Yeah, yeah," Bryan returned. "I'll get you next week."

"Next week we're skydiving," said Cullen.

"I do not want to hear this," said Daniel, hoping against hope that it was a joke.

Bryan finally sank the golf ball. "Relax, Dad. It's an easy jump."

"I knew we should have resorted to corporal punishment," said Daniel.

Cullen laughed. "Where are your clubs, Dad?"

Daniel squared his shoulders. His sons might be grown men, and he might not have control over their hobbies, but he was still their father. "I'm not here to golf."

Bryan returned the putter to his caddy. "Yeah?"

"And I wasn't at Boca Royce to swim this afternoon, either."

After a silent pause, Cullen raised an eyebrow. "Uh, thanks for sharing that with us, Dad."

He pasted each of his sons with a significant glare. "I was there to talk to your mother." Then he dropped his tone an octave, giving his voice that steely undercurrent he'd used when they were teenagers and got caught drinking beer or breaking curfew. "She told me about her law practice."

He paused and waited for their reaction.

Cullen glanced at Bryan, and Bryan shrugged.

"Her *defense attorney* practice," Daniel elaborated, trying to crack their poker faces.

Bryan turned to leave the green. "Is something wrong, Dad?"

"Yeah, I'd say something was wrong. Your mother is working for *criminals*."

Cullen followed his brother, cocking his head to one side. "Who'd you think she was working for?"

Daniel stalked through the rough. "Executives, politicians, little old ladies writing wills."

"She's a litigator," said Bryan. "Always has been."

"And you never mentioned it?"

Cullen peeled off his white leather gloves and tucked them in his back pocket. "We don't talk to you about Mom."

"Well, maybe you should have."

"Why?"

Daniel couldn't believe his sons would be so obtuse. "Because, she's in danger, that's why."

"Danger from what?" asked Bryan.

"Criminals."

"She's not in danger," Bryan scoffed as they turned onto the pathway that led up to the clubhouse.

Daniel squinted at his older son. He sounded very confident, very definitive. And Bryan was in the business of danger.

Wait a minute.

Maybe he knew something Daniel didn't. That was it. Daniel should have realized he could count on his sons.

He felt as if a weight had risen right up off him. "Are you having her watched by one of your associates?"

Cullen sputtered out a laugh, while Bryan stared at Daniel. "Dad, you've seen one too many cop shows."

Daniel rocked back. They were mocking him now. "Her clients are thieves and murderers."

"And she's their best friend," said Bryan. "Trust me on this, Dad. The mortality rate for defense lawyers is pretty damn low."

"Are you two going to help me or not?"

"Help you do what?" asked Cullen.

Daniel's original plan was to work on her image and her business. But if he found a good clothing designer, it would only attract a better class of criminals. Nope. This called for drastic action.

"Convince her to change careers," he said.

His sons drew back simultaneously. Cullen actually held up crossed fingers as if to ward off an evil spirit.

"Uh-uh," said Bryan with a shake of his dark head.

"Are you out of your mind?" Cullen asked.

Daniel stared at his two strapping, six-foot-plus sons. "Don't tell me you're afraid of her."

"Hell, yes," said Cullen.

Daniel squared his shoulders and crossed his arms over his chest. "More afraid of *her* than you are of *me?*"

Both boys snorted their disbelief.

"You're on your own with Mom," said Cullen, starting up the steep grade.

"We'll be doing something safe," Bryan said.

Cullen nodded his concurrence. "Like skydiving."

"He is making me very nervous," said Amanda to her ex-sister-in-law Karen Elliott where they sat in the solarium at The Tides, her former in-laws' palatial estate. Since her mastectomy this past winter, Karen had been recuperating out on the Long Island estate. Rays of sunlight streamed through the skylights, glowing against the hardwood floor and bringing out the pastels in the cushions covering the wicker furniture.

"Did he actually do anything?" asked Karen. A cup of herb tea in hand, she was reclining on a lounger next to the glass wall that overlooked the Atlantic. Seagulls soared on the rising air currents while storm clouds gathered on the far horizon.

"He suggested an extreme makeover." Amanda still bristled at Daniel's nerve.

"Like plastic surgery?" asked Karen.

"Like a haircut and a new wardrobe. But who knows what all else he had in mind."

"Whew." Karen blew out a breath. "You scared me for a minute. I thought maybe Sharon had completely corrupted him."

Amanda cringed at the mention of Daniel's recent ex-wife. Rail thin and strikingly beautiful, Sharon Styles was never anything less than a perfectly coiffed fashion plate.

Karen smoothed a hand over the colorful scarf that disguised the hair loss from her chemotherapy. "Personally, I'd kill for a good makeover."

Amanda gave a chopped laugh of disbelief. Karen didn't need a makeover. She was classy and gorgeous under any circumstances, from the glow of her honey-toned nose to the shine of her pedicured nails.

"I say we skip the makeover and kill off Daniel," said Amanda.

Karen suddenly sat up on the chaise, swinging her legs around the side and clinking her china teacup into its saucer. "That's exactly what I'm going to do."

Amanda feigned delight. "You're going to kill off Daniel?"

"I'm going to get a makeover. And Daniel's right. You should come with me."

"Hey!" Bad enough when Daniel criticized her appearance. She didn't need Karen jumping on the bandwagon.

Karen waved a dismissive hand. "Don't be so sensitive. We'll spend the weekend at Eduardo's. Mud wraps, facials…" Her hand went to her chest, and she rolled her eyes reverently. "Oh, one of those heated stone massages will make you feel like a new woman."

"I don't want to be a new woman. And I can't afford Eduardo's. One of those heated stone massages would bankrupt me. I don't *need* a makeover."

"When did need have anything to do with a makeover? And you can make Daniel pay."

Daniel pay? Let Daniel and his money anywhere near her life? Was Karen out of her mind?

"After all, it was his idea," said Karen with a calculating gleam.

Amanda shook her head. "I think you're missing the point of this conversation."

Karen grinned unrepentantly. "I'm not missing the point. They nuked my cancer, not my brain."

Amanda leaned forward in her armchair, folding her hands on the knees of her khaki pants, making sure she was perfectly clear this time. "I don't want to humor Daniel. I want your husband to help me get him off my back."

Karen copied Amanda's posture. "Maybe Daniel will get off your back if you get a makeover."

"If I get a makeover, Daniel will think I've taken his advice."

"Who cares?"

"*I* do. He wants me to stop practicing law. I give in on the makeover, you can bet what's coming next."

"It's not like he can have you disbarred."

Amanda paused. She supposed that was true enough. He couldn't actually force her to stop working. Could he? The Elliotts were powerful, but she had to believe there were limits on what they could pull off.

He'd have to catch her doing something unethical—which she wouldn't. Or he'd have to set her up—which he wouldn't. Her folded hands tightened. But Patrick might. If Daniel asked him to.

Of course, Patrick couldn't care less what Amanda did for a living, or whether she consorted with criminals. By the same token, neither should Daniel. Really, where on earth was this coming from?

Karen sat back in the chaise and gave an exaggerated sigh into the silence, smoothing the palm of her hand over her forehead. "I think a makeover would help me recover *so* much faster." She turned her head toward Amanda and shamelessly blinked her long lashes. "But I really don't want to go to Eduardo's all alone."

Amanda wasn't fooled for a second.

Karen was milking the situation for all it was worth. But she *had* been through a terrible illness. And if she wanted company at a weekend spa, how could Amanda refuse?

A gull cried against the sheer cliffs outside, a second answering it as the surf roiled up against the rocks.

"If I say yes," Amanda ventured, "we can't tell Daniel." If Daniel thought she was taking his advice, any of his advice, there'd be no stopping him.

A beautiful smile grew on Karen's face. "I say we let them dye your hair."

"No, we're not…" When Karen's expression faltered, Amanda paused. "You think I should dye my hair?"

"Oh, they can give you the most divine highlights. You'll love it. I promise."

Amanda didn't want divine highlights, and she sure didn't want to touch Daniel's advice with a ten-foot pole. But she did love Karen, and she supposed highlights wouldn't kill her.

"Okay. Highlights it is."

Karen all but bounced back up into a sitting position. "Great. My treat."

"No way." Amanda wasn't about to let Karen pick up the tab.

"Okay. Michael's treat. I'll make the reservations." Karen reached for the phone.

"Your husband doesn't pay, either."

"But you said—"

"Final offer. We go to Eduardo's, I pay my way and nobody tells Daniel."

"Yes! We have a plan."

Three

Daniel was a man with a plan. Of course, Daniel was always a man with a plan. But this one was better than most.

The door opened, and Cullen entered the office on the nineteenth floor of the Elliott Publication Holdings building. He tossed a sheaf of papers on Daniel's desk. "The new sales figures."

"Thanks," said Daniel, giving the report only a cursory glance.

Regina and Hopkins were probably his best bet. They were a reputable firm specializing in corporate law. He supposed getting Amanda a job offer up-front was probably too heavy-handed, but maybe he could drop a few hints regarding their billable hours and their profit margin. He was pretty sure Taylor Hopkins would give him that information.

"Last month's numbers look iffy," said Cullen, cocking his head in an effort to make eye contact. "We're not going to pull ahead with numbers like these." He paused. "It's so frustrating not knowing where we are in the competition."

"I see," said Daniel with a nod.

Amanda obviously didn't understand the amount of money to be made in corporate law. Or the fact that the money was all made during business hours. If she was invited anywhere in the evening, it would be to an art museum opening or a new production of *La Bohème*.

Daniel was willing to bet Taylor Hopkins had never, not even once, been called out at midnight to drop by the Fifty-Third Street lockup and arrange bail for a drug dealer.

"Dad?"

Not even once.

"Dad?"

Daniel blinked up at his son. "Yeah?"

"We're probably losing this race."

"You have your Mom's phone number programmed into your cell?"

Cullen didn't respond.

"Never mind," said Daniel, pressing the intercom button. "Nancy? Can you get me the number for Amanda Elliott, Attorney? She's in Midtown."

"Right away," came Nancy's voice.

"You're calling Mom?" asked Cullen.

"Somebody has to."

"Dad, I really think you need to back up and—"

"You said something about sales figures?"

"Oh, *now* you want to talk sales figures."

"When have I not wanted to talk sales figures?"

Cullen rolled his eyes. "We're not gaining any ground."

"We expected that."

Cullen pointed to a number on the top sheet. "This is a problem."

Daniel glanced down. That was a low number all right. "How are hits on the new Web site?"

"Increasing."

"People buying subscriptions?"

Cullen nodded.

"Demographics?"

"Eighteen to twenty-four is the fastest growing sector."

"Good."

"Not fast enough," said Cullen.

The intercom buzzed. "I have that number for you," said Nancy.

"I'll be right out." Daniel stood up and clapped his son on the shoulder. "Keep up the good work."

"But, Dad…"

Daniel slipped his suit jacket off the hanger on the corner coatrack.

"You're leaving?" asked Cullen, glancing from the sales report to Daniel and back again.

"I'm thinking you're right. A phone call is probably a bad idea." He'd drop by Amanda's office. That way she'd have a harder time saying no to a drink. He could call Taylor Hopkins from the car and have the facts and figures all ready to present.

Cullen walked backward, keeping himself between Daniel and the office door. "The reps will be expecting a conference call."

"We can conference call tomorrow."

Cullen came up against the door, effectively blocking Daniel's escape. "You do realize we're losing hope of catching Finola?"

"We'll make it up in Web sales. That was the strategy all along."

Cullen paused. "You do realize you're on a suicide mission with Mom?"

Daniel cracked a small smile. "Your faith in me is inspiring."

"Just laying out the facts for you."

"Your mother's an intelligent woman. She'll listen to reason."

Cullen put a hand on the doorknob. "What makes you think your idea is remotely reasonable?"

Daniel peered at his son. "Of course it's reasonable."

Cullen shook his head, his tone mocking. "Dad, Dad, Dad."

Daniel held up his index finger. "Watch yourself. I may not be able to spank you, but I can still fire you."

"You fire me, Finola will wax your ass for sure."

Daniel pushed Cullen's hand off the knob. "Young punk."

"You got your will in order?"

"I'm writing you out of it in the car."

Cullen gave him a mock salute and cocky grin as he stepped out of the way. "You're making a bold move here, Dad. A lesser man would be quaking in his boots."

Daniel hesitated for a split second.

Then he shook his head and opened the office door. He had twenty years of wisdom and experience on Cullen, and his younger son wasn't going to make him second-guess his plan.

Daniel noticed right away that Amanda's office was a startling contrast to EPH. It was smaller, darker, and where the Elliott building had lobby security, Amanda's storefront door opened directly into the reception area, inviting any passerby to come right on in.

The young, multiearringed, purple-haired receptionist didn't look as though she could stop a grandmother, never mind a criminal punk intent on harm. She stopped chewing her gum long enough to cock her head sideways in an inquiry.

"I'd like to speak with Amanda Elliott," said Daniel.

The girl indicated the closed, frosted glass office door with her thumb. "She's with Timmy the Trench. Be about five or so."

"Thank you," said Daniel.

The receptionist blew a pink bubble.

After checking a vinyl chair in the waiting room for dirt smears or chewing gum, Daniel sat down and sighed. The woman hadn't even asked his name or his business with Amanda.

When the majority of your clientele was likely armed and dangerous, a person would think rudimentary security questions would be in order. First thing Daniel would do was install a metal detector at the entrance, and maybe station a couple of former Green Berets on the sidewalk.

A meeting with Timmy the Trench.

Nobody named Timmy the Trench could be up to anything remotely legal.

Fifteen minutes later, while, out of desperation, Daniel was leafing through a six-month-old edition of a competitor's magazine, a short, balding man in a trench coat shuffled out of Amanda's office.

"Can you call Courthouse Admin?" called Amanda through the open door. "I need to know the new trial date for Timmy."

"Sure," called the receptionist, punching the numbers on her phone with long, dark fingernails.

She glanced Daniel's way and gestured to the open door. "Go on in."

Daniel rolled to his feet, tossed the magazine back on the untidy pile and headed into Amanda's office. He couldn't shake the knowledge that he could be anyone, after anything.

"Daniel?" Amanda lifted her chin, rolling back a few inches on her office chair.

"Yeah." He pushed on the door, and it rattled into place behind him. "And you're damn lucky it *is* me."

Her eyebrows shot up. "I am?"

He took one of the two molded plastic guest chairs opposite her desk. "That receptionist would have let anyone in here."

Amanda tucked her dark brown hair behind her ear. "I suppose we could issue membership cards."

He frowned. "You're being sarcastic."

"Am I? Care to guess why?"

Daniel leaned back and flicked open the button on his suit jacket. "It's a defense mechanism. You use it when I'm right and you're wrong."

"When has that ever happened?"

"I have a list of dates."

"I just bet you do."

He paused, taking in the flash of her mocha eyes. She liked this. Hell, *he* liked this. There was nobody on the planet who could spar with him like Amanda.

She was quick on her feet and downright brilliant. That much hadn't changed.

He remembered Cullen's parting words. Perhaps he had underestimated how easy it would be to lure her over to corporate law. But he was definitely giving it his best shot.

"Have dinner with me," he said on impulse. Then he saw her expression and realized his tactical error. Too bold, too up-front. It almost sounded like a date.

"Daniel—"

"With Cullen and Misty," he quickly put in. As the boss, he could order their son to join them, right? If that didn't work, he'd go straight to Misty. He'd heard through the family grapevine that she and Amanda had hit it off extremely well.

Amanda's eyes settled into a glow. "Have you seen Misty?

"No, but I saw Cullen earlier today."

"And everything's all right with the pregnancy?"

"Everything's fine." Not that Daniel had specifically asked. But Cullen would have told him if anything was wrong. Right?

Amanda picked up a pen and tapped an open spot between two file folders and her Rolodex. "So, what can I do for you, Daniel?"

"Have dinner with us."

"I mean right now."

"Now?"

"Yes, now. You went to all the trouble to come to Midtown. What do you want?"

Daniel hesitated. He hadn't planned to plunge right in, right here, right now. But what the heck, he might as well lay the groundwork. "I was talking to Taylor Hopkins earlier today."

"Let me guess, he wants my legal advice on a delicate matter."

"He's a lawyer, Amanda."

"I know he's a lawyer. I was making a joke."

Daniel shifted. "Oh, right."

She stood up.

Daniel quickly came to his feet.

She scooped up a stack of files. "Relax, Daniel. I'm just putting these away. You don't mind if I organize while you talk?"

Daniel glanced from the overflowing bookshelves to a desktop and credenza piled high with papers. "Of course not. But why doesn't Miss Gothic—"

"Julie," said Amanda.

"Fine. Julie. Why doesn't Julie do your filing?"

"She does."

Daniel scanned the room again, biting his tongue.

Amanda followed his gaze. "She's learning," she clarified.

"You mean it used to be worse?"

After some hesitation, Amanda set the pile down on a wide windowsill behind her. "Did you come here just to insult my staff?"

From his vantage point, it looked as if Amanda had blocked the air-conditioning. On a humid August day in the city. "How long has she worked here?"

"Two, two and a half—"

"Weeks?"

"Years."

"Oh."

"Don't 'oh' me like that."

"Like what?"

"Just because Elliott Publication Holdings restricts its administrative staff to Ph.D. candidates—"

Daniel jumped at the opening, narrow as it was. "I wasn't comparing you to EPH."

She arched a brow.

"I was comparing you to Regina and Hopkins."

The brow arched higher. "Who won?"

"Amanda—"

"Seriously, Daniel. How did I stack up to a cold, calculating, profit-obsessed, inhuman firm like Regina and Hopkins?"

Whoa. Where had that come from? Daniel blinked at his ex-wife.

She scooped up another armload of files and glanced around. "Thought so."

From what he could see, she was randomly rearranging the mess.

Or maybe she was nervous. Now, that wasn't a bad thing. It could give him an edge. "Why do you always treat efficiency and profit like dirty words?"

She smacked the files down on the one vacant corner of the credenza. "Because 'efficiency,' as you so carefully term it, is an excuse to treat people as profit generators."

Daniel shifted that through his brain for a second. "People *are* profit generators. You hire good people, you pay them a fair salary and they make money for your company."

"And who decides who the good people are?"

"Amanda—"

"Who decides, Daniel?"

He paused, trying to determine if it was a trick question. "The Human Resources Department," he ventured.

Amanda pointed at the office door, the edge to her tone increasing. "Julie is a good person."

"I believe you." He nodded, realizing he needed to pull back. Their arguments escalated so quickly, it was difficult to keep the conversation on an even keel.

"She might not be the best typist or filer in the world. And she'd never make it past the screeners at EPH, but she's a very good person."

"I said I believe you," Daniel repeated in a conciliatory tone, gesturing for her to sit back down.

Amanda drew a breath and plunked into her chair. "She deserves a chance."

Daniel sat, too. "Where did you find her?" He was pretty sure it wasn't through any of the reputable employment agencies.

"She's a former client."

"Is she a criminal?"

"An *accused* criminal. Jeez, Daniel. Just because they arrest you, it doesn't mean you're guilty."

"What was she accused of?"

Amanda's lips pursed for a split second. "Embezzlement."

Daniel stared at her in stunned amazement. "Embezzlement?"

"You heard me."

He stood up, taking a few steps across the small room, trying desperately to keep his composure. "You hired an *embezzler* to run your law office?"

"I said she was *accused*."

"Was she innocent?"

"There were extenuating circumstances—"

"Amanda!"

Her eyes hardened defensively. "This is really none of your business, Daniel."

Daniel clamped his jaw. He could see how she might have that perspective. They'd gotten off on the wrong foot again. It was his fault. He should have orchestrated the conversation more carefully.

He sat down. Then he leaned forward. "You have a soft spot, Amanda. You always have."

She leaned over the desk, looking directly into his eyes. "If by a 'soft spot' you mean I look at people as more than drones, you're right."

He clamped his jaw, resisting the urge to respond.

She linked her fingers together and stretched them out as if warming up for a fight. "You want to critique my hiring practices? Let's take a quick look at yours."

"My people are the best," he said.

"Yeah? Tell me about some of your people."

"My secretary, Nancy, has a college degree in business administration, and she's an expert with computerized office tools."

Amanda lifted her pen again, tapping it rhythmically on the desk. "Does she have any kids?"

"I don't know."

"Is she married?"

Daniel thought about that. "I don't think so." Nancy never had a problem working late. If she had a husband and a family, it might bother her more.

"Here's a pop quiz for you, Daniel. Give me the name of an employee's spouse. Any employee's spouse."

"Misty."

"That's cheating."

Daniel grinned. "You did say *any* of them."

"You know what your problem is?"

"I'm smarter than you are?"

She tossed the pen at him.

He ducked.

"You have no soul," she said.

For some reason, her words hit harder than they should have. "I guess that is a problem," he said softly.

She flinched at his expression, but then quickly recovered. "I mean you are so myopically focused on business and productivity and profit, you forget the world is full of people. Your employees have their own lives. They're not just extras in yours."

"I know they have their own lives."

"In the abstract, yes. But you know nothing about those lives."

"I know everything I need to know."

"Yeah?" she asked with skepticism.

"Yeah."

"Let's contrast, shall we? Ask me something about Julie."

"Julie?"

Amanda rolled her eyes. "The Goth receptionist."

"Oh, Julie."

Amanda waited.

Daniel searched his mind for a relevant question. "Does she have any previous convictions for embezzlement?"

Amanda sat back in her chair. "No. She has an apartment in the East Village. She has an on-again, off-again boyfriend named Scott. I think she's too good for him. She's taking night school courses in spreadsheet applications. Her mother is battling arthritis, and she has two nephews, from her sister Robin, that she takes to the zoo on Saturday afternoons."

"Yet, she can't file."

"Daniel!"

"I don't see your point, Amanda. She's your employee, not your best friend."

Amanda shook her head and pulled open a desk drawer, turning her attention to the jumbled contents. "Of course you wouldn't see my point," she muttered. "You hired Sharon."

"Whoa." Daniel's shoulders tensed. His ex-wife had nothing to do with this. "That was out of line."

"How is it out of line?"

"I didn't *hire* Sharon."

Amanda glanced back up. "Be honest, Daniel. Did you marry Sharon because you loved her sense of humor, her opinions on literature and her outlook on global events?" Her voice rose. "Or did you marry her because she could make small talk in three languages, whip up canapés in under an hour and she looked great in anything by Dior?"

"I divorced Sharon."

"What happened? The canapés get soggy?"

Daniel stood. "I shouldn't have come." He hadn't meant to upset Amanda. And he sure hadn't meant to talk about Sharon. Sharon was out of his life for good.

"Why did you come, Daniel?"

"It wasn't to talk about Sharon."

Amanda nodded. "Of course not." Her eyes softened to that mocha color he loved. "I'm sorry. Do you miss her?"

"I divorced her."

"But still—"

"I don't miss Sharon. Not for one second. Not for one nanosecond." Which, when he really thought about it, meant Amanda could be right. He frowned.

She stood up and moved around the end of her desk. "So it *was* the small talk and designer gowns."

"You've got me on the ropes, and you're willing to score points?"

"Absolutely."

Daniel sighed. What had attracted him to Sharon in the first place? His father had supported the marriage, but that couldn't have been all there was to it.

He was recovering from losing Amanda at the time. Maybe he simply hadn't cared whom he married. Maybe he thought

Sharon would be a safer wife. A wife that knew his world and wouldn't expect things from him that he simply couldn't deliver.

Like Amanda had.

"Daniel?" Amanda's voice interrupted his thoughts.

He focused on her face. She'd moved closer, and he could smell her perfume. "Yeah?"

"I asked you when."

"When what?"

Her mouth curved into a patient smile. "Dinner with Cullen and Misty?"

He stared at her smile. She was still so incredibly beautiful, with full lips, shiny hair, bottomless eyes.

He shifted from one foot to the other. "Oh. Friday, eight o'clock at The Premier."

"Sure."

"Good." He had a sudden urge to touch her hair. He'd always loved running his fingers through its scented, silky softness. It was one of his favorite things in the world.

"Daniel?"

He curled his fingers into fists to keep them still. "Yeah?"

"I'm sorry I brought up Sharon."

"Do you really think I hired her to be my wife?" He was genuinely curious.

"I think your priorities are mixed-up."

"How?"

She paused. "You're a very driven man, Daniel."

"Yeah? Well you're what's driving me crazy at the moment."

She tilted her head and a slow grin formed on her lips. "Then you should stop hunting me down."

"You're probably right about that," he breathed, daring to move a little closer. "But, apparently, I find you irresistible."

Her eyes widened.

He touched her hair—stopped fighting the compulsion and simply reached out. His fingers released its scent, and he was catapulted back fifteen years. "I'm trying to help you here, Amanda."

Her voice was breathless. "I don't need any help."

"Yes, you do." He kissed her lightly on the forehead. "And lucky for you, I'm available."

As the office door rattled shut behind Daniel, Amanda grabbed the corner of her desk for support.

I'm available?

What did that mean? *I'm available.*

And why had he kissed her?

Okay, so he hadn't exactly kissed her. But he had—

"Amanda?" The office door opened, and Julie stuck her head in the room. Her brows waggled and a secretive smile curved her dark purple lips.

"So, who was hubba hubba man?"

Amanda stared at her blankly.

"The guy who just left," Julie elaborated.

"Daniel?"

"Right." Julie mimicked a swoon. "Delectable Daniel."

"He's my ex-husband."

Julie drew back. "Hello? You *exed* that guy?"

"I did."

"What were you thinking?"

"That he was uptight, pretentious and controlling."

"Who cares?"

Good question. No, bad question. Amanda had left Daniel for some very good reasons, not the least of which were his single-minded desire for success and his refusal to maintain even the slightest independence from his father.

"I cared," she said to Julie.

Julie shook her head and gave an exaggerated sigh. "To each his own, I guess. So what did he want?"

Amanda pressed her fingertips into her temple. "To run my life."

"Going to let him?"

"Not a chance."

"Going to see him again?"

"Nope." Well, not after Friday. And that didn't count, since Cullen and Misty would be there.

Julie shrugged. "Okay, then. Your two o'clock's here."

Amanda glanced at her watch. "It's nearly two-thirty."

"I didn't want to disturb you."

She gave Julie a gentle shove toward the doorway. "He's a paying client. Disturb me already."

Julie strained to look back over her shoulder. "I thought you might be jumping Mr. Delectable on the desktop."

"Yeah, right," said Amanda, ignoring the rise in her pulse.

Julie chuckled low. "That's what I would have done."

Four

Amanda slid the hanger of her red Chaiken silk along the rod at the far end of her closet. She didn't mind that it was several years out of date. She *did* mind that it was too sultry for an evening in the same room as Daniel.

Next she peered at the V-necked Vera Wang. Nope. Too Vegas.

Then she frowned at the sequined Tom Ford. Nope again. Too princess.

Her ten-year-old, multicolored Valentino sunburst was the last one on the rack. As far as comfort went, it left a lot to be desired. It was strapless, and she'd have to wear one of those underwire torture devices to keep her breasts in the right position. But it was made of beautiful orange, yellow and red-streaked silk, snug across the bodice, with a flowing skirt and a scalloped hem that was very flattering.

It was elegant, without giving in to basic, New York black.

She glanced at her watch. Oops. For better or worse, this was the dress.

Tossing it on the bed, she headed for the shower. A light was blinking on the answering machine, but she ignored it. She'd stayed too late at the office reading a brief, and now she had five minutes to wash her hair, throw on a little makeup and strap herself into the torture underwear.

Halfway through the shampoo, she remembered she also needed shoes. More specifically, she needed those little gold sandals with the crossover straps.

They were in the front hall closet...maybe.

So much for makeup.

She ducked her head under the spray, scrubbing her nails furiously against her scalp. Then she shut off the tap, rubbed her skin with a towel and headed for the entry hall.

She dropped to her knees on the soft carpet in front of her closet and scrambled through the untidy pile of shoes. Black, beige, flats, sneakers...

Ah ha. Little gold sandals. Well, one, anyway.

She hunted for the other, coming up lucky.

She threw them by the door and dashed back to her room.

She snapped on the bra and stepped into a matching pair of panties. Thank goodness she'd shaved her legs this morning. Lately, she hadn't been as diligent about that as she should.

She shimmied into the dress, pathetically grateful when the zipper slipped up easily. In the bathroom she ran a comb through her hair. In the hallway, she stuffed her feet into sandals. Finally, she was set.

Purse.

Darn. She ran back to the bedroom and grabbed an evening purse. She spied a pair of garnet earrings on the dresser and slid them through her pierced ears.

There.

That had to be it.

Her hair would dry in the taxi.

She grabbed her keys and headed out the front door.

"Ms. Elliott?" A uniformed chauffeur was waiting at the bottom of the stairs beside a stretch limousine.

Amanda's steps faltered. "Yes?"

He opened the back door with a flourish. "With Mr. Elliott's compliments, ma'am."

Amanda stared at the car.

"He apologizes if you didn't get the phone message."

Amanda's first instinct was to send the limo back to Daniel. But then she mentally shrugged. Why chase down a taxi out of spite?

She smiled at the driver and crossed the sidewalk. "Thank you."

"Of course," said the driver with a nod.

Amanda peeked inside at a bar, a television, three phones and a video-game controller. It had definitely been a while since she'd ridden in this kind of luxury.

She glanced back at the driver. "I don't suppose you have a hair dryer in there."

The driver grinned. "Afraid not. Do you need a few more minutes?"

"No thank you. I'm already late."

"A lady's prerogative," he said.

She shook her head and stepped into the car. "They'll just have to take me as I am."

"You look lovely, ma'am," he said diplomatically.

"Thank you," Amanda returned, making herself comfortable on the bench seat. "And thank you for picking me up."

"My pleasure." He closed the door.

The limo glided smoothly away from the curb. Low purple lights came on around the perimeter and soft music floated out from unseen speakers.

"Would you care for a beverage?" asked the driver.

"No, thank you." Amanda leaned back and watched the surrealistic blur of traffic lights through the tinted windows. She really shouldn't enjoy this quite so much.

"Mr. Elliott asked me to apologize about the mix-up with the restaurant," the driver continued.

"Mix-up?" asked Amanda, straightening.

"He wasn't able to get reservations at The Premier."

Amanda hid a small grin. An Elliott turned down by a maître d'? That must have driven Daniel wild.

"So, where are we going?" she asked.

"To Mr. Elliott's apartment."

"His apartment?"

The driver nodded in the mirror. "Yes, ma'am."

Amanda's hand splayed on her stomach. Whew. Okay. Deep breath. She could do this.

Misty and Cullen would be there as a buffer. And there'd probably be a dozen or so kitchen staff. It wasn't as if she and Daniel would get all cozy on the balcony or anything.

It wasn't a date.

Although he *had* kissed her.

On the forehead.

Still, his lips had touched her skin.

She dropped her head into her hands.

"Ma'am…"

She straightened, flipping her damp hair back from her face. "I'm fine. It's nothing."

"Are you sure?"

"I'm sure." She gave him a reassuring smile.

She'd go to Daniel's apartment. Have dinner. Chat with her son and new daughter-in-law, maybe feel the baby kick then get out of there before things got awkward.

Simple.

* * *

Things got awkward faster than she'd expected.

"Misty wasn't feeling well," said Daniel as he closed the front door in an oak-paneled, skylighted entry hall.

"So they're not coming at all?" Amanda darted a glance at the exit, wondering if she should bolt before it was too late.

"Her back was sore."

Misty's health was definitely more important than dinner, but Amanda had been counting on their presence. An evening alone with Daniel was more than she could handle right now. "Why didn't you call?"

"I did call. I left you a message."

"Then why did you send the car?"

"The message was that we'd moved to my place, not that you weren't supposed to come."

"But…"

He gestured to the short staircase leading to his sunken living room. "Please come in."

She hesitated. But there was no way to bail without looking scared. And she wasn't scared. Not exactly.

"Amanda?"

She took a bracing breath, made her decision then stepped down the short staircase to the plush ivory carpet.

The room was nothing short of magnificent. Two stories high, it was decorated with sculptures and abstract oils. Camel-colored sofas were scattered with burgundy and navy cushions, alongside two plaid armchairs that formed a conversation group.

Pot lights were sunk into the high ceiling. There was a Monet above a white marble fireplace, flanked by two walls of double-decker windows overlooking the park.

The furniture gleamed, and the flower arrangements were fresh. A team of photographers could show up for a lifestyle shoot and not have to touch a thing.

"I ran into Taylor Hopkins earlier," said Daniel, crossing the huge room to a curved cherrywood bar.

"Oh?" Amanda took a cautious step forward. Even for Daniel, the room was pristine. There wasn't a single magazine on the tables, no papers, no dust, not even a track in the carpet. She wondered if it was Sharon's influence, or if he was spiraling down to some sort of perfection psychosis.

He retrieved two wineglasses from the hanging rack. "He was free, so I invited him to dinner."

Amanda's gaze shot to Daniel's back. "You invited who to dinner? When?"

"Taylor."

"Why?"

"Because he was free."

Taylor was free? The same Taylor that Daniel had mentioned on Tuesday? The same Taylor he'd held up as an example of lawyerly perfection?

"What are you up to?" she asked warily.

"Opening the wine. You want some?"

"You're telling me you accidentally ran into Taylor *after* Misty called?" She didn't believe anything in Daniel's life was random.

His shoulders tensed. "After *Cullen* called," he corrected. Then he relaxed and turned his head to look at her. "Glass of merlot?"

"Daniel, what's going on?"

He shrugged as he twisted the corkscrew into the wine. "Nothing's going on."

Yeah, right. "Why is Taylor really coming to dinner?"

"Because Stuart had already picked up the salmon, and because you and I were going to be alone." He popped the cork.

Alone? If alone was a problem for him, why hadn't he canceled?

A man in a white suit jacket entered the room. "May I help with the drinks, sir?"

"Thanks," said Daniel, abandoning the open bottle to the perfectly groomed gentleman.

"We could have rebooked," said Amanda.

"Then who would eat the salmon?"

Her eyes narrowed. There was something suspicious about that straightforward logic, but she couldn't quite put her finger on it.

"Care for a tour before dinner?" he asked easily, not a flicker of cunning in his eyes.

Maybe she was being paranoid. Maybe Daniel wasn't thinking up plans to interfere in her life. Maybe she'd over-estimated his interest entirely.

"Okay," she agreed slowly.

The man in the white jacket handed them each a glass of merlot.

"Thank you, Stuart," said Daniel.

"Thank you," Amanda echoed.

"Dinner in an hour?" asked Stuart.

"Sounds fine," said Daniel.

Then he placed his hand lightly at the small of her back. "Let's start upstairs."

Amanda forced herself to relax and take in the decor. The room smelled of beeswax and lemon polish. She ran her fingertips gingerly along the gleaming banister as they climbed the stairs.

When they stepped onto the landing, Daniel directed her along the hallway that overlooked the living room.

"Your house is very…neat," she offered.

There was a hint of a chuckle in his voice. "Why do I get the feeling that wasn't a compliment?"

"I don't know," she lied.

"You'd prefer it was messy?" he asked.

She'd prefer it had a soul. "Well, my house is definitely a lot messier than yours."

"Do you have a housekeeper?"

She glanced up at him. "Why?"

He didn't meet her eyes. "Just wondering if you might have hired a former client to do that, too."

Amanda resisted the urge to elbow him in the ribs. "I don't have a housekeeper."

"I see."

No rebuke. Nothing overt that she could fight with. Just a measured, judgmental *I see.*

"Regular people clean their own houses," she pointed out.

He opened a door and hit the light switch. "This is the library."

She gazed at another pristine room. Two leather love seats faced each other across an antique table. There was a reading desk in the corner with a diamond-tufted chair. And a lighted, saltwater fish tank was built into floor-to-ceiling bookshelves. The wood was deep and rich, in contrast to the muted neutrals in the living room and hall.

She wandered inside, running her finger along the leather-bound volumes.

"Shakespeare," said Daniel.

Of course it was. "Got anything lighter?"

"A first edition Dickens."

"Anything newer?"

"The Life of Pi."

"I give up." Maybe it wasn't an act. Maybe Daniel had truly turned into a paragon of perfection. His father must be proud.

"You give what up?" he asked.

"Mr. Elliott?" Stuart appeared in the doorway. "Your company has arrived."

"Thank you." Daniel smiled at Amanda and gestured to the library doorway.

"Taylor," he greeted over the railing. "Glad you could make it."

"Wouldn't miss it," Taylor responded, smiling at Amanda as she and Daniel made their way down the stairs.

"Amanda," he said, holding out his hand.

She reached out to shake.

"You probably don't remember," he said, grasping her hand warmly. "We met at a party once. Karen and Michael introduced us."

"The Ritz," said Amanda. She remembered. He'd been polite and friendly that night, with a quick smile and a courteous manner that made it hard to remember he was a cold, unfeeling profitmonger.

"You *do* remember." He flashed that boyish grin and prolonged the handshake.

"Merlot?" asked Daniel.

Taylor slowly let go of Amanda's hand, keeping his gaze fixed on her eyes. "Love some."

Daniel couldn't let Taylor's interest in Amanda bother him. Sure, he'd only invited the man over to talk business, not to gaze adoringly into Amanda's eyes and chuckle appreciatively every time she said something that remotely resembled a joke.

And he hadn't expected Taylor to pat her hand, touch her arm or inquire about her personal life. But Amanda was an attractive, sexy woman, particularly when her hair got disheveled and she kicked off her sandals to curl her legs up on the couch.

Daniel had to accept the fact that other men were going to find her interesting. He couldn't let it bother him.

Even now, when Taylor stood up and oh so casually offered Amanda a ride home, Daniel had to bite his tongue and set his jaw. None of his business if she wanted to accept.

Amanda glanced at him.

He kept his expression deliberately impassive.

"Thank you, no," she said to Taylor.

And Taylor accepted her answer with equanimity.

Daniel saw Taylor to the front door alone, trying to keep the spring out of his step. Her relationships with other men were irrelevant. He had to focus on the primary goal—getting her to change careers.

He thanked Taylor sincerely for joining them.

When he returned to the living room, Amanda was still curled up on the couch, sipping a second cup of coffee.

"I hope you had a nice time," he said, retaking his seat in the armchair across from her.

"Nice coincidence, you running into him at Boca Royce."

Daniel nodded. "It was."

"And so interesting, all those little details about his business," she continued.

He met her eyes. "I know I found them interesting."

"I had no idea corporate law was so easy and so lucrative."

"Makes me wish I'd become a lawyer," he joked.

"Me, too. Wait. I *did* become a lawyer."

Daniel grinned. She was fun when she relaxed.

"And, you know…" Amanda snapped her fingers. "Listening to Taylor makes me wonder why I've spent my entire career on criminal defense."

Daniel tried not to act too interested. "It does?"

She nodded vigorously. "Think about it, if I'd gone into corporate law right off, I could have a new Mercedes by now."

"You could," he agreed, with what he hoped was a thoughtful nod. He'd have to thank Taylor again tomorrow. The man had obviously hit exactly the right note.

"And I could sleep in every morning, get the best theatre tickets from clients and shop for clothes on Fifth Avenue."

Daniel rested his hands on the arms of his chair, trying not to look too eager. "*Snap* would be happy to give you some business, and an excellent recommendation."

Amanda bobbed her head up and down. "That would help. And I bet you could get me some uptown office space, too."

"Sure," said Daniel. He was surprised, delighted, actually, by the turn of the conversation.

"And you could rent a van, maybe pack up my files."

"I'd be happy to help in—"

"Heck, you could probably hire somebody to blow off my existing clients."

Uh-oh. Her dark eyes began to glitter, and Daniel's stomach slid down a few inches. "I…"

"And find me a new receptionist."

Daniel felt like a supreme fool. "You're yanking my chain, aren't you?"

She came to her feet. "Of course I'm yanking your chain! Did you really think that setup would work?"

Yeah, actually. Daniel rose. "I'd—"

"That Taylor Hopkins is a one-man press gang."

Okay, salvage time. What could he say? What could he do? "I was only thinking—"

"Yeah, yeah." She waved a hand. "You were only thinking about me. Tell me, Daniel, were Cullen and Misty ever really invited?"

He flinched. He hadn't expected that to come up again. He'd thought about inviting them, but it just seemed simpler to go straight to Taylor.

Amanda's hands went to her hips. "I knew it. Will you lay off my life? I'm doing perfectly fine, thank you very much."

"But—"

"No *buts*." She jabbed a finger at him. "You back off."

"Okay." At least temporarily.

She dropped her hand, a look of surprise coming over her face. "You will?"

He shrugged. "Sure." It wasn't as if arguing with her tonight was going to get him anywhere.

She gave a sharp nod. "Good choice." Then her voice dropped to a mumble. "It's not like *your* life is working out so well."

Daniel squared his shoulders. "Excuse me?"

"Nothing."

"That wasn't nothing."

"Fine. I said it's not like your life is working out so well."

"You're going to have to explain that one."

"Look around you," she gestured with her hand.

He looked around, and what he saw was—not to put too fine a point on it—pretty darned decent. "What exactly about this isn't working out so well?"

"It's pristine. It's perfect. There's absolutely no life in your life."

He squinted. "You win many court cases with arguments like that?"

She cocked her head and crossed her arms over her chest, pushing up her breasts.

Cleavage. Okay, that was helpful. He'd really be able to concentrate now.

"I'm beginning to think you need professional help," she said.

For a moment he was speechless. *She* was worried about *him?*

"You're the one whose life is out of control," he pointed out.

"At least I know what I want," she countered.

Ha. He had her now. If there was one thing Daniel's life had, it was direction. "I know exactly what I want."

"What's that?"

He took the easiest answer. "To be CEO of Elliott Publication Holdings."

"Do you, Daniel?"

"Of course." Just because success wasn't on Amanda's to-do list, didn't mean it wasn't on his. "Can we go back to talking about you now?"

"No. I'm not the one with the problem."

Daniel scoffed. "I've seen your office."

She scoffed right back. "And I've seen your apartment."

He opened his mouth, but then he paused, an idea twigging in his mind. She seemed fixated on his apartment. Maybe there was room to maneuver here. A deal of some kind. A swap. His apartment for her office.

"Tell me what you'd change," he said.

Her dark eyes narrowed.

He moved closer, lowering his voice. "Really. Tell me. I'm ready to take your advice."

"No, you're not."

"Yeah, I am." He moved closer still. If he took her advice, she might feel honor bound to take his. "Give it to me straight, Amanda. I can take it."

She was silent for a moment, but then her gaze turned pitying. "Okay. You want it straight? You've stopped feeling."

"Feeling what?"

"Everything."

That just plain wasn't true. Especially not now. Especially not at this particular moment.

She placed her small hand on his shoulder, and his muscle contracted beneath its warmth. "Feel," she urged.

"I am," he rasped.

Then her eyes turned mocha, and she came up on her toes. She tilted her head, parted those deep ruby lips and took his mouth against hers.

Memories saturated his brain, longing, passion, desire. He was catapulted back decades. His arms went around her, dragging her against him. He slanted his head, kissed her back, inhaling her familiar scent.

He reveled in the tender moisture of her mouth. Her body was imprinted on his brain, and his hands slid down the curve of her back, remembering. Oh, how he'd missed this. How he'd missed her.

He felt every molecule in his body hum to life. Colors and emotions swirled around in a kaleidoscope.

He let his mouth roam, and she twined her arms around his neck, her breaths puffing against his skin, nearly driving him out of his mind. He longed to lose himself in her, to tear off her clothes and lay her back right there and then on the soft carpet and relive every ounce of love they'd ever found in each other.

Her small moan vibrated against his mouth.

He whispered that he wanted her, so much, too much.

She drew back at that, blinking her big brown eyes in obvious confusion. Her cheeks were flushed. Her lips were swollen. And her chestnut hair was a messy halo of filtered light.

There'd never been a more desirable woman. Ever.

But she wasn't his.

She hadn't been his for a very long time.

He forced himself to release her.

"I'm sorry," he said. "I had no right…"

He didn't know what else to say. He never got carried away. He was the master of self-control.

An ironic half smile grew on her face. "Don't be sorry. We're making progress. You felt something."

He dropped his arms and stepped completely away. "That was *therapy?*"

She shrugged. "Of course."

Something inside him froze. That was what the kiss was to her? A point in her argument? He'd been out there on memory lane all by himself?

Yeah, he wanted her to change careers. But there was a limit to how far he'd go. And he had a feeling he'd just reached it.

Five

Amanda tipped her head back against the smooth headrest as the limo eased into traffic. Kissing Daniel *had* been therapy.

Memory enhancement.

For her.

It was only the years of practice, keeping her control in front of sharp-eyed judges, that kept her from swooning, or begging, or worse.

Daniel had always been a great kisser. From that very first night, he'd made the earth shift beneath her and pyrotechnics shoot off inside her brain.

As the limo accelerated away from a red light, she sighed her way into the memory. Their very first kiss— prom night.

Amanda had been more of a nerd than a jock back then, more likely to be found at photography club or the social activism office on a Saturday night than at an A-list party. So when her friend Bethany had wrangled an invitation to

Roger Dawson's after-prom party in the Presidential Suite of the Riverside, there was no way in the world she was missing it.

The event was a crush. The music was loud, the punch was spiked with something bitter and the snacks were being used as missiles. Amanda had been quickly separated from Bethany, so when she spotted Daniel standing alone near the door, she was thrilled to see a semifamiliar face. She'd eased toward him, squeezing her way between dancing couples and chattering groups of friends.

She and Daniel had met on several occasions early in the year when she was dating one of his friends. He'd always struck her as a nice guy, and he knew everybody. If she was lucky, maybe he'd introduce her to a few people, and she could stop standing around looking like a dork.

"Hey, Daniel," she breathed, yanking her arm from where it was trapped between two bodies.

"Amanda." He turned and smiled warmly down at her. "I didn't know you were coming."

"I came with Bethany." She gestured vaguely in the direction Bethany had disappeared twenty minutes ago.

"Hey, Elliott?" someone called from the crowd.

"Yeah?" Daniel called back.

"You got a room, right?"

Daniel nodded over the heads of the crowd. But Amanda was too short to see whom he was talking to.

"We need your ice bucket and some more glasses," the guy called.

"I'll get 'em," said Daniel.

Amanda's heart sank. Just when she'd found someone to talk to, he was leaving.

Daniel looked back down at her. "You wanna come help?

"Yes," Amanda quickly said.

"Let's go."

Daniel elbowed them a path to the door, and they emerged into the cool, quiet hallway.

"I'm down at the end," he said.

"You didn't want to drive home?" she asked, just to make conversation.

He chuckled a little self-consciously. "My older brother Michael rented the room. He figured I might get lucky."

Amanda swallowed and tried to make her voice nonchalant. "Oh. Uh, you're, uh, here with Shelby Peterson?"

Daniel shrugged. "I thought I was. But last time I saw her, she was dancing with Roger. Maybe Roger'll be the one to get lucky."

Amanda wasn't used to talking about sex, particularly not with guys, and definitely not with great-looking jocks who'd probably slept with half the cheerleading squad. Her face grew warm.

When she didn't answer, Daniel looked down. "Hey, I'm sorry." He gave her a friendly nudge with his shoulder. "That was tacky."

She shook her head, embarrassed that she wasn't as sophisticated as his friends. "No, it wasn't."

"Yeah, it was. Here we are." He stopped and unlocked the door, swinging it wide open.

Amanda had never been in a five-star hotel before. She hadn't seen much of the Presidential Suite, because of the crowd. Now she glanced around in wide-eyed amazement at the plump, burgundy couches, a curved wooden bar with a mirrored back ground, double French doors leading to a bedroom and a fern-filled bay window alcove with a Jacuzzi tub.

The door swung shut behind them.

"Go ahead and look around," said Daniel, dropping his key on the entry table. "This is going to take me a couple of minutes."

"Wow," said Amanda, not even pretending to be blasé

about the opulent room. "Michael must have thought you were going to get *very* lucky."

Daniel chuckled from behind the bar. "Michael's the optimist of the family."

Amanda wandered between the two couches, glancing down at the oak coffee table. There was a fresh flower arrangement in the middle, a dish of gourmet chocolates on one end and an arrangement of current magazines on the other.

More interesting was the rectangular gadget covered in colorful buttons. "Is that a remote control?" she asked, picking it up and aiming it at the television. She'd heard about them, but had never seen one in real life.

Daniel popped his head up from where he was rattling glasses. "I don't know. Try it and see."

She pushed the power button, and the television clicked to life. "All right!"

Daniel laughed at her exclamation.

She checked out the other buttons and began clicking through channels. "I think these are going to be really popular."

"I can't find the ice bucket," said Daniel, glancing at the glass shelves behind him.

"Want me to check the bathroom?"

He rounded the end of the bar. "I'll do it. Eat some of those chocolates, will you? Michael probably paid a fortune for them."

Amanda grinned, happy to oblige. She plopped down on the soft couch and peeled the gold foil from a chocolate truffle.

It was so much nicer here—cooler air, a place to sit down, nobody shouting obscenities or throwing food, no repetitive bass pounding against her eardrums. And, best of all, no crushing mortification because she was the only person in the room without a conversation partner.

"No ice bucket," said Daniel. He stopped behind the couch. "Is that *American Graffiti?*"

Amanda glanced at the screen. "I think so."

"Cool. Are the chocolates any good?"

She rocked forward and took another gold globe from the dish. "To die for." She handed it back to Daniel.

On the screen, a group of high school grads were out celebrating their final night together.

Daniel unwrapped the chocolate and gestured to the television. "Kind of like us," he said.

Amanda nodded her agreement. Like the characters in the movie, they were standing on the cusp of a brave new world. Sometimes she was excited, mostly she was scared. Her parents had saved the money for her first year of college, but after that it was going to be a struggle.

"These are great," said Daniel, coming around the couch. He picked up the dish, plunked it down on the middle cushion and sat down on the other end. "I say we eat them before we leave."

Amanda nodded her agreement and helped herself to another chocolate. "Seems a shame to let them go to waste."

She let the sweet, creamy candy melt on her tongue as they watched the movie in silence for a few minutes.

"So, what are you going to do?" Daniel asked, snagging another chocolate.

"After the party?"

"No. After high school. You had pretty good grades, didn't you?"

Amanda nodded. Given her slow dating life, she'd had plenty of time to study. "I've been accepted to NYU."

"That's great. What are you taking?"

"English lit and prelaw. What about you?"

"The family firm," he said with a tired smile.

"Guaranteed job," she offered.

He was quiet for a couple more minutes, his eyes fixed on the movie. "You know, what I'm really hoping…"

She waited, but he didn't continue.

"What?" she finally asked.

He shook his head.

"Tell me."

He shifted one leg onto the couch and angled himself toward her. "Promise you won't laugh."

Amanda Kedrick laugh at Daniel Elliott? Not in this lifetime. She shook her head. "I'm not gonna laugh."

"Okay." He nodded. "Here's the thing. I'm hoping I can talk my dad into starting a new magazine."

Amanda was impressed. It sounded so much more interesting than plain old law school. "Really? What kind?"

"Outdoor adventures, foreign lands, action. I could travel all over the world, write articles and send them back to New York."

Amanda swallowed, suddenly feeling boring and trite. She wasn't even planning to leave the state, and here Daniel was going on a global adventure.

"You think it's a dumb idea," he said, his expression falling.

"No," Amanda quickly assured him, moving a little closer. "I think it's a fantastic idea. I'm jealous is all."

He perked up. "You are?"

She nodded vigorously. "It sounds fantastic."

He took another chocolate, grinning as he unwrapped it and popped it into his mouth. "It does, doesn't it?"

They both turned their attention to the movie again.

After a few moments he rolled to his feet and went back behind the bar. "These chocolates are making me thirsty. Ever drink champagne?"

Her eyes went wide. "Where would we get champagne?"

He held up a green bottle.

"But won't you get in trouble?"

Daniel shrugged as he twisted off the wire cork holder. "Room's in Michael's name."

"So, they'll think—"

"I don't particularly care what they think." He popped the cork with his thumbs. It hit the ceiling and bounced to the carpet.

Amanda suddenly felt very daring. "I'd love some champagne."

He grinned and flipped over two of the long-stemmed glasses on the bar. Then he poured the bubbly liquid, scooped a bag of pretzels from the snack basket and rejoined her on the couch where Ron Howard's character was fighting with his steady girlfriend.

To a backdrop of fifties music, Daniel and Amanda leaned forward and touched their glasses together.

"Happy prom night," he whispered.

She gazed into his deep blue eyes, not feeling nearly as awkward as she had earlier. "You do realize you're not going to get lucky."

His eyes sparkled and a grin curved up the corners of his mouth. "I think that ship's already sailed." He glanced down at the empty bowl between them. "I mean, since you scarfed down all the chocolates that I was going to use to seduce the girl."

She smacked him on the shoulder. "I had a little help, you know."

He gave her a mock frown. "They were my secret weapon."

Instead of answering, she took a sip of the champagne. "Hey, this is good." She held the glass up to the light and watched the tiny bubbles rise to the surface. "I think the champagne should be your secret weapon."

"Yeah? Well, you're scarfing that down, too," he complained.

She smiled around another swallow. "Life sucks sometimes, doesn't it?"

He laughed and took a drink, glancing at the television screen. "What did I miss?"

"Terry the Toad is hoping to get lucky."

"Did Richard Dreyfuss find the blonde?"

"Not yet."

Daniel tore open the bag of pretzels and settled back into the couch.

Amanda sighed with contentment. She'd hated the party. Hated to admit it, but she hated her first teenage A-list party.

This was so much better, lounging on comfortable furniture, watching a funny movie, laughing and talking with Daniel and sipping on a beverage that didn't taste like orange-flavored gasoline.

She reached for a pretzel.

So much better to eat food she was positive nobody'd used as a missile.

By the time Richard Dreyfuss's character flew off in an airplane, Amanda had kicked off her shoes and the champagne bottle was half-empty.

"He never even got to meet her," Daniel complained.

They'd both editorialized throughout the movie, sharing surprise, suspense and laughter.

Amanda raised her glass. "She will forever remain the mystery woman."

"That sucks."

"It's fiction."

"It still sucks."

She laughed.

Daniel set down his glass. "A guy shouldn't let opportunities like that go by."

"Kiss ye blond bombshells while ye may?"

"Something like that."

She gathered the remains of their impromptu picnic and padded barefoot over to the bar, the carpet soft against her feet. "We should probably get back to the party," she offered reluctantly.

He stood up behind her, the glasses clinking together as he lifted them from the table. "I guess we should. We never did find the ice bucket."

"I have a feeling nobody's going to notice missing ice at this point." She turned around and came face-to-face with him, or rather face-to-chest, since he was a good six inches taller now that she wasn't wearing shoes.

He reached around her and set the glasses on the bar. "Not if they kept drinking that punch, they won't."

She shuddered again at the memory.

"Amanda?" His voice sounded unnaturally low.

She tipped up her chin to look at him. "Yes?"

He cocked his head sideways, and she was suddenly aware of a shift in the atmosphere.

"I was thinking," he said, moving almost imperceptibly closer.

His closeness should have made her feel crowded, but it didn't. His shoulders were broad. His chest was deep. And he towered over her, but she didn't feel the least bit intimidated.

She drew in a breath and smelled his spicy, masculine scent. "Thinking about what?"

"Missed opportunities." He smoothed a wisp of hair that had escaped near her temple.

She was pretty sure she wasn't misunderstanding his signals. But the thought of Daniel Elliott coming on to her was so far out in left field.

"You mean, the movie?" she asked.

"I mean graduation."

Confused, she squinted at him.

"We might never see each other again," he said.

"We might not," she agreed. Their paths barely crossed in the same school, never mind when she was at NYU and he was globe-trotting in search of exciting magazine stories.

"So…" he breathed.

"So?" she returned.

"What do we do about that?"

She watched his eyes darken, his smile fade, his lips part.

"Daniel?"

"It's now or never, Amanda." He smoothed his palm over her cheek, ever so slowly, giving her time to adjust to the change of mood, plenty of time to protest.

He twined his fingers into her hair, stroking her scalp. "I'm about to kiss you," he rasped.

"I know," she whispered, longing for his kiss.

It was perfect. It was right. Somehow she knew, intellectually, emotionally, cosmically, that this kiss at this moment was absolutely meant to be.

His lips touched hers. Firm, then tender, then moist, then hot.

She wound her arms around his neck, answering his pressure, parting her lips and tilting her head to deepen the kiss. Desire surged up inside her. She went hot, then cold, then hot all over again.

It was Daniel—Daniel Elliott—kissing her, holding her. His scent mingled with flowers. His taste overpowered the chocolate and champagne. Her skin prickled and her blood sang. She'd never felt remotely like this before.

Sparks of desire shot through her. She'd kissed boys before, but never like this, never where their touch took control of her body and soul.

She wanted it harder. She wanted it deeper. She parted her lips, inviting him in.

His tongue invaded her mouth, and she nearly whimpered with the pleasure.

His free arm circled her waist, settling across the small of her back, anchoring her firmly against his hardening body.

Yes. Closer, tighter. She wound her arms around his neck, pressing against him, tilting her head to deepen the kiss.

An ocean roared in her ears, and her hands clenched convulsively against him. The kiss went on and on. He swirled his tongue through her tender mouth. She opened wider, answering him back.

A sound emerged from deep in his chest as he arched her backward, over the bar. One strong hand traveled up her spine, traversing to settle on her rib cage, thumb barely brushing the underside of her breast. She felt her nipples tighten, sparks of pleasure shooting through her.

She wished he'd touch her, but she was too afraid to ask.

Then his other hand stroked down her neck. She tensed. She waited. And then his fingertips moved to her breast. She all but bucked under the intense sensation.

"Amanda," he rasped.

Her breath came in pants and she slid her palms up his chest, slipping beneath his suit jacket, working her way to the heat of his back and pressing her breasts harder into his hands. Her world contracted to him and her.

No wonder her friends got so carried away. No wonder they made love with their boyfriends in the back seats of cars and beneath the stadium bleachers. At the moment, she couldn't have cared less where they were.

A pounding need echoed in her brain and blotted out time, space and reason.

"Daniel." Her voice turned his name into a plea.

"This is—" He kissed her again and his hands burned through her silk halter dress. His thumb circled her hardened nipple, shooting sparks to the core of her being. She never knew such sensations existed.

Gone was modesty. Gone was shyness. She wanted Daniel with every single fiber of her being. Wanted him in a way she'd never wanted anybody ever before.

He moved to her neck, kissing her roughly, fiercely, abrading her tender skin with delicious furor.

She tipped her head back to give him better access. Her breath hissed through her teeth, and she tightened her grip on his back. His jacket had to go. She wanted to touch his skin, to feel his fire.

He kissed her shoulder. His lips moved to the hollow between her breasts, and she moaned in wanting. His hands went to the halter tie at the back of her neck.

"Tell me to stop," he demanded, even as he worked the knot. He breathed her in, his hot tongue flicking out to taste her skin.

"Don't stop," she said, breathless with need. "Don't stop." Electricity pulsed at the apex of her thighs, making her nearly desperate to assuage the burning need.

"Amanda," he groaned. The bow came free, and the slinky fabric slipped down to her waist.

Daniel drew back, his gaze fixed on her bare breasts.

She arched her spine, closing her eyes, boldly raking her fingers back through her hair and shaking it loose.

Daniel swore through clenched teeth. "You're beautiful," he groaned. "Unbelievably beautiful." His hand closed over her breast, and she moaned at the intense sensation.

She felt beautiful. For the first time in her life she felt beautiful and desirable and totally unselfconscious about her body.

She pushed his jacket from his shoulders, desperate to feel his skin next to hers. She might not know much, but she did know his clothes had to go.

The jacket hit the floor, and she went to work on his tie. He sucked in a tight breath as she loosened it.

"Amanda." His voice sounded desperate.

She kissed his mouth again, flipping open the buttons on his shirt.

"We can stop," he hissed. "It'll kill me, but we can still…"

Finally, skin. Her lips touched his bare chest, and his entire body convulsed.

"We're not stopping," she breathed against his warm skin. Of all the options in all the world, stopping right now was not one of them.

"Thank God." He found the tip of her breast and did something that made her knees nearly give way.

He clasped her tightly against him.

Then he lifted her into his arms, kissing her mouth as he strode for the bedroom doors.

She ran her fingers over his chest, reveling in the sparse, soft hair, palming his flat nipples, wondering if she was making him feel the same sensations.

He moaned her name one more time as he shakily set her on her feet next to the bed. Then he pulled her against his bare chest for another long kiss.

She flicked the single button at the side of the dress, and the fabric pooled around her ankles.

His hands stroked down her bare back, grasping her buttocks and pulling her hard against him.

She trembled a little at the thought of what would come next. But she was doing it. There was no power on earth that could stop her.

"Amanda?" he questioned, drawing back, gazing at her in the darkened room.

She pushed off his shirt, avoiding eye contact.

"You nervous?"

"No," she lied.

He paused. "You ever…"

This time she did look at him. No point in lying. He was going to figure it out soon anyway. She slowly shook her head. "Sorry."

He swore softly. Then his grip loosened. "Sorry?" He coughed. "You have just…" He tenderly kissed her mouth, then her cheeks, then her eyelids and her temples, drawing sensation after exquisite sensation up from her soul.

"If you're sure," he finally whispered.

"I am so sure," she breathed.

A smile formed on his lips and he traced his fingertip down her abdomen, dipping into her navel, over the downy curls, then he feathered a whisper-light touch on her tender flesh.

Her eyes went wide, and her jaw dropped open.

"You like?" he asked, his eyes burning into hers.

"Oh, yes."

His touch grew firmer, delved deeper.

She grasped his shoulders. "What should I do?"

"Nothing," he whispered.

"But—"

"You can't get it wrong, Mandy. There is absolutely no way for you to get this wrong."

Her muscles clenched and her eyes grew moist.

He gently laid her back on the bed, knees bent, feet still on the plush carpet.

"You tell me if I hurt you."

"You're not hurting me." He was so far from hurting her.

He left her for a second, kicking off his pants. But then he was back, and his hands were everywhere. She wanted time to stand still while she absorbed every possible sensation.

She took a deep breath, wanting to give back, wanting to make sure he was feeling half of what she was. She skimmed his chest with her knuckles, working her way lower across his taut skin. His abs contracted under her touch, and he gasped in her ear.

He groaned and kissed her mouth. She kissed him back, dueling with his tongue, arching into his touch, begging him with her body to go harder and deeper.

She wrapped her hand around him, and his heat seared her palm.

He swore, and she immediately jerked back.

"Did I hurt you?"

"You're killing me, babe."

"Sorry."

He gave a hollow laugh. "Kill me some more."

She did.

He shifted on top of her, his face showing the strains of control. "It's now or never."

She shifted her thighs to accommodate him. "Now," she said with conviction.

He pushed inside her in one swift stroke.

Her eyes widened with the pain, but he kissed it all away.

"It's going to be okay," he whispered in her ear.

It was already okay. The pain was fleeting, but the passion kept on.

He moved inside her, and her need blasted off. A driving pulse pounded in her thighs, her abdomen, her breasts.

As his pace increased, she kissed him hard, opening her body, her muscles stretching and tensing, reaching for something she couldn't identify.

Lightning burned behind her eyes. Electricity buzzed along her legs and a hot pool of sensation spread out from where their bodies joined.

He gasped her name, his entire body tensing as the world stood still for a microsecond.

Then relief pulsed through her, washing over her like summer rain, while the pounding pulse contracted her muscles and the lightning turned to streaks of color.

"Mrs. Elliott?"

A voice reached into her private thoughts. The limo driver.

She shook herself, her hand going to her chest as if to shield herself from the embarrassment of having been caught fantasizing about Daniel. "Uh, yes?"

He nodded to the brownstone building on the right. "We're here."

"Of course." Amanda moved shakily toward the limo door.

"I'll be right there."

She allowed him to help her from the back seat, thanked him and crossed the sidewalk to her front door, where she carefully inserted the key.

Still, the memories of that prom night refused to fade.

She and Daniel had made magical love all night long. They'd said a bittersweet goodbye the next morning, knowing they would probably never see each other again.

And they wouldn't have. She'd have gone to NYU, and he'd have trekked all over the world.

If not for Bryan.

Bryan had changed everything.

Six

Daniel pulled his silver Lexus to the curb in front of the courthouse, determined to change tactics. He should have known his impulsive plan with Taylor wouldn't work on a woman as smart as Amanda.

But this time, things would be different.

He was slowing down, going on an intelligence-gathering mission. By the time he made his next move, she wouldn't even see it coming.

He set the emergency brake and shut off the engine. First things first. It was easy for him to see what should draw her to corporate law. It was harder for him to understand what drew her to criminal law.

But that was about to change.

He opened the driver's door and stepped out of the car. Amanda's receptionist—bless the woman's unthinking friendliness—had told Daniel exactly where to find Amanda. She was arguing an embezzlement case.

Embezzlement.

Employees stealing from their employers.

He slammed the car door shut and clamped his jaw. It was a glamorous career his ex-wife had chosen.

He glanced at his watch as he trotted up the wide, concrete steps. They were nearly an hour into the trial.

He pulled open the heavy oak doors, crossed the wide foyer and located courtroom number five.

There he quietly slipped into the back row.

The opposing lawyer was conducting the questioning, but Daniel could see the back of Amanda's head. She sat at the defendant's table next to a thin woman in a tan blouse with straight, mousy brown hair.

"Can you identify the signature on the check, Mr. Burnside?" the other lawyer asked the witness.

The witness looked up from a plastic sheaf in his hand and nodded toward the defendant. "It's Mary Robinson's signature."

"Did she have signing authority?" asked the lawyer.

The witness nodded. "For petty cash, office supplies, things like that."

"But she wouldn't normally write a check payable to herself?"

"Absolutely not," said the witness. "That's fraud."

Amanda stood up. "Objection, Your Honor. Speculation."

"Sustained," said the judge. He looked at the witness. "Just answer the questions."

The witness's mouth thinned.

"Can you tell us the amount of the check?" asked the lawyer.

"Three thousand dollars," the witness answered, eyes hard.

"Mr. Burnside, to the best of your knowledge, did Mary Robinson purchase office supplies with that three-thousand dollars?"

"She stole it," spat the witness.

Amanda stood again. "Your Honor—"

"Sustained," said the judge, wearily.

"But she did," Mr. Burnside insisted.

The judge looked down at him. "Are you arguing with me?"
He clamped his jaw.

"No further questions," said the lawyer.

Good move, thought Daniel. Burnside didn't seem to be
helping the cause.

The judge looked to Amanda.

"No questions," she said.

"The prosecution rests," said the other lawyer.

"Ms. Elliott," said the judge, "you may call your first witness."

Amanda stood up. "The defense would like to call Collin
Radaski to the stand."

A man in a dark suit stood up and made his way toward
the aisle. Amanda turned to watch, and Daniel ducked behind
a woman two rows up who was wearing a broad hat.

The bailiff swore in the witness, and Amanda approached
the stand.

"Mr. Radaski, would you state your position at Westlake
Construction Company."

Radaski leaned toward the microphone. "I'm the office
manager."

"As part of your duties, do you approve payroll checks?"

He leaned in again. "Yes, I do."

Amanda walked back to the defendant's table and
picked up a piece of paper. "Is it true, Mr. Radaski, that
Jack Burnside instructed you to hold back holiday pay on
those checks?"

"We don't include holiday pay every month."

"Is it also true that overtime was paid to Westlake Construction employees at straight time rather than time and a half?"

"We have a verbal agreement with employees regarding
overtime."

Amanda raised her eyebrows and paused, making her disbelief known without saying a word. "A verbal agreement?"

"Yes, ma'am."

Amanda returned to the table and switched papers. "Are you aware, Mr. Radaski, that Westlake Construction has been breaking labor laws for over ten years?"

"What does that have to do with—"

"I object," called the prosecuting lawyer.

"On what grounds?" asked the judge.

"The witness is not in a position—"

"The witness is the office manager responsible for payroll," Amanda pointed out.

"Overruled," said the judge, and Daniel couldn't help a small smile of pride.

Amanda flipped through her notes.

Daniel was pretty sure it was all for show. The set of her shoulders told him she wasn't refreshing her memory. She knew exactly where she was going.

She looked up again. "Are you further aware, Mr. Radaski, that Westlake Construction owes my client four thousand, two hundred and eighty-six dollars in back overtime and holiday pay?"

"We had a verbal agreement," the witness sputtered.

"A verbal agreement of that nature has no force under New York labor law. Mr. Radaski, according to the accounting firm of Smith and Stafford, Westlake Construction owes current and former employees a total of one hundred and seventy-one thousand, six hundred and sixty-one dollars in back pay."

Radaski blinked at Amanda.

"Your Honor," she said, lifting a thick sheaf of papers from the table. "I would like to enter this actuarial report as exhibit D. My client wishes, at this time, to launch a countercomplaint against Westlake Construction for a settlement in the amount of one thousand, two hundred and eighty-six dollars, being the balance owed to her for unpaid overtime and holidays."

"But she stole three thousand dollars," shouted Jack Burnside from the galley.

The judge pounded his gavel.

Amanda's lips quirked in a small smile. "I'll be contacting current and former employees to ascertain their interest in a class action lawsuit."

The judge gazed at the prosecuting lawyer.

"I'd like to request a recess to confer with my client."

"I guess you would," said the judge. He brought the gavel down once again. "This case is adjourned until three o'clock Thursday afternoon."

Daniel quickly slipped out the door of the courtroom.

Okay, he could see the appeal. But surely those Perry Mason moments were few and far between.

Still, she was good.

Amanda stared at the small cardboard card that had accompanied a bouquet of twenty-four red roses.

Congratulations!

Puzzled, she flipped it over.

Saw you in court today. If I ever take up bank robbing, you'll be the first person I call.
—D

Daniel.

"Mr. Delectable?" asked Julie, breezing through the door with a stack of files.

"They're from Daniel," Amanda confirmed.

Julie leaned over to smell the roses. "This time you definitely have to do him on the desktop."

Amanda smiled at Julie's irreverence. "Daniel's not that kind of guy."

Julie toyed with the looped chain of her black choker. "It's a proven fact, sending red roses to an office means a guy wants to do it on the desktop."

"Where do you get these facts?"

"Didn't you read last month's *Cosmo?*"

Amanda cleared a space on the credenza for the flowers. "Afraid I missed it."

"I'll get you my copy."

Amanda set down the vase. "What do yellow roses mean?"

"Huh?"

"If a guy sends yellow roses to an office, what does that mean?"

Julie grinned. "Yellow means they want to do it on the desktop. Come to think of it, breathing means they want to do it on the desktop."

"Not Daniel." Amanda couldn't imagine any possible circumstances under which Daniel would make love on a desktop. It would be sacrilegious.

"Try him," Julie advised with a waggle of her dark eyebrows. "You'll be surprised."

"Daniel's not a surprise kind of guy."

"Were you expecting the roses?"

Amanda paused. "Nope. I have to admit, those were a surprise."

"There you go," said Julie.

"He's my ex." Amanda wasn't doing Daniel on the desktop or anywhere else. Bad enough that she'd kissed him.

"But he's hot."

He was hot all right. And he was still a fabulous kisser. And, unless she'd lost her mind, he'd responded to her kiss.

Which meant he was interested, too. Which meant they were both in big trouble.

"Amanda?"

Amanda blinked. "Hmm?"

Julie grinned. "You think he's hot, too."

"I think I'm late for a meeting."

A visit with Karen wasn't exactly a meeting, but as soon as Amanda walked out onto the veranda at The Tides, she was glad she'd come.

Karen was sitting on a deck chair with albums and photographs scattered around her.

"There you are," said Karen, pulling a brochure out of the mess. "I couldn't decide between a pedicure and reflexology."

"What are you doing?"

"I got us into Eduardo's for the twenty-fifth, but we should book our appointments early. You want a facial?"

"Sure," said Amanda, sitting in one of the other chairs. Now that she'd decided to do the spa weekend, she was getting a little excited about it.

Karen gestured to a pitcher of iced tea on a side table. "Thirsty?"

Amanda stood up again. "I'd love some. You want a refill?"

"Please." Karen put down the brochure and sat back in the padded chair. "Tell me about the world."

"The *entire* world?"

"Your world."

Amanda filled Karen's tall glass. "I won a case this morning."

"Congratulations."

"It's not exactly official yet. The judge will rule on Thursday, but I threatened Westlake Construction with a class action suit. They'll cave."

"Was that the Mary something embezzlement trial?"

Amanda nodded. "Sweet woman. Single mom, three kids. Nobody's served by her going to jail for six months."

"But she stole some money, right?"

Amanda sat down again. "She provided herself with an advance on holiday pay owed."

Karen grinned. "Will you be my lawyer?"

"You don't need a lawyer."

"I might. I'm bored. I'm thinking of taking up bank robbing."

"You been talking to Daniel?"

Karen's eyes sparkled. "No, have you?"

Amanda instantly regretted the impulsive joke. But backing off would only make Karen press harder.

"He sent me flowers," Amanda admitted. "He mentioned bank robbing, too. Is there something about the Elliott fortune you're not telling me?"

"What kind of flowers?"

"Roses."

"Red?"

"Yes."

"Holy cow."

"It's not what you think." Not that Amanda had any clue as to what she was supposed to think.

"How can it not be what I think?" asked Karen. "A dozen?"

Amanda hesitated. "Two."

"Two dozen red roses."

"They were congratulatory."

"Congratulatory for what?" Her eyes went wide. "What did you two do?"

Amanda quickly waved off the question. "It's nothing like that. He came to watch me in court. I won the case. He sent flowers."

Karen straightened one of the albums in front of her. "Daniel watched you in court?"

Amanda nodded.

"What for?"

"Beats me." She took a sip of the iced tea. "And, I tell you, he's making me nervous again. After the Taylor Hopkins thing, he said he was going to back off."

"What Taylor Hopkins thing?"

"Daniel invited Taylor to dinner, and Taylor gave me an indoctrination into the cult of the almighty dollar."

"Well, Taylor's definitely the guy to do it," said Karen. "Have you seen his new house?"

"Nope."

Karen sat forward and flipped a couple of pages in one of the albums. "Here it is."

Amanda stood up, coming around beside Karen. "Nice."

"It's on the shore. Fantastic tennis courts."

It was a nice house. But Amanda had never been overly impressed with expensive real estate. She glanced at the pictures of the extended Elliott Family. "What a wonderful picture of Scarlet and Summer."

"That was taken last year. Somehow we all ended up at Martha's Vineyard. Bridget went wild with the camera."

"Who's that with Gannon?"

"His date. I can't even remember her name. It was between rounds with Erika."

The mention of Erika reminded Karen of Gannon's recent wedding. "You have wedding pictures?"

"I sure do." Karen switched albums, opening to a formal shot of the bride and groom.

"Gorgeous dress," Amanda commented.

"She's a wonderful woman," said Karen. "So good for Gannon."

On the next page was a family shot. Amanda's gaze stopped on Daniel. He looked magnificent in a tux.

Then she saw the woman standing next to him.

"Oops," said Karen. "Sharon showed up. Nobody quite knew what to do about that."

Amanda squinted at her ex's ex. Sharon was petite and thin, with sculpted blond hair an expensive shade of platinum.

She looked younger than forty. Her makeup was perfect, and her dress fairly dripped with silver sequins. The spray of flowers in her hair made her a competitor for the bride.

"I'm nothing like her, am I?" asked Amanda, suddenly overtaken by a wave of inadequacy.

"You're nothing like her," said Karen. "Thank goodness."

"But she's what Daniel wants."

Karen turned to gaze at Amanda. "You do know he divorced her."

"But he married her."

"He loved *you*."

Amanda shook her head. "I was pregnant."

Karen squeezed Amanda's arm. "You are a kind, compassionate, intelligent, loving—"

"And she's thin and beautiful, with a flair for designer clothes and multilingual small talk."

"She's cruel and brittle."

"But she looks great in an evening gown." There was no disputing that.

"So do you."

Amanda smiled. "You haven't seen me in an evening gown for more than a decade. Heck, I haven't seen myself in an evening gown for years."

"Maybe it's about time you did."

"I wear underwires," Amanda confessed in a whisper.

Karen chuckled. "Well, at least I don't need those anymore."

Amanda froze in horror.

But Karen shook her head. "Thank you so much. That was my first breast joke."

Amanda cringed. "But I—"

"Don't you dare apologize. You don't care about perfection. You blithely brought up breasts because you've forgotten all about my surgery."

It was true. When Amanda thought about Karen she didn't think of a double mastectomy; all she thought about was her true and wonderful friend.

"That's why I love you so dearly," said Karen, squeezing Amanda's arm. "Physical imperfections mean nothing to you."

Amanda glanced back down at Sharon. "They obviously mean something to Daniel." That was why he'd complained about Amanda's clothes and hair.

"I don't think that's true."

"We both agree that Sharon has nothing going for her except her appearance."

"Yeah," said Karen slowly.

"Then that's what attracted Daniel." Amanda glanced involuntarily at her plain navy pants and her white blouse.

"Do you care what he thinks?" asked Karen.

Good question. Amanda shouldn't care. She didn't want to be attractive to Daniel. She only wanted Daniel out of her life.

Still, the kiss, the flowers, her memories… Something was happening here. And she didn't know how to fight it.

"Dad?" Cullen bumped Daniel under the boardroom table and slipped him a sheet of paper.

Daniel snapped himself back to reality and focused on the expectant faces of the senior management team of Elliott Publication Holdings. He'd been wondering if Amanda liked the roses.

Stalling, he glanced down at the paper from Cullen.

Say: Cullen has those figures,

it read.

Daniel looked up, leaning back slightly in his chair. "Cullen has those figures."

Attention immediately swung to Cullen.

"The Spanish and German numbers look promising," said Cullen. "French is marginal, and translation costs for Japan make it a nonstarter."

Ah, the translation offices. Daniel knew what they were talking about now.

Daniel's brother Michael nodded. "We found pretty much the same results for *Pulse*. I'd want to talk about French, giving low shipping costs to Quebec and some domestic potential. But Japan will definitely give us diminishing returns."

Daniel's sister, Finola, spoke up. "*Charisma* is ready for any market."

"That's because you're image focused," said Michael. "You could probably sell without doing any translation at all."

"Still," said Finola, "it's part of the mix."

"What about you, Shane?" asked Michael.

Attention moved to Finola's twin brother, and Daniel knew everyone was wondering if Shane would take the perspective of his magazine or back up his twin.

"*The Buzz* could go either way," he said.

"Why don't we shelve the Japan discussion for today?" Cullen suggested.

"How does that help?" asked Cade McMann, the executive editor of *Charisma*. "Nothing's going to change."

"What if we prototype two translation offices," Cullen suggested. "Spanish and German. We're unlikely to lose on either of them, and it might answer some of the outstanding questions."

The room went silent as everybody considered the idea.

Cullen gave a small smile. "I don't think anyone wants to incur unnecessary losses this year, do they?"

There were nods all around on that.

"I can run it by Dad," Michael offered.

"Works for me," said Daniel, proud of his son's straight-forward compromise.

"Then it's done," said Shane, smacking his hand on the table. "Can we adjourn? I've got a lunch meeting."

Everyone began gathering their papers and rising from their chairs.

Daniel pictured Amanda's smile one more time. He hoped she liked the roses. Maybe he'd call and ask—just to make sure they'd arrived.

"So much for the international advantage," said Cade as he and Finola paused behind Daniel's chair.

"I knew they'd vote Japan down anyway," Finola answered.

"Did you give any more thought to my concerns about Jessie Clayton?" asked Cade.

"My intern?"

"Yeah."

"I don't have an opinion. I've barely seen her. You know, it's almost like she's avoiding me."

"But why?" asked Cade.

"Who knows." Finola laughed. "Maybe I'm scary."

"I don't trust her."

"Then do some digging."

"Maybe I will." Cade's voice trailed off as they moved toward the exit.

"Got a minute, Dad?" asked Cullen as Daniel started to rise.

Daniel sat back down. "Sure."

The boardroom door closed on the rest of the management team, and they were alone.

Cullen pivoted his chair and leaned back, rolling a gold pen between his fingertips. "Okay, what's going on?"

"What do you mean?"

Cullen scoffed and shook his head. "I mean, I had to save your ass three times in that meeting. What's got you so distracted?"

"You didn't—"

Cullen tapped his finger on the note he'd passed Daniel.

"I was a little distracted."

"A *little?*"

"I was just wondering—"

"About Mom."

"About business."

"Yeah, yeah. It was the potential French market that put that twinkle in your eyes."

"I didn't have a twinkle."

Cullen set down his pen, suddenly looking every inch the senior executive. "What are you doing, Dad?"

Daniel searched his son's expression. "About what?"

"You went to her court case yesterday."

"So? I'm trying to get her to change professions. You know that."

Cullen shook his head, giving Daniel a sly smile. "Dad, Dad, Dad."

Daniel raised his eyebrows. "What, what, what?"

"Admit it."

"Admit what?"

"You've got the hots for Mom."

Daniel nearly choked. "What?"

"This isn't about her job."

Daniel didn't answer. He rocked back in his chair and stared incredulously at his son.

Cullen didn't know about the kiss. He couldn't know about the kiss. Even the Elliott grapevine wasn't that efficient.

Cullen straightened in his chair. "Dad, I talked—"

"To *whom?*"

"To Bryan. We both think it's a good idea."

"You think what's a good idea?" Him kissing Amanda, Amanda kissing him?

"You and Mom getting back together."

Daniel held up his hands. "Whoa."

"You might have a hard time convincing her—"

"Your confidence in me is inspiring."

"But we think it'll be worth it."

"Oh, you do, do you?"

"Absolutely."

Daniel leaned forward and stared hard at his youngest son. He didn't know what was going on between himself and Amanda, but whatever it was, he sure didn't need a misguided cheering section.

"Back off," he ordered tersely.

"Now, Dad—"

"I mean it, Cullen."

"I don't care what you mean. It's time to move past that corporate law stuff."

"No way." Daniel wasn't giving up.

"It's a ruse, anyway. Just go ahead and date her."

"She's not—"

"Send her flowers or something."

"I already—" Daniel snapped his mouth shut.

"You already what?"

Daniel jumped to his feet and scooped up his files. "This meeting is over."

Cullen stood, too. "You already what?"

"You're an impudent young punk."

"She hasn't had a boyfriend for a while."

That stopped Daniel. "What do you mean 'for a while'?" The thought of Amanda dating someone else sent a spear through Daniel's chest. It was the same reaction he'd had when Taylor had flirted with her.

"Roberto somebody or other proposed last Christmas."

"Proposed?"

"She said no. But I think you have a better chance."

Somebody else had proposed to Amanda? Another man had *proposed* to his wife?

The breath went out of Daniel's lungs. She could have said yes. She could have been married by now—out of reach, out of touch. And he wouldn't have had the chance…

To what?

What was he thinking here?

Cullen's palms came down on the tabletop. "Take her out on the town. Make her feel special."

Daniel stared blankly at his son.

"She likes lobster," said Cullen.

Hoffman's did a great lobster. Or Angelico's. Daniel pictured Amanda across the table from him in a softly lit restaurant.

She looked good.

She looked *really* good.

With a sinking certainty, Daniel knew his son was right. And that meant Daniel was in big trouble. He wanted to date his ex-wife.

Seven

Daniel had been on a hundred dates, maybe a thousand. He knew impressions mattered. And he knew enough to focus on the details. First thing he needed here was a skilled calligrapher and a single white rose.

There was a little print shop down on Washington Square that would do an elegant invitation and do it quickly. He could have the driver drop it all off at Amanda's later this afternoon.

He rocked back in his chair and buzzed Nancy.

Two hours later, he had his answer.

In an e-mail from Amanda.

An *e-mail* of all things.

He'd gone for style and elegance, and she'd chosen expediency.

He double clicked her name.

No, thanks, the message said. Could she have been any more terse and impersonal?

This gave him nothing. No explanation. No room to re-schedule. Nothing.

No thanks? He didn't think so. He hadn't brought *Snap* magazine this far by taking "no thanks" for an answer.

He hit the buzzer. "Nancy?"

"Yes?"

"Get me Amanda Elliott's office, please."

"Right away," said Nancy.

When the light on line one blinked, he picked up again. "Amanda?"

"It's Julie."

"Oh. Is Amanda available? It's Daniel Elliott calling."

"Mr. Delectable?" asked Julie.

"Excuse me?"

She giggled. "One moment, please."

Daniel rubbed his temple, taking a deep breath. He didn't want a fight. He just wanted a date. A simple dinner and some conversation so he could find out where things stood between them.

Her husky voice came on the line. "Amanda Elliott."

"Amanda? It's Daniel."

Silence.

"I got your e-mail." He kept his voice even and nonjudg-mental.

"Daniel—"

He played dumb. "Is Friday night bad for you?"

There was a pause. "It's not a scheduling problem."

"Really?" He leaned back in his leather chair. "What kind of a problem is it?"

"Don't do this, Daniel."

"Don't do what?"

"The roses were great. But—"

"But, what?"

"Okay." She paused. "Honestly?"

"Of course."

She drew a breath. "I don't have the energy."

He straightened his chair with a snap. "I take *energy?*" How did he take energy?

"Daniel." Exasperation built in her voice.

"*I'll* make the reservation. *I'll* pick you up. *I'll* pay the bill and *I'll* bring you home. How does that take energy?"

"It's not the travel arrangements that take energy."

"What is it, then?"

"It's you. You take energy. You said you'd back off, but then you came to the courthouse."

"I will back off. I *am* backing off."

"Yeah, right," she scoffed. "Spying on me is backing off."

"I wasn't spying." Well, maybe he was. But that was yesterday. Now he had a different mission. A better mission.

"You watched me in court."

"So did several other members of the public."

"Daniel."

It was time to go for broke, time to pull out all the stops. "You were right, and I was wrong, and I'll stop."

There was a long silence.

Then there was a hint of a smile in her tone. "Could you repeat that?"

He snorted. "I don't think so."

Another silence.

"What's the catch?"

He swiveled his chair, loving the breathy sound of her voice. "No catch. I'd like to take you to dinner. My way of apologizing."

"Apologizing? You?"

"Yes. I think we've made some good progress in our relationship, Mandy."

She inhaled sharply at the sound of her nickname.

"And I don't want to lose that," he continued. "And I

promise I will not venture an opinion on either criminal or corporate law for the duration of dinner."

There was a smile in her voice. "Will anyone join us at the last minute?"

"Not if I can help it."

"What does that mean?"

He couldn't remember doing quite this much work to get a date before. He must be slipping.

"It means," he said, "that while I cannot vouch for the behavior of all the citizens of New York City, I have not invited, nor will I invite, anyone else to join us."

"Is that a promise?"

"I swear."

Another silence. "Okay."

"Friday night?"

"Friday night."

"I'll pick you up at eight."

"Goodbye, Daniel."

"Goodbye, Amanda." Daniel grinned, holding his hand against the receiver for an extra minute as he hung up the phone. He'd done it.

Now all he needed was a pound of Soleil Gold chocolates and a reservation at Hoffman's.

Amanda was definitely underdressed for Hoffman's. She'd rushed home from the office and thrown on a black denim skirt and a cropped cotton blouse. Her makeup was light, and her hair was combed back behind her ears, showing off simple jade earrings. She'd suggested popping down to the bistro at the corner for a steak sandwich, but Daniel wouldn't be budged.

In true Elliott fashion, he'd wrangled reservations to the "it" place and was preparing to show off his money and his connections.

She didn't know who he was trying to impress. Fifty-dollar appetizers didn't do a thing for her. And she sure wasn't a trophy to flash in the faces of his society cohorts.

A tuxedo-clad waiter tucked them into a softly lit alcove, next to a bay window overlooking the park. Daniel ordered them each a martini.

Okay, she'd admit the high-backed, silk-upholstered chairs were comfortable. And the expensive art, fine china and antique furnishings were easy on the eyes.

The waiter laid a linen napkin across her lap and handed Daniel a leather-bound wine list. Since Elliotts measured the importance of an occasion in dollars, she knew something had to be going on here.

She leaned forward. "You swear this isn't part of some grand plan to coerce me into changing careers?"

"So cynical," said Daniel with a disarming grin.

"So experienced," said Amanda, watching his expression carefully. She half expected Taylor Hopkins to jump out from behind a Jacobean cabinet.

Daniel let the wine list fall open in his hands, scanning the first page. "You should relax and enjoy dinner."

"I will," she said. "As soon as the ah-ha moment is over."

He glanced up. "The ah-ha moment?"

"The moment when that final, significant piece of evidence is revealed, and all of this makes sense."

"You spend too much time in a courtroom."

"I spent too much time married to you."

Daniel closed the menu and gazed at her over the low candle. "Okay. Let me see if I can move things along here."

That surprised her. "You're going to 'fess up to the nefarious plot?"

A busboy in a short red jacket stopped to fill their water glasses and place a basket of fresh rolls on the table.

Daniel thanked him, then returned his attention to Amanda. "There is no nefarious plot. Bryan's the covert operator, not me."

"Ha. Everything he knows he learned from his dad."

"Everything he knows he learned from the CIA."

Amanda flinched.

Daniel reached for her hand, squeezing her fingers and sending a warm buzz up her arm. "Sorry."

She shook her head. "It's all right. It's over. That's what counts."

"It's over," Daniel agreed.

Amanda drew a breath, retrieving her hand. "Okay, confess. What's going on?"

"I wanted to tell you I thought you were terrific in the courtroom."

The compliment gave her a warm glow, but she fought the feeling. This was no time to go all soft over Daniel. He was still up to something.

"That's nice. But that's not why we're here," she pointed out, reaching for a roll. They were warm and fragrant, one of her biggest weaknesses in life.

"We're here because I realized when I watched you nail that guy that I was wrong to push you to change careers."

There was no ignoring that compliment. It wasn't glib, and it wasn't generic, and she knew deep down in her soul that it was sincere.

The waiter appeared and set a martini in front of each of them. "Are you ready to order?" he asked, stepping back.

"Give us a few minutes," said Daniel, his gaze never leaving Amanda.

The waiter inclined his head and withdrew.

Daniel picked up his martini glass to salute her.

Amanda lifted her own glass. "Let's say I believe you."

"I'd applaud your intelligence."

"But I still think you're up to something."

He shrugged. "What you see is what you get."

"Yeah, right. The Elliotts are known far and wide for their transparency."

He slowly focused his attention, his intense gaze thickening the air between them. "I'm being as transparent as I know how."

She waited.

"Think about it, Amanda. Candy, flowers, dinner…"

She blinked. "We're on a *date?*"

His smile held a hint of pride. "We're on a date."

She waved her silver butter knife. "No, we're not. You're apologizing. We're getting our relationship back on an even keel, for the sake of our children and our grandchildren."

Daniel shrugged in a way that emphasized his broad shoulders. "Whatever you say. I'm not going to argue with you, Amanda."

She stared at him in mutinous silence.

The waiter appeared at Daniel's elbow. "Are you ready to order?"

"Yes. Thank you." Daniel glanced at Amanda. "The lobster?"

The fact that he remembered her favorite meal gave her a little thrill. But she squelched it. This wasn't a date. He wasn't her boyfriend. Those stupid intimate details were just old habits.

"The scallops," she said, to be contrary, handing the waiter the menu. "And a garden salad."

Daniel's eyebrows quirked. "You're sure?"

She nodded.

"I'll have the scallops, as well," he said.

"But—"

He shot her a silent question.

"Nothing." She'd expected him to order a rib eye, but she wasn't about to admit that.

As a harpist began playing in the far corner, Amanda smoothed the napkin over her lap and regrouped. Tonight was about maintaining an even keel.

She searched her mind for a neutral topic. "So, uh, did you get your legal troubles solved?"

Daniel took a sip of his martini. "What legal troubles?"

"The employee manual."

"Ahhh." He nodded. "Those legal troubles. Unfortunately, it looks like we're going to have to fire the man."

"You're going to fire someone over the employee manual?"

"Afraid so."

An instant defensiveness bubbled up inside her. "You're pretty cavalier with someone's livelihood."

"Well, he was pretty cavalier with his job."

"What did he do?"

"Time theft."

"What's time theft?"

"When you're doing personal business on company time."

"What? Like making a hair appointment?"

Daniel gave a hard sigh. "You don't fire someone over a hair appointment."

"I don't, but it sounds like you might."

"He called in sick and then was spotted on Seventh Avenue by one of the managers."

"Maybe he was picking up a prescription."

"According to my sources, he looked hale and hearty."

Her eyebrows went up. "You have *sources?* Bryan really does get it from you."

Daniel stroked his fingers along the stem of his martini glass. "Even you have to admit that a company the size of EPH can't afford to have employees abusing sick leave."

Amanda didn't have to admit any such thing. "Did you ask the guy what happened?"

"Not personally."

"Did anyone ask him what happened?"

"He was offered a chance to bring in a doctor's note. He didn't take it."

Amanda leaned across the table. "Maybe he didn't see a doctor."

Daniel took another swig of his martini. "He signed for sick leave. He wasn't sick. That's fraud."

"Did he get a fair and impartial hearing?"

"Why? You want to take on the case?"

She met his level gaze with a challenging smile. "I'd love to take on the case."

Daniel pushed back his chair. "We should dance."

"Excuse me?"

He nodded to a staircase. "There's dancing on the veranda upstairs."

"But we just ordered."

He stood and held out his hand. "I'll get them to hold it. I think we should do something that doesn't require talking for a while."

Amanda opened her eyes wide and feigned innocence. "Am I ruining your perfect date?"

"Let's just say you're a bigger challenge than most."

"Maybe you should dump me."

"I'm a gentleman."

Amanda stood up without taking his hand. "Really, Daniel. You could cancel our order and take me home."

She tensed, waiting for his answer.

Getting out of here would be the smart thing to do. The safe thing to do. Dancing with him would be the stupid and dangerous thing to do.

"Don't be ridiculous." He captured her hand, and she hated the feeling of relief.

His fingers were warm and strong as they twined with hers, and the resistance evaporated from her body.

"This isn't a date," she affirmed as he led her toward the worn, wood staircase.

"Of course it's a date. I sent you roses."

"You know, my entire house smells like a florist."

He gestured for her to go first up the narrow staircase. "This is a bad thing?"

"It's a weird thing."

"Your old boyfriends didn't send you flowers?"

She twisted her head to look at him. "What old boyfriends?"

"Cullen told me about Roberto."

She tripped on a stair and grabbed for the handrail. Roberto had been intense, too passionate. She didn't need to save the *entire* world. She was just going for one small corner.

Daniel's hands closed on her waist to steady her. "I hear he proposed."

She regained her balance. "He did."

"You said no?"

"I did."

"Why?"

"None of your business." She pushed open a heavy door at the top of the stairs and the sound of a string quartet wafted over her.

Daniel reached over her head and took the weight of the door. "Fair enough."

Amanda had expected an argument so his words took her by surprise.

He put a hand on the small of her back and guided her onto the open-air dance floor.

She immediately realized dancing with him was a colossal mistake. But then, it was beginning to look as though this whole evening was a mistake. Amanda should have known better. When an Elliott pulled out all the stops, a woman was pretty much powerless to resist.

He drew her into his arms and she automatically matched his rhythm.

The evening breeze was cool. Even the stars were cooperating—shining brightly in an unusually clear sky. She wondered for a moment if the superrich could control the weather. Maybe there was a secret satellite network out there.

She tipped her head back and stared straight up at the scattering of silver flecks against midnight purple. "Is everything you do always so perfect?"

There was a chuckle deep in his throat. "So perfect?"

"Perfect flowers, perfect dinner, perfect sky."

He looked up with her. "All it takes is a little forethought and planning."

She tipped her head back down. "And you are the planner."

"I am the planner."

"Ever do anything without a plan?"

"Nope."

"Nothing?"

He shrugged. "What would be the point?"

The quartet segued into another waltz, and Daniel gathered her even closer. She shouldn't like this. Didn't want to like this. It was bad enough fantasizing about him when she was alone in the back of a limo. Fantasizing about him in his arms was downright dangerous.

"It might be fun," she said, forcing herself to keep the conversation going. Last thing she wanted was to give her sexy thoughts free rein.

"What's fun about disorganization?" he asked.

The wind gusted, blowing a strand of hair across her face. "I'm talking spontaneity."

He tucked the wayward hair behind her ear, his blunt fingertips brushing her cheek. "Spontaneity is just another word for chaos."

She shook the hair loose again. "Spontaneity is doing what you want when you want."

"That's just flighty."

"Are you calling me flighty?"

He touched his forehead to hers and sighed. "I'm not calling you anything. I'm just saying I don't change so much in a week that I want completely different things by the end of it."

"What about in a month, in a year?"

"There are different levels of planning."

Amanda drew back, her feet coming to a stop. "You actually have something planned for a year down the road?"

"Of course."

"No way."

"There's the annual budget cycle, reservations, conferences. You don't just hop on a plane to Paris and throw up an EPH display at the European Periodical League."

"But what if something changes?"

He pulled her back into the dance, stroking his warm palm along her spine and making her shiver. "What would change? I mean fundamentally?"

Despite her effort to keep up a good argument, her voice was growing softer, more sultry than the moist night air. "But don't you ever just want to live life on the fly?"

"No."

"Not even the little things?"

"Amanda." His voice went gravelly, and his hand continued its leisurely path up and down her spine. "There are no little things."

Now that was just plain crazy. "What about dinner? Wouldn't it have been fun to pick a restaurant on the spur of the moment?"

There was a chuckle in his voice as he danced them toward one of the outer railings. "You mean you'd have rather waited in line for two hours to get a table?"

Mustering her fading energy, she smacked her hand against his arm. "You're being deliberately obtuse."

"I'm being deliberately logical. Planning doesn't take the fun out of life. It keeps the fun *in* life because it takes out the worry."

She looked up at him again. "Get out on a limb once in a while."

"I don't think so."

"It'll make you feel alive."

He paused, brushing the wayward hair from her face again. This time her shiver was obvious.

"You think?" he asked softly.

"I know," she said with assurance.

"Okay. Here's something you probably didn't plan on."

Her interest perked up. "Yeah?"

He nodded, slowly drawing her toward him. "Yeah." He bent down, slanting his mouth.

Her eyes went wide. *Uh-oh.* There was spontaneity and then there was *spontaneity.*

"This," he whispered as his lips touched hers.

It was a gentle kiss. His lips barely parted, and the arm at her back eased rather than pulled her against his body.

It couldn't have lasted more than ten seconds, but a frenzy of desire thrummed to life inside her. The silver stars blurred inside her head and her knees went weak.

Then he opened his mouth, and the image melted. She clung to his shoulders, silently repeating his name over and over inside her head.

Just when her frenzied words threatened to break free, he ended the kiss.

They stared at each other, standing still amongst the swaying couples, breathing deeply for long minutes.

"Didn't plan on that, did you?" he finally asked.

She considered the glint in his eye. "Did *you?*"

"Oh, yeah. All week."

"What?"

He chuckled low. "I'm a planner, Amanda. That's just the way it is."

"But—"

"And I don't think my careful planning distracted from my enjoyment one little bit."

Amanda drew back. He'd planned to kiss her?

A frightening thought entered her head, and she tightened her grip on his arms to steady herself. "Please tell me you haven't got anything else planned."

His white teeth flashed in the lantern light. "It's probably better if I don't answer that."

Eight

Daniel's intercom buzzed on Monday morning, and Nancy's voice came through the speaker. "Mrs. Elliott to see you."

Amanda? Here?

Daniel could hardly believe it.

She'd seemed so jumpy after their kiss on Friday night, he'd decided to back off for a few days.

Maybe he'd been unwise to tip his hand. But he wanted to date her, and he wanted her to know that he was interested. The more he saw of her, the more he remembered what they had together, and the more he wanted to recapture the magic.

He stood up from his desk and straightened his tie, smoothing back his hair with one hand.

"Daniel?" came Nancy's voice again.

He pushed the intercom button. "Send her in."

The door opened and he put a welcoming smile on his face. Then the smile died.

It was Sharon.

The *other* Mrs. Elliott.

She marched into his office, all five foot three of her, almost painfully thin with hair that had seen way too many salon treatments. Her blue eyes crackled as she swung the door behind her. It closed with a bang.

Daniel braced himself.

"I don't know what the hell you thought you were up to," she hissed, advancing on his desk.

"Up to?"

"Hoffman's?"

He dropped down into his chair and shuffled through a stack of papers. "Is there something I can help you with, Sharon?"

She paced in front of his desk. "Yes, there's something you can help me with. You can uphold the terms of our divorce agreement."

"You got this month's check." She'd cashed it within hours.

"I'm not talking about the money," she all but screeched. "I'm talking about our agreement."

"Our agreement to what?" Daniel signed the letter in front of him, then moved his attention to a marketing report. "I've got a busy morning here." And he didn't want to waste valuable brain space focused on Sharon when he could be daydreaming about Amanda. He wondered if she was busy for lunch.

Sharon placed both her hands on Daniel's desktop and leaned forward. It was hard for an overbleached pixie to look intimidating, but she was doing her best. "Our agreement to tell our friends *I* was the one who left *you*."

"I never told them any different."

"Actions speak louder than words, Daniel."

He glanced at his watch. "Can we skip to the point? I've got a ten o'clock with Michael."

Her jaw clenched, and her eyes wrinkled up despite two

very expensive surgeries. "Nobody's going to believe me if you're necking on the dance floor with some other woman."

Daniel squared his shoulders. "That wasn't another woman. It was Amanda."

Sharon waved a hand. "Whatever, you just—"

"And we weren't necking."

"Stay away from her, Daniel."

"No."

Sharon's pale blue eyes nearly popped out of her head. "*What?*"

He stood up and crossed his arms over his chest. "I said no."

"How dare—"

"I dare because you and I are divorced, and I will see whomever I want whenever I want."

"We had an agreement," she sputtered.

"I agreed to lie once to save your reputation. It's over. We're done. You have absolutely no say in my life anymore. Got that?" Particularly when it came to Amanda. Daniel wasn't taking direction from anyone ever again when it came to Amanda. Well, maybe Cullen. But that was only because Cullen was smart, and Daniel happened to agree with him on this.

Sharon put on a pretty pout, and her expression was almost magically transformed. It was embarrassing to think he'd once fallen for that trick.

"But, Daniel," she whined, "I'll be humiliated."

"Why?"

"Because people will think you dumped me."

"If you want to save your reputation, get your own dates. Go out. Be happy. Show them all you're well rid of me."

Crocodile tears welled up in her eyes. But Daniel was unmoved.

She'd made her bed, and it was up to her to lie in it. He'd given her the house, the artwork, the season tickets and the staff. He was done.

He moved out from behind the desk, heading for the door.

"You're on your own, Sharon. Fool them however you want, but leave me out of it."

"But, Daniel—"

"No. I'm through. We're done."

She straightened and squared her shoulders. "At least keep that woman out of the public eye."

Daniel clenched his jaw on the words he wanted to hurl at her. He opened the door. "Goodbye, Sharon."

She sniffed, put her pointed chin in the air, tucked her clutch purse under one arm and marched out.

Daniel shut the door firmly behind her and stalked back to his desk.

Keep Amanda out of the public eye?

He didn't think so.

He buzzed Nancy. "We have any high-profile invitations for this weekend? Something splashy, with the who's who?"

"He *kissed* you?" asked Karen, her green eyes lighting up with a grin as she tamped soil around an African violet.

She was working in the solarium, hand tools, potting soil and fertilizer scattered on the table in front of her.

"Am I crazy?" asked Amanda, carrying a tray of seedlings to a shelf on the other side of the sunlit room.

"Crazy to fall for your ex-husband?"

Amanda groaned as she walked back. "It sounds so much worse when you say it out loud."

"It doesn't sound bad at all. It's really very sweet," said Karen, stripping off her brightly colored gloves and sitting down heavily in a wicker chair.

Amanda quickly went to her. "You okay?"

Karen nodded and smiled. "Just a little tired. But it's a good kind of tired." Her gaze went to the plants. "It feels great to accomplish something."

Amanda crouched down and squeezed Karen's hand. "It feels great to see you so energetic."

"Back to you and Daniel."

Amanda groaned, but Karen just laughed.

A phone rang.

Then it rang again.

Karen glanced at Amanda's purse sitting next to the African violet. "Is your cell turned on?"

Amanda jumped up. "Oh, shoot. I'll shut it off."

"See who it is," said Karen.

Amanda flipped it open and checked the call display. Her chest contracted—not a good sign. "It's Daniel."

"Pick it up," Karen urged, sitting forward.

Amanda squeezed her eyes shut for a second then pushed the talk button.

"Amanda Elliott."

"Hey, Mandy. It's Daniel."

She felt her cheeks heat, and Karen grinned.

"Hi, Daniel."

"Listen, are you free on Saturday night?"

"Uh, Saturday?"

Karen nodded vigorously.

"Let me…" Amanda paused, not wanting to look too eager. She didn't know what they were doing, or where they were going, but she wanted to feel that rush of excitement one more time. "Saturday's fine."

"Good. There's a museum fund-raiser at the Riverside Ballroom."

The Riverside? As in the hotel where they'd first made love?

Amanda opened her mouth, but nothing came out.

"Pick you up at eight?" asked Daniel.

"I… Uh…"

"It's black tie. For a really good cause."

Of course it was a good cause. Daniel always showed up

for the good cause. Just as he always showed up for the reporters and the movers and shakers.

Why couldn't they just go out for pizza?

"Amanda?" he prompted.

"Yeah?"

"Eight o'clock's okay?"

"Sure."

"Great. See you then."

Amanda closed her little phone.

"Another date?" asked Karen with a sly grin.

"The museum fund-raiser at the Riverside."

Karen's breath whistled out. "Now, that's a date."

"I have nothing to wear."

Karen waved a dismissive hand. "Sure you do."

Amanda tucked her phone back into her purse. "No, really. I've been through my entire closet. I have absolutely nothing to wear."

"Let's see if we can help you."

"How do you mean?"

Karen stood up. "Scarlet must have a hundred of her designs upstairs."

Amanda took a step back. "I couldn't."

"Sure you could. It'll be fun." Karen took Amanda's arm. "If it makes you feel better, we'll call her for permission when we find something. But she's going to be thrilled."

Amanda allowed Karen to tug her toward the door. "You think she'll let me wear her clothes?"

"Absolutely. And if we need alterations, we'll get her over here."

Amanda hesitated. "I'm not—"

"Humor me on this," said Karen. "I'll feel like I'm going to the party myself."

"You actually like that kind of thing?" Amanda asked as they headed up the staircase.

"It's fun getting all dressed up."

"Well, that's the difference between you and me." Amanda felt stiff and plastic in formal wear, not to mention heavy makeup and hairspray. Her expression would go tight, and even her voice would go formal. She felt as if she was making people dig through layers to get to the real her.

"So, are you going to kiss him again?" asked Karen.

"I hadn't thought about it." Now that was a lie. She'd fantasized about kissing, kissing and more kissing in the days since Friday.

"Well *think* about it."

They entered one of the spare bedrooms, and Karen opened the double doors of a walk-in closet.

"Okay. I'm going to sit down here and get comfortable," she said. "And I want you to give me a fashion show and a monologue on kissing your ex-husband."

Amanda laughed. "It was a short kiss."

"But a good one?" asked Karen, easing down into an armchair and putting her feet on the matching ottoman.

Amanda let her mind go back for the thousandth time. "A good one," she agreed. A very good one. An "I think I remember why I married you" good one.

"You should see the expression on your face," Karen clucked.

"I just wish I could figure it out," Amanda called as she entered the closet. "I mean, we're divorced. We're living completely different lives."

"Maybe he's just after your body."

Amanda leaned back out the door. "Hello? After Sharon?"

"Especially after Sharon. That woman might look good in pictures, but believe me, up close it's all makeup, *Botox* and putty filler."

Amanda choked out a laugh.

Karen laughed along with her. "She's frightening, particularly when she starts talking. You, on the other hand, get more gorgeous by the minute."

Amanda didn't believe her, but Karen was a very kind friend.

"Now," said Karen, "we are going to knock that man dead with a sexy dress."

"I'm not sure I can pull off sexy," said Amanda.

"Don't be silly. You can do sexy with one hand behind your back."

Even if she could pull it off, she wouldn't. "If I go out there all vamped up, you know what he's going to think."

"What's he going to think?"

Amanda frowned at Karen. "That I'm…you know…interested in him."

"You *are* interested in him."

"Not as a boyfriend."

"As what then?"

Amanda peeled off her blouse. She sighed. "Isn't that the million-dollar question."

"He can be your clandestine lover," said Karen.

"A secret affair? With Daniel?"

"It's not like you've never slept with him before," Karen said.

Amanda rolled her eyes.

Karen laughed. "May I assume it was good?"

"Of course it was good." Amanda peeled off her pants and laid them on the bed. Sex had never been the issue in their marriage. The issues had been Daniel's overbearing family, his drive to make money and his unrelenting pretension.

In the early years, they'd had something real, and it had broken her heart to watch it slowly slip away as Daniel retreated further and further into the shell of propriety. But the sex, ah, the sex…

"So, the sex was good but the marriage went bad?" asked Karen.

Amanda stepped into the closet again. "That's one way of putting it."

"You could have the best of both worlds," Karen called. "Sleep with the good lover, but live apart from the bad husband."

"That's—" Amanda stopped. She walked back to the closet door and stared at Karen. It was either crazy, or a pretty good idea.

"It is the twenty-first century," said Karen.

Daniel as a lover, and only a lover?

He'd already promised to back off on the career advice, so she wouldn't have to endure any more lectures. Could she really take advantage of his strengths and simply ignore his weaknesses?

"You are going to need one special dress," said Karen with a knowing wink.

Amanda couldn't put her finger on it, but something about this just wasn't quite right.

"I couldn't…" she began.

"Actually," said Karen, "you could. It's not illegal, immoral or unhealthy."

The Elliotts' housekeeper appeared in the doorway. "Do you ladies need anything?"

"Yes, Olive. We need champagne and orange juice," said Karen decisively. "We're celebrating."

"Are you allowed?" asked Amanda.

"In moderation," said Karen.

"I'll bring it right up," said Olive, exiting the room.

Karen pointed imperiously to the closet. "I want you to start with the dresses you'd be least likely to wear in public."

Amanda strolled into the museum fund-raiser in a black sheath of oriental silk. Sleeveless, it had a mandarin collar that eliminated the need for jewelry, and it was slit up the back

for easy walking. A floral silkscreen of gold and pink cascaded diagonally across the front.

One of Scarlet's designs, it was a compromise with
Karen—elegant but not overly flirtatious.

Scarlet had insisted on a thin golden anklet that winked
when Amanda walked and complemented her strappy
sandals. The heels were higher than she normally wore, but
Daniel gave her a steady arm to hang on to.

As they entered through an ornate archway, she took in
flamboyant floral arrangements and chandeliers dripping
with crystal teardrops. The ceiling beams were white with
inlayed gold. Perimeter tables were immaculately set and a
circular dance floor gleamed in the center of the room.

Cinderella's ball had nothing on this place.

Then she spotted Patrick and Maeve. Her stomach
clenched and she stumbled a step. "You didn't tell me your
parents were going to be here," she whispered to Daniel,
feeling eighteen and impossibly gauche all over again.

"Is that a problem?" he whispered back.

"Yes, it's a problem," she hissed.

"Why?"

What a question. "Because they don't like me."

"Don't be ridiculous."

She slowed. The glitz, glitter and orchestra music were
suddenly making her claustrophobic. She didn't belong here.
She'd never belonged here.

She needed to proposition Daniel and get out.

"Daniel, darling." A sixtyish woman dripping in sequins
and wearing enough diamonds to cancel the national debt
gave Daniel a kiss on each cheek.

Daniel smiled and clasped her papery hand. "Mrs. Cavalli."

"I saw your mother at the Humane Society quilt raffle
last week."

"I heard it went well," said Daniel with an easy interest.

"It did." Mrs. Cavalli's gaze strayed to Amanda.

Daniel put his hand on the small of her back. "This is my friend, Amanda. Amanda, Mrs. Cavalli."

Amanda held out her hand. "Pleased to meet you."

"Do you have any pets, dear?"

"Uh, no." Amanda shook her head. "I'm afraid I don't."

"You should consider adopting one from the shelter. That's where we got Buttons, three, maybe four years ago." Mrs. Cavalli turned to Daniel. "The little dickens got into some caramel candy last week."

"Did she?"

Mrs. Cavalli chuckled, her bosom jiggling. "Took the groomer three hours to get it out of her fur."

Then she turned back to Amanda. "She's a cockapoo. Big brown eyes. Just a treasure."

"She sounds adorable," said Amanda.

"Will we see you at the Children's Hospital tea, dear?"

Amanda glanced at Daniel.

"Amanda works during the day," he said.

Mrs. Cavalli drew back, her eyes rounding. "Oh, I see."

"Amanda is a lawyer."

"Well, that's lovely, dear. Perhaps another time?"

"Perhaps," said Amanda.

Mrs. Cavalli gave a fluttery-fingered wave. "I must go find Maeve."

"Nice to see you," called Daniel.

"Daniel!" boomed a hearty voice as a gray-haired man in a tuxedo reached for his hand.

"Senator Wallace," Daniel greeted in return.

"Did you catch the closing numbers in oil futures this afternoon?" asked Wallace.

Without waiting for an answer, he held up his palms. "We have *got* to drill in Alaska, that's all there is to it. Sooner the better as far as California is concerned."

"What about conservation measures?" asked Daniel.

Senator Wallace pointed his index finger at Daniel. "You show me an SUV owner willing to turn down his air-conditioning, and I'll show you a liberal Democrat about to support Adam Simpson." He laughed heartily.

Amanda smiled, even though she didn't really understand the joke.

"You get caught up in the Chesapeake scandal?" asked the senator.

Daniel shook his head. "I got out of tech stocks early."

"Damn accountants," said the senator. "No better than the lawyers."

Amanda's discomfort must have shown, because Senator Wallace acknowledged her for the first time. "Don't get me wrong, little lady. I'm a lawyer myself. But damn these upstarts, we've got to put the economic clout back in the hands of the Fortune 500."

Amanda clenched her jaw, and her hand tightened on Daniel's arm.

Daniel quickly redirected the senator's attention. "Senator, you remember Bob Solomon. Bob, come and say hi to Senator Wallace."

A man disengaged himself from a nearby conversation group and shook the senator's hand.

"Bob was a big supporter of the Nicholson campaign," said Daniel.

The senator's grin broadened.

Daniel eased Amanda away from the conversation.

"What I want to know," she said, "is, if the economic clout is no longer in the hands of the Fortune 500, who the hell does he think has it?"

"Let's move on," said Daniel.

"Let's move upstairs," said Amanda.

He glanced down at her. "Upstairs?"

Amanda stopped and faced him. She had planned to have a drink, maybe two or three before this moment, but she didn't think she could last much longer.

"I have a confession."

His brows went up. "Do tell."

"I rented a room."

"You *what?*"

"I—"

"Wait. Damn." He latched on to her arm and spun her around. "Keep walking. Don't look back."

"Is it your parents?"

"No, it's not my parents. Jeez, Amanda. They like you already."

"No they don't."

He scooted her around a corner where they were hidden from the main ballroom. Rich burgundy curtains accented paned glass doors that led to a balcony overlooking Fifth Avenue. It had started to rain, so nobody was outside. Wet droplets blurred the city lights and darkened the secluded corner.

"Who did we escape from?" she asked.

"Sharon."

Amanda blinked at him. They were hiding from his ex-wife? Why did he have to hide her from Sharon?

"She's been…" He tightened his jaw. "Difficult."

Amanda's stomach lurched. Maybe she'd got this all wrong. Maybe her imagination and Karen's enthusiasm had led her down a completely wrong path.

She took a couple of steps back. "Hey, if you've still got a thing for—"

Daniel reached out and grasped her arms, halting her retreat. "I do *not* have a thing for Sharon." He loosened his grip and closed the space between them. "It's just that she's loud and unpredictable. I didn't want her to insult you."

"Insult me?"

He shifted closer still, and his voice went gravelly. "Forget Sharon. Let's get back to the part where you rented a room."

Amanda's heart flip-flopped.

"You rented a room?" he prompted, his blue eyes smoldering with obvious desire.

She drew in a bracing breath. This was going to be even harder than she'd imagined.

His voice dropped to a whisper. "I rented a room here once."

"Yeah?" she managed.

His eyes twinkled like a moonlit ocean. "It was prom night. And I got very, *very* lucky."

Amanda ducked her head and focused on his chest.

"Hey." He tipped her chin up with his finger. "Is it possible that you're propositioning me?"

She slowly nodded. "It's possible."

A broad grin grew on his face. "All right."

His palm slid around to cup her cheek, and he dipped his head to kiss her.

She stretched to meet him, her muscles tense, her entire body humming with pent-up need.

His lips touched hers, and her limbs all but melted. He opened wide without preamble, stroking her tender mouth with the tip of his tongue. Her pulse pounded and their bodies fused with delicious heat.

Her hands twined around his neck, clinging to him, while he braced a forearm over the small of her back, holding her solid.

Their kiss deepened and lengthened. The orchestra music faded to the background and the pounding of the raindrops drummed in her ears.

"Mandy," he whispered, stroking her face with the pad of his thumb as he stared into her eyes for a long moment.

He returned to her lips. He grasped her buttocks, emphasizing his arousal. Amanda felt her bones turn to liquid.

"Daniel," she whimpered.

"Uh-hmm." A male voice sounded from behind her.

Amanda wrenched back, whipping her head around to see the senator, Sharon and two other people staring in shocked silence.

Nine

Daniel could think of a dozen directions this could go in. All of them bad. He'd wanted to thumb his nose at Sharon's orders, but this wasn't anywhere near what he'd had in mind.

Sharon's eyes glittered like granite; her mouth was drawn into a thin line of anger.

Senator Wallace looked faintly amused. He offered a quick salute with his single malt before turning to leave.

The Wilkinsons had the good grace to simply fade back into the party.

Sharon, on the other hand, advanced. "Have you lost your mind?"

"Do we really need to do this?" asked Daniel, keeping an arm around Amanda. The seven-figure settlement should have wedged Sharon out of his life for good.

"Yes, we need to do this. What did I ask you? What did I *tell* you?"

Amanda started to pull away. "I think I'll just—"

"Don't you go anywhere," Daniel demanded, tightening his hold on her waist.

Her eyes widened, and he moderated his voice. "Please wait." He turned to Sharon. "Go back to the party."

"Not a hope in hell. I'll be the laughingstock."

"Only if you act like it."

"You don't think this story has already circulated the room a dozen times?"

"It's been three minutes."

She leaned forward and poked him in the chest with her index finger. "You're the one who screwed up here, Daniel. And you're the one who's going to fix it."

"Don't be melodramatic."

"You are going to dance with me."

"What?"

"I mean it, Daniel. You get your butt out on that dance floor and let everybody see us laughing and talking together. That'll tamp down the gossip."

"Not in a million—"

"You owe me."

"I do not owe you anything."

Amanda shifted away again, this time breaking Daniel's grip.

He didn't blame her. Who wanted to watch a fight between a divorced couple? It probably brought back terrible memories for her.

He realized in an instant that if he wanted to get anywhere in his relationship with Amanda, he had to neutralize Sharon. And, right now, neutralizing Sharon meant dancing with her.

"Fine," he spat out reluctantly. He turned to Amanda. "This will only take a minute. Meet me by the statue?"

"Sure," she agreed with a shrug and an enigmatic expression.

Sharon grasped his arm, and he followed her onto the dance floor.

But halfway through the fake dance, Daniel spotted Amanda. She was leaving.

He swore under his breath and abandoned Sharon, practically sprinting for the exit.

"Amanda." Halfway across the foyer, he caught her by the arm. "What are you doing?"

She turned a glare on him. "You'd better get back to the party, Daniel. You wouldn't want people to gossip."

"I don't care if people gossip." He'd just left Sharon fuming in the middle of the dance floor. The gossip was well under way.

"Yes, you do," said Amanda.

"I was just trying to get rid of her."

"By dancing with her?"

"You saw what happened."

"Yeah. I saw exactly what happened."

"So you know—"

"Did you or did you not just blow me off for the sake of appearances?"

"It wasn't like that." He didn't care what people thought. He'd just wanted to get Sharon out of their hair.

"It was *exactly* like that. Not that I ever had any doubts." She shook her head and started walking again.

"Amanda." He matched his pace to hers.

"This was a mistake, Daniel."

"What was a mistake?"

"You, me, us. Thinking we could have the best of both worlds."

He blinked at her. "What best of both worlds?"

"Never mind."

"No. Not never mind. You have a room. *We* have a room."

She rolled her eyes and scoffed. "Right. We're going to sneak upstairs together. What if the senator sees you? What if your *parents* see you?"

"I don't care."

"Yes, you do."

He took her arm and tried to turn her around. "Let's go. You and me. Upstairs. Right now."

She shook him off. "Well, isn't that just the most romantic invitation I've ever had."

Daniel clenched his jaw.

A doorman pulled the glass door open.

"Good night, Daniel," said Amanda, shaking off his arm.

Short of throwing her bodily over his shoulder, Daniel had no choice but to watch her walk away.

"Good morning." Cullen strolled jauntily into Daniel's office. "I hear you had a date with Mom on the weekend."

"Where'd you hear that?" Daniel growled. He'd been trying to get Amanda on the phone for the past thirty-six hours.

"Aunt Karen told Scarlet, and Scarlet told Misty."

"Word travels fast in this family."

Cullen straddled a guest chair. "How'd it go?"

Daniel glared. He was pissed at Sharon and a little bit pissed at Amanda.

He'd done the right thing for them. He'd done the right thing for *her*. Sharon was poison, and they didn't need her out gunning for them.

"What?" asked Cullen, studying Daniel's expression. "I don't need intimate details or anything. 'Course if Mom's giving them to Karen, I'm going to hear eventually, anyway."

"Where are the weekly sales figures?"

Cullen drew back. "You want to talk *business*?"

"We're in the office, aren't we?"

"But—"

"And whatever happened with the Guy Lundin situation?" The time theft issue had been nagging in the back of Daniel's mind for a week. Not that he wanted to adopt Amanda's style of business management—far from it. He just wanted to understand what had happened, and how they could avoid it in the future.

"The time theft thing?" Cullen squinted. "Are you saying that me asking about Mom on company time is the same thing as a bogus sick claim?"

"Depends on how long you talk about her. Did we fire him?"

"I'm meeting with personnel this afternoon."

"What's your gut telling you?"

Cullen looked confused. "My gut?"

"Yeah. Your gut."

Cullen paused. "You already have all the verifiable facts."

He might have all the verifiable facts, but Daniel kept hearing Amanda's voice inside his head asking him how well he knew his employees. "What about the nonverifiable ones?"

"They're not relevant."

"Are there any?"

"Guy Lundin claims he was taking his mother to the cancer clinic."

"Did we check on that?"

Cullen sat down in one of the guest chairs. "There was no reason to check."

"Why not?"

"There's no provision for taking family members to medical appointments."

"So what do people do?" Daniel had taken Amanda out for a drink on company time. He'd ordered her flowers on company time. If she was sick, you can bet your ass he'd take her to the doctor on company time.

"About what?" asked Cullen.

"Family medical appointments. Emergencies. Crises."

Cullen held up his hands. "I don't know."

"Well, maybe we should think about it. Do you think Guy's mother is really sick?"

"He's not habitual about sick leave. He only took one day last year. Two the year before."

"Let's drop it," said Daniel, picking up his pen and flipping to a letter waiting for his signature.

"But my meeting—"

"Cancel the Personnel meeting. Give the guy a break."

"What about the other employees?"

"What about them?"

"What happens next time somebody has a sick family member?"

"Good question."

"Thank you."

Daniel pushed the intercom. "Nancy?"

"Yes?"

"Do we have a copy of the employee manual?"

"Yes, we do. Shall I bring it in?"

"Not yet."

"Okay."

Cullen leaned forward in his chair. "What are you doing?"

"Answering your question." Daniel waved him away. "Don't worry about it."

"You want to go over the sales report now?"

Daniel stood up and flexed his shoulders. "Nah. You take care of it. Let me know if there's anything I need to worry about."

Cullen stood with him. "You sure?"

"You're a good sales manager. I ever mention that?"

"Dad?"

Daniel rounded the desk and clapped his son on the shoulder. "No. You're a great sales manager."

"You okay?"

"Not really." He urged Cullen toward the door. "But I'm working on it."

Cullen looked at him strangely, but allowed himself to be ushered into the reception area.

As Cullen left, Daniel stopped beside Nancy's desk. "Can you do a little research for me?"

She picked up a pad and pen. "Of course."

"Find some comparable-size companies and see if anybody has family leave."

"Family leave?"

"For sick kids and stuff."

Nancy gazed at him.

"Time off. When your kids are sick, or your parents have medical appointments."

"Is this about Guy Lundin?"

Daniel smiled. "I definitely hired you for your brain."

"I'll get right on it," she said.

Daniel turned. Then he turned back. "How's your family?"

She squinted at him, hesitating for a second. "They're fine."

"Your kids are…"

"Sarah's nine and Adam's seven."

"Right. They like school?"

Nancy blinked. "Yes."

Daniel nodded. "That's good." He tapped his knuckles on her desk before turning to walk back into his office.

Sarah and Adam. He'd have to make a note of that.

He eased down into his chair again and picked up his phone. He had Amanda's office number memorized now, so he dialed it directly.

"Amanda Elliott's office," Julie answered.

"Hi, Julie. It's Daniel."

"I'm not supposed to put you through."

"Yeah, I figured that."

"You wanna bribe me?"

Daniel chuckled, liking Julie better and better all the time. "What'll it take?"

"Some more of those gold foil chocolates Amanda brought in."

"They'll be on your desk in an hour."

"Amanda can speak with you right away." The line clicked and went silent.

"Amanda Elliott."

"It's me."

Silence.

"I took your advice today." He waited.

"What advice?"

Bingo. He'd have put money on that line working. "I've ordered a review of family leave provisions for the employee manual."

"Ordered?"

"Okay. I asked my secretary to look into it. Her kids' names are Sarah and Adam, by the way."

"You had to find that out, didn't you?"

"I think the important point here is that I *did* find that out."

"Okay. I'll give you credit for that." There was a smile in her voice.

He jumped at the opening. "Go out with me again, Amanda."

"Daniel—"

"Anywhere you want. Anything you want. You name it."

"This is not going to work."

Panic surged in the pit of his stomach. "You can't know that. We don't even know what we're doing, where we're going. If you don't know what *this* is, how can you know that it won't work?"

"You ever thought of becoming a litigator?"

"What's your gut telling you, Amanda?"

"My gut?"

"Your instincts. You're the one who's big on instinct and spontaneity. Forget logic—"

"Forget logic?"

He slowed himself down. "Go with emotion on this one, Amanda. If I can take your advice, surely you can take it, too."

Her voice went soft. "That's not fair, Daniel."

He matched his tone to hers. "Who said anything about fair?"

She sighed. "Anywhere I want?"

"Yeah."

"A picnic. At the beach."

"Sunday at five."

She hesitated for another couple of heartbeats. "All right."

"I'll pick you up."

"No limo."

"I promise."

To be fair, Amanda had only specified that he couldn't use a limo. Too bad she hadn't thought to ban helicopters.

The chopper set them down on the helipad of the Carmichael estate on Nantucket. The Carmichaels were in London, but they'd given Daniel permission to use their private beach. And apparently they'd offered their staff, as well, or else Daniel had hired staff specifically for the occasion.

It *was* on the beach. And there *was* food. But that was where the resemblance to a picnic ended.

A round table had been set up on a flat stretch of sand between the lapping waves and the rocky cliffs. A white table-cloth flapped in the light breeze, held down by flowers, hurricane lamps, crystal and fine china. A maître d' stood at attention, and he appeared to be wearing a Secret Service headset.

Daniel pulled out one of the padded chairs and gestured for her to sit down. "I asked them to time the entrée for sunset."

"*This* is a picnic?" As soon as her butt hit the cushion, the maître d' sprang into action.

He muttered something into his microphone then laid her napkin across her lap.

"We're starting with margaritas," Daniel said, sitting down across from her.

"Margaritas?" asked Amanda.

"I hope you like them. If not, I can arrange—"

"I like them just fine. But, Daniel…"

"Yes?"

"This isn't a picnic."

He glanced around. "What do you mean?"

"A picnic is fried chicken and chocolate cake on a blanket, battling ants—"

"I think we can skip the ants."

"—maybe cheap wine in paper cups."

"Now you're just being ornery. People drink margaritas on beaches all over the world."

"At resorts. They don't bring a blender to a picnic. Where would you plug it in?"

"Who brought a blender?"

"That's how you get margaritas."

"The bartender is making them in the house. Now relax."

At that moment, the bartender appeared with two frosty lime margaritas in hand. At least Amanda thought it was the bartender. Perhaps Daniel had also hired a cocktail waiter.

Daniel thanked the man, who then withdrew back up the wooden stairs to the house.

Amanda took a sip of her margarita. It was delicious. It just wasn't rustic.

"We're starting with a shrimp Creole appetizer," said Daniel.

"Stop trying to impress me." She hadn't come here to see Daniel's money at work. She'd come here to see Daniel.

He sat back. "This is a date. Why wouldn't I try to impress you?"

Maybe it was time to tell him she was a sure thing. She smiled to herself. Before this night was over, she was going to fight her way through to the real Daniel, then she was making love to him.

"What?" he asked, watching her smile.

She tucked her hair behind her ears. "I was wondering about the employee manual."

"Nancy did a terrific job researching. We're putting forward a proposal to Dad."

"You're going to offer family leave?"

"We're going to propose it."

Amanda took a sip of the tart margarita. "What made you change your mind?"

"About looking at my employees as people?"

She nodded.

"You did, of course."

She felt a warm glow. "Thank you."

"No. Thank *you*. You push and prod and poke and probe—"

"You make me sound so appealing."

He grinned. "You are rather relentless."

"So are you."

"Hey, I gave up."

She stilled. He made an interesting point. Daniel had sincerely tried to understand her perspective, whereas she hadn't budged a single inch.

The rhythm of the waves increased and a group of gulls called on the air currents high above.

Amanda flicked her hair out of her eyes.

"What's wrong?" he asked.

She shook her head and revived her smile. "Nothing. Tell me about the CEO competition."

"What about it?"

"Are you going to win?"

Daniel shrugged. "We're coming up fast on Web site subscriptions."

"There are four months left."

"But *Charisma* always has a strong December."

Amanda nodded, toying with the stem on her frosted glass. "Will you be disappointed if you lose?"

He looked her straight in the eye. "Of course. I play to win."

"I know. But ego aside—"

"I don't have an ego."

Amanda laughed. "Oh, Daniel."

He looked genuinely confused. "What?"

"You mean to tell me having the job is more important than winning the game?"

"I don't know what you're talking about. It's the same thing."

She shook her head, flicking her hair again as the breeze freshened. "It's two completely different things."

"How?"

Another uniformed waiter appeared with their appetizer. After he left, Daniel asked his question again. "How?"

Amanda took a deep breath, trying to figure out how to say what she wanted to say. "Take off your jacket."

"What?"

"You heard me."

When he didn't move, she stood up and walked around to his chair. As she reached for his lapels, storm clouds rumbled on the distant horizon.

He pulled back. "What are you doing?"

She grasped his jacket and tugged it over his shoulders. "I'm peeling away the layers."

"The layers?"

"To get to the real you."

"I think that's metaphorical. And I *am* the real me."

She tugged on his sleeve. "How do you know?"

He finally gave up and shrugged out of his jacket. "Because I've been the real me my entire life."

Amanda went to work on his tie. "What does the real you want?"

He looked straight into her eyes. "You."

Okay. That was a good answer. "I meant professionally."

"I want to be CEO. Why is it so inconceivable to you that

I want the top job in a company where I've worked my whole life?"

She released the knot in his tie and pulled it from around his neck. "Because I think people, your family, have been putting things in front of you for forty years and then telling you you're supposed to want them."

"Like what?"

She dropped the tie on the table. "For starters? Me."

He looked to his right and then to his left. "I don't see my family urging me on here."

"I meant after high school."

He pulled her into his lap. "Hey, that was just you and me on prom night. Nobody *told* me to want you."

"They told you to marry me."

"You were pregnant."

"They told you to come back to the family firm."

"We needed the money."

"They told you to stay on this continent."

Daniel snapped his jaw shut. "I stayed for you."

She shook her head. "You stayed because they told you to stay. Whose idea was it for you to marry Sharon?"

"Mine." But he flinched, then went quiet.

"Whose idea was it for you to try for the CEO position?"

Daniel stared at her.

"What do *you* want, Daniel?"

Thunder boomed closer this time, and lightning flashed in the darkening sky as the first fat drops of rain hit the sand.

Daniel turned to the maître d'. "Have them bring out the canopy, Curtis."

Amanda jumped up from Daniel's lap. "No!"

"What?"

"No canopy."

"Why not?"

"Layers, Daniel."

He peered at her. "Are you, like, clinically insane?"

She leaned closer. "Can you send that man away?"

"Will I be safe alone with you?"

"Maybe."

He hesitated, and another thunderclap echoed against the cliffs. "You can go inside, Curtis. We'll be fine."

Curtis nodded and headed for the staircase.

"So, we're going to stay out here and get wet?" Daniel asked.

"Yeah. Life's messy. Get used to it."

"Can I put my jacket back on?"

"No."

"You want it?"

The rain began in earnest, and Amanda spread her arms wide. "No."

"Dinner's ruined," he pointed out.

"We'll order pizza later."

"What do we do now?"

"Now?" She climbed back into his lap, wrapping her arms around his dampening shirt and slicking back his wet hair.

This was Daniel. This was real. This was what she'd been waiting for.

"Now," she said, "we make love."

Ten

Daniel stared at Amanda's wet hair, her clingy blouse and her loose chinos.

He'd pictured this moment, pictured it a million times. But there was always a bed, satin sheets, champagne. "Here?"

"Yeah." She laughed, kicking out her legs. "Right here."

"You'll get cold."

"I don't care."

He glanced at the yachts moored in the bay. "Somebody might see us."

"They'd need a telephoto lens."

"Yeah." As if that had ever been a deterrent.

"Afraid you'll end up on the cover of your own magazine?"

"Don't be ridiculous, Amanda."

"Kiss me, Daniel."

He gazed at her moist mouth. It was tempting. Boy, was it tempting. "You'll get sand stuck to your butt."

"My butt will survive."

He wanted this to be memorable. He wanted this to be perfect. He wanted this to be a moment she'd cherish. "Can we at least go inside?"

She leaned forward and placed a quick kiss on his mouth. "Not a chance."

Her lips were cool and damp and sexy as hell.

"Amanda," he groaned in protest.

"Here and now, wet and wild, cold and sandy, risking yachting voyeurs." She kissed him again, longer this time, deeper, their lips warming to each other.

"I don't remember you being like this," he mumbled before initiating the next kiss.

"You weren't paying close enough attention." She plucked at the buttons of his shirt.

Losing track of the argument, he returned the favor, separating the fabric of her blouse and sliding his hand beneath it. "Oh, yes, I was," he breathed, inhaling deeply. "I remember every square inch of your skin."

"Every single one?"

"Yeah."

"You want to see them again?"

He spared one more worried glance at the boats bobbing just offshore. It was getting pretty dark. If he spread his coat behind the skirt of the tablecloth, her modesty would be well protected.

Curtis wouldn't let any of the staff come back down unless Daniel called for them.

"Yes," he answered, making the only possible decision. "Oh, yes."

Amanda pulled back, shifting so that she straddled his lap. Then she gave him a saucy, mischievous grin and slowly peeled away the wet fabric of her blouse, baring her breasts.

Lightning flashed, and her alabaster skin glowed slick in the white light.

His world stilled. Unable to stop himself, he leaned forward and kissed one breast, then the other, tasting her delicate skin, testing the texture with his tongue, drawing out the moment, second after exquisite second. Her skin was as sweet as he remembered. He used to crave her taste, revel in her scent, count the minutes until he could hold her and become one with her.

The raindrops clattered, and the waves roared onto the shore. The thunder rumbled the very earth beneath them, but he blanked out everything but the gorgeous woman in his arms. Her skin was slick and wet, and impossibly smooth. Her murmurs of encouragement stoked his desire.

He couldn't stop holding her, but he *had* to make love to her. He finally stood, lifting her with him and holding her close. Her legs wrapped around his waist, and she burrowed her face in his neck, lips suckling, tongue laving his sensitive skin.

He lowered her feet to the sand, kissing her deeply as he flicked his coat out on the wet beach.

She stepped back, peeling away the rest of her wet clothes, and the lightning flashes gave him tantalizing glimpses of her naked body—her rounded breasts, the tight pink nipples, her smooth stomach and the dark triangle that led between her legs.

Every muscle in his body grew taut, and he reached out a trembling hand to cup her hip.

It was like the Boca Royce pool, only better than the pool. Her curves were wet and smooth and ripe, but this time he could touch her. He could hold her. He could make the world melt away between them.

"You're gorgeous," he whispered, slowly drawing her toward him. His arms wrapped around her naked body, and raw lust overtook his system. There was something incredibly erotic about a naked woman on a dark, windswept beach. For a split second he wondered why they'd never done this before.

Then, impatient, he laid her back on the blanket of his coat, shucking his clothes, following her down, putting them out of the wind, behind the protection of the tablecloth.

She smiled at his nakedness, her gaze caressing his entire body. Then she reached for him, twining her fingers in his damp hair, cupping his face and urging him down for a long, searing kiss.

The raindrops practically sizzled against his heated skin. She was the sexiest, most amazing woman alive, and it was all he could do to keep from taking her in the next five seconds.

He gulped in mouthfuls of salt air and steeled himself against the onslaught of desire.

"I've missed you," she whispered.

A steel band tightened around his chest, and he thought it might explode. He cupped her face, kissing her sweet lips, absorbing her taste, reveling in her feel. "Oh, Amanda, this is so…"

"Real?"

He nodded.

Her hair was tangled with wet sand, her makeup was smeared in a rainbow, and droplets of water trickled over her cheeks. But he'd never seen a more beautiful woman. Sensation washed over him with the beat of the waves. "I remember."

"Me, too. I remember you were wonderful."

"I remember you were beautiful."

Her hands tightened on his upper arms. "I want you. Right now."

He shook his head. "Not yet." There was nothing he wanted more. And nothing would stop him, nothing could possibly come between them.

But he had to make this last. He had to imprint her on his brain all over again. There'd be many long, lonely nights ahead, and he wanted hot memories to see him through.

He was selfish, he knew. But he couldn't help himself.

He cupped her breast, feeling the press of her taut nipple against his palm.

She moaned.

"You like?" he asked.

She nodded her head.

He brushed a thumb across the crest, and her fingertips convulsed against him.

Her response was fuel to his fire, and he let his hands and lips roam free, changing her breathing to gasps and pants, reveling in his ability to please her.

He trailed his fingers up her thigh, finding the core of her heat, groaning aloud as he pressed into her softness. She welcomed him with a flex of her hips, and her mocha eyes went wide.

"Oh, Daniel."

"I know." He kissed her deeply. "I know. Just go with it."

She responded, running her fingers over his chest, finding his flat nipples, his navel, his abdomen, and sending shock waves straight through his body.

Then her cool, small hands roamed farther, grasping him, stroking him, urging him.

He shifted above her.

"Now," she asked again, tightening her grip.

His only response was a guttural groan. He pushed her thighs apart, kissing her lips, her cheeks, her eyes as he pressed inside her inch by careful inch.

She gasped his name.

He almost shouted "I love you." But that was a different time, a different place.

"Amanda," he gasped instead, surging into a rhythm as her hips rocked forward and her legs locked around his waist.

He cupped her breast, and she gripped his shoulders, her nails digging into his skin. Her head dropped back and she scrunched her eyes shut.

The thunder rumbled and the waves crashed their furor.

There could have been an armada of paparazzi moored in the bay and he couldn't have cared less. She was his. After all these years, she was his once again.

Her teeth clamped down on her bottom lip, and her breathing became ragged. He could feel her body arching against him, straining, struggling.

He waited, waited, waited.

"Daniel!" she cried, and he let himself go.

The lightning melted the sky and the earth shook with the force of his release.

When it was over, they lay gasping in each other's arms. Daniel supported himself on his elbows, using his body heat to keep her warm.

He kissed her forehead and lingered there, because he simply couldn't resist. He knew they should get dressed and go up to the house to dry off, but he didn't have it in him to let her out of his arms.

She smiled, her eyes still closed. "I just love spontaneity."

His heart contracted on the word *love*. But that wasn't what she meant. He brushed a lock of gritty hair from her check. "What makes you think I didn't plan this?"

Her eyes popped open. "You did not."

"Sure, I did."

"Daniel, this is not a plan you would make."

He nodded. "What's more, you planned it, too."

"Dream on."

"Counselor, are you trying to tell me you didn't plan to make love with me tonight?"

"I didn't know when, and I didn't know how."

He shifted his weight and leaned on one elbow. "That's still a plan."

She wiggled as cool air blew between their bodies and the slowing rain trickled over their hot skin. "No, that's an idea."

"Semantics."

"Philosophy."

He chuckled. "Admit it, your philosophy's not that much different than mine."

She shifted on his wrinkled coat, propping on her elbow, a gleam in her eye. "You think? Okay. Let's talk philosophy. Tell me again why you want to be CEO?"

He groped for his dress shirt, shook it out with one hand and draped it over her. "The corner office."

"You already have a corner office."

"Yeah, but this one's on the twenty-third floor."

"Weak, Daniel. Very weak."

"You're making more of this than actually exists."

She shook her head. "No, I'm not. Your father told you to fight for the CEO job."

"And I'm fighting because *I* want it. Not because somebody told me to want it." But even as he made the argument, he felt a crack in it.

Had he ever thought about becoming CEO before his father had issued the challenge? He'd jumped right in, along with his three siblings, but he'd never stopped to analyze the decision.

Amanda continued to challenge him. "Tell me the last thing you aspired to that wasn't suggested by someone else."

He focused on her earnest face. "Changing the employee manual."

Amanda made a negative buzzer sound. "That was my idea."

"Not specifically."

"But generally. You remember prom night?"

He tucked his shirt closer around her. "In detail."

"You remember your adventure magazine plan?"

"Of course."

She traced a fingertip along the ridge of his bicep, and suddenly his body was awash in heat. "That was you, Daniel. That was *all* you."

He nodded, thinking she was proving his point rather than her own.

"What happened to that?" she asked.

What a crazy question. "Bryan happened to it. *You* happened to it."

"You ever think about where you'd be if you'd done it anyway?"

Daniel shifted his gaze past the top of her head to the black cliffs and the faint lights of the mansion. "No," he lied.

"Never?"

He shrugged. "What's the point?"

She curled into a sitting position, his shirt falling to her lap. "There's every point. I wonder all the time what would have happened if I'd told Patrick to take a flying leap."

"A flying leap to where?"

She flipped her damp hair back. "You know. Told him to bugger off. Gone to court over Bryan, and sent you off to Africa or the Middle East."

A chill formed deep inside Daniel. Gone to court?

"Maybe he was bluffing." She got a faraway look, and Daniel pushed into a sitting position.

A sense of dread crept along his veins. "Bluffing how?"

Amanda bit her lower lip, a bleak vulnerability coming into her eyes. "You think a judge would have taken a baby away from its mother? Even back then?"

Daniel's throat went dry. He shook his head, sure he couldn't be hearing what he thought he was hearing. "Patrick threatened to take Bryan away from you?" he rasped.

"Yeah…" Her brown eyes darkened. She squinted at Daniel. "You didn't—"

He shot to his feet and paced down the sand before pivoting on his heel and raking a hand through his wet hair. "My father threatened to take Bryan away from you?"

She stood up. "It was a long time ago. I thought you…"

His hands tightened into fists as every muscle in his body clenched. "You thought I knew?"

She nodded. Then she shook her head. "I'm sorry. I shouldn't have brought it up. You're right, there's no point in discussing what-ifs."

Daniel forced himself to take three deep breaths. It wasn't Amanda's fault, nothing was Amanda's fault. She'd been forced to marry him.

This answered *so* many questions. All those years, she'd let herself be kept hostage for the sake of her children. It was a wonder she'd lasted as long as she did.

In an instant, Daniel knew Amanda was right. Patrick was more insidious than he had ever imagined. What else had he done? How much manipulation went on in the Elliott family?

Did Daniel want to become CEO?

He had nothing against being CEO. But was being CEO where he wanted to put all his effort, all his energy, all his time?

Not a question he could answer at the moment, and not one he had any intention of pondering while Amanda was shivering on a beach.

He drew a cleansing breath and moved toward her. "I'm the one who's sorry," he said, gently drawing her into his embrace. "My father should *not* have done that. I had no idea you'd been blackmailed."

She shivered in his arms. "It was a long time ago."

He nodded against the top of her head, kissing her sand-gritty hair. "It was a long time ago."

She tipped her chin to look up at him. "Can we do spontaneity again sometime?"

He stroked a hand over her hair. "Anytime, anyplace."

Her lips curved into a brilliant smile.

Daniel gritted his teeth as he crossed the twenty-third floor to his father's office at eight o'clock on Monday. He would have confronted him last night, but he didn't want to do this in front of his mother.

"Hello, Daniel," Patrick's secretary greeted.

"I need to see him," said Daniel. "Now."

"I'm afraid that's not possible."

"Take a good look at my expression. Now."

Mrs. Bitton pulled her glasses down the bridge of her nose. "Take a good look at my expression."

Normally, Mrs. Bitton intimidated the hell out of Daniel, but not today.

"Pull him out," said Daniel.

An unexpected grin tugged at the corner of her mouth. "Bad idea."

"I really don't give a damn what he's doing."

"He's at thirty-thousand feet over Texas."

Daniel paused. "When does he get in?"

"He'll be here at two. But he's meeting with the art director."

"Rebook."

"Daniel—"

"Look into my eyes, Mrs. Bitton."

She paused. "I can put it off until two-thirty."

Daniel gave her a sharp nod. "Good enough."

Amanda knew it was barely twelve hours since they'd left the beach. But Daniel *had* said anytime, anyplace. Plus, now that she'd wedged the door open a crack, she was determined to drag him out of his regimented little world.

She paused at Nancy's desk, holding up the bag of Buster Burgers. "Is he free?"

Nancy's eyes lit up and her lips curved into an amazed smile. She pressed her intercom button. "Mrs. Elliott to see you."

There was a silent pause. "Fine," said Daniel, his voice abrupt.

Amanda hesitated, but Nancy waved her toward the door. "Don't worry about it. He's having a tense morning. You'll cheer him up."

Amanda headed across the outer office. She sure hoped she would. Slipping through the door, she flipped the lock behind her.

Daniel glanced up from his desk.

His eyes widened, and he drew back. "Amanda?"

"Who were you expecting?"

He shook his head and stood up. "Nobody. Nothing." He rounded the wide, thankfully empty desk. "I'm glad you're here."

"Good. I brought lunch."

He looked down at the bag, and his eyebrows shot up. "Buster Burgers?"

"Ever tried one?"

"Can't say that I have."

She dropped the bag on his desk. "They're to die for."

His glance strayed past her. "You locked the door?"

She sidled up to him. "I locked the door." She ran her fingertips down his silver silk tie. "You did say anytime, anyplace."

His jaw dropped, and his hands closed over hers, stilling them. "Amanda."

She grinned. "This is anytime. This is anyplace. And I'm here for spontaneity."

"Yeah, right."

She shook her head and freed her hands, going to work on the knot of his tie.

"Are you nuts?"

"No."

"What if somebody—"

"Have a little faith in Nancy."

"But—"

She ran her tongue around the rim of her lips and gazed

deeply into his blue eyes. "I've been wanting to do you on the desktop since the first time you walked into my office."

His jaw worked, but no sound came out.

She pulled off his tie and started on his buttons.

"You want burgers first?" she asked, leaning forward to give him a hot, wet kiss on the chest. "Or you want me?"

He made a sound that was half groan, half curse and his arms wrapped tightly around her waist. He kissed her hair, murmuring her name over and over.

"We can be quick," she assured him, kicking off her shoes. "I'm alfresco under this skirt."

He dipped his head to kiss her mouth.

She opened wide, and liquid desire poured through her system. She pushed his shirt out of the way, reveling in the feel of his hot skin against her fingertips.

He held her close, while one hand snaked its way up her thigh.

He groaned when he reached her bare buttocks. Then he turned her and lifted her onto the desk, pushing her skirt out of the way without breaking their kiss.

He slipped his hands over her thighs, sensitizing her skin. Then he reached around to caress her bottom.

"What you do to me," he murmured as he massaged and kneaded, making her squirm against the smooth wood.

"What you do back," she breathed, burying her face in his neck, inhaling his scent.

"But I'm a little busy right now." His fingertips danced their way between her legs, tickling, teasing, tantalizing. "And I'm not sure this is the time or place—"

"Don't mess with me." She scrunched forward, urging his explorations to go further.

"Like you're not messing with me?"

"It's for your own good," she gasped, reaching down to press his hand into her.

He disentangled himself, but then dropped to his knees. "My own good?" He feathered light kisses along her inner thigh.

She sank back on her elbows. "Okay, this part's for my own good." Her muscles started to melt.

He chuckled against her, and moved higher, higher still, and then his voice vibrated on her tender flesh. "I think there's a company rule against this."

"Don't you dare stop."

"Maybe even two."

"Daniel."

He chuckled again, and then he kissed her, hard and deep, and a little bit of heaven zapped right down into *Snap*. She sucked in gulps of air, gripping the edge of the desk as he nearly drove her out of her mind.

She was soaring, flying, cresting…

Then she realized what he was doing, and she jerked away.

"What?" He looked up.

"Uh-uh." She sat up straight, latched on to his shoulders and pulled.

"You done?" he asked, slowly rising.

"Hardly." She went after the button on his slacks.

He grabbed her hand to stop her.

But she stroked him through the fabric and he groaned, grasping the edge of the desk with his free hand.

"You're mine, Daniel," she vowed.

"I can't…" He gritted his teeth, and the hand stopping her relaxed.

She popped the button. His zipper slid down easily, and her hand contacted searing hot flesh.

"Amanda—"

"Do me on the desktop, Daniel," she purred.

"You're out of your—"

She squeezed. "Now."

He swore.

She pressed forward, bringing him against her, guiding him inside her.

He swore again, but it sounded like a prayer, and he gathered her to him with a groan of surrender.

He slipped his hands right under her bottom, holding her in place while his body thrust, and his muscles bunched beneath his suit jacket, turning to tempered steel.

He whispered of how she looked, how she felt, how she tasted. She reveled in his words, his touch, his scent.

She lost track of time as the tension mounted and the room spun around. She frantically kissed his mouth, tangling with his tongue. His fingers dug into her as he groaned her name and jerked harder and harder against her.

Sensation radiated out like fireworks, and she slipped off the edge of the world, her body contracting over and over and over again.

When their heartbeats finally slowed, his hands were tangled in her hair. He gently kissed her temple, stroking his knuckles down her cheek.

"I'm beginning to love spontaneity," he breathed.

"You give a whole new meaning to the word," she admitted.

His chest puffed against her.

"Burger?" she asked.

Daniel laughed deep in his throat, and his arms contracted around her. "There's a bathroom through that door." He pointed. "If you want to freshen up."

She kissed his mouth. "Yeah."

He kissed her back. "Okay."

She kissed him again. "Hope you like cola."

He kissed her. "Sure."

She kissed him, and this time they lingered. "I guess we don't have time to do it again, huh?" she asked.

"Not and eat the burgers."

"You don't want to miss the burgers."

He stepped back, and she slid off the desk.

While she washed, and combed her hair, she could hear Daniel unpacking their lunch.

On the way back through the office, she scooped his tie from where it dangled over the back of a guest chair and looped it around her neck.

Daniel handed her a burger, taking the guest chair beside her.

"These aren't bad," he said after the first bite.

"Would I steer you wrong?" The waxed paper crackled as she unwrapped hers.

"Apparently not. Where did you get them?"

"Across the street. You know it's a national chain, right?"

"Really?"

She shook her head and laughed lightly. "There's a whole world out there you've never seen."

He stopped eating and gave her an intense stare. "You want to show it to me?"

Amanda felt a surge of guilt. He was coming around. He was willing to meet her halfway, to experience new things. And she still hadn't budged.

It wasn't Daniel's fault that Patrick was a Machiavellian genius. More than any of his siblings, Daniel had tried to exert his independence. And the fact that Bryan was the only Elliott who'd succeeded in breaking free was partly thanks to Daniel.

She swallowed, making a decision. "Only if you'll agree to show me your world."

He crumpled his wrapper and tossed it into the trash. "What do you want to see first? Paris? Rome? Sydney?"

"I was thinking more along the lines of The Met."

"You've already been to The Met."

"But you can get better tickets."

"*La Bohème,* followed by pizza?"

Amanda laughed and stood up, tossing her own wrapper in the trash. "I've got an appointment at one," she told him.

He moved in front of her, kissing her gently on the lips and reaching for his tie.

"Uh-uh." She shook her head and held the tie fast. "Souvenir."

"Fine," he agreed easily.

While she gathered her purse and took a last drink, he moved around the desk. He opened a drawer and extracted another tie.

Amanda dropped her paper cup in the bin and followed him around. She commandeered the second tie.

"Hey!"

"No tie."

He grabbed for it, but she backed away.

"What do you mean no tie?"

She looped the second one around her neck. "Price you pay for spontaneity."

"Nancy's going to know what happened."

Amanda shot him a grin. "Yeah, she will."

He took a step toward her. "Amanda—"

"Call me." She quickly scooted out the door.

Eleven

At precisely two o'clock, Daniel strode into his father's outer office. Making love with Amanda had taken the edge off his anger. Making love with Amanda had taken the edge off everything.

But then, making love with her had also reminded him all over again how cruelly his father had manipulated a frightened, pregnant teenager.

"Is he here?" Daniel asked Mrs. Bitton, barely breaking his stride.

"He's expecting you," she answered.

Daniel swung the door wide, then shut it firmly behind him.

His father didn't look up from the papers he was signing. "Do we have some kind of a problem?"

Daniel took a few steps into the office, struggling to keep a rein on his temper. "Yes, we have some kind of a problem."

Patrick glanced up. "And that would be…?"

"You blackmailed Amanda."

Patrick didn't flinch. "I haven't said more than three words to her in sixteen years."

Daniel took two more paces. "You threatened to take Bryan away from her." His voice rose, nearly shaking. "How could you do that? She was eighteen, pregnant, defenseless."

Patrick set down his pen and squared his shoulders. "I did what was best for the family."

Daniel smacked his palms on the desktop. "Best for you, yes. Best for the family, maybe. Best for Amanda? I don't think so."

"Amanda wasn't my responsibility."

"Amanda is my *wife!*" Daniel shouted.

"*Was* your wife."

Daniel clamped his jaw and sucked in a breath.

Patrick rose to his feet. "This is ancient history, Daniel. And I have a meeting."

"Don't you dare."

"Don't I *dare?*"

Daniel pointed a finger at his father's chest. Strangely, the man who had intimidated him all his life didn't look so intimidating now. "We're not finished with this conversation."

Patrick started around the desk. "We are *definitely* finished with this conversation, and you're damn lucky you still have a job."

Daniel stepped sideways, blocking his father's exit, folding his arms over his chest. "You are going to apologize to Amanda."

Patrick's eyes glittered and a muscle ticked in one jaw. "Amanda made her choice."

"You gave her *no* choice."

"She chose to sleep with you."

"You know nothing about what happened that night."

"Are you telling me she was unwilling?"

Something exploded in Daniel's brain. He doubled up his fists and leaned in. "Are you suggesting I raped her?"

"Did you?"

"No! Of course not!"

"Then she made her choice. There was a baby. An *Elliott* baby. I protected the family, and that's all I'm going to say on the matter." Patrick started to go around Daniel.

This time Daniel didn't stop him. His voice dropped to a growl. "You betrayed her, and you betrayed me."

Patrick's voice shook with anger. "I *protected* this family."

Daniel pivoted to glare at him. "You were wrong."

Patrick stared back for a long moment, then he walked out of the office.

Daniel hadn't had it in him to work the rest of the day. Going home held no appeal, and he was too upset to call Amanda.

He ended up at the family table at Une Nuit, Bryan's restaurant. Bryan wasn't there—just as well. Daniel was content to hunch in a dim corner and sip on his second single malt. He had a lot of thinking to do.

"Hey, bro." Michael slid into the chair in front of him.

"Hey," Daniel answered, checking to see if anyone was with Michael. He really didn't feel like company at the moment.

"Heard you reamed out the boss." Michael signaled to the manager for his usual drink.

Daniel nodded. He wondered how accurately the gossip had spread.

"Business matter?" asked Michael.

"Personal," said Daniel.

Michael accepted a martini from a waiter. "Amanda?"

Daniel squinted. "What did you hear?"

"That you ordered Mrs. Bitton to reschedule Dad's meeting—nice one, by the way—and that you went up one side of him and down the other." Michael took a swig of his drink. "And you're still standing."

"Still employed, too." Daniel was pretty amazed about that. Not that he'd cared at the time.

Michael snagged the olive from his martini and popped it into his mouth. "Only person I can think of that would make you go off like that is Amanda."

Daniel banged his heavy scotch glass on the table. "He threatened to take Bryan away from her if she didn't marry me."

Michael was silent for a moment. "I know."

"You *know?*"

Michael nodded. "He was afraid it would kill Mom to lose her grandchild."

"Why didn't you say something?"

"I was keeping my head low at the time. Remember, I was the guy who got you the suite."

"But later?"

"Later you two seemed happy. Then, when things fell apart, it hardly seemed like the kind of information that would help."

Daniel rocked back in his chair. "It was unconscionable."

Their brother Shane appeared and slid into the seat next to Daniel. "What was unconscionable?"

"Dad blackmailed Amanda into marrying Daniel," said Michael.

"When?" asked Shane.

Daniel turned to give his younger brother an amazed look. "In high school."

"Oh, that time."

"Was there another time?" Daniel asked.

"How'd he blackmail her?" asked Shane, ignoring his brother's comment.

Daniel chugged the last of his scotch, still seeing red at the thought of his father's actions. "He threatened to take Bryan away. He forced her to marry me in order to keep her baby."

Again, on cue, their sister Finola appeared and sat down next to Michael. "Could've been worse," she said.

Her three brothers' gazes swung her way.

Then they all went silent, remembering that Patrick had forced Finola to give up her own baby at fifteen.

Shane reached across the table and took his twin sister's hand. "Yeah, it could've."

"Aw, Fin," said Daniel, feeling like a jerk. At least he'd had the chance to raise Bryan.

Michael signaled for a round of drinks. "You ever wonder if this family needs therapy?"

Finola turned to look at her oldest brother, twin tears refusing to spill over her lashes. "What do you mean *wonder?* We're scrapping it out like a pack of dogs for our father's job."

Daniel dumped a sliver of ice into his mouth. "After this afternoon, it might be a three-way race."

Shane scoffed out a laugh. "What in the hell did you do?"

"I yelled at him," said Daniel.

"You *yelled* at Dad?" asked Finola, amazement clear in her voice.

"I ordered him to apologize to Amanda. I may have stopped him from leaving his office there for a minute, too."

"Bodily?" asked Michael.

"No blows were exchanged," said Daniel with a dark laugh.

Shane chuckled along with him.

"It may be a two-way race," said Michael.

Everyone turned their attention to him.

"With Karen's health I just don't have the energy for this. She needs me, and I am going to be there for her."

"Maybe I'll back out, too," said Shane.

"What are you talking about?" Michael asked Shane. "You have no reason to back out."

The waiter arrived and set drinks out all around.

"Don't be ridiculous," Finola said to Shane. "You love your job."

"I may love the job, but I hate being manipulated. He's hurt us all. At one time or another, he's screwed up everyone's life."

The other three nodded.

Daniel felt as though blinders had been peeled away from his eyes, and they could never be put back.

"When he made me take the job," said Daniel, "when Bryan was sick, and he told me it was the only way to clear the bills, it was the worst mistake I ever made." He pushed aside the memory of Bryan's heart defect, not wanting to relive the tense time before the surgery made his son whole.

Finola cocked her head. "But if you hadn't come back—"

"Amanda and I might still be married."

"Impoverished," said Michael.

"But married," said Shane, lifting his highball. "Chuck it, Daniel. Chuck it all and marry Amanda."

"Whoa," said Michael. "How'd we get there?"

Daniel laughed, but a small corner of his brain told him to take Shane seriously.

"You're bitter," Finola said to Shane.

Shane leaned forward and stage-whispered to his twin, "I'm cutting back the field. I'd rather have you in charge than Daniel."

Daniel elbowed Shane. "Hey. Why?"

"She likes me better than you do," Shane said to his brother.

"That's true enough," said Daniel.

Michael chomped down on his second olive. He waggled his eyebrows in Daniel's direction. "I don't think we can just let Finola walk away with it."

"Hell no," Daniel chuckled. "She's a girl."

Finola bristled. "Here we go again."

Amanda blinked, just to make sure it really was Sharon Elliott standing in her office doorway.

"Surprise," said Sharon, sauntering into the office in impossibly high heels, a black denim skirt and a black-and-white cropped sweater. Her hair was pulled back in a slick knot and her makeup was as bold as the outfit.

Julie made a face behind the woman's back and pulled the door shut.

Amanda closed her case file and came to her feet. "Can I help you with something?"

"Actually, it's me who's here to help you." Sharon pulled her deep red lips into a smile and sat down in one of the guest chairs, tucking her purse in the space beside her.

"Uh, thank you," said Amanda, dropping into her seat.

Sharon sat forward, jiggling her diamond teardrop earrings. The jeweled rings on her fingers flashed as she folded her hands. "I know what you're doing."

"You do?" Amanda was preparing closing arguments for the Spodek case, but she doubted that was what Sharon was talking about.

Sharon nodded. "And I can respect it."

"Thank you."

"But I think you might be fishing in the wrong pond."

"Oh?"

"Daniel is, let's say, challenging."

"Let's say." Amanda hoped being agreeable would get Sharon out of her office sooner.

Sharon reached for her purse, snapping open the clasp and retrieving a folded piece of paper. "I've taken the liberty of coming up with a list of potential men."

"For what?" asked Amanda.

"To date," said Sharon. She unfolded the paper, pasting on a just-between-us-girls smile. "They're all good-looking, intelligent, available and, most importantly, rich."

She held out the paper to Amanda.

Amanda gingerly took it. "You're showing me a list of your dates?"

Sharon's head tipped sideways, and her laughter tinkled though the office. "Not my dates," she said. "Yours."

Amanda dropped the paper. "*What?*"

Sharon shook her head. "Honey, Daniel is never going to fall for you again. Consider this a gift from one jilted wife to another."

Ah. It all made sense now. "I take it you want him back?"

"Me?" Sharon laughed again. It really was a lovely laugh. Probably lured men to their deaths all the time. "I'm not trying to get him back."

Sure, she wasn't. Sharon had decided to become dating.com out of the goodness of her heart.

Oh, wait. Sharon didn't have a heart. Which meant she was lying. She wanted Daniel back.

"Once you're on the outs with Patrick, you're on the outs," said Sharon.

Amanda supposed that was true enough.

"Though there was a time," Sharon continued, "that Patrick just couldn't get enough of me."

Amanda gave her head a little shake. "You *slept* with Patrick?"

"Of course not." Sharon dramatically fluttered her fingers against her chest. "He recruited me for Daniel. He knew exactly what he wanted in a daughter-in-law."

"And he got it," Amanda muttered, knowing Sharon was exactly what Patrick would have ordered.

"For a while." Sharon sighed. "Now, back to the list." She stood up and bent over to read upside down. "Giorgio is nice, not too tall, but very well-groomed. He has a penthouse overlooking the park, and—"

"Thank you," said Amanda, folding the list closed again. "But I'm not looking to date anyone."

Sharon straightened, her mouth drooping into a little-girl pout. "But—"

"I'm afraid I'm very busy." Amanda held out the list.

Sharon didn't take it. "You're dating Daniel."

"Not really." She was only sleeping with Daniel. That was

as far as the relationship was likely to go. Sharon was right about one thing, though: to get Daniel, first you needed Patrick.

The door opened, and Julie stuck her head in. "Amanda?"

Amanda could have kissed her receptionist.

"There's someone here to see you." Julie actually seemed flustered.

Amanda didn't care who it was, just so long as they got Sharon out of the office.

Amanda tucked the list into Sharon's hand. "Thanks for stopping by."

Julie opened the door wider.

Sharon glanced from one woman to the other. For a second, Amanda thought she was going to refuse to leave. But then she gritted her teeth, stood as tall as she was able and stalked to the door.

Suddenly, she halted in the doorway and swiveled her head to look back at Amanda. "It appears I underestimated you."

Before Amanda could decipher the cryptic message, Sharon was gone, and Patrick Elliott himself was entering the office.

She squeaked out a desperate signal to Julie, but Julie had already scooted out of the way.

"Amanda." Patrick's nod was terse as the door closed behind him.

"Mr. Elliott." Amanda nodded in return, her stomach clenching reflexively against her backbone. She couldn't remember the last time she'd been alone with him.

"Please, call me Patrick."

"All right." Now she was even more off balance.

He gestured to the guest chairs. "May I sit down?"

"Of course."

He waited, and she realized he expected her to sit first. She did, surreptitiously wiping her damp palms over her slacks.

He then took his own seat. "I'll get right to the point. My son tells me I owe you an apology."

Amanda opened her mouth. But then his words registered, and she promptly shut it again. She stared in silence at the man she'd feared for decades.

"I disagree with Daniel," Patrick continued. "I am not sorry."

Amanda let out her breath.

Okay, now he was sounding like himself. His hair might have gone completely white, and the line of his chin might have softened. But his ice-blue eyes were as shrewd as ever. The last thing in the world he'd do was arrive at her law office, hat in hand, begging for forgiveness.

"I'm not sorry I kept Bryan in the family," he continued. "And I'm not sorry I ensured Maeve had her grandchild. But I am sorry…" He paused, and his blue eyes thawed ever so slightly. "I am sorry that I didn't have your best interests at heart."

Amanda gave her head a little shake. Her ears must have been playing tricks on her. Had Patrick Elliott just apologized?

The corners of his mouth turned up. But it looked more like a grimace than a smile.

"It was a long time ago," said Amanda, realizing belatedly that she should have thanked him. Maybe. What on earth was the proper etiquette in these circumstances?

He nodded. "It was a long time ago. But Daniel's right. You were alone and frightened and I took advantage." He held up his palms. "Oh, I know I did the right thing. On balance, Bryan deserved to grow up an Elliott every bit as much as we deserved to know our grandchild. But…" His mouth pursed. "Let's just say I didn't have the same appreciation for collateral damage back then."

Amanda's spine stiffened ever so slightly. "Is that what you considered me? Collateral damage?"

Could a person actually live and breathe this many years without a soul?

"I considered your circumstance…unfortunate," he said.

"Yet you played God." Despite his apology, decades of anger surged through her bloodstream. She hadn't deserved his manipulation then. And Daniel didn't deserve his manipulation now. Neither did his other children or his grandchildren.

"I don't consider myself God," said Patrick.

Her tone was bitter. "Then why do you act like it?"

He stood up. "I believe this meeting is over."

"I'm serious, Patrick." She couldn't let it go. She knew deep down inside that this was her one and only chance to save Daniel, maybe to save Cullen and Bryan. "You have to stop."

His brow furrowed. "Stop what?"

"Holding on to your family with an iron fist."

"I guess you haven't heard. I'm stepping down as CEO."

She gave a scoffing laugh. "While making them pawns in your emotional chess game."

"Is that what you think I'm doing?"

"Isn't it?"

They stared at each other in silence for a moment.

"With all due respect, Amanda, I don't have to explain myself to you."

"You're right. You don't. But you'll eventually have to explain yourself to Daniel." Amanda shook her head. "One day he'll wake up. One day he'll see you for what you are."

"I think that day was today."

"Then you see my point."

Patrick considered her for a long moment. "No. But I think I see something else."

She waited.

"I think I see what you are to Daniel."

Amanda drew back. "What?" Did he know about their affair?

Patrick ran his knuckles along the back of her guest chair. "It seems my mistake wasn't in making you marry him. My mistake was in letting you divorce him."

"Letting me—"

"He still needs you, Amanda." Patrick gave a calculating smile, and it was even more frightening than his frown.

"Back off, Patrick."

"No, Amanda, I don't believe I will. Good day."

Twelve

Daniel figured it would take at least one lap around Central Park to work up his courage. And it might take another lap to convince Amanda they had a chance.

He pocketed the three carat diamond ring and double-checked the champagne he'd stashed under the seat of the carriage.

Julie had been a willing accomplice in getting Amanda to the park entrance at the right time. He didn't know what methods she'd used, but he could already see the two women walking up Sixty-Seventh Street.

He adjusted his tie, patted the square bulge in his breast pocket and started toward them along the crowded sidewalk.

"Amanda," he greeted.

"Daniel?"

"Gotta go," said Julie, quickly melting away.

Amanda spun toward the sound of Julie's voice. "What—"

"She must have had something to do," said Daniel, taking Amanda's arm and steering her around a cluster of tourists.

Amanda skipped a step, coming into pace with him, craning her neck. "She wanted me to look at a pair of shoes."

"Maybe she changed her mind." He slid his hand down to grasp hers.

Amanda blinked up at him dubiously. "Where did you come from?"

He jabbed over his shoulder with his thumb. "The park."

"Were you out walking?"

Daniel nodded. That seemed like as good a story as any.

He smiled down at her, and lowered his voice, ignoring the crowds parting around them.

"I missed you," he said, squeezing her hand.

Her expression relaxed, and her mocha eyes glinted with mischief. "I could stop by the office again."

He moved in closer. "I'll buy another tie."

She grinned, and he grinned right back, feeling giddy as a kid on Christmas morning.

She'd agree to marry him.

She *had* to agree to marry him.

Then they could make love every night, wake up together every morning, visit their grandchildren and grow old together. He lifted her hand and kissed her knuckles.

Daniel suddenly wanted nothing more than to grow old with Amanda.

Well, there was one other thing. But they could talk about that after he convinced her to marry him. He had a feeling she'd be in support of his career move.

"Or you could come to my office." She pulled their clasped hands toward her lips and kissed him back. "I've had this fantasy…"

"Oh, I like the sound of that."

Her expression turned slumberous.

"For now," he said, drawing back, forcing himself to concentrate on the proposal instead of future lovemaking, "I have a little fantasy of my own."

"Is it sexual?"

"Better than that. It's spontaneous."

She quirked an eyebrow.

"Come on." He tugged her through pedestrian traffic and into the park.

He stopped next to the reserved carriage.

"Hop in," he said to Amanda.

"*This* is your fantasy?"

"You're going to get picky on me?"

She shook her head. "No. No, of course not."

"Then hop in." He offered her a hand up.

She put one foot on the running board and stepped into the carriage.

He followed her up, closed the half door and signaled to the driver to start.

The horse's hooves clip-clopped on the pavement. Dusk was falling over the city, and skyscraper lights began to illuminate the skies. The trees around Tavern on the Green lit up as they passed.

Daniel stretched his arm across the back of the seat.

"It's beautiful at night," said Amanda.

He wrapped his arm around her shoulder. "You're what's beautiful out here."

"Yeah, yeah. You use that line often?"

"Nope."

She scoffed in disbelief.

"Hey, how often do you think I take women riding through the park?"

She turned to look at him. "I don't know. How often?"

"Rarely."

"But you have done it before."

"You're saying spontaneity only counts if it's a brand-new activity?"

"No. But you get bonus points for a brand-new activity."

"I wish you'd told me that earlier."

She laughed and leaned her head on his shoulder.

He felt her chest rise and fall as she breathed. Suddenly, his world felt perfect.

He kissed the top of her head and took her hand in his across their laps.

The sounds of the city faded, and the horse's hooves, the squeak of the carriage and the jangle of the harness brass filled the night.

He wanted to ask her the question, but first he wanted the ride to last forever.

"Champagne?" he muttered against her hair.

She sat up straighter. "Where are we going to get champagne."

He gave her an eyebrow waggle, pushed aside the lap robe and revealed the cooler. He popped the lid and pulled out a bottle of Laurent-Perrier along with two fluted glasses.

"Spontaneous?" she asked with a raised brow.

"I only thought of it this morning."

She shook her head, but her smile was beautiful.

He couldn't resist kissing her sweet mouth.

She wrapped her arms around his neck, eagerly participating.

"Who needs champagne?" he muttered, drawing her close and delving into the recesses of her mouth.

She pulled back and glanced pointedly at the champagne bottle. "Wouldn't want to screw up your carefully planned spontaneity."

He reached for it. "As long as you promise we can kiss later."

"We'll see."

"Would it kill you to plan *something?*"

"I like to keep my options open."

He handed her the glasses and then twisted the wire holder off the cork.

"I want you to consider me an option," he said, and popped the cork out with his thumbs.

The champagne bubbled out the top of the bottle, and Amanda laughed.

"An option tonight," said Daniel as he poured the effervescent liquid into the glasses. "And an option every night."

Her mouth pursed in confusion.

"Amanda," he breathed, wondering if he should drop to one knee. That would be the proper thing to do. But Amanda didn't have too high an opinion of doing the proper thing.

"Yes?" she prompted.

"These past few weeks...together." He took a breath. "They've meant a lot to me."

Her lips curved in a shy smile. "They've meant a lot to me, too," she said.

"I've remembered things." He glanced off into the dark trees and the city lights beyond. "I've felt things that I haven't felt in years."

He looked back into her eyes. "I've realized that my feelings for you were buried, but they hadn't changed."

"Daniel—"

He put a finger over her lips. "Shh."

He slowly drew his hand back and reached into his inside suit pocket. Retrieving the ring, he flipped the velvet case open with his thumb.

"Marry me, Amanda."

Her eyes went wide, and she sucked in a tight breath.

He rushed on before she had time to react. "I love you very much. I've never stopped loving you. I haven't been living these past fifteen years, just existing."

Her gaze shot from the ring to his face and back again.

"This is—"

"I know you think it's sudden. But we've known each other so well and for so long—"

"I was going to say, unbelievable." The tone of her voice wasn't quite right. It was flat, almost accusatory.

"Amanda?"

"He couldn't work this fast. Nobody works this fast."

Daniel stared at her. To be fair, it had been a few weeks. And they weren't exactly strangers. And they'd made love twice.

"I've given this a lot of thought."

"Have you? *Have* you?"

He flipped the conversation over in his mind, trying to figure out where it had gone off the rails. "Yeah."

She glanced at her watch. "He only left my office two hours ago."

"Who?"

She shook her head and laughed coldly. "No, Daniel. I won't marry you."

Her answer was like a stake in his heart.

"I won't be your family's pawn," she said.

Panic invaded his system as he scrambled for a way to change her mind. "How'd my family get into this?"

She dumped her champagne over the side. "Your family's been into it from the very start."

He stared at the empty glass. So that was it. He wasn't worth it.

"You're saying our love won't trump your aversion to my family?"

She dropped the empty glass into the cooler. "I'm saying take me home."

He snapped the case shut. "Right."

All night long, Amanda assured herself she'd made the right decision. Daniel didn't want to marry her. He didn't want to marry her any more than he wanted to be CEO of Elliott Publication Holdings.

Patrick had them all brainwashed, and there was nothing she could do to change that. The best she could do was save herself.

She'd definitely made the right decision.

And when her alarm clock went off, she was still telling herself just that.

She kept saying it all through her shower.

But over granola and tea she started asking questions. Scary, insidious questions.

Had she made the right decision?

Sure, Patrick was behind it, and Daniel might not have proposed again without his father's urging. But there was something there. There was magic between them. And she could have spent the rest of her life exploring it.

She dropped her granola spoon and buried her face in her hands. What if she'd made the biggest mistake of her life?

That had been one perfect ring.

It had been one perfect proposal.

And Daniel was one perfect guy.

Her arms suddenly felt empty. Ridiculous, considering she'd spent sixteen years without him and only a few weeks in his company again.

She was losing it here.

She had to get him out of her brain.

She picked up the telephone, automatically dialing Karen's number.

Olive put her right through.

"Hello?" came Karen's voice, cheerful despite the early hour.

"Karen? It's Amanda."

"Oh my God," Karen burst out. "Michael told me what happened."

"He did?"

"The whole family is talking about it."

Amanda sat back in her chair. "They are?"

"Of course they are. We can't believe it."

Amanda wasn't sure she was getting this right. Daniel had put his marriage proposal out there on the Elliott grapevine?

Unbelievable.

"Cullen overheard," said Karen. "And he called Bryan—"

"Cullen overheard what?"

Karen whistled low. "Patrick must be just fuming."

"Because I said no?"

There was a silent pause. "Because none of his children have ever dared yell at him before."

"I didn't—"

"I'd have paid money to see it. Michael said Daniel went up one side of him and down the other. Now they're all placing bets on who'll blink first."

"What do you mean who'll blink?" If they fought, they'd already made up. Because Patrick had apologized. And then he'd told Daniel to marry Amanda.

"They're no longer speaking to each other."

"No. That can't be right. They talked yesterday." In the afternoon. After Patrick had seen her. After Patrick had decided to make Daniel propose.

"No they didn't," said Karen. "Definitely not."

Amanda raked her fingers into her damp hair. This didn't make sense. Unless… Her eyes went wide. *Oh, no.*

"Amanda?" Karen's voice seemed to come from a long way off.

"I have to go."

"What—"

"I'll call you later." Amanda quickly hung up the phone. Something was seriously wrong. If Daniel hadn't talked

to Patrick, then he'd proposed all on his own. But that
couldn't be. Because that would mean...

Amanda swore out loud.

Daniel dropped the neatly typed letter on the top of his
desk. He'd pictured Amanda here for this, pictured her
smiling with pride, hanging on to his arm, making plans for
a simple wedding—maybe on a boat off Madagascar.

He was ready to give her everything she wanted, everything she'd made him want. But she hadn't even let him make
his case last night. She hadn't even listened to his plan, she'd
simply written him off along with the rest of his family.

As if Daniel didn't have a life of his own. Sure, he liked
to keep his family happy. It was usually easier to go with the
tide than to fight it.

Truth was, he hadn't really cared a whole lot since Amanda
had left him the first time.

But he'd come back to life.

She'd brought him back to life.

He was about to do every damn thing she'd ever asked of him,
and she wouldn't even give him the courtesy of a fair hearing.

He plucked a gold pen from the holder on his desk and
signed the letter of resignation with a flourish. Looked as
though he was going to Madagascar alone.

His office door burst open.

He looked up, expecting Nancy, but Amanda rushed
into the room.

She slowed her steps when she saw him, gazing quizzi-
cally, as if he'd sprouted horns.

Nancy quickly appeared behind her, clearly ready to escort
Amanda back outside.

"It's fine," said Daniel, waving his secretary away.

Nancy nodded, pulling the door closed and leaving them
alone.

"Something I can help you with?" he asked Amanda, focusing on the seascape behind her left ear. He wanted to cling to his anger, not take a good look at everything he was losing.

"I…uh…" She took another tentative step toward him. She cleared her throat. "I wanted…"

He plunked the pen back in its holder, not bothering to disguise his impatience. It was proving quite easy to hold on to his anger.

He crossed his arms over his chest, feeling strong enough to look into her dark eyes. "I'm a little busy this morning."

Her eyes were wide, liquid and strangely vulnerable, but he steeled himself against them.

She swallowed. "Why, Daniel?"

"Why what?"

She was silent for several heartbeats. "Why did you ask me to marry you?"

"I thought I made that pretty clear."

"I thought your father had talked to you."

"He talks to me all the time."

"Did he tell you to marry me?"

"Not since the seventies."

Her tone turned pleading. "Then, why?"

He shrugged. "Oh, I don't know. Since I have no brain of my own, I called one-nine-hundred, proper behavior, and they told me I should propose after the fifth—"

"Daniel."

"—date. They also suggested a carriage ride and champagne. Shipped me the ring, and gave me a wallet card full of catch phrases. You want to see it?"

"Daniel, stop."

He sighed. "I've got a big day coming up. Can you say whatever it is you came to say and get out?"

She recoiled from his anger.

Too bad. He wasn't feeling particularly charitable at the

moment. Especially not with her standing there looking so sexy and desirable, reminding him of what might have been.

"You're glaring at me," she accused.

"No, I'm not."

"Yes, you are. I can't say what I want to say with you glaring."

He let his arms drop to his sides and tried to soften his expression. Now he just wanted to get this over with. "Fine."

"I came to say I'm sorry." She moved in a little closer. "I also came to say…" She raked her teeth over her bottom lip. "That was one perfect ring."

His body went still, and her scent swirled out to tease him. She gently touched his arm, making him flinch.

"I'm sorry I misunderstood," she said. "But after your father—"

"My father?"

"He stopped at my office yesterday to apologize."

Daniel all but staggered against his desk. "My father *apologized* to you?"

"He said you told him to."

"Yeah, well…" Daniel nodded. "I did." But he never thought his father would do it. Not in a million years.

"Then he told me you still needed me. And then you showed up with a ring, and I—"

"Put two and two together?"

"And came up with seven. I'm so sorry, Daniel." Her hand trembled on his arm and she gazed into his eyes. "I really loved that ring."

A weight lifted from his shoulders. His chest tightened and his heart thudded deeply. "You saying you want it back?" He'd already returned it, but he could fix that with one phone call.

"It was perfect," she said.

"You hate perfect."

"Yeah? Well, I'm working on that." She slipped her arms

around his waist and settled her body against his. "Because you're perfect, and I really, really want you."

"I don't have the ring," he confessed.

Her eyes mirrored her disappointment.

He felt like a cad. He should have been prepared for this. He usually had contingency plans for his contingency plans.

Then his gaze caught the paper clip holding his letter of resignation.

On the other hand, he could try for spontaneity. He slipped the paper clip off and twisted it into a loop.

He held the makeshift ring out to Amanda. "But will you marry me anyway?"

She grinned and presented her finger, giving him an eager nod. "Yes. But don't think this gets you out of a big diamond and a well-planned proposal," she said.

He slipped the paper clip over her finger. "You hate it when I plan."

"I was thinking a suite at the Riverside. A few dozen roses. Champagne. A string quartet."

"Think I'll leave that one to you." He reached behind him and lifted the letter from the desktop, holding it in front of her eyes. "Because I have other plans to make."

"What's—" She adjusted the focal length and started to read. "I don't understand?"

"I'm offering Cullen my job as editor in chief."

She stared up at him. "Why?"

"I'm going traveling."

"Where?"

"Everywhere. I'll be looking into a new adventure magazine."

Her eyes went very wide. "Your father agreed?"

He shrugged his shoulders. "I don't know."

"You haven't asked him?"

"It was a spontaneous decision. You want to come along?"

A grin grew wide across her beautiful face. "You bet."

Amanda smiled to herself as she snuggled up to Daniel's bare chest.

Cullen had accepted the position of editor in chief of *Snap*, and Patrick had agreed amazingly easily to let Daniel investigate an adventure magazine for Elliott Publications. Bryan and Cullen were ecstatic about the reunion and made their parents promise to get married before they left on their travels.

They had no plans so far, but Amanda wasn't worried. Sooner or later, Daniel would give in to temptation and rent a ballroom somewhere.

She kissed his chest. "Have I mentioned lately that I love you?"

Daniel kissed the top of her head and gave her a squeeze. "Not for about thirty minutes. But that yodel thing you did was good for my ego."

She elbowed him. "I did *not* yodel."

"Sure, you did."

"Are you going to keep making stuff up?"

"Yeah."

Then he stroked her hair with his wide palm. "No more planning. From now on, I'm making stuff up as I go along."

Her chest tightened. "I don't want you to change for me."

"I'm changing for me. And partly for you, because you're the best thing I never planned. I love you, Amanda," he whispered gruffly and drew her into his arms.

The phone beside his bed interrupted their kiss.

Amanda checked the clock. "Who on earth—"

Daniel picked up the phone. "Hello? Cullen?"

Amanda sat straight up.

"Is she okay?" Then Daniel grinned. "Are *they* okay?"

They?

Daniel covered the mouthpiece. "It's a girl."

Amanda jumped out of bed and grabbed for her clothes.

"Seven pounds, six ounces," said Daniel. "Maeve Amanda Elliott."

Amanda's chest contracted and her eyes filled with tears.

"Come on," she whispered to Daniel.

"We're on our way," he laughed into the phone.

"We're grandparents," said Amanda as she climbed into her slacks.

They made it to the hospital in less than fifteen minutes.

While they stood at the nursery window, scanning name tags, trying to locate their new granddaughter, a harried Cullen burst through the swinging doors of the maternity wing.

"Mom," he cried, his yellow paper gown flapping around the knees of his pants. He immediately pulled Amanda into a tight embrace. She had to gasp for breath as he rocked her back and forth.

He kissed the top of her head, his strong voice cracking. "I can't believe what you went through for me. How can I ever thank you?"

Amanda's chest swelled, and she blinked back a sheen of tears. "You don't have to thank me," she whispered against his chest. "You were the most wonderful son in the world."

Cullen pulled back to look into her eyes. "Oh, Mom."

She grinned at him, smoothing back his damp hair from his forehead. "Congratulations, Dad."

He shook his head in disbelief.

Then he turned to Daniel and held out his hand. "And, Dad. You did this. You did this twice!"

Daniel chuckled, shaking Cullen's hand and pulling his son into an embrace.

Amanda wiped away the tears as they spilled over her lashes.

Cullen turned to gaze through the nursery glass to where

a nurse was wheeling in a bassinet. "There she is," he sighed. "Oh, she's so tiny."

"She's supposed to be tiny," said Daniel.

Amanda moved up to the window while the nurse placed the bassinet in the center of the front row, giving them a warm smile.

"I'm almost afraid to touch her," Cullen confessed.

Daniel patted him on the back. "You'll be fine, son. You'll feed her, change her and bathe her, and before you know it, she'll be begging you for bedtime stories."

Cullen gave a forced chuckle and put an arm around each of his parents. "I just hope I make it through the first twenty-four hours."

Amanda leaned her head against her son. "She's beautiful."

"She is," he agreed.

"How's Misty?" asked Daniel.

Cullen blinked rapidly. "She's perfect. She's wonderful." He drew a breath. "She's sleeping now."

"Hey, bro. Way to go!" Bryan and Lucy arrived and the three separated so Cullen could greet his brother.

Daniel shifted closer to Amanda as the Elliott family began streaming into the nursery hallway. She felt the familiar stirrings of unease as first five, then nine, then twelve of them crowded around the window, talking and joking with each other.

By the time Patrick and Maeve rounded the corner, Amanda's stomach was cramping with insecurity. What had she gotten herself into?

"It's going to be okay," Daniel whispered into her hair, sliding an arm around her waist.

But Amanda wasn't so sure.

Then Patrick gave her a nod and a smile of greeting. Karen called her name and sent her a wave across the crowd. And Daniel pulled her tight into the circle of his strong arms.

Little Maeve opened her mouth in a wide yawn, and there was a collective sigh from the assembled adults. It was obvious their hearts had melted then and there for the newest Elliott.

Amanda leaned her head against Daniel's chest and drew hope from the enduring bonds of his family. There might be bumps on the road ahead, but they were going to make it this time.

Together.

* * * * *

THE INTERN AFFAIR

BY
ROXANNE ST CLAIRE

Roxanne St Claire is an award-winning, national bestselling author of more than a dozen romance and suspense novels. Her first book for Desire™ was nominated for the prestigious RITA® Award from the Romance Writers of America, and she is also a recipient of the 2005 MAGGIE Award and multiple Awards of Excellence. In addition, her work has received numerous nominations, including the SIBA Award for Best Fiction of 2005, the National Reader's Choice Award and the Booksellers Best Award. Roxanne's first book was published in 2003, after she spent nearly two decades as a public relations and marketing executive. Today she writes full-time, while raising two preteen children and enjoying life with a real-life alpha hero. She lives on the east coast of Florida and loves to hear from readers through e-mail at roxannestc@aol.com and snail mail, care of the Space Coast Authors of Romance, PO Box 410787, Melbourne, Florida, 32941, USA. Visit her website at www.roxannestclaire.com to read excerpts, win prizes and learn more!

This one is for my dear friend Jane Palmer who
taught me never to hesitate on the great
street corner of life.

One

Cade McMann smelled trouble all around him.

At the moment, trouble smelled like honeysuckle, or at least what he imagined honeysuckle would smell like if he had the opportunity to sniff some. Sort of sweet and fresh and…inviting. And, truthfully, the scent was not all around, but definitely wafting from behind, if he wasn't mistaken.

And Cade made it a point to avoid mistakes at all costs.

Trouble cleared her throat. "Did you want to see me, Cade?"

He spun his chair around from his view of Park Avenue seventeen stories below and looked across his desk at the young woman whose expectant expression was only partially covered by the hideous horn-rimmed glasses with lavender-tinted lenses. She hadn't worn those in her interview six months ago, of that he was certain.

But since the first day of her internship at *Charisma* magazine, Jessie Clayton had hidden behind the glasses and kept her waist-length auburn hair pulled tightly back in a braid or a bun. Although, by the end of the day, some silky strands usually slipped out of their prison and caressed the creamy complexion of her cheeks. *Caressed?*

Oh, boy. Serious trouble.

He forced himself to focus on the business situation, not his suddenly poetic imagination.

"I did need to see you, Jessie." He indicated one of the empty guest chairs. "Have a seat."

She clutched a cheap vinyl-covered day planner to her chest, her gaze still on him as she sat. "Everything cool, Cade?"

No. As a matter of fact, nothing was cool when this vivacious twenty-something was in the room. A situation that a man who ran a predominately female staff and boasted of having four younger sisters didn't relish.

"Totally cool, Jessie." He let his mouth kick up in a smile as he spoke, and was rewarded with a quick and easy laugh that had become as common a sound in the cubicles of *Charisma* magazine as a ringing phone.

"Careful, Cade. You're starting to sound less like the boss and more like one of *Charisma's* loyal readers." She brushed one of those careless strands away. Of course, it was past four o'clock. The braid would start to give way soon.

"I'm only thirty, Jessie. I can say *cool.* Plus," he reminded her, "I'm not the boss. I'm just her right-hand man."

But, of course, he was the executive editor, and way up the publishing food chain in this intern's eyes. "And speaking of our illustrious editor-in-chief, I have some very exciting news for you."

He could have sworn some color drained from those creamy cheeks, leaving behind a dusting of freckles as natural as the darker streaks in her cinnamon-colored hair.

"Really?" She made a show of opening her day planner and getting out a pen, to take notes.

"You don't need to write this down. I know you won't forget."

She looked up at him, hesitancy in her smile. "I won't?"

"You've been selected as Finola Elliott's shadow intern."

The smile froze as she stared at him, pen poised. Then it faded, replaced by a little crease in her forehead. She swallowed, dry-throated enough for Cade to see that she had to struggle with the action. "Shadow intern? It sounds…mysterious."

"It's not. Every year we pick one intern who gets to shadow the editor-in-chief for one month. Fin goes to a meeting, you go to a meeting. Fin previews the next month's issue at the printer, you preview the next month's issue at the printer. Fin gets wined and dined by an advertiser, you get—"

She held up her hand. "I get the idea."

He waited, and watched her try to swallow again.

The reaction validated the very suspicions that motivated him to pick her as the shadow intern. Sure, she had all the professional qualifications—she was smart and hardworking and well-liked—but something was *off* about Jessie Clayton.

And, he reminded himself as he forced his gaze to stay on the colored lenses, he'd better start paying attention to her bizarre behavior instead of the concave dip in her throat, just in case it had anything to do with the business of *Charisma* magazine. Although, for some reason, when Jessie Clayton was around he thought less about business and more about…Jessie.

"It's funny," he said slowly. "I would expect you'd be a little more excited about this opportunity."

She gave her head the tiniest negative shake and pushed her glasses firmly into place. "I—I can't take that assignment."

"Pardon me?"

"I'm sure there are other interns more deserving. And Scarlet just gave me this incredible layout project to handle myself and, with the whole place upside down trying to…well, you know, working so hard to win the family thing…I just don't think the timing is right."

Cade took a deep breath and tipped his chair back as he regarded her. "By the family thing, I assume you mean the ultimate management of Elliott Publication Holdings."

She shifted uncomfortably. "Well, I mean, everyone knows that Patrick—Mr. Elliott—has pitted the four magazines of EPH against each other to see which of his offspring will run the overall company."

Of course, from the boardroom to the janitor's closet, the whole of EPH was discussing the "contest" among the four Elliotts and the magazines they each ran. The lucky one would replace Patrick at the helm, and the competition among the four editors-in-chief to make the highest profit was getting downright dirty.

It didn't surprise him that Jessie Clayton would know about the situation. Especially if his suspicions about her were correct.

And her response was only confirming those suspicions. Why would she be reluctant to accept what had to be a coup among the interns at one of the world's most successful fashion magazines?

"Let me make sure I understand this. Are you saying you don't *want* to be Finola Elliott's shadow intern for the month of September?" He didn't bother to hide the incredulity in his voice.

Her tongue darted over her lips as though they were as parched as her throat. "That's right. That's what I'm saying."

He let out a small choke of disbelief. "You know this is the most coveted assignment for an intern at the magazine?"

Her eyes widened, but the color was so hard to discern

behind the tinted glasses. "I am honored and grateful, Cade.
I can't imagine why I'd get picked, but—"

"Because you are an excellent candidate," he interrupted.
"Because your ideas are fresh, your energy is constant, you've
never been late or out sick in five months, and you've shown
great promise in the world of high fashion publishing."

*And you've made a point to avoid any contact with
Finola Elliott.*

But he didn't add that little piece of information. She didn't
know that her unusual behavior had landed her on his radar
screen. Of course, her silky hair and slender body, that porcelain complexion and melodic laugh also got his attention. Too
much of it, actually. But it was her proactive avoidance of the
woman most interns did handstands to impress that had ultimately landed her in his office.

"You're a model intern and you've earned this reward."

She opened her mouth, then closed it again. One more
time she adjusted the frames of her glasses. "No. Thank you.
I'd rather not."

Every highly trained cell in his body screamed in alert.
Before him sat a young woman who was smart, attractive,
qualified and ambitious enough to work for nothing but
exposure to the business. Why would she turn down a plum
high-profile assignment?

"Why not?" he asked.

"We're days from the editorial deadline for January, and
Scarlet let me have this whole Spring Fling layout for March,
which will mean I'll have to go to the photo shoot and meet
with…" She trailed off and wet her lips again. "I just would
rather not take on that kind of assignment right now," she
finished quietly.

There was only one explanation that occurred to Cade.

She didn't *want* Finola's close attention and examination. And there could be a very good reason why.

Business instinct told him that nothing he asked could get her to reveal that reason. He couldn't scare it out of her, even though he'd been known to intimidate a few employees on occasion. He couldn't coax it out of her, even though he'd seen her react with a sweet blush to his friendly teases.

No, neither his MBA training nor his legendary management skills were going to do the trick here. He'd need to resort to something more ingenious, something a little trickier and lot more appealing.

"You know, Jess." He leaned forward a bit. "I'm just not buying this."

This time there was no doubt that some blood drained from her cheeks. "You're not?"

He shook his head. "You're not telling me something."

Behind the tinted lenses, he saw her eyes widen. If he was right, and she was a mole from *Pulse* or *Snap* or even *The Buzz,* then one of Finola's family had picked a lousy liar for the spy job.

He'd get the truth out of her. He just needed to take down her defenses a little.

"Tell you what." He put his elbows on the desk and lowered his voice. "Why don't you meet me for a drink after work, and we'll talk about it in some friendlier surroundings? Maybe you need a little time to think about it."

"A drink?" She backed up ever so slightly.

Now he had her disarmed. Lying about something, and not sure if she had just been asked out on a date by the magazine's executive editor. "You know the Bull and Bear? At the Waldorf?" When she nodded, he said, "Good. Then we can talk about the shadow assignment there."

He held her gaze for a moment too long. Which wasn't difficult at all, because he'd been fighting the urge to flirt with the redheaded dynamo from the minute he'd first interviewed her. But professionalism demanded that he never, ever date employees of the magazine. That would be a serious mistake.

However, this wasn't really a date. This was the only way to get a woman to confess everything.

Jessie Clayton was hiding something, and he intended to find out what it was and how it would impact his magazine.

"What do you say, about six o'clock? In the bar?"

"I don't know…."

He winked at her. "Come on, Jess. It's just a drink."

She straightened her glasses again. "Okay. Six o'clock. At the Waldorf."

If he could just see into her eyes, he might be able to figure out what she was hiding. What would he have to do to get her to take those glasses off?

"I'll see you there," he promised.

She left his office, but there was no mistaking the pretty aroma of trouble that lingered in her wake.

At exactly five-forty, Jessie dialed Lainie Sinclair's extension. "Is he gone yet?" she asked her roommate, who had a birds-eye view of the executive editor's office from her cubicle.

"He left a few minutes ago," Lainie said softly, "Stopped in the men's room first, came out with his tie straight, but no new hair gel or cologne."

"You'd make a great spy, Lainie." Jessie laughed. But she knew Cade McMann wouldn't gel up his burnished gold hair. He wore it tousled, and casual. *Touchable*. For the fortieth time since she'd left his office, her stomach flipped. "Wish me luck."

"What do you need luck for? Your boss's boss has plucked

you from intern obscurity for the coolest job in the company. I still don't get why you're turning it down."

The urge to confess all welled up in Jessie. Lainie had befriended her on the day of her internship interview, and then became her roommate and closest companion in New York City. If she were ever to confide in someone, Lainie was the one.

But the time wasn't right. Lainie was a doll, as trustworthy and true a girlfriend as there could ever be, but Jessie's secret would be the most sizzling gossip to hit EPH since Patrick Elliott announced his year-long battle for the boardroom. Even Jessie's new best friend might not be able to hold in the truth. Lainie had been bouncing off the walls for the past hour and all she knew was that Cade had offered Jessie a great assignment and was taking her for a drink to discuss it.

If Lainie knew the truth…

"I told you, Lainie. I don't see shadowing Fin as a great plus for me. I'd have to give up the Spring Fling layout Scarlet offered me."

"Spring Fling Schmling. You're nuts. Did you talk to Scarlet?"

"She's out at a photo shoot today," Jessie said, peering at the empty cube where *Charisma*'s flamboyant assistant fashion editor worked in a sea of photos, clippings and fabric swatches. "Which I guess is why Cade delivered the news, since Scarlet is technically my boss."

"But it doesn't explain why he wants to drag the meeting into a swanky hotel bar for further discussion." Lainie paused, then added, "Think he got a room upstairs?"

"Get real, Lain." Not that the same thought hadn't occurred to her. But, for once, fantasies of rolling around on high-end sheets with Cade McMann were not what caused the flipping in her stomach. "It's just a drink." An invitation to a drink, she had to admit, that was issued with a look that practically singed her down to her toes.

But Lainie *did* know one of Jessie's secrets: She nursed a crush on Cade McMann the size of her daddy's south eighty acres in Colorado. And, to her credit, Lainie had kept that secret for months.

"Just hear him out," Lainie said. "You might be able to work it out so that you don't lose the layout assignment *and* you get to do the shadowing."

There was no way Jessie was spending all that time with Finola Elliott. But there was also no way to explain that to Lainie. "We'll see," she said vaguely. "I better go."

"Should I wait up?" Lainie asked with a little tease in her voice.

"I'll be home by eight," Jessie promised.

"Tomorrow morning?" Lainie chuckled.

"Very funny."

As Jessie pushed open the lobby door of EPH and stepped into the evening bustle of Park Avenue, an early September breeze danced over the tops of the trees that lined the gardenlike median strip. Momentarily taken with the possibility of inhaling clean air, Jessie sucked in a deep breath, only to taste the fumes from a cab that pulled out from the curb.

Colorado seemed so far away. She paused to get her bearings, because even after almost six months in New York, Jessie had to glance at street signs and do a little grid math before she could figure out exactly where to go. Which was pretty sad for a girl who grew up knowing north from south strictly by the color of the sun streaks on the mountains.

Stepping onto the sidewalk and dodging a man walking

three dogs, Jessie gazed down the endless corridor created by the skyscrapers that lined Park Avenue. A different kind of valley from the acres of green and gold that surrounded the haven of Silver Moon Ranch. This one was made of steel and glass, and smelled of car exhaust and sausage vendors, and she couldn't remember the last time she felt a mountain breeze in her hair.

Well, she could. The day she left Colorado on this crazy, irresistible fact-finding mission.

But the only facts she'd found—

A man talking on a cell phone jostled her, and a woman carrying an armload of shopping bags excused herself as she hustled past Jessie.

Sighing, she paused at the street corner. Some brave natives were crossing against the light. Someday she might have the nerve to do that. But for now she waited for the green Walk sign.

When her cell phone beeped out the chorus of "Rocky Mountain High," she seized it like a starving woman who'd been handed a rare rib-eye.

"Hi, Dad!" she fairly sang into the phone as she started across Park Avenue, still checking both ways; she didn't trust those cabbies. "You'll never guess where I am!"

"Tell me, angel." Travis Clayton's booming baritone sounded as rich as if he were sitting across from her on the patio, gazing at the snow-tipped mountains that surrounded the Silver Moon Ranch.

"Crossing Park Avenue." Jessie let out a little laugh. "Pretty cool, huh?"

"Be careful, honey," Travis warned. "Those drivers are crazy in New York."

She accepted the long-distance parenting without even

rolling her eyes, the bittersweet ache of homesickness too sharp to tease her father. "How are you, Daddy? How's Oscar?"

"I had him out for a ride today," he said. "I swear that gelding misses you."

Jessie closed her eyes for a moment and imagined climbing into a saddle with a single movement as natural to her as breathing. Another pang of homesickness threatened.

"Of course he hasn't forgiven you for that name."

Jessie just laughed. "Where are you, Daddy? Out on the porch?"

"I am. I have to go back over to the barn in a bit, but I thought I'd catch you on your way home from work."

"I'm not going home," she told him. "Get this. I'm about to walk into the Waldorf-Astoria. How does that sound?"

"Like you're a long way from Colorado, angel." She could hear the wistfulness in his voice.

Even though it had been three years since her mother died, maybe leaving Dad alone in Colorado hadn't been the smartest thing Jessie'd ever done. It had certainly been the most impulsive. But she had to know.

"What are you doing at this fancy hotel?"

A valet opened the door to the Waldorf with one of those appreciative smiles that men in New York gave to pretty women, and Jessie beamed right back and thanked him.

"I'm having a meeting with the executive editor of the magazine, if you can believe that." In the softly lit lobby, a vast center table featured a bouquet of fiery and exotic autumn flowers exuding a luscious fragrance.

"Oh? Think they're finally going to start paying you?"

She glanced around for the entrance to the Bull and Bear, and then spotted a silk-covered settee against one wall. She perched on the edge to finish her conversation. "The internship lasts a year and trust me, Dad, any of my classmates at the Art Institute would kill for this opportunity. Don't worry, I'm watching every penny."

"I know, sweetheart." His voice softened, and Jessie could imagine that his brilliant blue eyes did the same. "Your mother left you money to do anything you want. If living in New York City and working at a big magazine—for *free*—is making you happy, then it would have made her happy."

She closed her eyes and imagined her mother's face for a moment. Her *real* mother. The one who raised her, the one who—

Suddenly, the need to confide in her father squeezed her chest so hard, she thought her heart would pop right out.

"So what's this meeting all about, Jess? Do you have time to tell me?"

She glanced at her watch. How long would it take to tell him the truth? More than the three minutes she had until six o'clock. But, oh, the need to share was sharp.

"I've been offered an opportunity to shadow the editor-in-chief, Finola Elliott." She deliberately waited a beat to see if he reacted to the name. "But I'm not sure I want to take it."

"Why the hell not?" His voice bellowed as though he were hollering to one of the Silver Moon hands. "That sounds like a fantastic break and you wouldn't have been picked if they didn't see your brains and talent."

She took a deep breath. "I'm just not sure I want to spend that much time with Finola Elliott."

"Doesn't spending time with the boss increase your profile…and the chance that they'll hire you for a job that actually gets a paycheck?"

Jessie had to smile. It was killing Dad that the internship was unpaid. "It might," she agreed.

"Then why wouldn't you jump at the chance?"

"I'm not sure I want to be under Fin's close scrutiny."

"Why not?"

She took a deep breath, closed her eyes and whispered the words that had been reverberating in her head for almost a year. She had to say them. She had to tell someone.

"Because Finola Elliott is my birth mother."

Two

Jessie was a full ten minutes late when she entered the darkened atmosphere of the Bull and Bear. Her head still rang with her father's reaction and warnings, although the room hummed with soft chatter and conversation.

Don't expect some sort of hallelujah chorus when she finds out… She's a city woman who probably wants no part of facing a past she gave up twenty-three years ago… If she wanted a reunion, honey, don'tchya think she'd have found you?

Even the fact that Finola's name was listed on an adoption finders Web site didn't convince Daddy that Jessie's birth mother may be conducting the same search with the same hope and trepidation that seized Jessie.

Jessie loved that dream, loved imagining a moment when Fin Elliott would look at her and throw her arms open to exclaim "My baby!"

But Daddy might be right. After observing Fin for five

months, Jessie had seen absolutely nothing that would indicate the thirty-eight-year-old workaholic would be interested in finding, and knowing, and loving, a child she'd given up for adoption when she was only fifteen years old.

Revealing the truth could be a huge error in judgment, one of those prayers that are best left unanswered.

The sight of a golden-haired god at a corner table brought Jessie back to the moment. From the day she'd walked into Cade McMann's office for an interview five months ago, Jessie had felt a tickle of…desire. At first it was just his looks—six perfect feet of solid muscle, dark blond hair that in the summer he'd let grow over his collar, and those see-right-through-you smoke-gray eyes. And it didn't take long for Jessie to get past the great looks and realize that Cade also had a leader's sense of order and a survivor's sense of humor.

From the sidelines, she'd watched a man who thought through every decision he made, who considered all the angles and rarely, if ever, made a mistake.

So why, then, would he ask an intern out for drinks?

And why was he standing there now, looking at her like a man who wanted something? What could he want?

His handsome face broke into a slow smile, and her heart skittered around for a second. She wasn't sure what he wanted, but she sure wished it was her.

"Sorry I'm late," she said as he pulled out a chair for her.

"Don't tell me. Scarlet called from the photo shoot with twenty things for you to do before you could leave."

She put her purse on the floor next to her and touched the frame of her glasses to make sure they completely covered her green eyes. Even in the dim light of the bar, he might recognize the similarity in shape and color to the woman he worked for.

"Actually, I was on the phone with my father and didn't have the heart to hang up on him."

He raised his eyebrows in interest. "He's in Colorado, right?"

Did he remember that from her interview? Or had he been checking on her background? "Yep. We have a cattle ranch not far from Colorado Springs."

He signaled for a waiter, who took their orders for drinks. Jessie planned to slowly sip a chardonnay; the last thing she needed was to lose control. Anyway, just being this close and personal with a man she'd been admiring—okay, *lusting* after— for five months was about all the intoxication she needed.

After they ordered, Cade slipped off his suit jacket and tossed it casually over the back of a chair. Jessie congratulated herself on keeping her gaze from meandering over the solid muscles that strained the crisp white linen of his custom-tailored shirt.

"So how exactly did a girl raised on a ranch in Colorado land in the jungles of New York City?" he asked, leaning back in his chair and absently running a hand over his jaw. By the end of every day, he had just enough stubble to make her want to rub it.

"I mentioned this in my interview," she reminded him gently. "I graduated from the Art Institute of Colorado with a bachelor's degree in graphic design. But all my minor classes were in fashion. Where else would I go but New York?"

"To combine your love of art and fashion?" he prompted.

"I've been reading *Charisma* since I was fourteen," she admitted. "I've always loved the magazine and always loved fashion." But the day she found out that her birth mother was the editor-in-chief was the day her world changed forever.

"So this is your dream job," he said.

"You could say that."

"Except for the pay." He winked and it sent a little quiver through her body.

The waiter brought her wine and a beer for Cade.

She gave a nod to his Coors. "The Colorado girl in me says thanks for that."

He smiled and tilted his head toward the bar. "Mostly martini drinkers in here."

"It is more old-world than new-age." She adjusted the napkin under her wineglass. "Why did you pick this place?"

"I knew there wouldn't be any EPH people here." He poured the beer into a glass, then looked up at her, his gray gaze direct and meaningful. "The other magazines have spies everywhere, you know."

"I wouldn't know," she said, lifting her glass. "But I hope *Charisma* wins." She forced herself to add, "For Finola's sake."

He tapped her glass with his. "We plan on winning," he said, his voice rich with confidence.

As she sipped, he asked, "Did you interview at the other magazines before you came to *Charisma? Snap* has a great internship program and *Pulse* is one of the most respected newsmagazines in the business."

"I didn't even consider the other magazines," she said, eliciting a flash of surprise on his face. "While the celebrities covered in *Snap* are appealing and I'm impressed with what Michael Elliott's done with *Pulse,* my heart has always been in fashion."

A statement that was the absolute, honest truth. And when she discovered that her birth mother was the editor-in-chief of her very favorite magazine, Jessie had been in an emotional upheaval that even two-hour-long rides on Oscar hadn't calmed.

"The week after I graduated," she continued, "I came to New York and *Charisma* is the very first place I interviewed."

"How did your parents feel about you going so far away?"

She touched her glasses. They'd become her favorite crutch ever since she saw Lainie wearing a pair, and Jessie discovered she could disguise her eye color and look somewhat hip at the same time.

"My father," she said softly. "My mother passed away three years ago."

"I'm sorry." His fingertips grazed her knuckles. It was the most natural gesture in the world, but the contact sent a wholly different rush through her.

"Thank you. She had an aneurism. It was sudden, and difficult."

"My father died five years ago," he said, surprising her with the gentleness in his voice. "It was really hard on my mother and the girls."

"The girls being the four younger sisters I've heard about." She relaxed a little, hoping the spotlight would be on him for a few minutes. "Where are they?"

"Near my mother. Believe me, I've got my own cheering section at home in Chicago."

"No wonder you're so good with all the ladies at *Charisma.* You know your way around a sorority house."

"I'm lucky that way." He took a sip of beer, then set the glass down with a thud. "But no changing the subject, which is *you.* Do you have brothers and sisters?"

"I'm an only child." Should she tell him she was adopted? Or might that send up a warning flare? Did anyone know about Finola's past? She had been trying to find that out since she'd arrived in New York. She lowered her voice and added a purposeful glint to her eyes. "You want to know a secret?"

He leaned forward as though she had him on a string and had tugged it. "You have no idea how much."

"This is the first time I've been east of the Rockies."

He dropped back in his chair. "No way."

She nodded, enjoying the unbroken eye contact and the glimmer of a smile tipping the corners of his lips. Had she ever really noticed just how perfectly shaped his mouth was?

Oh yeah. Several times, as a matter of fact.

"You're acclimating very well, then," he said.

She crinkled her nose. "Well, I still can't cross the street unless there's a Walk sign."

He "tsked" as though he were disappointed in her. "Are you hailing taxis yet?"

"I can't afford cabs." She tapped his knuckles playfully just for the fun of touching him again. "You don't pay me, remember?"

"Oh, yeah." He regarded her for a minute. "So how can you afford a Manhattan apartment? And clothes? And food?"

She spun the stem of her wineglass, then slid her fingers up and down it thoughtfully. "My mother left me some money and I've decided to use it to support myself while I learn this business. I room in a rent-controlled studio with Lainie Sinclair, the proofreader and keeper of The Closet keys." She gave him a knowing smile, since it was common knowledge that the only perk for the low-ranking staff was the chance to borrow clothes from *Charisma*'s well-stocked fashion closet. "And I don't eat much."

Still, he didn't say anything, and Jessie suddenly wondered if he doubted her. The way he looked at her...it was almost as if he didn't think she was telling the truth.

"Do I look like I eat a lot?" she asked with a half smile.

He shook his head slowly. "No."

"Then why are you staring at me as though I'm guilty of something?"

He laughed self-consciously. "I'm just thinking about where I should take you to dinner. Somewhere great, since you don't get to eat much. What do you like?"

You, she thought daringly. *I like you.*

"French. Mexican. Japanese. Fusion. I'm a starving intern. I'll eat anything."

Had she just accepted a dinner date with her boss's boss— and Fin Elliott's right-hand man?

By the look on his face, he was as surprised and pleased as she was.

This wasn't going at all as he had planned. While Jessie visited the ladies' room and he paid for their drinks, Cade took a deep breath and remembered that his goal was to find out why she was avoiding Fin, what she was hiding.

Not how far one date could actually go.

Get a grip, man. Falling into the sack with an intern might not be forbidden, but it was definitely less than professional.

It could be a mistake.

And he hadn't plowed to the head of the class, the top of the team and the pinnacle of a career by making mistakes. But something about Jessie Clayton made him want to take chances.

She'd confirmed everything in her file from the school she'd attended to the fact that there were no other interviews at the other magazines in the personnel computer system. He even knew that her mother had passed away three years ago, while she was studying at the Art Institute. So she wasn't lying about her background.

But still Cade's sixth sense screamed that Jessie Clayton was hiding something. And with the competition hot and furious among the four top magazines of EPH, he didn't put anything past the Elliotts.

Elliotts played to win and that was why Cade liked being around them. But would they be conniving enough to pick an innocent girl from Colorado to spy for them?

He had to find out.

And that was why he asked her to dinner.

It didn't have anything to do with that flashy smile or a laugh that sounded like…like the prettiest thing he'd ever heard.

He stood and grabbed his jacket, catching sight of her returning to their table. Of course she wore those glasses and she must have rebraided her hair before she left the office, because it was held securely back now. And although her simple black skirt and white blouse was classic, it certainly didn't have the *au couture* flair of some of the models and society girls he'd dated in the past few years. Even though she had the long, lean body for it.

Must be all that horseback riding. The thought tightened his gut, and a few muscles below that.

Easy, boy. No mistakes. This is research.

She flashed him that easy, genuine smile as she approached, as vivacious and bubbly as she was in staff meetings.

Maybe she was hiding something; but if she was, she had hidden it in a beguiling package. There was something so unaffected and real about her. Something he'd missed with the women he'd been seeing.

Not that this was a date.

"So what'll it be, Cade?" Jessie asked as she picked up her handbag. "French, Japanese, Fusion? I know this great Chinese place in Times Square."

He had to keep this focused on research. "You know, it's amazing you'd never been to New York before, and you just arrive, get an apartment, a job, friends…"

She gave him a sidelong glance as they walked toward the

lobby. "Actually, I got the job before the apartment," she said. "After I interviewed, I was chatting with Lainie who mentioned that her roommate was getting married. That was pure serendipity."

"I remember interviewing you," he said as he held the door and they stepped into the waning light casting long shadows on Park. He dipped a little closer to her ear and lowered his voice. "Before you entered your horn-rimmed phase."

He didn't expect her to pale at that. He really expected a light, melodic laugh…and maybe she'd slip the glasses off. Instead, she tapped the frames as though she needed to be sure they were still there.

"I can't wear contacts," she said, a note of apology in her voice.

He suddenly realized she must have taken it as an insult. "Jessie." He stopped walking and held her elbow so that she stopped, too. "I didn't mean that you aren't…" *Pretty.* "I just noticed that you didn't wear them before."

She eased her elbow out from his light grasp. "They're part of my whole New York look," she said with a lightheartedness that sounded just a tad hollow. "So, where are we going?"

"French. Soho. You'll love it." He guided her toward the corner. "But we need to get a cab headed in the other direction."

With a quick glance at an opening in the traffic, he put his hand on her back and started across Park. She took a few steps and stopped, her attention on a taxi barreling into the intersection.

He gave Jessie a little prompt and hustled her along. "Don't hesitate. Ever." They dashed across the intersection and the taxi flew behind them. "Never show them you're uncertain. Never pause, never scuttle, never show them they have any power. Those are the rules of the city." The rules of his life, too.

"It's a little like horseback riding then," she said, laughing. "You've got to let them know who's in charge."

"Exactly." Cade raised his arm and instantly a taxi pulled over for them. "I've seen all those pictures in your cubicle. You must love horses."

He let her slide into the back seat first, and then he spoke through the safety glass to give the cabbie the address. Leaning back, he stayed in the middle of the back seat, much closer than he would ride with any business colleague.

He ignored the thought and draped his arm over the seat behind her. It was too natural, too…nice. And she didn't seem to mind. In fact, she still wore that fresh smile he'd elicited with the lecture on how to cross city streets.

"I do love horses," she told him. "I miss Oscar most of all."

He choked out a laugh. "Oscar? That doesn't sound like a horse. Horses are supposed to be called Silver and Gypsy."

She gave him a light punch in the rib cage and his body tensed. "Spoken like a true city boy. As a matter of fact, my horse is named after a famous designer."

"De la Renta?"

"Is there any other Oscar? I told you I love fashion. That's why I came to *Charisma*." She dropped her glasses just a smidge to peek out over the rims. "Or don't you believe me?"

Oh, they were green. No, no. They were way more than green. They were deep, endless, intriguing seas of emerald And all Cade wanted to do was gaze into those eyes for hours.

"Why wouldn't I believe you?" he asked. "You're not lying about anything, are you?"

She slipped the frames back up. "Certainly not about a horse named Oscar."

He laughed at that, and about two hours later, he was still laughing. Tucked in the back corner of an ultra-trendy Soho restaurant, sharing a pear sorbet Jessie had called the most sinful piece of fruit she'd ever tasted, Cade nearly forgot the reason he'd asked her to dinner.

Because Jessie was as cool and refreshing and tangy as the dessert that finished their perfect meal. And Cade found himself sharing stories he'd never dreamed of telling the women he'd been dating.

Not that this was a date. The mantra was definitely not working because the closer they got to each other, the more he wanted to kiss her. And that did not qualify as research or work. That qualified as a mistake.

"Believe me," he said, setting down his spoon as he pushed the dish back to her. "I never missed another ballet recital after my sisters pulled that stunt."

She slipped another slow, sensual taste of the icy concoction between her lips, a soft moan of appreciation rumbling from her throat. "They sound intriguing."

What was intriguing? Her mouth over that sorbet? "Who?" he asked.

Her lips twitched in a sneaky grin. "Your sisters." She slid some more sorbet on the spoon and held it toward him. "You want some more, Cade?"

What he wanted was to taste the smidgen that remained on her lips. "Nah. But I'm having fun watching it melt in your mouth."

She smiled and looked down at her plate, then back at him. Man, she was *flirting* with him. "I don't get a lot of fine French cuisine."

"You're making me feel guilty about our intern policies."

"Don't. It's a standard industry practice and I'm happy to pay my dues."

"But not happy enough to take the shadowing assignment,"

he said, giving himself a mental pat on the back for getting back on track.

She let the spoon clink softly against the porcelain dessert dish. "I told you I'd rather not."

"Why don't you tell me the real reason you don't want the assignment, Jessie?"

She dabbed her mouth with the corner of her napkin, then folded it next to her plate. A little twinge of disappointment poked at his heart at the finality of the act. Flirting and shared dessert were over.

"Never mind," he said impulsively. "Just think about it some more. We'll talk about it tomorrow."

"Okay." She gave him a quick smile that probably didn't reach her eyes. He'd know if he could see behind the damn glasses. "Let's get back to your sisters. Are you planning to go home to see your family anytime soon?"

He shook his head. "I doubt I'll be taking any time off this year."

"Because of the pressure for *Charisma* to finish the year with the highest profits?"

Great. She just brought the topic back to something that made him suspicious instead of just plain intrigued. "How about you, Jessie?" he volleyed back without answering the question. "Will you get home to the ranch this year?"

"I plan to go home for Christmas. I really miss my dad."

"And Oscar," he said with a teasing wink. "The high-fashion horse."

She put her elbows on the table and balanced her chin on her knuckles. "I do miss Oscar," she said wistfully. "Believe it or not, I miss the smell of horses, the clip-clop sound of their hooves."

"You sure don't get a lot of that in New York City."

"Or mountains, rivers, valleys and flowers."

He gave an apologetic shrug. "There are some plants in the traffic island on Park Avenue. Do they count?"

"Mmmm." She smiled. "They count. This spring, when I got here, the Parks Department had planted some lilacs in that median strip."

"I don't think I noticed."

"No, probably not. But lilacs were my mother's favorite. She had a whole field of them on the ranch and every April and May they would explode in the most incredible sea of lavender and violet you can imagine and oh, the glorious smell." She closed her eyes and inhaled as though she could sniff the fragrance she described. "I thought, when I moved here, that the lilacs were like a message from my mother. Telling me that coming here was the right thing to do."

"How could it not be?" he asked. "You love fashion and design, and doesn't everyone want to take a stab at life in the big city?"

She didn't say anything for a moment, the flicker of the candle casting just enough light for him to see a whisper of sadness behind her tinted lenses.

"Anyway," she finally said with a sigh, "I love that smell. I even wear lilac perfume sometimes, to remember it."

"Oh." This time he inhaled softly, taking the excuse of her perfume to move a little closer to her. "I thought it was honeysuckle."

She didn't back away, not an inch. "Honeysuckle is much sweeter."

"Smells pretty sweet to me." He sniffed again. "You left a trail lingering in my office today. A whole trail of trouble."

At the word, her jaw slackened and she let out a disbelieving laugh. "Me? Except for not wanting to accept your assignment, I've never been any trouble at *Charisma*."

"That's not what I mean," he said lowering his face close enough so that he could practically taste a kiss. "And you know it."

He couldn't help it. Wordlessly, he reached up and slid her glasses off. She flinched at first, then held his gaze. "So, who is hiding behind these things, Jessie Clayton?" he teased.

Her eyes widened, and stayed on him. Cade stared back into her tempting eyes, as green as the deep sea and just as dangerous.

"I'm not trouble and I'm not hiding anything," she said.

"Yes you are."

"I am?" Her voice cracked with just a hint of trepidation but she didn't look away. And neither did he.

"You're hiding your beautiful eyes."

There was absolutely no way he could stop himself from kissing her. Her lips were cool from the sorbet, but as soft as he'd imagined they'd be. A shimmer of heat lightning streaked through him as their lips touched.

He didn't even try to invade her mouth; he just let their lips meld, let the electricity arc, let the promise of more spark in the air. And then he very slowly broke the contact.

"Are you sure you wanted to do that, Cade?"

He'd never been more sure in his life. "If you have to ask, then I did something wrong."

"No, not wrong." Then she quietly slid the glasses back on and that sense of loss and disappointment punched him again. "Just surprising."

"Do you have to wear those?" he asked, aching to take them off again. To gaze into those eyes until the sorbet in the dish was nothing but a puddle of pears and sugar and she was his for the night.

"I only take them off to kiss."

Leaning into her ear, he let his lips graze a few strands of silky hair. "You might need to give contacts another shot, Jess."

She gave him a questioning look. "Why's that?"

Cade only hesitated a moment before he took any caution he'd brought to this dinner and cast it to the wind. "Because I'd like to kiss you. A lot."

Three

"I need your bosom."

The announcement snapped Jessie to attention. She looked up from the staff memo she'd been reading—well, the words had been in front of her, but they hadn't exactly reached her brain—to see the humor sparking in Scarlet Elliott's pale green eyes as she propped against Jessie's cube wall.

"You have a fine bosom of your own, Scarlet," Jessie replied. "Just ask John Harlan if you need a second opinion."

Scarlet's smile deepened at the mention of the man she loved. "He's partial to mine, it's true," she said with an audacious wink. "But I've decided you have the perfect cleavage."

Jessie didn't like the sound of that. "Perfect for what, Scarlet?"

"I have to doctor up the 'Color Me Charismatic' feature again. The January theme is 'How Low Can You Go' and I think you—" Scarlet leaned over and eased out the V of

Jessie's cotton blouse enough to show the edge of a very functional white bra "—can go nice and low. In something from The Closet, of course."

"No way." Jessie pulled back and grasped the armrests with both hands. "I'm no model."

"First of all, you could be if you'd lose the frames and let that hair down. But you know this feature. We never show the face. I sent two photographers out this weekend to get me some colorful cleavage shots, and this is what they came back with."

Scarlet slapped two proof sheets on top of the staff memo, each showing an array of deeply cut blouses and sweaters on women walking the streets of New York City. The colors were blah and the shots unremarkable.

"Oh, these won't do," Jessie agreed. "Color Me Charismatic" was one of *Charisma*'s most popular monthly features—a candid photograph of an anonymous woman on the street wearing something in a maverick, memorable color and making it work for her. They always had a theme like "Skirts that Flirt" or "Watch Your Back" and the photographers usually managed to get an angle where the woman's face was at least partially obscured, which protected the magazine and the unwitting "model."

Scarlet tapped one manicured nail on the mess of pictures. "You have a good eye, Jessie. I knew you'd recognize dreck when you see it. So, come on, I have an outfit in mind and a body. Yours. Let's go."

Jessie narrowed her eyes at Scarlet. Why today? Today she wanted to hide in her cube and relive every single moment of last night's "date" with Cade. Especially the last kiss at her door. Or maybe the one in the cab, when his tongue touched hers and—

"Why don't you ask someone else, Scarlet? I have so much to do."

Scarlet tugged the staff memo out from under the pictures and peered at it. "You have to read a staff memo that came out last Monday?"

Busted. The memo was the first thing she had grabbed to look busy while she relived the way Cade held her hand. The way he smelled and sounded and, oh saints alive, the way he kissed.

"Hel-*lo?*" Scarlet leaned a little closer to Jessie and waved a hand in front of her face. "You with me today, Jess?"

Jessie started to laugh. "I'm just a little tired this morning."

"Great, I've got just the color to wake you up." Scarlet managed to pull Jessie from her chair. "You have to be the 'Color Me Charismatic' woman on the street sometime during your tenure as an intern. Them's the rules, darling."

Sighing deeply, Jessie left her cube and followed Scarlet down the hall to where Lainie protected a closet stocked full of clothing samples from the top designers in the world and every imaginable accessory. The Closet was located perilously close to Cade's office, but he hadn't arrived yet this morning. Since he was never late, Jessie assumed he had a meeting out of the office.

Which was just as well, because she'd probably melt at the sight of him.

"I see you found a victim," Lainie said dryly as she handed an oversize key ring to Scarlet.

"Why don't you do it?" Jessie asked her roommate.

Lainie slapped her hands over her breasts. "Evidently my little double A's don't make for great cleavage."

Jessie glanced down at her chest. "I'm just a B."

"A B-plus," Scarlet insisted as she slipped the key into the door and reached in to flip on the light. "And I have a bra in here that will take you to a C in record time. Lainie, undo her braid, will you?"

Jessie automatically protected her head. She didn't want anyone to notice her hair, the color and texture of so many other Elliotts'. "Can't my hair stay back?"

"Not a chance," Scarlet said from inside the closet. "And don't even think about wearing those glasses. That's an order."

Twenty minutes later, Jessie was out on Park Avenue, wearing a screaming yellow sweater with a giant black zipper up the front and black leather pants, her hair whipping in the breeze and her glasses somewhere on Lainie's desk. And all Scarlet could do was tug that zipper lower and lower.

"Any farther and you'll run into my pants," Jessie said as she brushed a hair from her face.

"That's next month's feature," Scarlet said dryly. "'Hips You Want to Hug.'"

"Count me out," Jessie said as she inched the zipper up just enough to cover the single front clasp of the black lace bra she now wore. "By the way, this isn't a bra. This is an optical illusion."

Scarlet chuckled and snagged the zipper down again. "That cleavage is real. Just…enhanced." She stepped back and eyed her work, signaling over her shoulder. "We're ready, Nick."

A few passersby glanced at them, but for the most part they were ignored by the pedestrian traffic. Scarlet gave Jessie a little push toward the freelance photographer they used for lots of *Charisma* shoots. "Walk straight to Nick. Think sexy thoughts."

Sexy thoughts? Now *that* was the first thing she'd been asked to do that felt easy.

Sexy thoughts…Cade McMann.

"Chin up, shoulders back, think about something provocative," Scarlet ordered.

Provocative…Cade McMann.

From behind her, Scarlet fanned Jessie's long hair over her shoulders. "Keep going toward Nick," she said as she dodged out of the frame. "Push your chest out. Look toward the street and think about something absolutely *lusty.*"

Oh, lusty would definitely be Cade McMann.

Turning toward the noise and traffic, Jessie thought about Cade's smile. His silvery eyes. His incredible mouth.

And then she stumbled on a crack in the sidewalk as she stared right into all three.

The subject of her fantasies leaned against a street sign, his arms crossed, a wide smile on his face. "Now that is what I would call a *charismatic* cleavage."

Cade levered himself off the sign pole and ambled toward her, his gaze drifting all the way down to her toes, and back up again to settle in the V of her neckline. The rush of heat in her lower half could melt the leather pants.

"You run this photo, Scarlet," he said as he approached Jessie and continued to sear her with his stare, "and zipper sales will skyrocket within an hour and yellow will be pronounced the new black."

For a moment, Jessie couldn't breathe. She looked up at Cade, her heart thundering like a thousand horses over the Colorado prairie. As he neared her, he locked on her eyes and she realized with a start that she had left her glasses upstairs.

But she couldn't look away. His wolflike gaze swallowed her up, and all of Park Avenue just disappeared into the background.

He leaned into her ear and whispered, "You look like a bumblebee who could seriously sting the most unsuspecting victim."

Chills danced down her spine as she laughed and threw him

a teasing look. Somewhere in the distance, she heard Nick's camera clicking and ticking.

"Out of the frame, Cade," Scarlet snapped, nudging him away. "I'm trying to get a shot here."

"Don't worry, Scarlet," Nick called from his spot a few feet away. "I got the shot. You'll love it."

"Glad I could help." Cade winked, and as he continued into the EPH building, he called to Scarlet, "Let her keep that sweater, okay?"

Jessie watched him disappear into the building, his broad shoulders filling up the doorway, his golden hair grazing the back of a very expensive suit jacket.

"Oh, that's adorable!" Scarlet exclaimed as she studied the digital image captured in Nick's camera. "Look at this, Jessie."

Scarlet held out the camera and Jessie peered into the screen on the back. Nick had caught Cade leaning down as though he were kissing Jessie's hair, his gaze aimed squarely at her breasts.

"Just look at your face," Scarlet said, jabbing Jessie with a little elbow.

Nick had captured her teasing, flirtatious glance and the flash of unadulterated lust on Cade's face. It was, for "Color Me Charismatic," a perfect shot.

"Don't forget the face blur," Jessie said. "'Color Me Charismatic' is anonymous."

"Are you kidding?" Scarlet waved her hand in one of her flamboyant gestures. "That's just to protect us from lawsuits. You can sign a model release. This shot is so sexy. You know, if I didn't know better I would say you've missed your calling as an actress. You look downright infatuated with Cade in that picture."

"I took an acting class in college," she said quickly. And she'd barely passed. She hadn't been *acting* infatuated. She was.

* * *

Cade dug his hands deep into his trouser pockets and squinted down at the scene far below his office window. Although he stared at the splash of red-and-orange flowers spilling across the median strip, all he could really see was the vision of Jessie, her yellow curves and auburn hair and green eyes dancing as she flirted with him.

The same vibrant woman he'd kissed over dessert…and in the cab…and at her door. She was everything bright and alive and attractive.

He'd always thought she was pretty and spunky, but after spending all that time talking to her, he was just mesmerized by her. What was it about her?

He peered at the flowers below.

Had there really been lilacs in that cement garden last spring? He'd never noticed the flowers on Park Avenue before. Was it possible he walked down that street every day and never noticed lilacs in the spring, or the colors of the trees?

I even wear lilac perfume sometimes.

His intercom buzzed and Chloe Davenport's distinct voice broke his reverie.

"Fin's waiting, Cade. In her conference room."

Damn. He glanced at his watch and realized he was ten minutes late for a management meeting. What the hell was the matter with him? He was staring out the window thinking about trees and flowers while his very future hung on *Charisma*'s balance sheet.

He reached over and hit the speaker to respond to Fin's assistant. "I'll be right there, Chloe."

"She's got two things on the agenda," Chloe added. "The P&L from last month and the staff assignments for September."

"Will do." From his credenza, he picked up the file folder

he'd been looking at yesterday, right before Jessie Clayton came wafting into his office and turned down the shadowing assignment.

Some fact-finding mission he'd gone on last night.

He still didn't know any more about Jessie's reasons for avoiding Fin than he did when the evening began. He'd tried a dose of seduction and it backfired. Instead, he'd been the one damn near seduced.

By the time he watched her slip into the door of her apartment building, he'd forgotten why he'd asked her out for drinks and dinner and could only think about how much he enjoyed the evening with a charming, sweet, energetic young woman who talked about flowers.

Damn, that wasn't like him. But, still, he couldn't remember the last time he'd enjoyed himself so much. And then when he got out of that cab and saw her on the street this morning, her hair blowing, those clothes hugging her curves, her expression lost in some fantasy…

He grabbed his phone and dialed. Chloe answered on the first ring. "Finola Elliott's office."

"Tell her five more minutes," he said quickly. "I have to make one call."

"Make it fast." He could imagine Fin's assistant rolling her blue eyes or crinkling her nose in distaste.

"I will," he promised. And he meant it. Because if he gave this too much thought, he might talk himself out of it. He could tell himself he was just trying to get to know Jessie Clayton better, for business reasons, but he knew that was an excuse for a little more time with her.

He started calling immediately, until he found what he wanted. It took him a full ten minutes to convince the man on the other end of the phone, but once he got a commitment,

Cade grabbed the files he needed and headed to the conference room connected to Fin's office. He used the hallway entrance, which gave him the chance to glance over to the editorial cubes and peek at Jessie's empty chair. She might still be down on the street shooting "Color Me Charismatic"…or right around the corner in The Closet getting changed. Sliding that big black zipper down over the lace of that—

"Earth to McMann."

He turned back to the conference room doorway at the sound of Fin's impatient voice. "Sorry, Fin," he said with a little laugh. "I was just checking out the action in the cubes. It's Friday and you know the natives tend to lose their focus."

At the head of an oval mahogany table, Fin brushed a sleek strand of auburn hair over her shoulder and gave him a smile that made her eyes sparkle like Tiffany emeralds. "You seem distracted, Cade. Are you sure you're not the native losing his focus?"

"Get real, Fin." He pulled out a chair and dropped the financial files on the table, glancing at the wall where the first few finished pages of the January issue had been hung for the staff to review. "The next issue's going to be great, Fin, but the monthly numbers aren't nearly as attractive."

She frowned and flipped open the file, studying the spreadsheet. "Not hopeless, but you might want to get on Liam's calendar for a chat."

"I already did." Not that he needed to schedule a meeting with EPH's top financial executive. They'd been friends for so long they were more like brothers.

Fin looked up from the spreadsheet, all sparkle gone from her eyes. "We are going to win this, aren't we, Cade?"

"Yes," he said with total assurance. "You've earned it, Fin, and we can do it. We were the leader at the six-month mark, so if we don't make any mistakes between now and the end of the year, we should be in."

She nodded. "We have to stay completely on task. No distractions, no mistakes."

And that, he reminded himself sternly, should really include dalliances with interns under the guise of figuring out her motives. The job of running Elliott Publication Holdings was the brass ring that Fin, a certified workaholic driven to success, wanted more than anything.

But Patrick Elliott wasn't basing his decision on who wanted the job the most. Like every decision the patriarch of the Elliott clan made, the answer lay in the bottom line. Whichever editor-in-chief produced the most significant profit margin for the year won the prize. So the competition for advertising, subscribers and cost-cutting had never been fiercer among the executives who ran *The Buzz, Snap, Pulse* and *Charisma* magazines.

And Cade wanted that honor as much as Fin did. Not only would it mean an automatic promotion for him, but he deeply respected and admired Fin, and genuinely believed that EPH would be a better company with her at the helm. Plus he loved nothing more than the challenge of avoiding any errors and winning the game.

As she looked back at the file, he studied her. There was always an undercurrent of sadness to Fin, like she worked with such fury and concentration because it helped her escape. As long as he'd known her, she'd had extremely strained relations with her parents, especially Patrick. Of her brothers, only her twin, Shane, the editor-in-chief of *The Buzz*, seemed to share a close relationship with Fin.

Fin looked up at him, and Cade expected her to comment on the numbers. But her eyes softened for a moment instead. "You will make an excellent editor-in-chief when I move up to EPH, Cade. I can't imagine a person more qualified to run this magazine."

He recognized motivation when she dangled it in front of him. "Thanks, Fin. We're a great team. We can do this."

"We will," she said decisively, and they launched into an hour-long review of every line item on the spreadsheet.

As always, Fin asked question after question, rarely satisfied with the first answer, always digging for a better solution. And when they were finished, she seemed satisfied that they'd attacked the numbers as best they could.

"I'll make a point of talking to Liam," Cade said as he closed the financial files.

"Yes, but in the meantime, keep a very tight rein on the January issue. We have three months left, Cade. A lot can happen in three months."

"I know," he agreed. "Are you ready to move on to staff assignments?"

She nodded and after they'd reviewed responsibilities for upcoming issues, Fin pulled the last item from his staffing file. "It's September," she said. "Don't I get to wear a new shadow this month?"

No mistakes. That was his rule. So how to handle the issue of the shadow intern? "Maybe under the circumstances, you'd rather not. Some of your meetings this month will be extremely sensitive."

"We could do a half-day shadow," she suggested. "I'll schedule my confidential appointments for afternoon. I like this program, Cade. We don't pay the interns and we have to be sure they are rewarded and trained."

"No argument there."

She glanced at the list of five intern names in his file. "Have you picked one yet?"

"I have one or two in mind." One in mind constantly, as a matter of fact. "But I'm still interviewing." Interviewing. Yeah, that was a good word for it.

"Who's your top choice at the moment?"

Why lie? She *was* his top choice. For a number of things. "Jessie Clayton."

Fin raised one beautifully arched eyebrow. "We've discussed her before. She's made a science out of avoiding me. Have you figured out why?"

"No, not yet." But he would. "Anyway, Scarlet has her on a big assignment for the March issue and I'm not sure if the timing will work out for the shadowing project." *And she turned the opportunity down.* But something in him wanted to protect Jessie, so he purposely kept that piece of information from Fin.

"I like her work and Scarlet raves about her ideas on layout and design," Fin said, looking hard at him. "But you mentioned last month that you wanted to do some digging into her background."

"I did. She checks out. I don't know why she avoids you, but she has done excellent work at the magazine."

"None of the other interns stands out this year," Fin said, looking at the list again. "She seems to be popular and smart."

And smells like a spring garden. Cade cleared his throat and took the file from Fin. "I'll find the right intern for you by next week."

Fin seemed to accept that as they packed up to leave. Just as they stepped into the hall, a sudden burst of female "Ooohs" and "Ahs" erupted from the sea of cubicles.

He looked down the hall to see the receptionist carrying an oversize bouquet of lilacs toward the editorial cubes.

Cade managed not to smile. The florist had given him a

hard time but he knew, in New York, you could get anything for the right amount of money. He stepped a little farther into the hall, just in time to see the priceless look on Jessie's face when the vase was placed on the corner of her desk.

"My, my, my," Finola said from behind him as she observed the scene. "Looks like our intern has an admirer."

"No surprise," he commented, purposely casual, as he watched Jessie open the card. "She's a very pretty young woman."

Fin looked hard at Jessie, whose infectious giggle was almost drowned out by her colleagues' comments and jokes. "It's hard to tell. She never takes those silly glasses off."

As Fin walked away to pick up a message from Chloe's desk, Jessie read the card to herself and smiled. She shook her head when someone tried to take it, holding his invitation to her chest without sharing.

Then she looked down the hall, toward the conference room, straight at him. It was nearly imperceptible, but he caught her tiny nod.

As Finola flipped through her messages, she asked, "So are you doing anything this weekend, Cade?"

"As a matter of fact, Fin, I have a date tonight."

She glanced up, curious. "Someone special?"

"Very." He couldn't wipe the smile off his face and, of course, Fin was too classy to pursue it.

Four

Jessie dodged across 57th Street with a few other intrepid New Yorkers, and the cab at the corner slowed for her. Maybe it was the yellow sweater…or her decision not to hesitate.

The thought made her smile, something she'd been doing since the arrival of the most incredible bouquet of lilacs, and a note that took her breath away.

Meet me at Columbus Circle at 6:00 tonight for some wide open spaces and a horse…New York style.

Lainie had taken the lilacs home for her, and, being a true friend, hadn't even teased Jessie about who might have sent them. Nor did Jessie reveal the truth to Scarlet or any of the other *Charisma* associates. Somehow, she managed to get through the afternoon, then swapped her white blouse for the yellow sweater and blessed her decision to wear nice black slacks to work.

Dressed for a date she hadn't known she was going to

have, Jessie made her way to Columbus Circle in the midst of the late Friday-afternoon bustle of New York City.

A troupe of break dancers wowed a crowd at the corner, their thumping beat of hip-hop music guiding Jessie's determined steps. As she headed toward the hub of activity known as Columbus Circle, she let her gaze travel up across a sea of high-end stores that dominated the busy area and up the towering skyscrapers that loomed over Central Park West.

For a second, her steps slowed as she scanned the crowds of people for a six-foot-tall hunk with golden hair and mesmerizing gray eyes. There were plenty of men that height, but none who took her breath away. None who gave her stomach that roller-coaster dip. None who made her whole being shiver in anticipation of a kiss or a touch, the way Cade McMann did.

A clip-clop of horse's hooves approached from behind. Still not used to the hansom cabs and the turned-out ponies who pulled them through Central Park, Jessie paused to check out the dappled coat of a jaunty mare pulling a bright red carriage. At the reins, a young man in a tuxedo smiled broadly at her.

But when he stopped and Cade leaned forward from the carriage seat, Jessie sucked in a breath of total surprise.

"Here she is," Cade said to the driver, who immediately stopped the carriage so Cade could get out.

For the second time that day, she stood speechless on a street corner staring at Cade.

He indicated the horse with a flourish. "The closest thing I could get to Oscar in New York City."

All she could do was laugh, shake her head and take his hand. "You're too much."

Helping her into the carriage, he said something quietly to the driver, then settled in next to her. Very close to her.

"I just don't want you to get so homesick for horses and open spaces that you run back to Colorado."

She took a deep breath, the familiar scent of horse mixed with the not-yet-familiar scent of Cade washing over her like the late afternoon sun.

"Your evil plan is working," she confided with a contented sigh. "Thank you for this treat."

"You're welcome." His gaze dropped to the zipper, which wasn't nearly as low as Scarlet had wanted it that morning. "I see you took my advice and kept the sweater."

And the magic bra, which, from the look on his face, was still creating optical cleavage illusions. "Scarlet said I'd earned it after my impromptu photo shoot."

He draped his arm behind her and lowered his head to hers. "You looked gorgeous this morning. Still do."

More warmth spread through her and it had nothing to do with the setting sun. "Thanks."

"You seemed to see pretty well, too."

She drew back and blinked at him. "Excuse me?"

"I was forty feet away from you when you spotted me on the street." Slowly, he slid the glasses down her nose. "You don't need these, Miss Clayton."

There was something so intimate about the way he removed her glasses. Something so sensual about being inches from Cade with nothing on her face to come between them. Anyway, it wasn't as if he was going to look at her and suddenly declare, "You have Fin's eyes." She was being too cautious.

"They're a fashion statement," she said softly, taking the glasses and closing them. With a sly smile, she reached over and slid them in the pocket of his suit jacket. "I can keep them off for you."

He rewarded her with a sexy wink. "I'm honored. Now, would you like some champagne?"

"Champagne?"

Reaching to the floor of the carriage, he flipped open the top of a wicker basket to reveal a bottle of champagne in ice, two crystal flutes and a few covered containers.

"Are we celebrating something?" she asked, taking the empty flute he handed her.

"Friday night? Horses and open spaces?" He drizzled a few drops of golden liquid into the glass and it fizzed with the same burst of excitement that bubbled in her blood. "Take your pick."

"I think I'd like to celebrate how different you seem," she said.

"Different?"

"You're so relaxed out here in the world," she teased. "Like you left 'the boss' at *Charisma* and you're just a regular guy." A fun, sexy, intriguing regular guy who was seriously easy on the eyes and appeared to be totally into her.

"As regular as a guy can be who's traveling around Central Park in a horse and carriage."

He'd done this for her. He'd done this all for her.

The realization hit her heart like the clopping hooves on the asphalt drive.

"So what are we drinking to, Jessie? Horses and wide open spaces?"

"And surprisingly regular guys."

He winked as their crystal touched and rang softly. In the background, Jessie heard the occasional shout of some teenagers playing Frisbee on the lawn, and the very distant hum of New York traffic and horns. The carriage rocked and the champagne tickled her nose and lips.

It suddenly seemed very unreal and magical.

"When did you arrange all this?" Jessie asked as she glanced at the rolling vista of green hills and autumn-dipped trees around them.

"This afternoon."

"Right after you ordered the lilacs."

His lips tipped up in a smile. "I couldn't resist."

She gave him a dubious look. "I'm not that irresistible, even in my bumblebee sweater."

"I'll be the judge of what I can't resist," he said, leaning back against the leather seat. "And you whet my appetite for horses and fresh air."

"So you probably don't want to know how much I miss the cattle."

He laughed and put his arm around her, tugging her just a little closer to him. "Let's not push it."

Colorado seemed a million miles away. And for the first time in more than five months, Jessie didn't care.

An hour later, as they passed the carousel and skating rink, the sun dipped lower over the skyline of New York turning the treetops a fiery orange-red. The driver stopped at the edge of a lush park, announcing that they were at the Sheep Meadow, a vast green field dotted with dozens of other couples, families and small groups playing football or enjoying a blissful evening in the park.

Within a few minutes, they carried the basket and a blanket to a clear spot.

"He'll be back in a little while," Cade told her, indicating the hansom cab driver. "Are you hungry?"

"Starving. What's in your basket?"

"I have no idea," he admitted. "I just asked for a deluxe picnic dinner from that deli near the office. It's not like I actually packed it."

As they set up the picnic and discovered they had shrimp cocktail and crispy chicken, fresh bread and even chocolate-covered strawberries, they talked about New York and how difficult—or, for Cade, how easy—it was to get used to.

"Once I bought my apartment, I knew I was here for good," he told her as he settled next to her on the blanket and picked up the container of shrimp.

"Where do you live?" she asked.

He tilted his head in the general direction of south. "Columbus Circle."

"In one of those towers? The new ones?"

He nodded and offered her a piece of juicy shrimp. "It's not huge," he said. "But it's on the twenty-ninth floor, so the view is indescribable and the location is insane."

"Twenty-ninth, huh?" She squinted in that direction, able to see the tips of the buildings. "Does it feel like you live in the air?"

Laughing, he bit into his shrimp. "No. I have a floor and walls. Want to see it?"

A blast of heat shot through her. "Are you asking me to go back to your apartment?"

He snagged her gaze, his expression serious. "Only if you want to."

For a moment, she said nothing, caught in the reflection of his gray eyes, absolutely unable to look away. "Let me ask you something, Cade. Is this a date?"

He touched the corner of her lips and used his finger to slide a teeny bit of cocktail sauce into her mouth. "Yep."

At least he was honest. "Why?"

"Why?" He let out a quick laugh. "Because I like you."

"But why?"

He grinned. "You want a mirror? It's pretty easy to see why."

"But you don't date *Charisma* employees, Cade. I've watched you for five solid months."

"Yeah?" He teased her with that half smile. "Well, that makes two of us. Because I've watched *you* for five solid months."

"What I don't understand," she said, shifting a little on the blanket as she carefully phrased her thoughts, "is why someone as by-the-book professional as you would suddenly decide to break the rules and date an intern."

"There are no rules about dating anyone at EPH."

"Unspoken? Unwritten?"

He shook his head. "It's up to the individual manager. Which, in this case, is me."

As much as Jessie wanted to follow her father's ageless advice about not looking gift horses in the mouth, something somewhere didn't quite fit. She decided to press on. "And you were just suddenly so overcome by attraction that you impulsively asked me out?"

"Jessie," he said, with a little note of exasperation in his voice, "you ask too many questions. You're like Fin."

The words shot the hairs on the back of her neck to full attention. "I am?"

"She always asks questions, wants to get to the bottom of things. In fact," he said, dipping another shrimp tail in a spicy red sauce and holding it up to his mouth, "she was asking about you today."

All of Jessie's cool confidence evaporated. Could he know? Could Fin? "Really? Why would she care about an intern, with all she has on her mind?"

He popped the shrimp into his mouth and chewed it while he regarded her. "Her attention to the staff is one of the keys to her success. She likes to know everyone at *Charisma,* professionally and personally."

She didn't know Jessie. Because Jessie had made sure to stay out of Fin's range. "So, what did she ask?"

"If you were going to be the shadow intern."

Jessie busied herself trying to open a bottle of water. "And what did you tell her?"

"That I was still considering the candidate."

Her hand froze on the twist-off lid. "Did you tell her I wasn't in the running?"

"No." He reached over, took the bottle and opened it easily, then handed it back to her. "I told her I would let her know next week."

Jessie took a long drink of water, letting the liquid cool her suddenly dry throat. Could she do this? Could she date Cade and keep a secret this big from him?

"She thinks you avoid her on purpose."

Jessie choked and sputtered the water.

"You okay?" Cade laid his hand on her back, patting her gently.

"Yes." She gasped for air and coughed again. "The water just went down the wrong pipe."

He slid his hand down her back and pulled her ever so slightly toward him. "Do you?"

"Do I what?" As if she didn't know.

"Avoid Fin on purpose?"

A million responses flipped through her brain. The only one she'd never tell him was the truth. But she didn't want to lie, either. How *could* she date Cade and not reveal her secret? The only way was to avoid the subject of Fin altogether.

Slowly, she turned to him and touched his face, loving the way his eyes darkened at the contact. "Will you do me a favor?"

He looked as though she could ask him for the moon and he'd say yes. But he just nodded.

She stroked the rough shadow of his whiskers with her fingertips. "Since we've established that this is an official date, can we not talk about work?"

He dipped his head to kiss her fingertips while he held her gaze. "Whatever you want."

"Then let's leave the office at the office."

For a split second, she thought he was going to disagree, but then he said, "Consider it done."

"Thank you," she said and then gestured toward the picnic basket. "And thank you for all this. For the lilacs, and the horse and the…space. You took away all my homesickness."

"It's my pleasure," he said, his gaze dropping to her mouth. When his lips captured hers, all Jessie could do was hang on for the thrill of it and make a mental note to stop asking questions like Fin.

"You taste like strawberries," Cade teased in between kisses in the back of the hansom cab.

"You taste like chocolate." Jessie closed her eyes and kissed him again with a soft moan.

"Gotta love dessert." He pulled her into him, vaguely aware that they were getting closer to Columbus Circle. The carriage ride had to end, but, he hoped, not the night. Not yet.

Their picnic had long ago finished on a high note as they fed each other chocolate-covered strawberries, and he and Jessie remained curled up in the warm leather of the carriage, torturing each other with long, wet, lazy kisses. He glided his hand over the silky skin of her throat, slipped his fingers into her braid and guided her mouth back to his for another taste.

He ached with hardness and need for more of her but still, he hadn't touched her. At least, not in all the places he wanted to.

He hadn't tugged that black zipper on her bumblebee

sweater and eased it open. He hadn't lifted her from her seat and guided her legs around his hips. He hadn't slipped his hand around her backside and braced her against him so she could feel exactly what she did to his body.

But, man, he wanted to. His breath tight in his chest, his hands hot from the need to touch her, he finally managed to give the word to David, their driver, that they could end the ride.

Jessie leaned forward to gauge their location. "I can grab the train up to my apartment."

As Cade paid with a wad of twenties, he shot a disbelieving look to Jessie. "You're not taking a subway at this hour."

She smiled as he helped her out of the carriage. "All right, I'll take a cab."

As the horse trotted off, Cade tugged her into him for a long, close embrace. "Don't go," he whispered into her hair.

She leaned back and looked up at him. He could see the desire and arousal in her eyes that matched what he felt.

"Cade," she said, "we work together. You're the boss, for God's sake. I'm an intern."

"Hey." He put a finger over her lips. "No talking about work. You made me promise."

"Yes, but, now…"

"Now what?"

"Now we should say good-night."

She was right, of course. Making sense, thinking straight. He dipped down and kissed her lips, gliding his tongue between her lips and along her teeth to see if he could get rid of all that sense and straight thinking. This was too good. She was too good.

"You don't want to leave any more than I want you to leave," he told her.

Her only response was to moan softly and squeeze her arms tighter around his neck.

"Was that a yes?"

Closing her eyes, she nodded and he didn't give her a second for her to change her mind. Or for him to change his, as unlikely as that might be. This night, this time, Cade didn't feel like monitoring his mistakes. Turning her in his arms, he started toward the doors of his building, threading his fingers into the thick braid that hung down her back.

"Good," he said softly. "'Cause I'll die if I don't see your hair down again."

Wordlessly, they walked over the glossy marble floor of the ultra-modern lobby, past the boutiques still humming with tourists and shoppers, down to the teak-paneled bank of elevators that would take them to the twenty-ninth floor.

Cade didn't waste one second pulling her into his arms the minute the doors closed behind them and they were alone in the elevator.

"Jessie," he said huskily, as he reached down to kiss her. "You're sure you want to stay, right?" He braced himself for any answer, ready to turn right around and get in a cab if he had to.

"I want to stay."

At the simple declaration, he kissed her again, and again as they reached the hall, and again at the apartment door, and again as they stepped into the entryway.

Easing her against the wall, he fully invaded her mouth with his tongue. She sucked on him, her hands traveling under his jacket, pushing it back, as hungry to touch him as he was to explore her.

He began to unbraid her hair. It fell in thick sections against his fingers and he let out a soft groan of pleasure when he finally got his hands into her mane.

"Your hair is amazing," he whispered, peppering her throat with kisses. "You are amazing."

When the braid was free, he pulled the locks forward, over her shoulders, and let it tumble down to her chest. He stroked the strands, and his palms covered her breasts.

Under her sweater, he could feel her nipples bud, her breath coming through her parted lips in tight, ragged bursts.

"Time to unzip Jessie," he said into a kiss, finally hooking his finger into the zipper hoop that some designer had added to the sweater just to torment men. "I haven't thought about anything but this all day."

The first few zipper teeth scraped open. She arched into him, riding his erection and offering him her breasts. A strip of a black bra appeared under the sweater.

His throat went bone-dry at the sight.

"Courtesy of The Closet," she said with a little laugh.

He trailed a kiss down the flesh of her throat, dipping into the rise of her breasts, sliding his tongue over the silky, feminine flesh. "Remind me to thank Scarlet."

"Don't you dare," she gasped.

He chuckled, easing the zipper lower with one hand, then spreading the sweater back.

He traced the black lace with his tongue and she rose on her tiptoes to offer him more. His thumb grazed her nipple, sliding against the satin of the bra.

"Cade." Her voice was raw with tension and desire. "Please. I can barely stand."

She didn't need to say more. Wordlessly, he picked her up in his arms, kissing her mouth as he carried her across the living room to the bedroom. As he laid her on the bed, she pulled him down on top of her.

In a tangle of wild, wet kisses and hungry hands, he took

off her sweater and pants, and she lay on the bed in the sexiest black bra he'd ever seen, and black lace panties, her hair spread like fiery silk over his bed.

"I can't believe this," he said, the awe and ache making his voice hoarse. "You're even more beautiful than I imagined."

Her smile was dubious as she started to unbutton his shirt. "You never imagined."

He snorted. "Wanna bet?"

Her fingers froze and she looked up at him. "You imagined this? I mean, before tonight? Or last night?"

Cade closed his eyes and let her finish the job of unbuttoning his shirt, then he shimmied out of it. Sliding down next to her, he lined up their bodies, easing his hand over her tiny waist to turn her toward him. He took a deep breath and willed his aching arousal to resist her for just a few more minutes.

He would be inside her. He knew that. But first, she had to know that this was not just a convenient office affair.

"Listen to me," he said. "I want you to know this before we make love."

In the dark, she looked at him, her eyes wide, her lips parted. He could feel her heartbeat hammer through her whole slender body.

"I noticed you the minute you walked into *Charisma*," he said, thinking back on the first time the auburn-haired beauty walked in his office. The first time he smelled that hint of spring and saw the grass-green eyes of Jessie Clayton. "I remember the first word I thought of when I looked at you."

"What was it?"

"Fresh." He tipped her chin toward him, so he could look into her eyes as he shared the memory. "Not like other New York women. You're so…well, there's always been something different about you—"

She backed up and laughed a little self-consciously. "Different? Like odd?"

"I mean that in a good way," he said quickly. He stroked her skin, gliding one finger over her lovely breast and into the cleavage he'd been thinking about since he saw her on the street that morning. "You're unaffected and real. And there's something about you that's…"

He felt her stiffen. He wanted to say *familiar.* But would she take that wrong? Like she reminded him of one of his sisters or something?

It wasn't that. It was just that she was…comfortable. "You make me comfortable," he admitted.

"Yeah? Well, that's funny because you have just the opposite effect on me."

"Really?" He tightened his grasp a little. "I make you uncomfortable?"

"Completely," she said, her lips quirking in a smile. "When I walked into your office for that interview I was totally and completely uncomfortable."

"Why?" He'd been friendly, easy to talk to. Hadn't he?

"Because I thought that you were—are—the sexiest guy I ever met."

He almost choked. "You did?"

"And, let me tell you, it's very uncomfortable to be so…" She pressed her hips against him and slid one leg around his waist. "Hot. And tingly. During an interview."

"Oh, man," he murmured a helpless groan and dropped his head into that irresistible cleavage, gently leaning her on her back. "If I had known that, I would have…"

"What?"

"Well, I would have…" He licked her flesh and with one hand, unclasped the front of the bra.

"You would have what?"

He eased the satin over her breasts, the rosy tips of her nipples jutting out for his mouth. "I would have never let you be uncomfortable. I would have just done…this."

She started to laugh, but drew in a sharp breath as he closed his mouth over one of her breasts and began to suckle her, his hand caressing the other.

She moaned under his ministrations, her hips writhing against him. Licking the hardened bud, he trailed his fingertips over her stomach, down to where her hips moved to the natural rhythm of sex.

"Are you still uncomfortable, honey?" He inched his fingers into the lace of her underpants.

She nodded. "Terribly."

He dipped further, touching the tuft of hair, then the moist and swollen bud of her womanhood. "Still?"

"I might die of it," she said breathlessly.

He eased one finger into her, eliciting a low rumble of pleasure from the throat he kissed. "I don't want you to be uncomfortable," he whispered into her ear, taking the tender lobe in his teeth as he stroked and caressed her slick flesh with his finger.

She shook her head, unable to talk, her breath ragged and trapped.

He started to kiss his way down to where he touched, anxious and hungry to taste her, dying to make her wildly, insanely and hopelessly uncomfortable.

As he eased her panties down, her fingers dug into his hair, guiding his head. She quivered as his tongue curled against her.

She whispered his name as he blew a soft breath over her. She murmured a plea for more and he tasted her again. Her thighs tightened around his head as he licked her, loving how she trembled and rocked and finally shuddered helplessly with a long, sweet climax.

Kissing the delicate skin of her inner thighs, and nibbling at the dip of her stomach, the underside of her breasts, the heated column of her throat, they finally managed to get him undressed.

"Still uncomfortable?" he asked teasingly.

She half sighed, half laughed. "Not as uncomfortable as I'm about to make you."

She closed her hands over his shaft and stroked him, making him swell with a surge of blood. He dropped back on the bed, as pain and pleasure and raw need shot up his back, down his legs, blinding him. She feathered his body with kisses and caressed his erection, her soft woman's hair tickling his chest and stomach as she took him into her mouth.

He groaned in ecstasy, his whole body on fire. Her lips were like satin gloves, her hands steady and relentless as she suckled and stroked and cupped him until he thought he'd scream.

"C'mere, Jessie." He gently brought her up, as she covered him in more kisses.

The room smelled like sex and flowers, and her lips were salty and smooth. He managed to slide over to the nightstand, retrieve a condom and sheath himself without really ending one long, juicy kiss.

He positioned himself over her, his erection seeking the heat of her. When she lifted her hips to him, he slid in slowly, watching the pleasure unfold over her features, seeing the flush darken her skin and harden her nipples.

She said his name and pulled him down for a kiss, arching sharply to drive him into the warm, wet envelope of her body. As her legs wrapped around his hips, he sucked in a breath,

unable to believe the burn, the hot, wicked ache she caused
in every cell in his body.

With each thrust, she whispered his name, begged for all
of him, dug her nails in his back. Mind-numbing pleasure
licked over him as he thrust into her, lost in her sweet,
womanly body. Lost in the pretty, fresh sex of Jessie.

She quaked furiously, her muscles spasming around him.

And then he was just so deep and far gone and so utterly
lost inside her that he let go until he'd released everything he
had inside her.

They didn't speak or separate or move for a long, long time,
until their breathing became normal, and their mixed perspi-
ration chilled their skin. Then he eased himself off her to look
at the woman he'd just made love to.

Her hair was everywhere, and her eyes were wide pools of
the prettiest color green he'd ever seen.

He'd known she was pretty. Known she was sexy and
charming and attractive. But he'd never realized that Jessie
Clayton was stunning. He'd never realized she was beautiful.

He broke their peaceful silence. "If I ask you a personal
question, will you tell me the truth?"

That made her smile. "If you can't get the truth out of me
now, when we're naked and basking in the proverbial after-
glow, then we're sunk."

"You're right." He leaned up on one elbow and fluttered
some strands of hair through his fingers. "But I really need to
know this. To know something about you."

"What is it, Cade?"

"Why do you hide your eyes and your hair?"

The way she looked at him made him think, *We're sunk.*

Five

Cade's question yanked Jessie from a state of pure rapture to one of stark terror.

"Excuse me?" Her response was a time-buying ploy, accompanied by a not-so-subtle shift in her body that could distract him.

But he wasn't diverted. "What are you hiding?"

"Cade." She tried to laugh as though the question were simply ridiculous. Then she leaned up on her elbow to show him her bare, flushed body. "Do I look like I'm hiding something?"

He shook his head, sliding his hands over her waist and backside. "At work, I mean."

"We're not talking about work, remember?"

"I just think a woman as beautiful as you would show it off a little."

She made a face. "I'm not beautiful, but thank you. And, hey, I like my look. If you don't like it—"

"I like *you*," he countered, kissing the tip of her nose for emphasis, then inching down to her mouth. "Can't you tell?"

She sighed and rubbed her legs over his, their bodies all lined up perfectly again. "I can tell. The question is…"

"Will everyone else be able to tell, too?" He finished her thought perfectly, his eyes glimmering like burned coals.

"We have to be discreet," she said. "No sex in your office."

"What about the conference room?"

She narrowed her eyes, but couldn't help laughing. "Maybe in The Closet."

His chuckle was just a low and sexy rumble that tickled her insides. As they cuddled into each other, Jessie let the newness of the sensation wash over her. Cade was her lover. Cade McMann was her very own amazing, fabulous lover.

"What about Fin?"

His question jerked her back to reality and she cursed herself for the little gasp she gave in response. "Fin? What about her?"

"She'll figure it out."

"I don't want to shadow her, Cade." Jessie pulled back enough to look in his eyes. "And you don't need to tell her about this."

"I won't have to. She's smart. She knows everything."

Not everything. She doesn't know her own daughter. "Let's just try to keep this quiet. It might not—"

"Yes it will," he said with a tiny squeeze. "It will last."

Slowly, she raised her face to his. Did he *mean* that? He answered her with one long, sensual kiss that made her head spin and her body ache for him all over again.

Then he showed her that it could last, at least another hour.

Saturday morning slipped into Saturday afternoon with the same ease that Jessie moved around Cade's hardwood floors and his comfortably elegant apartment in an oversize Chicago Cubs T-shirt that he lent to her. She called Lainie and told her she'd be home…sometime. He went out for coffee and brought her a toothbrush, then they took a shower in a sparkling marble stall with glass block that poured sunlight over their naked bodies and two shower heads that thoroughly soaked them. They made omelets and made love all afternoon.

In the evening they ordered Chinese and watched *Top Gun* on a movie channel and afterward, Jessie found a photo album in one of the wall-to-wall mahogany bookshelves, and she "met" his family in Chicago.

His four sisters were as attractive as he, and his mother looked like a modern version of Donna Reed. He walked her through the album, which his mother had lovingly made him when he moved from Chicago to New York. The only sadness in his voice was when they'd come to a picture of his dad, a strapping man who seemed to radiate happiness from every picture, his love for his wife and five children obvious even in the two-dimensional snapshots. Jessie could only imagine how palpable that love must have been in real life.

"Your family is like a storybook of midwestern perfection," she said, closing the album. "Did you ever argue?"

He chuckled and put the album back on the bookshelf, returning quickly to snuggle with her on the burgundy leather couch. "The girls fought plenty. Over everything. Boys, clothes, who stole whose hairbrush. And, God, don't even start on how much time they wasted in the bathroom."

"It must have been fun with all those kids," Jessie mused. "My siblings were horses and ranch hands. No one ever fought over a hairbrush. Well, maybe a horse's hairbrush."

"But you got the bathroom and all your parents' attention. I had to achieve perfection—in grades and sports and life—

to compete with all those girls." He pulled her into a horizontal lounge, lining their bodies exactly like they'd been most of the past twenty-four hours.

"I had plenty of attention, that's true," Jessie agreed. "God knows they wanted me."

"Then why didn't they have more kids?"

Jessie swallowed hard. She'd never, ever lied about being adopted. Why would she start now? Why would she keep that secret from her lover?

"I'm adopted," she said, glancing up for his reaction. "My parents couldn't have children."

His eyes flashed at the news. "Really? I didn't know that."

"Well, why would you?"

"I don't know." He pulled her more securely against him. "There's a lot I don't know about you yet. But I'm glad they adopted you. God, just think about it. I'm so glad…" His voice trailed off, as people often did when they thought about the choice some young unwed mother had to make.

Except that, in this case, that young unwed mother was his boss.

He had to feel the quickening of her heart as she waited for the next question. The one every friend asked: *Have you ever tried to find your birth mother?*

Before he asked, she slid her hand under his T-shirt and caressed his chest. His low, satisfied groan told her how much he liked her touch. Easily, effortlessly, she trailed her fingers over his skin, dipping into the waistband of his jeans and gliding over the tip of an erection he always seemed to have.

Cade rocked into her fingertips, starting the dance that was already becoming as familiar as it was thrilling. Thank God he was easy to distract. She nibbled his jaw and then his mouth with a long, soulful, openmouthed kiss.

In a matter of minutes, they were shedding clothes and giving in to the temptation to taste and touch each other again.

Naked and ready, Jessie rubbed herself against the muscular planes of his broad chest, the coarse golden hairs tickling her breasts. Cade steadied her hips with his powerful hands and guided her over his erection.

As he entered her, she closed her eyes, dropping her head back as the force of his thrust touched her in the deepest part of her body.

"You didn't let me finish my thought," he said softly.

Her eyes popped open, unable to believe he'd go back there now, when they were...

"I know what you were going to say," she whispered, dipping down to kiss his cheek. "I'm glad she did, too."

And that, she hoped, would be the last discussion they would have about her birth mother.

But the lie of omission made her heart heavy and when Cade climaxed into her, rasping endearments and words of sweet, honest affection, she closed her eyes and realized that if they got any closer, she'd have to tell him the truth.

And that would change everything.

When they were done, she clung to him, inhaled his scent and selfishly, foolishly, put off the inevitable.

"What are you doing?" Cade tapped on the partially opened bathroom door and it creaked inward. "You're dressed?"

"Can you imagine?" Jessie laughed at the incredulity in his voice. But, to be fair, she had spent most of the past two days *not* dressed. She tugged up the black zipper of her new favorite sweater and added, "Sorry, but it's almost five on Sunday afternoon, Cade. I have to go home and get ready for work tomorrow."

Cade rubbed the beginnings of a late-afternoon shadow that

darkened his cheeks even though he'd shaved that morning. Jessie had perched on the side of the tub and watched, an act almost more intimate than any of the things they'd done to each other's bodies over the past forty-eight hours. Which, she had to admit, had gone way past intimate.

"I don't suppose we could both call in sick." He grinned at her. "Might raise some eyebrows."

"Yeah," Jessie agreed. "It might. Because, as you noted a few days ago, I've never once called in sick."

"Me neither." He leaned against the doorjamb and studied her with a slow, hot gaze, his sexy mouth curled up in a smile. "But this is just cause."

Laughing, she turned to the vanity to put away the few items of makeup she'd taken out of her purse. As she picked up the toothbrush he'd bought her, his hand closed over hers.

"You can keep that here."

She looked at his reflection in the mirror. His smile was gone. "Are you sure?"

"Of course." He held her gaze. "I told you, Jessie, this is not some quickie office affair."

"It was anything but quick," she said, attempting a breezy chuckle.

"I mean it." His eyes narrowed and his hand tightened on her wrist. "I want you to come back. A lot. Often."

For a moment, she couldn't speak. A million thoughts warred for space in her head. How could they be an item and work together? How would they keep it quiet? How could she keep her hands off him at work?

"What about Fin?" Somehow, of all her mental questions, that was the one she let slip out.

"I'll handle Fin," he told her. "Anyway, I told you, there's no rule about dating co-workers."

"But you…" They covered this last night, but the question still nagged her. "You don't make mistakes, Cade. That much I know from watching you."

"I try not to, that's true. But this isn't a mistake. It just might be a little complicated." He managed to slide the toothbrush out of her grasp and placed it next to his. "But we can manage our way around the complications."

Could they? There were complications he hadn't even dreamed of. "This could be difficult."

In a second, he turned her from the mirror, to look at her face instead of her reflection. "This could be wonderful." His voice was husky, but not from desire or arousal. "You are so different, Jessie." He pushed her hair back from her face, his gaze sliding from her eyes to her mouth and back up to her eyes again. "I've never met anyone like you. I'm willing to take a risk and face some complications."

"I'm the same girl I was last week," she said. "You just got behind my glasses."

"And I like it back there." His lips hitched up in a knowing smile. "You do know this is real, don't you?"

She sighed, the idea of real making her dizzy. "I know, Cade."

"Good." He kissed her forehead gently and pulled her against his chest.

Jessie closed her eyes and laid her head on his shoulder. "I don't know how you do it, Cade," she whispered, "but you're really good at making me not care about…other stuff."

"You have the same effect on me."

The buzzer from the lobby reverberated through the intercom box on the wall. "Cade? It's Fin. Are you home?"

Fin? A surge of adrenaline propelled Jessie out of his arms as she stared at the intercom. *Fin?*

Surprise sparkled in his eyes. "Speaking of complicated…

Guess who's in the lobby?" He reached over and pressed the button to talk. "I'm here, Fin. What are you doing?"

"I was on my way to the office and thought I'd drop by and leave some updated spreadsheets for you to study before you meet with Liam. Can I come up?"

He closed his eyes for a second, and gave his head a quick shake. "She never stops working," he mouthed. As he leaned back to the intercom, Jessie slipped out of his arms, certain he would feel the hammering of her heart.

Fin was *there*. In Cade's apartment building. On her way up to his front door. With shaking hands Jessie finished packing up her makeup, left the toothbrush, and slid by Cade as he buzzed Fin up.

"I don't want to be here when she comes in," Jessie said when he found her in the living room. As Cade started to argue, she held up her hand. "Please, Cade. I'm an intern. You're the boss." *And Fin's my real mother.*

Jessie buried the thought, concentrating instead on getting out of there. Her gaze darted around the room and she practically pirouetted in a desperate search for her handbag.

"God, I hate this," she murmured, frustration and guilt bubbling through her. "It feels…" Spotting it, she scooped up the bag and started toward the door.

Cade grabbed her shoulder with one firm hand. "Jessie, stop. I want to take you home myself. I don't want you to run off like this."

"I'm not running off. I don't want to see her, Cade."

"Jessie, there's nothing wrong with this. We're both single and free and we like each other. A lot."

She eased away, backing toward the door. "It's just that…"

He regarded her closely, pinning her with his gaze. "Would you tell me why you always avoid her?"

"I don't avoid her." *Liar, liar.* "Is it so hard to imagine that this intern would rather not run face to face into the editor-in-chief when it is painfully obvious that I am sleeping with the executive editor?"

"But you always have avoided her."

The doorbell rang and Jessie didn't know whether to curse or thank God for the interruption.

"Let's get something straight," Cade said quietly, stilling her with a gentle grip on both shoulders. "I am not ashamed of how I feel about you."

The words touched her, as honest and affectionate as his fingertips. This had nothing to do with being ashamed of Cade or the fact that they liked each other, and she knew it. He didn't, but she did.

For one crazy minute, Jessie thought about confessing everything. About opening the door and standing in front of Fin and saying "I am your daughter."

But something told her that if she did, her whole world would fall apart. And right now, for the first time since she'd come to New York, her world actually felt together.

"Come on," he said, guiding her toward the door. "You can leave if you prefer, but I'm not going to hide you like some back-door quickie. I'm too proud of you."

Buoyed by the words, Jessie squared her shoulders and stood next to Cade as he opened his front door.

Fin's green eyes widened as she stared at Jessie. "Oh," she said with a soft gasp. "Hello, Jessie."

"Hello, Fin," she said, offering her warmest smile. "I was just on my way out when you rang."

Cade opened the door wider. "Come on in, Fin. Jessie, feel free to stay. Fin's just dropping off some papers."

She pulled her bag higher on her shoulder and inched

toward the door. "Thanks, but I really have to go. See you tomorrow, Fin."

Fin was processing the whole scene, Jessie could tell. But she was too much of a lady to say anything but goodbye as Jessie walked out.

"I'll be right back, Fin." Cade walked with Jessie to the elevator, slipping his hand into hers. "I really would prefer to take you home in a cab."

"Maybe next time." She tapped the down button. Twice.

"No maybe about it," he countered. "And there will be a next time."

"Of course there will be. I left my toothbrush." She reached up and gave him a quick hug as the elevator doors opened, and whispered, "And thanks for making me so *comfortable.*"

She heard him chuckle as the doors closed and it wasn't until that moment that she realized he still had her glasses in the pocket of his suit coat.

When Cade returned to his apartment, Fin still waited in the entry, amusement dancing in her expression.

"Well, color me astonished, Mr. McMann."

"Glad I can still surprise you, Fin." He didn't close the door behind him, fighting an undercurrent of irritation that she'd interrupted his last few hours with Jessie. "Do you have the files?"

"I'm sorry," she said quickly. "If I had known you were, uh, preoccupied, I wouldn't have stopped by."

He crossed his arms and gave her a warning look. Everything in him wanted to protect Jessie and her reputation. "It's not casual."

Fin met his gaze. "That's fine. Except that she's…"

"She's what?"

"Whoa." Fin held up the file folder in mock defense. "No

need to get all testy about. But, honestly, she's an intern at *Charisma*. And quite a bit younger than you are."

He tamped down more irritation. "I'm familiar with the EPH employee handbook, Fin, and there are no rules against employees dating each other. And she's twenty-three, which makes her seven years younger than I am. Hardly a generation gap."

"And she's your choice for the shadow intern."

He latched the door behind him and strode past Fin into the living room. "Not yet."

She stayed on his heels. "When this gets out, and she's been chosen as my shadow, there'll be talk of favoritism."

"Then she shouldn't be your shadow." He walked to the galley kitchen and yanked open the refrigerator. Beer or water? "I'll pick a different intern."

"But she's the best candidate."

He grabbed a beer. "You want something to drink?"

When Fin didn't say anything, he flipped the twist-off cap into the trash and returned to the living room. Fin stood in front of the picture window, the file discarded on a table, her attention riveted on the expanse of Central Park and the New York skyline that filled the view.

"There's something very…special about her," Fin finally said.

He snorted. "No kidding."

As he took a long pull on the bottle, Fin turned, an expression of determination on her face. An expression he knew well. He never fought that determination; it was a waste of time.

"I want her to shadow me," Fin declared. "We can fend off claims of favoritism with the truth: I'm making this decision, not you."

His chest tightened. He didn't know why, but Jessie really

didn't want that assignment. Would he be betraying her by agreeing to this?

"Fin, this isn't about suspecting her of spying on the magazine, is it? Because she's not. I'm sure of that."

"Are you?" She lifted a dubious brow. "I mean, she got in pretty tight with you in a hurry."

He slammed the bottle on an end table. "I've known her since April."

Fin held up both hands. "Stop it, Cade. I am not accusing her of anything. And who you sleep with is your business, as long as it doesn't impact the magazine."

"Oh, of course." A healthy dose of bitterness colored his tone. "That's the only thing that matters to you."

"Cade!" Her eyes darkened in disappointment, the color and shape suddenly reminding him of the woman he'd just spent the weekend making love to. Everything was going to remind him of Jessie; he might as well face that right now.

He blew out a disgusted breath, angry with himself for making the snide remark to Fin.

"It's true," Fin admitted softly. "The magazine may be the only thing that matters to me, but I want you to be happy. You know, you're like a brother to me."

Her declaration only deepened the guilt that nipped at him for the comment. "Sorry, Fin. I'm just not thinking straight."

She smiled and put a hand on his shoulder. "I've heard love can do that to you."

"Love?" He choked at the word. "This was our first date."

Her eyes sparkled. "The one that started on Friday night and ended on Sunday afternoon?"

He grinned. "Yep. That'd be the one."

"Mmmm. Okay. Then let me put it this way, I've heard *lust* can mess with your mind, too."

He picked up the beer bottle and rubbed the label, thinking about how to respond. "I don't think it's lust, either." Although there was plenty of that, too.

"Listen," she said. "While you figure out exactly what it is, I'd like to get to know that girl better."

"Woman." Cade glanced up from the label of his bottle. "She's not a girl."

Fin smiled. "Young lady. I have no problems with you dating Jessie, but I still want to know what she's all about. Even more so, if you're dating her. Think of me as the older sister you never had."

He rolled his eyes. "I have enough sisters, thank you."

"Too bad. I have plenty of brothers, too. You can always use more. And listen, Cade, she's the sharpest and most qualified of the interns for the job, so *not* picking her would be a disservice to the magazine."

He took a sip of his beer, eyeing her. She was right, damn it. "Well that's a typical strategy-driven Fin Elliott decision if I ever heard one."

"Good. Then you agree. She starts tomorrow morning as my shadow intern from 8:00 a.m. to noon, every day."

He tried to swallow the beer, but it got stuck in his throat. Jessie wouldn't like it, and he still didn't know why.

But come tomorrow morning, he was sure he'd find out.

Six

Jessie hadn't even tried to hide the truth from Lainie, confiding enough about her new romance to satisfy her roommate's curiosity, but not so much that Jessie felt she'd betrayed the intimacy she shared with Cade.

This was too new, too special, too wonderful to be chatted about like a mild flirtation. And it was too all-consuming for Jessie to concentrate on anything at work on Monday.

Cade had stopped by her cube early in the morning with a cup of coffee mixed exactly the way she liked it with extra milk. His gaze was just as warm as it had been over the weekend, and he looked even more breathtaking in a suit…now that she knew what he looked like out of one.

Before he went to his office, he'd quietly set her glasses on her desk, without a word, and she donned them the minute he disappeared. An hour passed where Jessie managed to get through e-mails, but mostly she gave in to the full-body tingles every time she relived the sensation of taking Cade inside her, of watching him lose control, of his sincere expression when he asked her to leave her toothbrush.

"It must be love."

Jessie jerked around from her computer screen to see Scarlet perched on the only chair in the cube, her long legs crossed lazily, her hands behind her head.

"Excuse me?"

"I've been sitting here for five minutes," Scarlet said with a sly smile. "And you not only didn't hear me, but, for the entire time I've been here, you've been reading the same four-sentence e-mail about a new mail-room procedure."

"I have?" Jessie felt the blood rush to her face. "I mean, I have. Because, you may not know this, Scarlet, but an intern has a very close relationship with the mail room. I make it my business to know every piece of mail that comes in and out of the editorial department. Their procedures down there are critical to our success up here."

Scarlet grinned and flipped one of her springy curls over her shoulder. "Cut the kiss-up, Miss Clayton. You got the job."

"The what?"

"The brass ring of internships. As a matter of fact, you're late for your meeting with…" Scarlet consulted a page of the notebook she carried. "The ad sales manager."

"Why would I be in a meeting with the ad sales manager?"

"I believe a review of the January spreads is on the agenda, but Fin wasn't specific."

At the mention of Fin, Jessie's stomach contracted. It couldn't be. He wouldn't do this to her. "What are you talking about, Scarlet?"

Scarlet's teasing expression morphed into one of pure joy as she reached over and gave Jessie a hug. "Congratulations, you are Finola Elliott's shadow intern and, sweetie, you have earned the honors."

All the blood that had warmed her face drained down to a puddle in her toes. "Her shadow intern?" She'd asked him not to. She'd *asked* him. Did she need to tell him why?

"Are you sure?" she managed to ask Scarlet. "Because there are a few other really great—"

"Here's the memo." Scarlet held a piece of paper and all Jessie could see was *From: Cade McMann* on the second line. So he'd made the decision, drafted a memo and released it without even coming over to tell her.

The creamy coffee she'd been sipping suddenly turned metallic in her mouth.

"Don't worry," Scarlet said reassuringly. "Cade told me you didn't want to lose the Spring Fling layout, and you won't have to. You only shadow Fin from eight to noon every day. In the afternoons, you can still work on our projects." Scarlet's face lit with excitement. "It's perfect. And almost guaranteed to end in a job offer. A paying job."

Jessie couldn't process this. He'd talked about her schedule to Scarlet? And not to her?

"Jessie? What's the matter?" Scarlet asked. "You don't want pay?"

Jessie couldn't even laugh at the joke. "I don't feel good."

Scarlet's green eyes filled with concern and she touched her fingertips to Jessie's forehead. "Do you have a fever?"

Oh, yeah. That was one way to describe it. "I just…I think I have to go home."

Scarlet's expression registered a mix of worry and shock. "Are you sure?"

Jessie nodded. She had to get out of there. If she didn't, she'd march into Cade McMann's office and demand to know why he said all sorts of things about this being real and how he'd handle Fin and *complications* and… Oh!

"That's why I've been so spacey, I guess," Jessie said quickly, opening her bottom drawer to grab her handbag. "I'm just sick. I'm taking a sick day, Scarlet."

"Do you want me to get you a cab? Maybe Fin's driver is still downstairs."

"No!" At the sharp retort and Scarlet's surprised reaction, Jessie cleared her throat. "No, thanks. I just want to— I'll go home and take something. I'll be fine. I just need to take the rest of the day off."

She was halfway out of the cube when, way down the hall near Lainie's desk, she saw the door to Cade's office open.

She could face him down or leave him cold.

Feeling completely chicken and desperate to be alone, she made her choice.

"Bye, Scarlet. I'll call you."

Cade fought the urge to shove the director of subscriptions out the door, instead of using every people skill he had to close the meeting diplomatically and quickly.

How long could that guy blow hot air about demographics and distribution? Couldn't he read the edge in Cade's body language? He didn't want to sit and listen to a presentation on tip-in cards, for God's sake. He wanted—no, he *needed*—to get to Jessie before the memo he'd signed was printed, distributed and discussed. But his assistant had scheduled the meeting in his only open block for the morning and he'd been yanked into the conference room before he could get to Jessie.

Hustling down the hallway, he prayed she kept lunch open. He had to explain, had to—

Was that Jessie's auburn braid flying out the lobby?

As he turned the corner to her cube, all he could see was Scarlet standing there, hands on her hips and a look of utter dismay on her face.

He jerked to a halt and glanced at the empty chair at Jessie's desk.

"Where is she?"

Scarlet's eyes widened a bit at his demand. "She just went home sick."

Oh, man. "What's wrong with her?"

"Well, I would have chalked it up to lovesickness based on the fact that she got flowers on Friday and still looked loopy on Monday, but I don't know."

"Did she say what was wrong?"

Scarlet shook her head. "It was the weirdest thing, Cade. I told her about the shadow internship and she—"

"You told her?"

"Well, duh. She works for me. What is the problem with telling her?"

There would be no problem if he weren't sleeping with her and making promises he hadn't kept.

"Nothing," he said absently, noticing she'd left her computer on and her desk in a state of disarray. He swallowed an angry curse at the director of subscriptions. If he hadn't been delayed…

No, that wouldn't have made any difference. He'd screwed up all by himself.

"She wasn't that excited about the shadowing job," Scarlet said.

No surprise there. "Would you do me a favor, Scarlet? Would you tell my assistant to cancel the rest of my appointments today?"

She frowned at him. "Yeah. But why?"

"I'm going home sick."

He turned and headed for the lobby, but still heard Scarlet's parting shot. "Does someone want to tell me what the heck is going on around here?"

There was only one person who would understand. One person Jessie could talk to. She prayed he wasn't out riding or roping or ranching.

She needed her daddy. Mom would have been better, but she buried the ache that accompanied that thought and managed to get home on the subway without shedding a single tear.

She waited to call until she'd let herself into the cluttered studio apartment she and Lainie shared. It was only nine o'clock in Colorado, but Travis Clayton could be anywhere on the Silver Moon at that hour.

To Jessie's relief, her father answered his cell phone on the first ring and admitted that he was still at the kitchen table drinking his coffee. With the time difference, that wasn't so unusual. Except he was an early riser, a hard worker. Since her mother had died, however, Dad spent a lot of time in the kitchen, thinking. Travis wasn't even fifty years old; he should start to think about a life. A new life.

But that wasn't the purpose of her call.

In ten minutes, she'd explained the situation, leaving out the fact that she'd spent the weekend with Cade. Some things a father didn't need to know.

"You shouldn't have run off, Jess," Travis said immediately. She knew that already. She'd decided that on the subway ride home. She should have confronted Cade. But what was done, was done, and now she needed to figure out a plan.

"I know, Dad. But it's complicated." *Complications.* Didn't

Cade say they could avoid them? Then, wham. One big, fat, nasty complication called *deceit*.

"In this man's defense, honey, he doesn't know the situation. He doesn't understand why you wouldn't want a job that is—what did that woman call it—the brass ring of internships? And the ticket to a paying job?"

"Daddy," Jessie sighed and curled deeper into the second-hand sofa she and Lainie had recently recovered in shiny polished cotton. "I told you why I came here. It's not about the money."

"You shouldn't have gone there without telling me why." She heard the note of gruffness in the reprimand. The note that usually meant his heart felt something different than what he was saying.

"You would have tried to stop me."

"For good reason." In the background, porcelain clinked and she imagined her father drinking from his favorite white mug, surrounded by a country kitchen that overlooked the most beautiful valley and mountains in the world. "There's nothing to be gained by dredging up that lady's history, Jessie. She was a fifteen-year-old girl when she had you. I've no doubt the last thing a woman running a big New York City magazine wants is a twenty-three-year-old reminder of her past."

"All the more reason for that past not to shadow her around for half the day."

"Honey, listen to me. She has no reason to suspect you are her daughter."

"Daddy, listen to *me*." She stood as though it would help her make the point to him. "I am the *daughter* of Travis and Lauren Clayton and no amount of irrefutable DNA can change that."

"Aw, angel, I know that."

"But, Daddy, it's just that…" *Mom's gone.* "If there's any

chance Fin and I could have a relationship...well, I'd really, really like that."

"Do you feel any kind of connection at all to this woman, this Fin?"

Jessie sighed. The only thing connected to Finola Elliott was *Charisma* magazine and Elliott Publication Holdings. She didn't seem to have any other life. "Well, there's definitely a resemblance. Maybe you'd have to be looking for it, but it's there."

"That's not the kind of connection I meant."

"I know. Well, no. I've just watched her, and stayed out of her way."

He was silent for a moment. Then he sighed and said, "Maybe you need to get in her way."

He was right. "Dad, she registered her name on an adoption Web site. Don't you think that might mean she's hoping to find me? Hoping for the same relationship I want?"

"I don't know, honey. She's living in a different world and from what you say, she's a Type A workaholic. She's never had children, Jessie. She doesn't sound too maternal."

You got that right. Unlike Jessie's mother, who had doted and adored her daughter. "She's not," Jessie acknowledged wistfully.

"I just don't want you to get hurt, sweetheart. By any of these people."

Too late for that. But Jessie didn't want to cloud the issue by discussing her relationship with Cade. That romance wasn't going to last anyway. She couldn't trust him. He didn't even tell her about the decision. She squeezed her eyes against the pain that seared her every time she thought of it.

"You're probably right, Daddy. You usually are."

She heard his soft chuckle. "Listen, if there was some way you could find out that she is looking for you, more than just registering on a Web site, but really looking, then I'd feel better about you telling her who you are."

"Yeah, I would, too. This is like living a lie." Jessie paced from one end of the tiny studio to the other. "I hate it."

"I bet you do. And maybe the shadowing thing is just the ticket, Jessie. You can really get to know her and maybe you could find out if she's willing to face her past."

She paused by the door and flipped through some envelopes that Lainie had left in the bill basket they'd hung on the wall. "I guess you're right. The shadowing would give me the perfect opportunity to do some digging."

"She won't be suspicious of you," her father reassured her. "Just be yourself and take advantage of what they've offered you."

"I know, I feel so bad acting all creepy about the assignment. It's a vote of confidence and, you know, I may have started this little secret job for one reason, but I really like the business. And I'm good at it."

"I have no doubt about that. Does that mean you're never coming home?" He couldn't hide the note of disappointment in his voice.

"I'll be back," she promised. But then she thought of Cade. Not only did she love working at the magazine, she loved being with him. But that feeling might not be mutual, and her father sounded like he needed a little reassurance, too. "Hey," she said with a heavy injection of warmth in her voice. "You know how much I love you."

"I just want you to be happy, sweetheart."

"I know." And she was happy…yesterday.

Cade stood with his knuckle in midair, about to knock. He'd raced to Jessie's apartment, charmed his way in the front door when another tenant left, found her apartment number on the mailbox, and bounded up the four flights of stairs two at a time.

His heart hammered steadily, but not from tearing up the stairs. Through the thin wooden door, he heard her voice.

And froze at the sound of her words.

This is like living a lie. I hate it.

What was like living a lie? He leaned an inch closer to the door.

I guess you're right. The shadowing would give me the perfect opportunity to do some digging.

His gut clenched as he listened to her describe a "secret little job."

I'll be back. Hey, you know how much I love you.

The words punched him so hard, he almost reeled right down the stairs. Without ever knocking, he turned and got as far from Jessie Clayton's door as he could.

Chloe Davenport looked up from the filing cabinet that took up part of the long wall that ran along the sides of Cade and Fin's executive offices.

"He's not in, Jessie," Chloe said. "And Diana's not here either." Although the two assistants were technically assigned to each executive, they often stepped in for one another.

"Is he expected in today?" Jessie asked, adjusting her glasses out of habit as she looked at the lovely brunette and mentally noted that she'd never seen Chloe wear that shantung silk dress before. Of course she hadn't. As Lainie noted long ago, Chloe never repeated.

"He should be in shortly. Do you have a meeting scheduled with him, Jessie?"

"Well, no, not really." Maybe she should get on his calendar. That might be the only way he'd ever talk to her again. She still couldn't believe he hadn't called her all afternoon or all evening. She'd checked to see if the phone was working so many times that Lainie started to tease her.

Even though it had been no teasing matter. To avoid the discussion, Jessie had gone to a movie alone, relieved when her roommate crashed early. Jessie had risen at five, and was out the door to work before Lainie had stirred.

"I'll have him call you when he gets in," Chloe said, then she narrowed her blue eyes. "Are you feeling better, by the way? Scarlet said you went home sick yesterday."

"I am, thank you." Jessie took a deep, steadying breath. "And I'm ready to start my shadowing assignment today."

Chloe's face brightened. "Yes! Congratulations on that. Fin is usually in way before eight, but she had to run an errand this morning. I'll buzz you when she's here, so you can get started."

"Great. I can't wait."

"You can't wait for what?"

Jessie's legs threatened to give way at the sound of Cade's voice. Mustering more indifference than she could have imagined possible, she turned to see him strolling toward his office.

"Shadow intern, here." She gave him a sassy mock salute. "Reporting for duty."

His eyes narrowed so imperceptibly she was certain Chloe hadn't noticed. But then Chloe hadn't spent forty-eight straight hours memorizing every expression on his face.

"Glad you're feeling better," he said, just pointedly enough to make the hair on the back of her neck stand up. He paused at his assistant's desk and picked up a few pink message slips, and when he looked down to read them, instead of at her, Jessie cursed the disappointment that kicked her as hard as Oscar's hind leg.

"Cade." The word was out before she could check herself in front of Chloe.

He looked up. "Hmmm?" Speaking of indifference. What was going on with him?

"No complications, huh?" Forget Chloe. This was too important.

He drew back at her words, searching her face. "Jessie," he said slowly, indicating his office with one hand, "why don't you come in here so we can talk?"

He let her wait for a few minutes alone in his office while he looked through the same messages that had been on Diana's desk since the night before.

Two could play this game, Jessie Clayton.

Finally, he strolled in and closed the door behind him. Just in case the resolve he'd swore he'd have around her melted and she ended up in his arms.

"So what made you change your mind?" he asked, purposely keeping all emotion out of his voice. "I hadn't expected enthusiasm."

She turned from the window. In the time he made her wait, she'd taken off her glasses. So she really wanted to play dirty.

"I don't see that I have a choice," she said, her voice unnaturally bright. "And I think I've acted foolishly. Of course I want the opportunity to shadow Fin."

He nodded thoughtfully, but didn't make a move. The only sound in the room was the soft ticking of the brass clock on his desk.

"What is the matter with you?" she finally asked. "Why are you acting so weird?"

He released a little breath he hadn't realized he'd been

holding. "Why don't you tell me how mad you are that I made that decision after you asked me not to?"

He'd give her a chance to tell him the truth. Maybe she would.

She waved her hand casually. "Oh, I'm over it."

Or maybe she wouldn't. "Really? That was easy."

"Cade." She took a step closer, as though physically unable to keep this far away from him. He knew the feeling. "You're the one who broke my trust. I wish you had told me first, but—"

He held up his hand to stop her. "Just tell me the truth, Jessie. What changed your mind?"

She shrugged. "I realized it was a good opportunity and I should take it."

"Uh-huh."

"And what changed yours, Cade?"

"Mine? Honestly, it was Fin's decision to choose you. But I never had a chance to tell you that."

She looked dubious. "You had a chance, but that's not what I mean. What changed your mind about me? Why are you acting like a different man than you were Sunday afternoon?"

"We're at work," he said coolly.

"I thought you weren't ashamed."

The crack in her voice squeezed his heart. "I'm not," he said, forcing a casual tone. "I figured you'd be so angry at me that—"

"I'm not, Cade." She moved closer, her fresh floral scent torturing him. "I'm going to make the best of the situation. It's a great opportunity and I'll take advantage of it."

Take advantage being the operative phrase.

Well, two could take advantage of a situation. Let her think she was getting inside information. She wouldn't find out anything that would help one of their competitors; he'd make sure of that.

And, in the meantime, he could take advantage of the situation, couldn't he? His arms already itched to hold her and he could taste her kiss.

As though her mind was on the same wavelength, she closed the space between them and looked up at him. Her arms slid around him and no force of nature could keep him from embracing her.

"I missed you," she whispered, looking up with nothing but total sincerity in those lovely green eyes.

"I missed you, too," he said. And that was no lie.

As he covered her mouth for the kiss she offered, the torture just increased. Sweet, blissful, achy torture.

Her tongue slipped into his mouth and he took it, pulling her into him to feel the response he couldn't fake under any circumstances.

As much as he tried to think of this as taking advantage of an opportunity, he knew he couldn't make love to Jessie anymore.

That would be a huge mistake.

Seven

Jessie arrived in the empty *Charisma* conference room a few minutes before eight-thirty. Fin would be in any moment for the morning meeting she held with various staff members every day. This would be the fourth session Jessie had attended as Fin's shadow intern, her fourth day in her new assignment.

And although he'd done everything he could to avoid anything resembling personal contact, Cade McMann was scheduled to be the only staff member in attendance at this, a management meeting, so she'd see him, too, in a matter of minutes.

She took a slow, deep breath at the prospect of being in the room with both Fin and Cade. Because the only thing more perplexing than the cool shoulder she was getting from Cade was the contrasting impression Fin had been making over the past few days.

Finola Elliott was tough, driven, smart, patient and strategic. She wore exquisite clothes and hid a small sprinkling of freckles with a light coat of makeup, but by the end of the day, the dusting of delicate pigmentation was visible. She always had an easy smile, and a very subtle sense of humor.

Fin was a woman of contradictions and that made Jessie like her—something Jessie wasn't sure she wanted to happen. What if Jessie liked Fin and revealed her secret, but Fin—

"Oh my God, wait until you see this." Scarlet breezed into the conference room, a swooshy tangerine skirt flipping around her legs as she practically ran to the last empty space on the layout wall. "C'mere!" she demanded to Jessie. "Check this out!"

Jessie circled the oval table in the center of the room, her gaze locked on a splash of bright yellow on the oversize page proof. Scarlet pushpinned the image into the corkboard with an air of complete victory.

"Look at you!" Scarlet exclaimed, standing back to admire the work.

Jessie stared at the picture, and her heart reared up like a stunned stallion. "Oh!"

The photographer had captured it all: her sideways glance of flirtation, along with a come-peek-at-me smile of invitation to a man who did just that. Cade's hungry eyes combined with just enough slack in his jaw to prove the timeless power of a half-unzipped sweater and a black lace bra.

"Is that not the sexiest 'Color Me Charismatic' we have ever had?" Scarlet half giggled with delight. "You two look like you're about to run off to the next bedroom and—"

"You should blur the faces."

Jessie jumped at the sound of Cade's voice behind her.

Scarlet whirled around and sliced him with a look as if he'd suggested heresy. "Are you out of your mind, Cade? The faces are the whole shot. All that chemistry! It's a wonder the page doesn't ignite. Good heavens, that designer will move ten thousand of those sweaters in January, thanks to every woman who dreams of having a man drool over her that way."

Jessie turned back to the picture, because the sight of Cade in two dimensions was only slightly easier to bear than Cade in real life. Especially when he wore that grim expression he only donned when he was about to make a directive that his staff wouldn't like.

"Blur the faces," he said again, ignoring all of Scarlet's exuberance and dropping some files and an electronic day planner at his usual seat. "That's the magazine's policy."

"Only when we use anonymous women-in-the-street shots, and we risk getting sued," Scarlet countered. "We're wasting a tremendous opportunity if we don't leave your faces in this picture. Don't you agree, Jessie?"

She felt both their demanding gazes on her. If it were up to her, she'd turn the thing into a billboard in Times Square. She loved the picture, but obviously, it didn't have the same impact on Cade.

"I have no intention of suing," she said calmly, as she made her way around the conference room table to where her notebook and files sat next to Cade's. Wordlessly, she slid her stuff down to leave a few empty chairs between them. "If you think the feature will be more effective leaving the photographer's subjects unblurred, go right ahead." She managed a blank look at Cade. "Unless you're worried about your reputation, Cade."

He opened a file, his face impassive. "I'm not."

Scarlet snorted softly. "I guess hearts could break all over Manhattan when they see his attention snared by the Lady in Yellow."

"No hearts will break," he said, using an apathetic tone Jessie imagined he'd practiced on his four sisters to deflect teasing. "I think we should keep it consistent with what we do every month. Our readers expect anonymity in this feature. It's part of the beauty of why CMC works so well."

Raw disappointment squeezed her throat. So much for Mr. There Will Be No Complications, the man who would be *proud* of her, of their relationship. He was ashamed. Embarrassed. Mortified that he'd ever drooled.

Jessie didn't trust her voice, so she merely took a seat without saying a word.

"Let Fin decide," Scarlet suggested, as their boss walked into the conference room.

"Let Fin decide what?" Fin threw a friendly smile at the group, smoothing her silk skirt as she took her seat. "What am I deciding now?"

"Look at this 'Color Me Charismatic' layout," Scarlet insisted, quickly unpinning the page to bring it to Fin. "Isn't it fabulous? Cade wants to blur the faces."

Fin leaned forward and studied the art.

Scarlet tapped her foot expectantly.

Cade casually poked at his electronic device, as though the decision didn't really concern him at all.

And all Jessie could do was hold her breath.

"This is…" Fin looked up slowly, her gaze zeroing in on Jessie. "Amazing."

Jessie managed a tight smile, the air still trapped in her lungs.

Fin tore her attention from Jessie, looked down to the picture and back up at her again, giving both a healthy dose of scrutiny. *Oh God.* "You look…"

Jessie's heart walloped against her chest, stealing every drop of blood from her head and threatening never to send any back. She blinked away a splash of light-headedness. *Here it comes. Here it comes.*

"You look…"

Like me. "Yes?"

"So different without your glasses, Jessie. You should get contacts."

Relief forced out her breath in a whoosh and she covered it with a quick laugh. Touching the frames of her glasses, she leaned back into her chair. "You think?"

The total lameness of the response must have been lost on Scarlet who clicked an impatient fingernail on the layout. "To blur or not to blur, Fin. That is the question."

"Well, I don't know." This time Fin looked at the picture and up at Cade, her expression morphed into a tease. Of course, Fin wasn't stupid. She'd walked in on Jessie and Cade together in his apartment. Surely she suspected that something more than intern training had been going on that afternoon. "You look pretty hot yourself, Cade. This expression could move some sweaters *and* magazines."

Cade shrugged. "I like when CMC is anonymous. I think it gives the whole feature a mysterious quality that readers like. But, hey, if you guys want to use me as the poster boy for sweater worship, feel free." He shot a lazy grin at Jessie that fried her nerve endings.

Scarlet swooped up the layout with a smug look of satisfaction. "Sweater worship. You're brilliant, Cade. That's the headline."

She tacked the layout back up and flitted out the door. "Have a great meeting, you guys."

And somehow Jessie survived the next forty-five minutes, but only by not taking one more look at Cade in two *or* three dimensions.

Until the very last moment, when Fin closed up her leather portfolio and stood to leave, tilting her head toward the picture that hung on the wall.

"Perhaps this is uncomfortable," she said quietly. "I didn't want to make a point of it in front of Scarlet, but if either of you prefers anonymity in that photo, I'll back you on that."

Jessie felt Cade's gaze on her, but she kept her attention on Fin. "Thank you, Fin. That's very kind of you."

Fin nodded. "Why don't you discuss it privately for a few minutes?" She scooped up her papers and headed toward the door. "I have a personal phone call to make, Jessie, but after that, I'll meet you in the lobby. We're off to the Revlon offices for an advertising meeting."

Before either of them could argue, Fin left the room, and closed the door behind her.

"That was awkward," Cade said.

"That was sweet." Their simultaneous assessments cancelled each other out.

"Sweet?" Cade choked the word out. "What was sweet about it?"

Jessie swiveled her conference room chair in his direction, something she hadn't done for the entire meeting. Did she think he wouldn't notice that she didn't look at him? He braced himself as she reached up and took off her glasses, and gave him one endless gaze rich with question and meaning.

The only problem was, he didn't know the answers and couldn't interpret her look.

"I think she was being very classy," Jessie said quietly. "She realizes this might be prickly for us."

"Precisely. Awkward, as I said."

"It doesn't have to be, Cade."

For the zillionth time, Cade wondered exactly how she'd react if he'd told her he'd overheard her telephone conversation. That he knew she saw the shadowing assignment as a chance to "dig around." That she'd promised *someone* that she'd be back. And that she loved that same someone, whoever he was.

"I'm just keeping things professional," he said simply. If he showed his cards now and called her on the corporate espionage, she'd run away. And he'd hurt in a wholly different kind of way.

Besides, he rationalized, if she disappeared, he'd never know who'd hired her and he wouldn't risk making that mistake. He'd made enough mistakes where Jessie Clayton was concerned; at least he would find out who sent the mole into his operation.

"As far as that is concerned—" He indicated the layout wall. "I still believe we should blur the faces."

She followed his finger to the image, a smile tugging at her pretty mouth. "I like it."

"Of course you do," he said wryly. "You've got me by the…eyeballs in that picture."

A hint of color darkened her cheeks. "That's not why I like it."

He waited, expecting her to elaborate.

"I like it because…" Her gaze slid to him and she leaned closer, a whisper of her perfume landing on him with the impact of a blow to the chest. "That was a special day."

She was either a trained actress or a natural-born liar. Because everything in her face and eyes screamed that she was telling the truth.

"Yes, it was." Past tense being all important.

Surprising him, she stood, and nothing could stop his gaze from traveling down over the khaki-colored pencil skirt that hugged her slender body and the black knit top that curved into her waist and over her rounded breasts.

Cursing the blood rush to his loins, he forced himself to look at his PDA. He picked up the device and absently clicked today's schedule. "We better make a decision. I have a meeting and you'll be late for Revlon."

When he looked up, she stood in front of the layout wall, her hand on one hip, her heart-shaped backside notched maddeningly to one side as she studied the picture.

The remembered feel of that backside under his hands and against his body clutched at him, and he mentally cursed the reflexive response of his body.

"Well," he said, forcing his tone to belie the strain she was causing in his lower half, "what do you think?"

She spun on her heels and faced him. "I think we need to talk. Can I come over tonight?" Unconsciously, she smoothed her hands over her hips and they rested on her thighs.

Was that a nervous gesture, or some subtle body language to seduce him? God, would he ever trust a woman again?

Maybe seducing him was part of her game. Well, hell, he wasn't a moron. He could have sex and not spill company secrets all over the sheets.

Why not? If she was offering it? He didn't have to listen to some inner voice that said she was special, different, fresh.

Of course not. He was a red-blooded American male surging with testosterone. He could have casual sex. It didn't have to rock his world just because last weekend had.

"Sure," he said with a forced half smile. "I'll be home tonight."

"Great."

He could have sworn she paled a bit. Was she expecting him to say no? Had he called her bluff?

"And what about the 'Color Me Charismatic' picture?" she asked. "Shall we hide or go public?"

"I have nothing to hide, Jessie. Do you?"

She brushed a strand of silky hair from her face, but didn't look away. "We'll talk tonight," she said.

Unless she planned to be brutally honest with him, he doubted they'd be doing much talking. And the thought left him with a jumble of mixed emotions and a hard-on that threatened to return all day.

Jessie had resisted the urge to wear a little extra makeup or some seriously tight jeans for her visit to Cade's that night. She felt uncomfortable as it was, having to initiate the date. Her only concession to vanity was to lose her glasses and unbraid her hair.

But as she stood outside Cade's door, she suddenly wondered if that would be enough to melt the iciness she'd been feeling for four days.

No. She didn't have to pretend to be some kind of supermodel for Cade. She wasn't here to jump his bones, anyway. She wanted some answers. If Cade had changed his mind and did a three-sixty from "leave your toothbrush here" to "I'm just being professional," then she had a right to know. And to know why.

She tapped on the door.

No more wondering. No more fretting. No more trying to analyze his every nuance. They'd slept together and whispered intimate endearments. They'd explored each other's body and tenderly given and taken the most exquisite pleasures.

They'd—

Cade opened his apartment door and all Jessie could do was stare. And imagine doing all those things again. Immediately. Without talking.

He wore jeans. And nothing else but an expression that somehow mixed disdain and expectancy.

"Hi," she said.

"Hi."

Her gaze dropped to the bare, broad planes of his chest, to the smattering of dark golden hair that curled deliciously between his nipples and then flattened in a single line that traveled over a well-defined six-pack and led directly to his unbuttoned fly.

Not fair, she almost whispered. So not fair.

"Come on in." He widened the door and stepped back.

She glanced at his bare feet, where worn jeans broke over his arch and the tiniest golden hairs on his toes matched the sleek tuft on his chest.

"Are you busy?" she asked.

Stupid question. He was half-naked, with weary shadows around his eyes. He'd probably been resting, or watching TV, or…

As she followed him into the living room, she saw the answer to her question all over the table in his dining area. Files and papers, an open laptop, a few layout pages from *Charisma*.

"You're working."

"Yep." He directed her away from the pile of papers to the living room and turned to go into the kitchen. "And I'm just about ready for a beer. Are you thirsty? Hungry?"

She watched the corded muscles of his back tense as he moved. Yes. She was starved and parched. For *that*.

"I'll have some water."

He returned in a minute with a beer in one hand and a bottle of water in the other. "You can sit down," he said, handing her the water.

She perched on the edge of a club chair. "What are you working on?" she asked as she opened the bottle, trying to ignore the fact that he didn't open it for her.

He took a long drink of beer and dropped onto his leather sofa. The one where they'd made love just a few days ago.

"Numbers," he said. "I've got a meeting with Liam Elliott tomorrow morning."

"Liam." She spun through her mental file of Elliotts. "He's the financial operating officer of EPH, right?" And Michael Elliott's second son.

Cade nodded. "He's also a good buddy of mine, so he generally cuts me a lot of slack on the financials. But, now…" His voice trailed off and he took another deep pull of beer.

She watched his throat work the liquid and her own got extremely dry at the sight. "Now, what?"

His gaze tapered over the bottle. "You know what's going on at EPH, Jessie. The future CEO of the company hinges on one year's profit percentage."

She sipped her water and he continued to watch her expectantly. This was going to be all up to her. "Cade, I didn't come over here to talk about financials."

He cocked an eyebrow. "What's on your mind, Jessie?"

"Are you serious?" She let her shoulders drop as the disappointment thunked to the bottom of her stomach. "Am I supposed to act like last weekend never happened? Are you going to pretend it didn't?"

He set the bottle on the table and leaned all the way forward, resting his elbows on his knees and melting her with a smoky gaze. "How would you like me to act, Jessie?"

She blew out a disgusted breath. "I don't want you to *act,* Cade. That's the point. I want the real, honest, kind, loving—"

"Loving?"

Her fingertips tingled with numbness at the incredulous way he said it.

"Well, yes." She squared her shoulders and looked hard at him. She hated to say it, but she had to. "Or was that purely physical lust with absolutely no possibility for anything else?"

His gray eyes warmed imperceptibly, a change that only a woman who'd made a science out of studying him would notice.

"Love," he said softly, "is irrevocably tied to trust."

She stared at him. "What do you mean, Cade? You are acting like *I* did something to breach *your* trust. You were the one who issued an executive edict that went directly against my wishes." She shook her head, the point so clear to her and yet he looked like *she* was lying. "And you were the one who didn't bother to tell me, but let me find out through the grapevine. And you—"

"And *you* are in love with someone else."

Her jaw dropped as she processed the words. "What?"

"Not to mention the fact that you are using *Charisma* and Fin and me to dig around for competitive information."

All she could do was blink at him. "What on earth are you talking about?"

"I heard you," he said quietly, his whole body stone-still as he delivered his announcement. "I went to your apartment on Monday afternoon and I heard you on the phone telling someone this was an opportunity to dig. Telling someone you loved him."

Relief and understanding and something she couldn't begin to define practically shook her down to her shoes. "Oh my God, Cade." She fell back into her chair as realization punched her. "I was talking to my father."

This time he blinked, then his gaze turned chilly again. "About spying on *Charisma?*"

"What are you talking about?"

"First you avoid Fin like the plague, then you don't want to take the shadow intern assignment, then you do a three-sixty, take the job and tell someone that you're only doing it to get information."

What was he implying?

"This is a very competitive situation, Jessie. I don't put anything past the Elliotts when they want something."

Realization morphed into a tidal wave of disbelief. "You think I'm *spying* for one of the other magazines?" Just the sound of it was so ludicrous that she laughed.

But he didn't even smile. "Can you sit there and deny that you told someone that you were living a lie, and that you referred to the shadowing assignment as a means to 'dig for information' and that you made a promise to someone that you'd be back because you loved them? Can you, Jessie? Because I heard you."

She started to speak, then closed her mouth as the whole situation crystallized in her mind. And another realization hit her: The only way to make him believe her would be to tell him the truth about Fin.

In fact, she realized as the puzzle pieces started snapping into place with wicked clarity, if she didn't tell him, she had no explanation for what was, under the circumstances, a reasonable assumption.

Of course he would think this. Of course. And if he knew the truth—if she revealed to him that Finola Elliott was her birth mother and what she was digging for was confirmation that Fin wanted to meet her too—then what? Would all be forgiven and understood? Would he take her in his arms and kiss her again?

She had to know.

"If I could prove to you that you're wrong, Cade, absolutely wrong without a shadow of a doubt, what would you do?"

He stood slowly, looking down at her. "If you could prove to me I'm wrong, Jessie, then…"

"Then what, Cade?"

Love is irrevocably tied to trust.

"Then I would feel like a complete jerk."

Despite the emotion squeezing her, she laughed softly at that. "You're not a jerk, Cade. At least, you weren't until Monday afternoon."

He reached a hand to her and she let him gently pull her out of the chair to stand in front of him. Neither one said a word as they looked at each other, heat and electricity ricocheting through the few inches that separated them.

"Prove to me I'm wrong, Jessie." As though he couldn't stop the power of nature, he reached for her, pulling her just a little closer. "You have no idea how much I want to be wrong."

His voice was husky, the scent of his bare skin dizzying as he brought her against his chest.

"I know you hate the idea of this," she said, lifting her face toward his mouth, nearly tasting his kiss, her body already moist in anticipation, "but you've made a mistake, Cade. This time you've made a mistake."

His mouth came down hard on hers, a kiss pent up for four long days and four endless nights. She pressed her body against his, loving the substantial erection that pushed against her stomach and the velvet-over-steel feel of his bare muscles under her fingers.

From deep in his chest, he groaned softly, sliding his tongue farther into her mouth as she arched her breasts against his chest. He buried his hands in her hair as he held her head, angling her face to get the full impact of their kiss.

"Jessie," he murmured into her mouth, kissing her face, her ears, her throat. "If I made a mistake, tell me. Tell me the truth. Tell me I'm wrong."

"You are, Cade. I promise."

His hands grazed her shoulders and slid over her breasts, squeezing them in his palms before he dipped under her arms to pull her closer. "So? Tell me. What were you talking to your father about? Digging for information about what? Why does it feel like you're living a lie?"

They were perfectly legitimate questions.

She opened her eyes and backed away from the dizzy, sexy heat of his hands to think clearly. She couldn't tell him before she told Fin.

And she couldn't tell Fin yet.

As much as she saw a kinder, softer side of Fin this week, it was still too soon. She had to have some kind of proof that Fin would welcome the news.

"Tell me," he insisted, pulling her back to caress her backside and drive her against his erection. "Because I want to make love to you so bad, Jessie. I want you so much, so much." His voice was hoarse, his breathing tight.

Between her legs, a slow, achy throb had begun and creamy moisture already dampened her underpants.

"You have to trust me, Cade," she whispered between kisses. "You have to just trust me."

Suddenly, his body stiffened, then slowly, agonizingly, pulled back. His eyes were charcoal with lust and arousal, his mouth slack from the passionate kisses.

"I want to trust you, Jessie, but you have to trust me, too. Tell me why you said those things to whoever you were talking to."

She heard her own breath turn slow and ragged. "I told you, I was talking to my father."

"Okay." He might as well have said "Yeah, right," it was so clear he doubted her word. "Then what were you talking about?"

"Cade, if we are ever going to have a chance at anything, if there's any hope that this could be more than lust, then you have to do this for me." She looked hard into his eyes. "I can't tell you. You have to trust me."

He took a step back as though the only way he could have control was if there was physical distance between them. "Why can't you tell me?"

"I can't."

His eyes flashed. "You can't or you won't?"

"I can't." Please, Cade. Please don't make this a showdown. "And I won't."

Very slowly, he shook his head. "I don't believe this."

"I'll tell you this much. There is something. But I am not some corporate spy and I am not trying to get information from you and I am not in love with anyone else."

He stared at her.

"Do you believe me, Cade?"

His eyes turned cool, his mouth set in that grim line. Bad news straight ahead. "I want to, but—"

But. Without another word, she stepped past him and walked out without looking back.

Eight

Liam Elliott looked over the cheeseburger he held between two large hands, a glint of pure devil in his blue eyes. "You're not seriously asking me for relationship advice, are you?"

Cade laughed and set his own messy burger on the plate, wiping his hands, then placing them on the stainless steel tabletop of the EPH cafeteria booth they shared. "Well, you know women."

Liam looked skyward. "The wrong ones." He took a bite and chewed while he continued to eye Cade skeptically. "So, you met a lady. You like her. But you think she's not being straight with you and won't tell you why. Do I have this right?"

"Basically," Cade agreed.

How much should he tell the financial operating officer of EPH, anyway?

To be sure, Liam's official executive role ended when they left the conference room after a morning-long financial meeting. They'd already examined the bottom line for a few hours and Cade knew the *Charisma* numbers could be better, but they weren't completely in the tank. He had decent news to report to Fin. But now he and Liam were eating lunch, having chosen the far more casual cafeteria over the executive dining room, and the only numbers up for discussion were the Jets' lousy passing record in the first two games of the season.

Once they covered that, it was only natural the conversation would turn to women. Cade had purposely steered the discussion that way; he needed some advice. Liam may have a checkered history with the ladies, but he was a true friend.

"So where'd you meet her?" Liam asked.

Cade glanced away, his gaze traveling over the ultra-modern decor of the crowded cafeteria. Even though it was just a few minutes past twelve, the room hummed with hungry EPH employees. He didn't see anyone in particular. Not that he was looking.

Liam blew out a breath of disbelief as realization dawned on him. "Whoa. Haven't you ever heard the expression 'don't get your meat where you get your bread'?"

A wave of resentment roiled through Cade. "This is meat." He held his cheeseburger up. "She is not."

"If you say so."

They ate in silence until Cade abandoned the meat in question in deference to the tightness in his gut. Liam already figured out the woman was an EPH employee; it would only be a matter of time until Cade told him the truth.

"She's an intern," he finally said.

"An int—" Liam choked on a gulp of water. His eyes widened as he coughed and managed to swallow. "Not that redhead with the funny glasses who's been following Fin around?"

"Her name's Jessie. And she looks a lot better without the glasses."

"She doesn't look bad with them," Liam noted. "But she's young."

"She's twenty-three. Hardly illegal and long past the cradle."

"All the women in New York City and you pick a twenty-three-year-old intern at *Charisma*."

Cade speared him with a look. "As if I need the world's worst judge of women to point that out to me."

"Hey, you brought the topic up."

"I know. Because I need some help. This is complicated and not funny."

"Okay." Liam held up a hand. "No jokes, I promise. Talk to me."

Cade took a deep breath and looked back into the sea of employees filing into the cafeteria. "I overheard a conversation she had and I know that she's hiding something from me. And she told me I just have to trust her and eventually, she says, she'll explain everything. Should I trust her?"

Liam shrugged one well-developed shoulder. "I guess it depends."

"On what?"

"On how much you like her. On how bad you want to get her in bed. On how big her secret is." Liam wiped his mouth and balled up his napkin before discarding it on the table. "Start with the first one. How bad do we have it?"

Cade snorted softly, not even sure there were words to describe his feelings. Certainly not words he'd share with Liam.

"I'm going to take that as 'real' bad." Liam laughed, then his look grew serious. "Don't tell me you've graduated from 'like' to…the big one?"

Damn. Had he? "I don't know about that. But it's serious. Not casual. Not just sex."

"Not *just* sex? So you already had her in the sack."

Distaste roiled through him. *Jessie* and *the sack* didn't belong in the same sentence. "We've made love."

"Oh, brother." Liam held up a hand, fighting more laughter. "I'm sorry. I'm not making jokes. But you're pretty far gone, pal."

If he was that far gone, why did he let her walk out last night? Why didn't he just act on the lust that pulled at both of them, and take what she would have offered if he hadn't pushed her to confide in him? Why couldn't he say he trusted her and get her in the sack, as Liam so poetically put it?

"So let's ask ourselves the third question," Liam said, copping the voice of authority he used in business meetings. "How big is her secret? What do you think she's keeping in the dark?"

If the financial operating officer of EPH suspected something like corporate espionage, he'd have to look into it, and if Cade's suspicions were even remotely right, Jessie would be gone and her professional reputation trashed.

"It's complicated," he said, purposely vague.

God, was he protecting her? Even as part of him believed the worst? For a careful man who avoided mistakes, he sure was flirting with disaster.

"You know what I think?" Liam leaned forward and put his elbows on the tabletop, a bit of humor remaining in his eyes. "I think you are well and truly in love, my man."

This was definitely not the advice he'd been seeking from Liam. "This from the man who hasn't made it to the fourth date without boredom setting in. Suddenly you're a love expert."

Liam grinned. "And how many dates have you had with her?"

"One." At Liam's threat of laughter, Cade added, "A long one."

"You're in love."

"What I am is sleep-deprived and distracted."

"Same difference." Liam paused, lowering his voice for emphasis. "Listen, Cade, seriously. If you really like her, give her the benefit of the doubt. What's to lose, really? How bad can it be? She has a stalker ex-boyfriend or she's got a lunatic aunt hiding in her attic? Whatever it is, you can handle it. It's not as if she can mess with your job or your life."

Yes, it was.

Before Cade could respond, Shane Elliott passed their table, carrying a tray of food and wearing a broad grin.

The men greeted each other, and Cade and Liam both offered some room in their booth. Despite the competitive environment Patrick had fostered with his contest, Cade was disappointed when Shane declined to join them. Cade genuinely liked Fin's twin brother and wouldn't have minded getting a little intel on how things were going at *The Buzz*.

"Thanks, but I'm meeting with some of my editorial staff." Shane tilted his head toward another table, a glimmer in eyes so much like Fin's, it was eerie. "We're not ready to rest on our laurels yet," he added lifting his tray slightly in a mock salute to Liam. "But thanks again for the news."

Nodding goodbye, Shane walked away, leaving Cade to look questioningly at Liam.

"What was that all about?" Cade asked.

Liam raised his eyebrows. "File it under Patrick's contest."

"He's ahead?" Cade asked in disbelief. "*The Buzz* took over the lead?"

Liam gave Cade a look of sheer discomfort. "You know I'm not at liberty to say."

Cade rubbed his jaw and regarded his friend. Liam couldn't reveal who was ahead, and Cade didn't want to push him to a breach of ethics. "But that's what Shane implied. Or was that a fake just to psych me out?"

Liam cleared his throat. "Numbers don't lie."

Cade stood slowly. "They're ahead," he stated again.

"It's only September, Cade. There are four months left in the year. Anything can happen. The Jets could make it to the Super Bowl."

Anything could happen, and if it was up to Cade, that wouldn't include mistakes of any kind. "I sure as hell better get my mind off the intern and onto business."

"Now you're talking," Liam said, standing as well. "Although I have to say, I've never seen you like this over a woman."

Cade exhaled softly, acknowledging the truth. "She's not like any woman I've ever met. I can't stop thinking about her."

"Whoa. Way, way far gone," Liam muttered with a chuckle.

They dropped their trays onto the rolling conveyor belt and headed for the door. Cade stuck his hands deep into his trouser pockets, not even trying to deny how far gone he was.

"Is it possible you're being too harsh on her?" Liam asked as they reached the elevator. "Maybe you're jumping to the wrong conclusion?"

Liam may not be able to commit to anything that lasted longer than a dinner date and a possible breakfast, but at the moment, he sounded remarkably balanced and insightful.

"I suppose it's possible."

"If she's that great," Liam added as he hit the elevator call button, "she's worth the risk."

Jessie had asked for Cade's trust. And, frankly, she'd done nothing wrong but have a conversation that he'd only heard half of. She deserved more than the rush to judgment he'd taken. And, yes, she *was* that great.

"You know what? I think I will give her the benefit of the doubt." Suddenly, he had an idea. "And something else." Cade stepped away from the elevator, toward the lobby doors. "I'll see you later."

Liam frowned as the elevator arrived. "Aren't you going back to your office?"

"I have something to do first."

As he bounded out the doors to Park Avenue, Cade wondered if he could be fined by the City of New York for what he was about to do.

Didn't matter. It would be worth a lousy fine to see the spark in Jessie's eyes again.

Chloe Davenport swung around the door frame of Fin's office and tapped on the wall for Jessie's attention.

"Hey there, Miss Shadow," Chloe teased lightly. "Fin still gone?"

Seated at the round table in the corner of the spacious office, Jessie looked up from the typeset page in front of her. "Hi. She said she wouldn't be back until mid-afternoon."

At Chloe's inquisitive look, Jessie added, "We finished up in here this morning, and I stayed to proof this one last article on hemlines. I have such a hard time concentrating out there in my cube."

"Boy, do I hear you," Chloe agreed with a knowing nod. "I can barely spell my name when the phones are jangling like mad. Stay in here as long as you like."

Bingo. Permission from the gatekeeper herself to be in Fin's office. Jessie's heart rate accelerated to a light trot. "Thanks, Chloe. It won't take me much longer to finish."

"Well, since you're here, I wonder if you could do me a favor. Cade's assistant is at an all-day computer class, and I don't expect anything earth-shattering to happen, but I'm dying to get something to eat and—" she wrinkled her nose guiltily "—I'd really like to stop by Saks for a quick look-see at the fall stuff on sale."

God bless Chloe's shopping habits. "I'll cover the phones," Jessie offered quickly. "You take your time."

"It shouldn't be busy," Chloe promised. "Cade's up in operations most of the day and neither one has anything on their calendars this afternoon. If you wouldn't mind—"

"If Fin's phone rings, I'll take a message." She waved her hand with what she hoped wasn't too much enthusiasm. "Go shop."

Chloe blew her an air kiss. "You are a doll, Jessie. I'm so glad you were the one to get the shadowing job."

Jessie smiled, hating the sudden shame that squeezed at her chest. "Thanks, Chloe. I'm learning a ton." And, when she was safely alone, she could learn a lot more.

Enough, she hoped, to make a decision about how and when to tell Fin who she was. She had to. If she didn't want to lose Cade, she had to come clean. And, like her father had said, she just needed some indication that Fin would welcome the news.

After Chloe left, Jessie waited for a moment, taking a deep, calming breath.

All she wanted was some shred of evidence that would show her Fin had an interest in finding her birth daughter. She had no earthly idea what that would be or where to find it, but she had to try.

Jessie glanced at Fin's desk, as neat and organized as the woman who normally sat there. Most people kept their private files right there, at their desk. Not out in the hall, where Chloe would manage them. And probably not over in the dark wood credenza that doubled as a file cabinet and a piece of furniture. They would be in her desk.

Blood sang through her ears as she stood, casually approaching Fin's chair.

She had permission, she reminded herself. Chloe had asked her to answer the phones. If someone walked in, it would be perfectly understandable for Fin's shadow intern to be jotting down the name of someone who'd just called.

She was covering for Fin's assistant.

But who would she say called? Jessie tamped back the roadblock. That was the least of her problems if she got caught.

She eased into the leather chair, leaned to the right to peek into the empty vestibule outside of Fin's office, then listened for any sounds of approaching feet.

The carpet would silence them, but Jessie would sense if someone was coming. She placed a clean pad of paper and a pen at the edge of the desk. As soon as she heard anything, she'd act like she was writing a message. The phone was inches from her hand. She could even lift and drop the receiver as though she were hanging up the phone.

With one more shaky breath, she reached over and gave the desk's lone file drawer a tug. Unlocked, it rumbled open. Thank God Fin was trusting.

A little pang of guilt accompanied that thought as Jessie began to finger through the neatly typed filing tabs.

There were four folders with the names of foundations where Fin had done some philanthropic work. Two labeled with doctor's names, perhaps personal medical files. One called "Design and Decorating" and another with the name of the woman Jessie recognized as Fin's housekeeper. The last file was marked with an address, but when she slid it out, she realized they were condo association documents and she quickly replaced the folder in its slot.

They were personal files, all right. But nothing so personal it was labeled Child Given Up For Adoption. Jessie almost laughed at the stupidity and naivete of her plan. Of course Fin wouldn't keep files like that.

But Jessie had one irrefutable fact. Fin had contacted and listed herself and Jessie's birth date on one of Canada's premier adoption finders Web sites. And Jessie had been born in Canada, at a convent, and her birth mother had been a fifteen-year-old girl by the name of Finola Elliott. That much she'd pieced together from bits of information her mother had given her and what the Mother Superior had told her when she called.

She glanced at Fin's computer, where the *Charisma* logo bounced around as a boldly colored screen saver. On a lark, she tapped a key to bring the monitor to life.

Enter Password.

There was no way she was attempting to hack into Fin's computer. This wasn't *Mission: Impossible.* This was real life. Maybe an impossible mission, but her real life.

Her skittishness and nerves had been replaced by a fine sense of frustration. Dropping back into the chair, Jessie's gaze moved around Fin's beautifully appointed office, the monument to a Type A overachieving woman.

A woman, Jessie thought miserably, who probably wouldn't want a reminder that she'd slipped up twenty-three years ago.

Maybe Jessie should just forget the whole thing. She knew Fin. And she liked her. Did she need more?

Yes. She needed to stop lying to a man she cared for. If there was any chance, any chance at all, then he had to know the truth behind what he'd heard her say. She'd been hurt and angry when she'd left his apartment last night, but during a sleepless night, she'd decided that she was asking a lot of him to just "believe" her. If they were going to have a chance, she'd have to tell him the truth. And she'd have to tell Fin.

She blew out a long, disgusted breath as she arrived back at square one.

The phone startled her out of her reverie. Reaching for it, Jessie pressed the talk button and copped her most professional voice. "Finola Elliott's office. May I help you?"

"Jessie?" Fin's voice lifted in surprise. "Is that you?"

"Oh, hello Fin. Chloe had to run out and I'm covering the phones."

"Let me guess. Sale at Bloomie's?"

Jessie chuckled, liking that Fin knew so much about her employees and kept all judgment out of her tone. "No, Saks."

"Well, I'm glad you're there. Can you do me a favor?"

"Sure. What do you need?"

"On top of my credenza, I left a file on freelance writers. Can you grab it for me? I need a phone number for David Luongo."

"No problem. Hold on a second, I'll see if I can find it."

The stand up file rack on the credenza held a few manila folders, and Jessie found one labeled Freelancers in a matter of seconds. "Here you go, Fin." She read the requested number and closed the file.

"Thanks, Jessie. I appreciate the help. Did you get that hemline article proofed?"

"Sure did. It'll go to production this afternoon."

"Awesome. You're doing a great job, Jessie. I'm going to get a little too dependent on you by the end of September." Fin's voice was rich with warmth and honesty.

And why did that send silly shivers of hope down her spine?

"Thanks, Fin. I'm having a blast."

When they hung up, Jessie walked the folder back to its proper place, a smile tugging at her lips. Fin really liked her. They'd clicked.

How bad could it be for her to know the truth?

She'd come to New York to find out who her birth mother was. And now she knew. But it wasn't enough. Now Jessie wanted a relationship with her.

But did Fin?

On an impulse, Jessie yanked open the credenza drawer to search more files. These folders were work-related, all the tabs indicating they contained information on staff and personnel, which sent a frisson of discomfort through her. She didn't want to spy on her colleagues.

In the drawer to the right, the files were all specific to finances: accounts payable, profit and loss by month, payroll. God, that was even more intrusive than employee files. The last thing she wanted to do was see payroll.

At the very back of the drawer, the last file was labeled Stimpson, P.I.

P.I. Private investigator? Of course, they probably used one once in a while for employee background checks. But wouldn't that be over in the personnel drawer? Had it been misfiled?

Her fingers closed over the manila folder and she slid it out.

Frozen, guilty, terrified, she stood with the closed file in front of her. She had no right to do this.

It was wrong.

But it was necessary.

Laying the folder on top of the open drawer, she flipped to the first page and stared at the creamy letterhead.

Robert F. Stimpson, Private Investigator.
Dear Ms. Elliott:

Jessie swallowed and forced herself to read.

We have received your check in the amount of $2,500 as a retainer for a adoption record's search you requested for the country of Canada registered for the year of 1982.

Her entire being thumped as her heart kicked into a full gallop. Lord above, Fin had hired a P.I. to find her.

Somehow she managed to close the file and gingerly replace it in the back of the drawer, her legs trembling as adrenaline and happiness surged through her.

With a soft yet definitive click, she closed the heavy file drawer until the carved wood blended with the rest of the piece of furniture.

"Find anything good?"

A gasp caught in her throat as she spun around.

The accusation in his tone was as piercing as the disappointment in his eyes. But the worst part of all was the cluster of yellow flowers Cade gripped in his hand.

Nine

Blood drained from Jessie's face as she stuttered, and her body visibly quaked. Getting caught red-handed did that to a person.

"Don't even try to lie," Cade said quietly. "I've been standing here for a few minutes."

Ever since he'd heard her voice on the phone, and he'd approached Fin's office with a handful of high hopes and trust. But what he found when he rounded the corner and peeked into Fin's office dashed any and every hope he'd had for a future with Jessie Clayton. And every shred of trust wilted faster than the flowers would.

If she had been anywhere but those files, maybe. But there was only one reason to snoop in there.

"I'm not going to lie," she said, her voice strong considering how guilty she was.

He squeezed the ridiculous bouquet of flowers he'd just

pilfered from the Park Avenue median. His grip was so tight that a few of the stems cracked in his palm.

"I can explain," she continued. "But not right away."

"Of course not," he countered, his own tone dripping with sarcasm. "You'll have to check with whoever's paying you to sniff around this place."

She shook her head. "Cade, you need to—"

"No." He fought the childish urge to throw the flowers on the ground. "*You* need to leave. Now."

Her head jerked as though he'd slapped her. "Are you firing me?"

Was she serious? "Jessie, I just saw you reading confidential financial records. There's no reason, no real or imagined reason, for you to be in that file drawer other than to access information to share with competitors."

She opened her mouth but he held out his hand to stop her lies. "Don't even bother. Fin would never send you in there for something, so don't make something up. Just get your stuff and leave. I won't call security."

"Security?" She choked out a soft breath. "Cade, you're going to be really sorry when I tell you what a mistake you're making."

His gut twisted. "I'm already sorry. I'm sorry I trusted you. I'm sorry I didn't listen to my gut. I'm sorry I—" No, he wasn't sorry he slept with her. He wouldn't have given up that pleasure, that connection for anything. "The only mistake I made was falling for you. I can get over that."

She just stared at him. Slowly, a hint of color returned to her cheeks as she notched her chin up to a defiant angle. She walked across the room toward him, her shoulders square, her gaze direct.

For one agonizing and insane moment, he thought she was going to kiss him.

Instead, she paused in front of him, removed her glasses with maddening deliberateness, then dropped them on the floor. Without taking her eyes off him, she stomped her heel over the frames and snapped the plastic.

"You didn't fall for me, Cade. You have no idea who you fell for."

She marched out, leaving behind the overpowering scent of trouble in Fin's office and one mangled pair of glasses on the floor.

Jessie perched on a smooth rock on a hill in Central Park, with Rollerbladers and bikers and, of course, a few young lovers, cruising by. Lucky people. Not one of them had just been handed the greatest gift and the biggest heartbreak in their lives in the span of one minute.

We have received your check…adoption records search you requested for the country of Canada…

Of course it was possible Fin only wanted to know that her daughter was alive and had been raised in a happy home. Jessie knew enough about adoption searches to realize that not all birth parents actually sought a reunion, as much as they needed assurance they'd done the right thing.

True, Fin was a driven career woman. But Jessie had seen glimmers of warmth. A spark of affection for all of her staff members.

With a deep sigh, Jessie closed her eyes and tried to picture what Fin would look like the moment that she'd learned the truth.

But all she saw was icy gray eyes looking at her like she was a criminal. And he wouldn't let her explain! He just denounced her.

The only mistake I made was falling for you.

The pain seared through her again, almost unbearable in

its intensity. She could never, ever forget that he was willing to write her off and able to fire her without even listening to an explanation.

After all her character assessment and people watching, she'd trusted the wrong *Charisma* executive. Cade was the one who put work before relationships. Not Fin. Cade was the one she should have avoided. Not Fin. Cade was the one who turned her away.

And Fin?

She glanced at her watch. Fin should be back by now.

Steeling herself with one long inhale of the sweet and earthy smell of Central Park, Jessie pushed herself off the rock and started to walk toward the bustling traffic of Manhattan.

But this time, she never hesitated at a single street corner.

She was no longer scared of New York.

Cade slumped in the guest chair across from Fin, still holding the broken glasses in his hand.

"Stop punishing yourself," Fin said sharply as she shrugged out of her business jacket, down to a black tank top. "You aren't the first man to get bamboozled by a woman with an agenda and you won't be the last."

He snorted and let a sharp piece of plastic dig into his palm. "I wasn't bamboozled, Fin."

She just raised an eyebrow. "Can we agree that you weren't thinking with your brain?"

"I wish it were that simple."

Fin regarded him closely. "Are you saying you really cared about her?"

"Yes, I'm saying that. I did."

"Well," Fin acknowledged, "she is a dear girl. I mean, in just a week, she'd totally grown on me."

Cade shot her an "I told you so" look. "She's good, isn't she? And then, she marched out of here threatening that I hadn't heard the last of her."

"What exactly did she say?" Fin asked. "It seems so out of character for her to make threats."

"Who knows what her character is? She just told me, 'You have no idea who you fell for.'" At Fin's frown, he shifted in his seat. "I told her I was sorry I fell for her."

"That was a lousy thing for you to say."

"Fin! She was digging through your files, reading confidential financial information, for God's sake. What do you want me to say? 'Gee, you look cute over there spying for the competition. Can I help you find anything in particular?'"

Fin glanced at the credenza thoughtfully. "Which drawer was she in?"

He vaguely indicated the right side. "Financials. But she went through the payroll stuff, too. I watched. I just couldn't believe it." He shook his head, reliving the moment that he'd frozen in the doorway, having heard her voice on the phone. He knew now that she'd been talking to Fin.

Fin's attention remained riveted on the offending file cabinet.

"And speaking of the competition," Cade added dryly, "I totally forgot the best part of this banner day."

"What?"

"*The Buzz* is ahead."

"Excuse me?" He had her full attention now. "How do you know that?"

"Liam…well, Liam didn't exactly tell me. But I saw Shane in the cafeteria and you couldn't wash away the smirk from his face with a fire hose. Liam didn't confirm or deny, but he said the numbers didn't lie."

Fin fell back into her chair with disgust. "We can't lose, Cade."

"I know. Maybe your twin brother is the one who hired our spy."

She shook her head. "Not Shane. And I just don't see Michael or Cullen stooping to that level."

"Something Daniel might have done before he and Amanda decided to leave and start an adventure magazine? Maybe when Cullen took over *Snap,* Michael forgot to tell him he'd sent a spy?"

Fin shook her head.

"Gannon?" Michael's son and right-hand man held the same position as Cade for *Pulse* magazine, executive editor.

"I doubt it. Marriage to Erika has mellowed him."

An unfamiliar pang of jealousy pinched his gut. "Happiness doesn't erase anyone's determination to win the contest."

"I can't believe Shane's winning," Fin said absently.

"Hey, he's your twin brother, Fin. All that competitive DNA runs in both your veins."

"It runs in the whole family," she said. "That's why I can't completely negate your theory that Jessie Clayton was hired as a spy."

"Fact, not theory." Cade pushed himself out of the chair and scooped up the wilted flowers along with the broken glasses. He held them over the desk. "Throw these away for me, will you?"

She took them, looking at the flowers with a bittersweet smile of sympathy. "I had no idea you were so romantic, Cade."

"So stupid, more like."

"You're not stupid, Cade. She just turned out to be a better actress than any of us gave her credit for."

He pointed to the glasses. "She even wore her own disguise."

Fin stared at the twisted frames, thinking. "I wonder why she wanted to hide."

"Because she was a farce from beginning to end. A phony. A liar."

Dropping the glasses in the trash, Fin gave him a sincere look. "Don't let love make you bitter, Cade."

"Love?" He spat the word. "That was a long way from love. I only went after her in the first place because I was so suspicious of her."

"Really? Well, that plan backfired, didn't it?" Fin offered a wry smile.

"Yep. All I wanted was to know why she was avoiding you. I should have pressed her more on it."

"Does she know that's why you asked her out in the first place?" Fin asked.

He shrugged. "Probably not. But it's moot now, because I found her out. And that's all that matters."

"No, that's *not* all that matters."

Cade jerked at the sound of Jessie's voice, spinning to see her standing in the doorway, her auburn hair tumbling over her shoulders and her emerald eyes sparking like the crown jewels.

"What are you doing here?" he demanded.

"I need to talk to Fin."

Cade consciously stepped to one side, as though he could block Fin from the attacking enemy. "She doesn't have anything to say to you."

"Well, I have something to say to her. And I deserve the opportunity to say it."

"I'll call security, Fin," he said, stepping toward the phone.

"Cade." Fin stood up and rounded her desk. "I'll hear her out."

"Thank you," Jessie said to Fin. "Finally somebody is willing to listen to an explanation."

"But I won't listen to lies," Fin stated sternly.

"No lies," Jessie said. "But I want to talk to you privately."

"No," Fin responded quickly. "I have no secrets from Cade. You made the decision to deceive him, and he has a right to hear what you have to say."

"You don't want him to hear what I'm about to tell you, Fin. Believe me."

Cade caught the bewildered expression on Fin's face, her normally smooth brow suddenly pinched as she stared at Jessie.

"This is private," Jessie said softly, taking another step into the office. "This is between you and me."

Fin's breath caught in her throat. Her eyes, as green as Jessie's, widened slightly as she stared. "How old are you?"

Cade backed up as Fin asked Jessie the question. How old was she? Was her age suddenly an issue now?

But Jessie didn't flinch at the question. In fact, she took a step forward and lifted her chin a notch. "I'm twenty-three, Fin." She said it as though it really mattered.

Fin still stared and all of a sudden Cade saw the fine hair on her bare arms rise with a spray of goose bumps.

Cade turned to Jessie, taking in her trembling mouth and glistening eyes. God, was she crying?

Was Fin?

What the hell was going on?

"In the file, I found a letter," Jessie said, her voice so rough that she could barely say the words. "So I hope you really are looking for me."

"Oh my God." Fin covered her mouth, tears now sliding over her bloodless face. "It's you. It's you. Why didn't I see that it's you!"

The two women folded into each other's arms, as Fin let

out a strangled cry. Jessie buried her face against Fin's neck, her narrow shoulders shuddering.

"I didn't know if I should tell you," Jessie mumbled through her own tears.

"You have no idea," Fin whispered. "No idea how long I've dreamed of this."

Nothing, absolutely nothing of what he saw made sense. Why were they crying? And hugging? He cleared his throat noisily. "Does someone want to tell me what's going on?"

Fin turned toward him, still clinging to Jessie as though her very life depended on the act. Tears streaked her makeup and her mouth quivered.

"Jessie is my daughter."

Her *daughter?*

The words sucker punched all the breath right out of his gut. Her *daughter?*

Jessie managed to pull just far enough out of Fin's grasp to look at him. He searched her face for answers, for an explanation, an apology, a look of anything that could reconnect them.

But all he could see was what she'd been trying to hide for five months.

Her eyes were exactly the same color and shape as Fin's.

He took a step backward, holding up both hands as though he could stop the emotional waves that rolled off the two women, as though he could stop the surge of a new and different kind of disappointment when he realized Jessie had deceived him for a very good reason.

And he'd willingly, stupidly, foolishly believed the worst.

"I'll let you two be alone," he managed to say. "I'm sure you have a lot to talk about."

Fin closed her eyes and squeezed Jessie back into her

embrace, but Jessie held his gaze long enough to deliver one unambiguous message.

She'd never forgive him for not trusting her.

Ten

Fin couldn't let go. Every time Jessie drew back to say something, Fin clutched her tighter, grasping her with a soft moan of disbelief and ecstasy.

Precisely the same sensations rocked Jessie right down to the bone as she held her birth mother. Vaguely aware that Cade had left and closed the door behind him, Jessie gave in to the overwhelming relief that flowed through her.

It was done. The truth was out. The secrets and lies, the wondering and observing and, best of all, the fear of the unknown response, were all over.

Fin backed Jessie just far enough away to scrutinize her face.

"You're an Elliott," Fin announced with a soft laugh of dismay. "How could I have missed that?"

"I did my best not to let you figure it out."

"Why?" Fin gave Jessie's shoulders a quick squeeze. "Why

did you wait? Why didn't you tell me right away? When did you find out? Oh my God, you took this job just to meet me, didn't you?" Then her eyes darkened as she stole a glance at the credenza. "You weren't spying on *Charisma* today. You found my investigator's file."

"I'm sorry, Fin, I—"

Fin placed a single finger on Jessie's mouth. "I understand."

An unbearable weight lifted from Jessie's heart. "Thank you, Fin."

"For wanting to know you? Are you kidding? I've been dying to find you. Ever since I was old enough to get out from underneath my father and look."

"Your father?" An image of the gruff, white-haired man Fin had only seen from afar came to mind. Her biological grandfather, Patrick Elliott. "Did he know? Did he not want you to find me?"

Fin closed her eyes and exhaled. "We have so much to talk about."

"Yes, we do," Jessie agreed. "Twenty-three years' worth."

"I can't believe it's you," Fin repeated, her voice still breathless with wonder. "Right here in front of me. And, Jessie," she touched Jessie's face again, her soft fingertips grazing her jawline. "You're so beautiful. And sweet. And smart."

Jessie laughed self-consciously. "You're biased."

"You bet I am. But I'm also proud of you."

"And I'm proud of you," she said, finally able to look Fin directly in the eye. "I think you're amazing."

Fin's blinked back tears. "How did you find me?"

"Sister Tarsisius."

"Excuse me?"

Jessie grinned. "The head nun at St. Theresa of the Little Flower finally told me your name. It took some tracking, but based on what my mother told me before she…" Jessie trailed off and sighed. "My mother—my adoptive mother—passed away three years ago."

"Oh, honey." Fin's shoulders slumped in sympathy. "I'm sorry. I bet you were close to her."

Jessie watched Fin for signs that talk of her adoptive mother might be uncomfortable. She didn't know why it would be, but then, she'd never been in a situation like this before. "We were very close. And I'm close to my father, too."

"He's in Colorado?"

"Yes, I grew up on a ranch outside Colorado Springs."

Fin beamed. "You're a cowgirl."

"A horse girl. But my dad is a rancher. He's the real deal." Jessie stopped for a moment. "I mean my adoptive dad."

Fin took her hand and clasped it between both of hers. "Honey, you don't have to qualify that. Your parents raised you and loved you and did a supremely fine job of both. I owe them a debt of gratitude."

Jessie cursed the tears that welled up again. She laughed and took a swipe at her eyes. "I think we better get a box of tissues."

"Oh, yes. We will need tissues…and time." Fin's voice cracked slightly. "I want to be alone with you, and absolutely no interruptions from anyone until we've caught up on twenty-three years."

Chloe cracked the door open and inched her face in. Her dark eyes flashed at the sight of the two women embracing.

"Are you all right?" she asked.

Jessie stiffened. Would Fin want the world to know about her daughter?

"We are wonderful!" Fin exclaimed. "But, Chloe, you need to do me a favor."

Chloe opened the door a little further, frowning as she regarded Fin, then Jessie. "Are you guys crying?"

Fin stepped forward protectively. "We are having a moment, Chloe. All women are entitled to moments."

"Of course," Chloe agreed, still a little tentative. "What do you need, Fin?"

"Cancel every single thing on my calendar for the rest of the day, and all of next week."

Chloe almost choked. "Are you serious? You have some critical management meetings, including one with your father."

"My father can take a leap from the top of this building." The other two women gasped slightly but Fin just smiled. "He owes me this time and I'm taking it."

"But what about the contest?" Chloe asked. "And the bottom line?"

"The bottom line just moved," Fin said brightly, putting her arm around Jessie and squeezing her shoulders. "And Cade can look after it for the next few days."

Chloe blinked again and struggled for a response. "Okay. If you say so." She looked hard at Jessie, as though she were really seeing her for the first time. "And, I guess, you're still shadowing Fin."

"Yep." Jessie grinned at Fin. "You might say that."

"We're taking the rest of the day off," Fin announced. "No explanations to anyone. Just inform everyone that I'm taking personal time and do not want to be disturbed, for any reason."

Chloe nodded, backing out of the room. "Do you want to tell all this to Cade before you leave?"

Fin opened her mouth, and then froze as though she was rethinking her response. She looked at Jessie. "I bet you want to talk to him."

Did she? What satisfaction would it give her? He'd apologize or maybe he'd be mad she didn't tell him, or he'd offer some explanation for why he asked her out when all he was doing was investigating her.

She could still hear the words she'd caught him saying as she marched up to Fin's office, her confession ready.

I only went after her in the first place because I was so suspicious of her.

Is that why he slept with her? Did he think she'd confess her traitorous activities in the throes of all that sexual pleasure?

Distaste spiraled through her. No. There was nothing left to say to Cade. At the bottom of all their misunderstandings was a big bad case of distrust. He was determined not to make a mistake and she turned out to be one giant error in judgment for him.

"I don't want to talk to him," Jessie said quietly.

"But I want to talk to you." Once again, he stood in the doorway, his gray gaze looking far less accusatory than the last time he'd walked in on her. "If I could."

Cade had never, ever seen Fin cry. But there she was, tearstained and shuddering. She glanced at Jessie and nudged her with an elbow. "Go." She tilted her head toward the empty conference room adjacent to her office. "You should talk to him before we leave."

Cade shot Fin a grateful look as Jessie quietly walked to the conference room. Once in there, she went immediately to the bank of windows and stared out at New York, while he closed the door behind him.

Where the hell should he start? Knowing women as he did, his gut told him to get the hard stuff out of the way as soon as he could.

"I'm sorry, Jess."

She didn't turn from the windows. "For what, Cade? For asking me out under false pretenses, for making assumptions about my motives, or for threatening to call security when I wanted to talk to Fin?"

She finally turned, the backlighting from the windows enhancing the flare in her green eyes. The look she gave him stabbed as much as the bitterness in her voice.

"All of the above," he said, propping a hip on the corner of the conference room table. "I should have trusted you. I shouldn't have made the comment about security. And I didn't ask you out just to find out the truth."

Her tight grimace told him exactly how much she believed that.

"And, more than anything, Jess, I didn't make love to you for any reason other than the fact that it felt…" Good? Amazing? "Real."

She closed her eyes and didn't respond.

After a moment, he asked, "Why didn't you just tell me?"

"Fin had a right to know first."

Of course she did. That much he'd figured out in the last ten minutes as he sat in his office and tried to piece it all together.

"Anyway, Cade, you wouldn't have believed me." She crossed her arms and took a step toward him. "I'm not going to get ugly or nasty. What just took place in that room, with Fin, is the most monumentally happy thing that's happened in a long time. I've waited…my life, really, to know if—" Her voice cracked and he instinctively reached for her.

"Jessie, I'm happy for you." She stiffened as he took her shoulders. "How did you know Fin is your birth mother?"

She met his gaze. "I found out her name and saw she'd listed herself on an adoption finder's Web site."

"So, you came here just to meet her?"

She slid out of his light grasp. "I do have a degree in graphic design and a minor in fashion, if that's what you're implying."

He blew out a breath. "I'm not implying anything." They had so far to go to get back to the closeness they'd had last weekend.

"When I found out that Finola Elliott, the woman who'd edited my very favorite magazine, was my birth mother, well, it just made sense. The fashion and design gene," she said with a weak smile, "must be pretty strong. I wanted to get to know her, to determine if she really wanted to meet a child she'd given up for adoption. So I applied for the internship."

"Why did you avoid her, then?"

"I thought she'd take one look at me and see this." She indicated her face with two hands.

How could he have missed how much she resembled Fin? The arch to her brows, the slight upward tilt in her green eyes, even the delicate jaw and that pepper spray of freckles. "Funny how you don't see things when you aren't looking for them," he mused. "Even if you hadn't worn those glasses, I don't think I would have made the connection."

For a moment, she just regarded him, doubt and pain so evident in those wide green eyes. "You really hurt me," she finally said.

The simplicity of the statement cut through him. "God, I'm so sorry, Jessie. Can you forgive me?"

He waited while she decided, while she searched his face and, no doubt, her heart. "I can forgive you, Cade. I can even understand why you would think what you thought."

He reached for her, but she stepped back, avoiding his touch.

"But I saw your true colors, Cade."

"My true colors?" He hated the sound of that. "I was watching out for—"

She silenced him by holding up one hand. "You did what you thought was right. You put your company and work first and that's very admirable."

"But?" There had to be one.

"But you made love to me and all the while you doubted me."

"I didn't. Not after I'd spent any time with you at all." How could he get her to believe him? "But then I heard you on the phone talking about secrets. When you wouldn't answer me, it all made sense," he repeated, hearing the miserable defense fall flat between them.

"It doesn't make sense to me."

"Jessie." This time he grasped her hands and pulled her against him, wrapping his arms around her. "Please give me another chance."

He lowered his head and kissed her soft, sweet-smelling hair. He'd give her time. He'd give her the opportunity to handle what was surely going to be an Elliott-rocking event. But then he would show her that…

That what?

She slipped out of his hold. "Cade, I've waited too long for this day to let it be ruined." Then she walked back into Fin's office without turning around.

He closed his eyes and let the ache roll over him. When he opened them, his gaze landed on a burst of yellow on the layout wall. In the picture, she looked so sexy, so pretty, so fresh. All the stuff he loved about Jessie captured in one candid shot.

Loved?

Oh, yeah. Why fight it? This was love, and this was real.

And this might very well be over.

For a man who hated making mistakes, he'd just committed a whopper.

* * *

Sipping the dry chardonnay after a long and satisfying dinner at Fin's apartment, Jessie tucked her bare feet under her and looked out at the darkened skyscape of New York and the smattering of lights throughout Central Park.

It had taken a full fifteen minutes just to absorb the view from Fin's magnificent Upper East Side apartment. But it had taken the remainder of the afternoon and well into the evening for Fin and Jessie to absorb the overwhelming newness of their relationship. For hours, they'd talked about everything. And still they hadn't covered a few important topics.

Like who was Jessie's father, and why had Fin decided on adoption.

Instead, Fin seemed focused on inhaling moments of Jessie's life that she'd missed. How old Jessie had been when she took her first steps, when she talked. What her high school years had been like. Why she was so mysteriously drawn to fashion and design. What it had been like to grow up on a Colorado ranch.

But now, as night took hold of the city, Fin finally seemed ready to share.

"I always told myself if I found you, I might be able to forgive my parents." Fin fingered the fringe of a silky throw pillow she cradled in her arms, her high heels long ago abandoned for comfort as she, too, tucked herself onto the same sofa with Jessie.

"So what happened back then?" Jessie asked gently. "How did you…" She wanted to ask, "How did you get pregnant?" but that seemed like a laughably stupid question. Still, more than anything, she wanted to know about her biological father. But she'd take her cues from Fin. "How did you finally make the decision to give up your baby?"

Fin let out a soft, unladylike snort and flipped back her shoulder-length hair, rolling her eyes to the ceiling. "I didn't make the decision, honey. I was fifteen, the daughter of the most intimidating, controlling man you'd ever want to meet, who was married to a woman who didn't dare oppose him, at least not publicly. And don't forget, I'm an Elliott and we have quite a reputation to maintain."

The image of a scared, troubled, pregnant teen in that particular scenario clashed with the ambitious, dynamic woman Jessie had come to know. Her heart clutched a little as she related to how frightening it must have been for Fin.

"I'm sorry," Jessie whispered.

Fin's eyes flashed. "It was not your fault, honey." She plucked at the fringe again, studying the pillow for a long time before she met Jessie's gaze. "His name was Sebastian Deveraux. And, yes, I loved him." Her expression softened as she offered up a wry smile. "As much as a fifteen-year-old can know about love."

"Sebastian Deveraux." Jessie let her biological father's name play over her lips for the first time. "He sounds sexy."

Fin laughed softly. "Oh, he was that."

"Was?" The word slipped out before Jessie could check herself. "Do you know where he is now?"

Fin sat up, reaching over to touch Jessie's hand. "He died, sweetheart."

Jessie sucked in a soft breath. "When?"

"About five years after you were born, he was killed in a car accident. I never saw him again, after my parents found out I was pregnant. He was from the same kind of family, with all the trappings of our country club lifestyle, and his parents were no happier about the situation than mine. They sent him to a military academy shortly after mine sent me to a 'finishing school.'" She made air quotes around the term. "Which, as you know, is a euphemism for St. Theresa of the Little Flower, where I had you."

"Did you…" Jessie's stomach tightened. "Did you think about keeping me?"

"Oh my God." Fin flipped the pillow to the floor as she reached to hug Jessie. "You have no idea. When that nun carried you away…" Fin's voice cracked as she leaned her cheek against Jessie's. "I'll never forget that moment as long as I live. That woman, that horrible woman in black disappearing with my tiny, wailing baby." She shuddered and squeezed Jessie tighter. "They never let me hold you. The one nurse, though…she whispered, 'You have a perfect baby girl.'"

Jessie's heart tumbled.

"I've said those words to myself a million times since then," Fin admitted. "I have a perfect baby girl. Somewhere."

Jessie let out a soft moan as they clung to each other for a long time.

"Of course, I blamed my father," Fin continued, as though she couldn't stop now that she'd started the story. "He told them not to let me hold you, not to let me have one minute with you. I hated him for that and hated my mother for going along with it."

"Oh, Fin."

Fin shook her head. "You'd think a woman who gave birth to all those children would be more sympathetic."

The impact of Fin's words settled over Jessie. Would her grandparents refuse to accept her now? Worry gripped her. Would they want her to disappear again?

A light tap on the door of Fin's apartment surprised them both.

"Doesn't the doorman call you before someone comes here?" Jessie asked.

"Not if my visitor lives in the building," Fin said, rising to answer the door.

"Who do you mean?"

"Get ready, Jessie. You are about to meet your first Elliott as an Elliott." She padded in her stocking feet across the expanse of the living room to her front door. "That you, Shane?"

"Fin, what's going on?" Shane Elliott's baritone rumbled through the door. "Why did you run off today? Chloe said—"

Fin whipped the door open and faced her twin brother. "Chloe said what?"

Shane looked beyond her, his gaze falling on Jessie. "So you did leave with her." He looked back at Fin. "Chloe said you were crying and acting weird."

"They were tears of joy, Shane." Fin tugged the door wider and indicated for him to enter. "Come on in, I want you to meet someone."

Jessie stood slowly. She'd met Shane Elliott once, at an EPH function, and had seen him in Fin's office and around the building. It wasn't like anyone could miss a version of Fin that came wrapped in six-feet-two of strapping male complete with the moss-green eyes and just enough oxblood in his dark hair to brand him as all Elliott.

And her blood uncle.

Oh, Lord. It was one thing to reveal herself to Fin, but now that the deed was done, Jessie had to face all of the Elliotts with no guarantee any of them would welcome her.

Shane stepped into the apartment, offering his easy smile to Jessie, but tempering it with a wary glance at his sister. "Are you in the middle of a meeting or something?"

Fin put her arm on Shane's shoulder and guided him into the living room. Her eyes sparkled and her mouth tipped up in a secret, triumphant smile that gave Jessie a much-needed injection of confidence. She had Fin's support. Wasn't that all that mattered?

"Shane, this is Jessie Clayton."

He nodded and reached out a hand in greeting. "I think we've met. Aren't you a *Charisma* intern?"

Jessie tilted her head in acknowledgement as they shook hands. "Among other things."

"Shane." Jessie could see Fin's fingertips tighten her grasp of Shane's arm. "Look at her."

He did. Hard and long. A bubbly brew of anticipation and dread numbed Jessie's limbs.

"Look at her," Fin repeated, abandoning Shane's side to stand by Jessie and wrap an arm around her waist. "Guess who this is? Can't you see?"

Shane frowned, saying nothing, studying Jessie, then Fin. The crease between his eyes deepened as he volleyed his gaze again. Then he took one step back, his jaw loose. "No."

Fin squeezed Jessie's waist. "Yes."

"Holy—" Shane's expression shifted from shock to elation. "You found her, Fin!" He shoved his fingers into his hair, laughing and shaking his head as he stared at Jessie. "You found her!"

"She found me," Fin said softly.

In an instant, Shane bolted forward and circled Jessie in a powerful, spontaneous bear hug. "I don't believe it!"

Firecrackers of delight popped in Jessie's head as she closed her eyes and let Shane embrace her with the unabashed enthusiasm of a favorite uncle. Like Fin, he drew back, inspected her and squeezed her again. Like Fin, he had a million questions and kept interrupting them to express amazement that she was such an Elliott and had slipped right in under their notice. And like Fin, he made Jessie feel utterly welcome and wanted.

Then talk turned to Patrick Elliott, and Shane and Fin shared a look that spoke volumes. Volumes that Jessie didn't think she wanted to read.

"Give it to me straight," she said from her comfy chair, looking at Fin and Shane on the sofa. "Is he going to hate me?"

Neither one said anything.

"What about your mother?" Jessie asked.

Again, they just exchanged silent glances, then Fin folded her arms defiantly. "I don't give a damn what either one of them says. They stole you from me—well, my father did. My mother just let him."

Shane placed a comforting hand on Fin's shoulder. "So many years have passed, Fin. I can't believe he'd hold onto old anger."

Fin gave him a look that said "get real." "This is Patrick Elliott we're talking about. Control freak and keeper of all that is Elliott and sacred."

"Do you think he'd flat-out reject me?" Jessie asked. "And your mother would, too?"

Shane shook his head. "Mom will do what is best for the family, but she does take her cues from Dad."

"The fact that their fifteen-year-old darling got pregnant was a sore spot twenty-three years ago," Fin said.

"I imagine it's still going to be a little tender," Jessie said

But Fin gave her a loving smile. "I'll watch your back. And if anyone tries to mess with you, they have to deal with me."

"And me," Shane said, shooting to his feet. "In fact, this calls for a celebration."

Fin looked up at him. "What do you have in mind?"

He grinned. "An official welcoming of Jessie. I think it's time the Elliotts leave the competition at the door and put on our dancing shoes."

"Dancing?" Jessie laughed.

"Precisely," Shane said. "Dancing, champagne, black tie, the works. This is a major event in the history of the Elliott family. Like a wedding, a birth, a golden anniversary."

"Oh, Shane!" Fin exclaimed, clasping her hands together in delight. "The official welcoming party. I love the idea."

Shane crouched down in front of Jessie. "You know, Jessie, we've lost a few members of the family over the years." He glanced at Fin, sadness in his eyes. "Our brother and his wife were killed in a plane crash fifteen years ago. There's been a hole in the family ever since."

"And in my mother's heart," Fin added softly.

"What could be more worthy of a celebration than finding someone who's been gone?" He took her hand and squeezed it. "I want to do this for you, Jessie. I want to throw a gala event that will show our family and the world that we welcome you. May I?"

Jessie blinked and looked at her uncle. Then at Fin, who didn't bother to wipe the teardrops that meandered down her cheeks.

"I can't believe how lucky I am."

"No, Jessie," Fin whispered, picking up that pillow and hugging it to her heart. "I'm the lucky one."

"We need to make an invitation list," Shane announced. "Everyone in the family, close friends, the executives of every magazine—"

"No." The word was out before Jessie could stop herself. At their surprised looks, she added, "This is just family and friends, right? Not work."

"Most of our friends are work," Shane said dryly. "Or at least we pretend like they are."

Fin gave Jessie a knowing look. "Is it Cade, honey?"

Fin knew, of course, that she and Cade had been together. And she'd been there when he'd accused her of spying. But Shane knew nothing of her affair with the executive editor of the magazine.

And, after all, it was an affair. Because if it had been anything else, anything more meaningful or lasting, Cade would have trusted her.

"You know, Jessie," Fin finally said, "I suspect Cade McMann is nursing a couple of black-and-blue shins from kicking himself tonight."

The thought gave her little satisfaction. "Then he'll have a hard time dancing at our party, won't he?" She managed a sly smile at Fin. "Sure, add him to the list. Why not?"

In spite of everything that had transpired that day, the truth was, Jessie still ached for Cade.

Eleven

"Where's the key to The Closet?" Jessie asked into the phone, keeping her voice low even though the *Charisma* offices were completely deserted.

"What are you talking about?" Lainie's voice was heavy with sleep and no small amount of irritation at the wake-up call. "Where are you?"

"I'm at work right now, and I need the key."

Jessie had crashed at Fin's on Friday night after Shane left, and Saturday too. On Sunday, she made two calls: to Lainie and to her father. Dad had been overjoyed that Fin had welcomed Jessie into her life, but Lainie had a million questions that Jessie had left unanswered. And she didn't want to launch into them now. Not while she was on a mission.

"What time is it?" Lainie asked, still sounding sluggish as she struggled to wake up. "What are you doing there?"

"It's about eleven-fifteen," Jessie said. "I left Fin's a while ago and I was going to come straight home, but I remembered that Spring Fling project needed to get moved into preproduction."

"Why don't you do it tomorrow?" Jessie could hear Lainie shifting in bed, probably reaching for the lamp and blinking madly.

"Fin and I are taking this whole week off. We're just going to hang out and catch up and get ready for the party I told you about. I really don't want to come back in here for a week."

The truth was, she wasn't ready to face the whole company yet. She didn't want to face Cade. Not yet. Her thoughts and feelings were still too jumbled and too raw. "I just stopped in here so I could handle that one production thing, so Scarlet wouldn't have to worry about it."

"Jessie, you're Fin Elliott's daughter," Lainie said with her best get-a-clue tone. "I think your *cousin* Scarlet will stop being your *boss* Scarlet and let you slide on this one."

"Lainie, don't do this," Jessie warned. "I'm the same person. And I still have a job to do."

"Okay. Fine. You're too devoted for words. But what do you want in The Closet?"

"That mint-green de la Renta."

"Oooh," Lainie cooed. "Killer dress. And I think it's your size, too."

"Fin said I could wear it to my welcoming party."

"Oh, man, with your eyes and body, you're right. You *need* that dress."

"Thank you. So, where's the key? Hurry up, this place is pitch-black and a little creepy."

"Open my bottom desk drawer."

Jessie did.

"Reach to the far left corner in the back. Feel the leather pouch?"

"Got it. What is this?"

"The key to where I keep the key." At Jessie's exasperated exhale, Lainie defended her security system. "That de la Renta alone is worth about six grand, sweetheart. The whole closet has about two hundred thousand dollars of clothes and accessories. I don't want just anyone burglarizing it in the middle of the night."

"Just your roommate."

"Well, you are Fin Elliott's daughter."

"Stop," Jessie chided. "Not another word from you."

"I cleaned the apartment."

Jessie scowled at the abrupt change of subject. "Why?"

"Won't I need to find a new roommate now that you're—"

"Cut it out, Lainie. I'm not going anywhere." She thought she heard a sound from the hall and peered out into the darkness. Nothing. "Except in that closet. Bye."

Key in hand, Jessie slipped into The Closet and put on one soft light behind the curtain of a dressing area. She didn't want to draw attention to the night security guard if he happened by. Might be tough to convince him that the editor-in-chief was her birth mother and she'd given permission for Jessie to borrow a designer dress for a party given in her honor.

No, she'd rather avoid that conversation and the ensuing arrest.

Tiptoeing across the cluttered central area, she ignored the racks of clothes and shoes and a three-way-mirror, heading straight to the back where the de la Renta hung. With reverent hands, she unzipped the black cloth protector and let a million yards of pale celery silk sigh over her fingertips. From the moment she'd seen this dress, she'd been in love. The top was a simple strappy camisole, fitted to the hips, but the whole bottom half was made of about twenty fluffy, filmy layers of organza frills that cascaded to the floor.

The man was a genius. How could she not name her horse after him? She might have to name her first *child* Oscar. Jessie eased the dress off the hanger, seized by a sizzling temptation. She didn't want to cart this creation home on the subway without being absolutely sure she wanted to wear it for the party. She simply *had* to try it on.

In a flash, she slid off the jeans she'd borrowed from Fin, and then stripped off the white T-shirt that she wore. She unhooked her bra and glanced down at her underwear. Serviceable, but a crime under this dress. She slid off her panties and walked naked to the lingerie cases, pulling out a whisper of peach-colored silk and lace that had only been photographed on a table for a special feature on "Undercover Agents."

She slid on the thong, then carefully climbed into the frothy organza, nearly giggling with delight as the magical fabric tickled her legs.

Of course, it was made for a five-foot-nine model, so the last two rows of ruffles pooled around her five-foot-six body. From a shoe cubby, she grabbed a pair of sky-high silver sandals and slipped them on, standing in front of the three-way-mirror and grinning like a fool. Then she did one slow, graceful pirouette.

"I love you, Oscar de la Renta." This dress was perfect for the night she would be welcomed by the Elliott family. She'd feel beautiful, confident, glorious.

And Cade would see her.

Sighing, she unclipped her hair and shook it out, letting it tumble like her own Oscar's sorrel-colored mane, imagining how she'd wear it next Saturday, along with a tiny bit of makeup that would make her eyes sparkle and match the amazing dress.

And then he'd dance with her.

The possibility made her tingle right down to the three-inch heels. She stared in the mirror, but instead of seeing herself, she visualized his expression when he saw her dressed like this. She imagined his powerful hands as he would reach for her to touch this dress. She practically tasted his long, soulful kiss at the end of a slow, sensual dance.

She froze, put her hands over her mouth and stared at the agony mirrored in her green eyes. She missed him so much it hurt. "Was he the best thing that ever happened to me? Was I wrong for pushing him away?" she murmured into her hands. "How can I live without him? I love him."

"Are you sure?"

With a gasp she blinked into the mirror at the image of Cade, standing in the partially opened doorway.

She twirled around, the skirt whooshing as fast as the blood in her head. "What are you doing here?"

"Listening to you worship at the altar of de la Renta." With his toe, he gently kicked the door open wider and leaned against the jamb, raking her with one long, hungry gaze. "And totally enjoying the view."

She touched the dress and speared him with a look. "No need to call security. Fin said I could borrow it."

"Jessie." His voice softened. "I didn't make any accusations." His gaze traveled over her at a maddeningly slow pace. The room was silent and still and very, very warm.

"That dress," he said, his words as lazy as his wandering gaze, "was made for you."

"Thanks." She plucked at a silky frill, but her attention was really on the way his black T-shirt clung to his muscles and on the temperature-rising bulge of his faded blue jeans. Silk and organza were nice, but denim and cotton had had a fine place in the world, too.

"So, you can't live without him. You love him."

"I was talking about my horse," she said quickly. "And you seem to be very adept at overhearing me."

He notched an eyebrow. "I saw the light under the door and had to see who was in here. And why."

"What are you doing here at this hour?"

"Working."

"At eleven-thirty on a Sunday night?"

"I blew off the weekend," he said with a casual shrug.

"What did you do?"

He crossed his arms with a pitiful expression. "It wasn't pretty."

What had Fin said? His shins would be black and blue from kicking himself? "You'll be okay," she said, fueled by the confidence that came from wearing a beautiful dress and having a gorgeous man stare lustily at the woman in it.

"Ya think so?" He took one step further.

She had to stop this game. Before she lost. "You'll get over me," she said simply.

The soft light cast a shadow over the stubble on his cheeks. She'd bet he hadn't shaved since Friday.

It wasn't pretty.

"I don't want to get over you, Jessie."

"Then what do you want?" She heard the temptress in her voice. White lightning zinged through her veins and a familiar ache started low in her belly.

"You."

"Cade." His name tumbled out of her lips, but she hardly heard it for the thundering rush of blood through her head.

He was an arm's length away, taking all the air and space and probably the common sense right out of the room. Who needed to breathe? Who needed to move? And, to be honest, common sense was overrated.

"Jessie." He reached for her, settling his hands on the sliver of silk at her waist. As carefully as if he were turning a priceless Ming vase, he rotated her around, so that she faced the mirror.

All she saw was a sea of lime sherbet silk, and Cade behind her, holding her, lowering his head to kiss her bare shoulder. His lips skimmed her flesh, his teeth nipping at the spaghetti strap that held the dress on her.

"I made the worst mistake of my life," he whispered, sliding his finger under the strap as though he were testing it. "And I want to undo that mistake."

What he was about to undo was the world's most beautiful dress. Along with her reason and ability to resist.

Wasn't she mad as hell at him? Didn't he break her heart, her trust, her spirit? She tried to muster anger and resentment, but not one ounce of either one would surface.

"Listen to me," he insisted, holding her gaze in the mirror. "I am so, so sorry I hurt you. I would do anything to take it back. To have another chance. To not make the mistake of losing you."

She tried to say his name, but no sound came out as she stared at his reflection, at the sincerity in his eyes.

"Jessie, I won't walk away," he continued, his raspy tone softened by his tender hands that caressed her arms and clasped her bare shoulders. "I won't get over you." Easily, he glided one shoulder strap to the side, then started nudging the other one. "I won't forget you." Both straps loose, the bodice of the dress dropped dangerously low over her breasts. "I won't stop…" He inched it down, down, down. The darkened circles of her nipples peeked out of the fabric's edge, torturing her breasts with the breath of silk. "Unless you want me to."

She lowered her head back into his chest, surrendering to the sensation of pleasure and need and want and Cade.

What she wanted was this.

Six thousand dollars' worth of mint-colored organza and silk billowed to the floor. To the front, the right, the left and in a million echoes of reflected mirrors, she stood naked but for a flash of peach lace and a cloud of green pooled at her feet.

In the mirror, she watched his powerful hands close over her breasts, and gasped as pleasure coiled between her legs and nipples budded against his palms. Slowly, he circled her breasts, tweaking the darkened peaks, weakening her knees and dissolving every ounce of willpower.

Gradually, leisurely, he slid his hands over her stomach, pulling her into him so she could feel the roughness of his bulging jeans grazing and growing against her bare backside. His fingers, so long and dark and masculine against her pale skin, reached the triangle sliver of silk and the skinny straps that held the thong on her hips.

Jessie stared, mesmerized.

One finger dipped into the top of the tiny triangle and stroked once over her tender mound. Her legs nearly buckled as frissons of delight shimmied up and down her thighs.

He glided his hand to the side, and using only his index fingers, he slid the thong down her thighs, exposing the dampened curls between her legs.

Once again, he pulled her against him, his ragged breaths warming her ear, the steady hammer of his heart against her shoulder blades, the relentless pressure of his erection right in the small of her back.

Then he glided both hands over her stomach and dipped

them between her legs, easing one finger into the slick folds and eliciting her low groan of pleasure. She rocked helplessly into his hand.

His mouth closed over her shoulder. He sucked the concave of her collarbone and throat with the same deliberate rhythm that he used to delve his finger into her.

"Let me inside you, Jessie," he whispered against her skin. "Let me make love to you again."

She closed her eyes and nodded, unable to speak.

In one move, he gingerly lifted her over the mountain of organza, and pushed it aside with his foot. Then he swirled her around and backed her into the mirror.

She couldn't think about the dress, the room, the possibility of getting caught. All she could comprehend was the sudden cold surface against her back and the power and size of Cade confining her against the glass.

He trapped her there with his body and gaze and amazing, delicious hands. He lowered his head and captured her with a furious, openmouthed kiss, and a deep moan torn from his chest.

"Nothing," he murmured into her mouth. "I have thought of *nothing* but you for forty-eight hours." He pressed against her, his hands roaming her body.

She turned her head as he trailed his lips over her cheek and teased the edge of her ear with his tongue, opening her eyes to see the vision of Cade in his jaw-dropping black T-shirt and sexy blue jeans, all hard and muscular and touching every inch of her naked body. The reflection in two mirrors, in a million dimensions, seemed to go on forever and ever.

"It's magic, honey," he whispered, seeing where she looked.

"It's madness," she responded. "And I hope it's—"

He narrowed his eyes at her. "Not a mistake," he finished for her. "Believe me. I've made a few. This isn't one of them."

It might be tomorrow, she thought. But she just sighed and closed her eyes.

Then he started kissing his way down her body. No force of nature could close her eyes and stop her from watching the endless reflections of him crouching before her, adoring her breasts with his sweet mouth, dragging his hands over her ribs, licking her navel, kissing her womanhood.

He tasted the flesh of her inner thighs as he lowered the thong over her knees, her calves, and then carefully guided it over her high-heeled sandals.

Glancing up, he gave her a wicked grin. "The shoes can stay."

When he straightened to his full height, he looked down at her, his pewter eyes intense and focused, his jaw clenched, his breathing tight and quick. "Absolutely not a mistake," he said again.

"You've been wrong before."

"Not this time." He rocked into her. "I'm not wrong. This isn't a mistake."

"Even if it is." She tugged at his T-shirt to free it from his jeans. "I want to make it."

In one move, he swiped the T-shirt over his head and threw it to the floor. He pushed her higher up the glass, nearly lifting her feet from the ground. Fire and moisture mixed between her legs as she arched into him, moving in an unstoppable, natural beat, riding the ache and his hardness.

She reached to the snap of his jeans, yanking at the zipper with a soft laugh under her breath. "Come on, Cade."

"Wait," he insisted, reaching into the back pocket of his jeans, yanking a condom package out. "Hold this for a second." He stuck it between her teeth. "But don't take your hands off me."

She laughed around it as he finished undressing and she

raked her free hands through the rough hairs of his chest. He flipped his jeans and boxers to the side, and they landed incongruously next to the minty mountain of designer fluff.

He snagged the condom and ripped it open, barely taking his eyes from her. Sheathed, he slid his erection between her legs, urging her naked body up the slick glass as she opened her thighs to take him.

Kissing her, he penetrated her mouth with his tongue at precisely the instant he entered her. Everything was hot and wet and excruciatingly *right*. She clung to his broad shoulders and wrapped her legs around his hips, as he thrust in to the hilt. She sucked in the scent of sex that filled the little room, grinding out his name with each movement. Sweat and friction heated their skin, as they slid against the glass, against each other.

Again and again he plunged into her, his face dark with the intensity of the pleasure and the helpless, mindless charge toward satisfaction.

"Look at us," he demanded, using his chin to turn her face toward the side mirror. She gasped at the vision, at the sight of this glorious man's body making love to her.

The beauty of it, the realness and the rawness sent her right over the edge. As her body coiled and tightened and creamed for release, she closed her eyes. But when she quaked with pleasure over and over, she finally opened her eyes and watched. In the mirror, she could see him grit his teeth and let out a long, low groan of ecstasy and satisfaction as his orgasm took over, thrusting into her with sharp, hard strokes as his backside tensed and his arms squeezed her.

Finally, spent, he dropped his head against her shoulder, closed his eyes and then she saw his mouth move, saw him say the same words ringing in her blood-drained head.

I love you.

But then, he didn't know she could see him. And saying it out loud might be the biggest mistake of all.

"I feel like a vagabond." Jessie curled into Cade's side, wrapping her silky bare legs around his thighs, the lingering scent of lilac and sleep all over her.

He stroked her skin from throat to navel in one long caress, loving the way she felt as smooth as polished marble and as soft as air. "I don't think a vagabond ever felt like this." He nuzzled in to kiss her neck and she shivered as his tongue touched the little dip in her throat.

"I mean, I haven't slept at home in days. I spent Friday and Saturday night at Fin's, and last night I came here to your place."

"Sorry, but I wasn't about to sleep on The Closet floor and my apartment was closer, and empty. Anyway, you're no vagabond. You have a toothbrush here."

"I have one at Fin's now, too. See? I'm a drifter."

He eased her a little higher on top of him, his morning erection already anticipating the warmth of her body. "Drift up here for a while. I don't have to leave for work for an hour."

"And I'm taking this week off, so there." She climbed up and slid her legs around his hips, and cradled his head in her arms. Her russet-colored hair spilled over his face and neck.

"You may never have to work again," he said, inhaling the dizzying scent of her as his hands cupped her bottom and positioned her on him. "You're the editor-in-chief's daughter, your supervisor's cousin and…"

She arched up, her eyes slit in demand. "Say it."

"Okay." He laughed and lifted his hips and let the burn begin. "You have a special relationship with management."

Her pretty smile faded and, without warning, she tumbled

off him to the side. On her back, she draped one arm over her face and moaned quietly. "This was so not supposed to happen."

"Baby, don't worry." He turned, tucking her closer. "It doesn't change anything."

She lifted her arm to peer at him. "It changes everything."

For a moment, he just let her think about it, while he worked to resist the urge to drop a kiss on the sweet underarm she exposed.

"What exactly changes because we're lovers?" he finally asked. "The situation with Fin, well, that will rock the EPH boat just for sheer gossip and shock value. And, yeah, it sounds like you have some hurdles to overcome with Patrick and Maeve, but we're…" *We're what?* How did he tell her that this wasn't just sex, that this felt so much bigger, so much better than that?

"I didn't plan on any of these new complications when I came here. I just wanted to meet Fin."

"So, I'm back to being a complication." He wasn't sure if that disappointed him or not.

"And work is a complication."

"What do you mean?"

She let out a long, slow breath. "I want a job."

"You have a job. And the way you're working on the shadow assignment virtually guarantees you an editorial assistant position when the internship ends. You know that."

She turned on her side to line up with him. "I want it fair and square," she said, a determined glint in her eye. "Not because you wanted to sleep with me—"

He opened his mouth to protest and she put her hand on his lips and continued, "Or because you wanted to figure out why I was avoiding Fin. Or because of the circumstances of my birth. I want it because I'm good at what I do."

"You are," he assured her. "You would have been picked for shadowing even if you hadn't gotten my attention for avoiding Fin." He couldn't resist. He traced a single line over the sweet skin of her arm. "Or even if you hadn't got my attention, period. Scarlet had already given you rave reviews."

She regarded him for a moment. "Will everyone know that?"

He shrugged. "Cube chatter is part of work, Jess, and you have to rise above it. You prove yourself on every issue of *Charisma* and I want you on the staff. To me, that's the end of the discussion."

"Until we break up."

He froze and stared at her. "We won't."

She scooted higher and challenged him with a look. "How can you be so sure? You know, I proofed an article on this very subject. The lower person on the corporate ladder invariably loses the job and references when an office affair ends. This might not impact your career, but it could wreck mine."

"First of all, you've been reading too many magazines." He leaned closer. "And second of all, this is not an office affair."

"A 'closet' affair?" she laughed.

He moaned at the memory. "I love that closet."

"Seriously." She nudged him. "These are the facts. And coupled with the revelation that I've got Elliott blood in my veins, no one will believe that I earned my spot."

He couldn't argue that she had legitimate concerns. "I understand you feeling that way," he said. "But what can we do? Hide how we feel? Pretend it's not real? Act like we aren't in…interested in each other?"

"Yes."

His chest knotted. "I don't want to hide this. I mean I don't want to flaunt it, but, Jessie, I don't want to hide." He let slow grin cross his face. "Unless it's in The Closet."

"I want it kept secret," she said, ignoring his teasing remark and grasping his shoulder to make her point. "Please, Cade. I don't want anyone to know. Let me get through this time, through this hurdle, as you call it, with the Elliotts."

How long would that take? "Can I see you in the meantime?"

"Secretly."

"I'll take that, then. I guess I have to." But he didn't have to like it.

Twelve

Jessie dialed her dad's phone number as soon as she emerge[d] from the subway station. The week had flown by as sh[e] juggled her days with Fin and a few select members of th[e] Elliott family whom Fin invited to lunch and dinners wit[h] them, and stole away for long, blissful nights with Cade.

Friday evening, however, she'd begged out of dinner wit[h] Fin or Cade for a much-needed stop at her apartment and a[n] evening at home in preparation for the party the next nigh[t.] She still couldn't believe the power of the Elliott name.

She'd been certain Shane couldn't find a location for th[e] grand party he wanted to have, but through a business contac[t] he'd learned that a cold-footed bride had pulled out of a weddin[g] in the ballroom of the Waldorf-Astoria, leaving the venue avai[l]able. Invitations were sent by e-mail and half a dozen admini[s]trative assistants were tasked with handling the RSVPs.

"Hey, Dad," Jessie said as she rounded the top of th[e]

subway station steps and started the walk through the Upper West Side. "Remember me?"

"I don't know," he teased. "Aren't you my best ranch hand who ran off to New Yawk City?"

She giggled at his lousy accent. "Oh, Daddy, I'm sorry I've been scarce. This has been an unbelievable week."

"I'm getting that impression. Still enamored?"

Her heart jumped. "With Fin? Of course. We're having a great time." Her fist tightened around the two Bloomingdale's bags she carried. "She's quite a shopper, and a talker and, well, she's becoming a good friend."

"I'm glad, sweetheart. Now, when are you coming home?"

She paused as she reached Amsterdam, gauging the traffic pattern for a quick cross. "My internship lasts until next spring." She swallowed hard and blurted out the next sentence as she stepped confidently into the street, beating a cab by a good three seconds. "And I hope to have a full-time job at *Charisma* after that."

Someone behind her earned a honked horn, and that filled the silence on the other end of the phone.

"Dad? You still there?"

"I'm here," he assured her. "Just thinking."

Only a daughter would catch the tiny hitch in his voice. "But I'll come and visit before that, I promise."

"Or I'll come to New York. I miss you, Jessie." There was no hitch that time, just raw, fatherly love.

"Oh, Daddy. I miss you, too." Jessie stood at the next corner, staring up at the red bricks of her studio walk-up and blinking back a sudden tear. Was this home now? This aging, metropolitan building with thirty-six stairs up to an apartment the size of Oscar's stall?

Yes. It was. But that didn't mean she couldn't visit the

Silver Moon. That was home, too. "Why don't I come back for a long weekend next month?"

"I'd love that," he replied, his voice rich with relief. "Pick a date."

And then an idea took hold. Fin had told her just that afternoon that she wanted to meet Jessie's father. Quid pro quo, she called it, for all the time Jessie was taking to get to know the Elliotts. "I'd like to bring Fin there, Dad. To meet you."

He snorted. "That city woman wants to come out to a cattle ranch in Colorado? Does she know there's no shopping here?"

Jessie bit back a smile. Was he intimidated by the idea of Fin Elliott on his ranch? Her big, tough cowboy of a dad?

"You know, I think you'll like her," Jessie mused. Maybe that was a stretch, but Jessie clung to the hope that she could make everyone happy with this impulsive offer. "How about Columbus Day weekend? We'll have closed the February issue and Fin and I can come from Friday to Tuesday."

She could be away from Cade that long, couldn't she?

"That's perfect."

As she opened the lock to the front door of her building, her attention was drawn to the floor. And the steps. And the landing to the first floor. "Oh my…"

"What is it?" her father asked.

"Lilacs," she whispered.

"Lilacs?"

Everywhere, as far as she could see, every square inch of the ground and the stairs was blanketed in a snowfall of lilac petals.

"Oh, Cade." Her heart just folded in half from the pressure of how much she loved him.

"What are you talking about, honey?"

"Oh, it's nothing, Daddy." Well, it was something. She jus

didn't know *what*. "Someone left something for me at my apartment."

Gingerly, she tiptoed over the petals and turned the corner at the next floor. More lilac petals.

"Who is Cade?"

It must be a father's job to assume the "never miss a thing" responsibility when a mom was gone. "He's, uh, a guy I work with."

"The executive editor," her father said knowingly. "The one you had drinks with a while ago. About the shadowing job."

The stairs to the third floor were no different. A blanket of lilac petals. "Wow, this is unbelievable."

"What is?"

She suppressed a giggle of delight. "That you really pay attention, Dad. To everything I tell you."

"Of course I do. Is he there now, this Cade?"

Sort of. She climbed the last set of stairs to the fourth floor. "Uh, no. I'm home, at my apartment. Oh, there's more!"

At the door was a giant bouquet in a glass vase, with a card tucked into the green fronds between the puffs of lilacs.

"More what?"

"I'm sorry, Dad. I have to go. I just got home and…there's a message here."

"Honey, are you being straight with me about this Cade?"

She lifted the card and leaned on the door, her gaze traveling over the bed of petals all around the hallway. "Well," she said, "I am sort of…"

"You're in love."

She let go of the laugh that had been caught in her chest. "Yeah. I don't know. Maybe."

"Well you better bring him along next month," Dad said softly. "I'll want to see how he does on a horse."

"No, I can't," she gasped. "He can't come back to Colorado with me."

"Why not?"

"Because I want to keep it secret. We work together. He's my boss, sort of."

Her father cleared his throat. "Angel, I can guess who will take the brunt of this thing if it doesn't work out. I don't want to see your heart broken."

Jessie slid the card open and read the words.

Make no mistake about it, the outside read. She didn't open the card, but answered her father. "I'm watching my heart, Dad."

"And, you know, an affair with a co-worker, especially your boss, well, it can be career suicide."

Affair. The word cut through her. "I've heard that, too."

"So what's more important to you? This guy or this job?"

She flipped open the card.

I'll miss you tonight. Love, Cade.

"Can't I have both?"

"I don't know," he said quietly. "I wish your mother were around to ask. She'd know what you should do."

Jessie's gaze fell on the lilacs, the familiar, comforting scent wafting up from the bouquet.

"She's around," Jessie whispered.

Everything in the Starlight Roof ballroom high above New York City sparkled. The crystal champagne flutes, the tapered candles on the tables, the tiny white lights that floated above the room named for them. But most of all, Fin sparkled.

Jessie marveled at how beautiful her birth mother looked, floating between the round dinner tables to check last-minute changes in seating, a strapless black dress clinging to her slender build, the blunt cut of her auburn hair grazing her shoulders. Every time Fin glanced at Jessie, she beamed.

Jessie stood next to one of the massive arched windows that lined one long wall of the legendary room, drinking in the beauty of the setting, plucking at one of the ruffles on her Oscar de la Renta dream dress and letting the surreal wonder of it all settle over her.

No matter what happened with Patrick and Maeve, she felt loved and welcomed. Now she had two families, and that was a blessing she'd never really expected.

Would they ever blend, her two lives? How would her gritty, gruff father take to the champagne-sipping executive who'd given Jessie birth? For some reason, Jessie wanted her father to like Fin as much as she did, and to realize that although she and Fin would be friends and confidantes, Jessie would always be Travis and Lauren Clayton's daughter.

But tonight, she had to deal with the New York side of her family.

With Patrick and Maeve…and Cade.

"He's not coming." At the whispered words, Jessie wheeled around to meet Shane Elliott's green eyes.

"Cade?"

A flicker of surprise brightened his expression. "No, I believe Cade RSVP'd the day the invitations arrived. I meant Patrick."

"Elliott?"

Shane lifted one handsome brow. "I don't know any others."

Before she could respond, Fin swooped in. "What's the matter?"

Shane and Jessie shared a quick look and in her peripheral vision, Jessie caught sight of Fin's chin lifting a bit in defiance.

"I knew he wouldn't come," she said.

"We're not sure," Shane responded. "But Liam told me that

when he left the office yesterday, Dad said he and Mom were spending the whole weekend relaxing at home."

Home, Jessie knew, was a luxurious Hamptons estate called The Tides. Patrick commuted by helicopter, so getting to and from the city, even on the weekend, was no issue for him.

If he wasn't coming, it wasn't because he couldn't. It was because he wouldn't. She hated the disappointment that formed a lump in her throat, and hated even more that she could see the same emotion on Fin's face.

"It's all right," Jessie said softly. "Really."

"It's all wrong," Fin countered. "But I don't care."

She did, and Jessie knew it.

Liam Elliott joined them with a drink in hand, the first of three hundred people invited to the spontaneous gala.

It was no surprise that Liam's steely blue eyes locked on Jessie as he approached. He may have seen her around the offices, but now she was a bit of a curiosity and she braced herself for the onslaught of stares and conjectures from the hundreds of people she'd meet.

Fin put her hand on Jessie's shoulder. "Have you met my nephew, Liam Elliott?"

"Not formally," Jessie said.

As Liam reached them, Fin said, "Liam, let me introduce Jessie Clayton, who I'm enormously proud to announce is my daughter. Jessie has been raised by her adoptive parents in Colorado, as you know, and I hope you'll join me in welcoming her to the Elliott family."

The words sent a shower of chills cascading down Jessie's bare arms. She slid a grateful glance to Fin before shaking Liam's hand. "It seems we're cousins, Liam," she said with a warm smile.

"Welcome to the family, Jessie." He shook her hand, studying her face closely. Looking for a resemblance he would no doubt find. Then he leaned closer and added, "I can certainly understand why Cade has officially removed himself from the market."

Jessie's jaw slackened.

"Cade?" Shane asked. "Removed himself from what market?"

Liam winked at Jessie but Fin put her hand on his arm. "Is Shane right? Did my father tell you he wasn't coming tonight?"

Liam's gaze softened. "I don't think he is, Fin."

She blew out a disgusted breath and closed her eyes.

Jessie slid her arm around Fin's waist. "Don't let it spoil the night for us."

"You're right. And look who's here!" Fin's face lit up with a smile. "Summer and Zeke, who get the award for coming the farthest on the shortest notice."

Jessie had met Scarlet's twin only once and had immediately liked the "softer" version of the beautiful sisters. But her gaze fell on Summer's fiancé, the world-famous rock star, Zeke Woodlow. The cubicles of all the EPH magazines still vibrated with the story of how Summer met Zeke when she was posing as the more flamboyant twin.

Fin tugged Jessie in the direction of the new arrivals. "Let's make you official with more cousins, and you can meet the bad boy of rock and roll."

Zeke whispered something to Summer and when she laughed, his handsome features softened with pleasure.

"He doesn't look so bad," Jessie said under her breath.

Fin laughed. "It's all an act. He's a cupcake inside, especially when it comes to Summer." As they greeted each other, Fin launched into introductions, eliciting a squeal of delight from Summer and a nod of welcome from Zeke. A minute later, Scarlet and her fiancé, John Harlan, joined them.

"Save your 'she's special' speech, Fin," Scarlet said as she draped an arm around Jessie. "I love her already."

Then Gannon Elliott stepped into the circle, his arms around his pregnant wife, Erika.

"The best thing about Fin finding you is this," Gannon said, indicating the steadily crowding ballroom around them.

"The party?" Jessie asked.

Gannon gave Fin a smile. "A wonderful reason to stop competing for a night and enjoy our family and friends, which keeps growing." He laid a hand on Erika's protruding belly. "One by one."

Everyone laughed and chattered about the twins' planned double ring ceremony, with lots of teasing about the possibility of even more Elliotts.

Scarlet and Fin made sure Jessie was included in the conversation, so that one by one, the Elliotts would get to know her. Most of the Elliotts, anyway. The absence of her birth grandparents niggled at the back of Jessie's mind. And Fin's, Jessie noticed, as they'd both glanced expectantly at the door a few times. But they weren't looking for the same man.

They knew where Patrick Elliott was…but where was Cade?

Within an hour, the ballroom burst with gowns and jewels and tuxedos, and the strains of a soft jazz band filled the multi-tiered room, just loud enough to blend in with the laughter and party talk.

Even though Jessie had met nearly every one of the Elliott family, or had seen them around the EPH offices, Fin made formal introductions every time, each exchange slightly different, but always with the same irrefutable message: *This is my birth daughter and we welcome her with open arms.*

Fin held Jessie's hand, moving from one group to another, pausing just once to take champagne flutes for the two of them from a passing tray. "Here, have some bubbly and stop looking at the door. He'll be here."

Jessie smiled and they let the crystal flutes ding lightly. "You're looking, too, Fin."

Fin sipped the champagne and lifted a narrow shoulder. "I wouldn't be human if I didn't want my father here. And my mother. They owe that to me. To you."

Jessie gave her an understanding look. "He'll come around, Fin. It'll take time."

"I don't care," she said, a little too flippantly. "Anyway, what about Cade? I know he's coming. He told me he wouldn't miss it. He said he can't wait to see you in that dress." Fin waited one beat too long and added a sly smile. "Again."

Jessie felt the heat rise as she touched one of the zillion layers of mint organza that floated around her. "I may have mentioned to him that you let me borrow the de la Renta."

"Keep it," Fin said, taking another sip.

"Fin, I can't!"

"Yes, you…" Her gaze slid past Jessie to the door and suddenly the blood drained from her face as the sly smile disappeared. "Can."

Jessie followed Fin's eyes and the champagne glass almost slipped from her hand as she stared at the distinctive gray-haired gentleman and felt the piercing gaze of eyes the color of a hot gas flame. The patriarch of the Elliott family stood as tall and proud as any of the men he'd sired or grandfathered, and next to him, the gentle Irish woman who'd been at his side for fifty-seven years.

Only the music filled the air as Patrick and Maeve Elliott stood like royalty under the marble rotunda entrance, because all of the guests took a moment to stare, hold their breath and wonder exactly what would happen next.

"I don't believe it," Fin whispered, more to herself than to Jessie.

Jessie squeezed her hand. "Believe it."

Fin's narrow shoulders squared and her delicate jaw hitched up a notch as she met her father's level gaze. The fifty or so people between them seemed to part in slow motion, allowing the two women to stride, hand in hand, across the room. Jessie's chest constricted as her heart pumped wildly, and she could feel Fin's pulse doing the same dance.

Jessie chose to look at Maeve, seeing a mix of warmth and curiosity in the green eyes that were so much like her own. Her seventy-five year-old skin was careworn, but surprisingly few wrinkles appeared on her face. Was that because she wasn't smiling?

Why wasn't she smiling?

Jessie stole a glimpse at Patrick, who still stared at her and not Fin.

It seemed to take forever to cross that room, to cross that gulf that separated father from daughter and granddaughter. Then, Fin and Jessie reached the rotunda and all four of them seemed to freeze.

As Fin cleared her throat, Jessie followed her lead and looked directly into the unwavering gaze of her grandfather.

"I'm so happy you came," Fin said, her voice steady but soft. "And I'm delighted to introduce you to Jessie Clayton. This is my—"

"Ooh." Maeve let out a soft cry as she reached out to Jessie. Automatically, Jessie took her hands and Maeve clasped them tighter. "Look at you," she whispered, her soft Irish lilt already musical to Jessie's ears. "'Tis no doubt you are one of us."

Jessie dared a glance at Patrick. His gaze had moved to Fin and they stared at each other wordlessly.

"Dad, I'd like you to welcome Jessie Clayton to our family." It was a demand, not an invitation.

Behind her, Jessie felt a movement and glanced to see Shane walk up and take her other side. "Isn't it fantastic?" he said, putting an arm around Jessie. "After all these years, we've found her."

"If the truth be told," Maeve said, squeezing Jessie's hands but looking up at her husband, "she found us."

"And for that," Fin said, "I am eternally grateful."

One single vein pulsed in Patrick's neck as he stared at his daughter. "I did what I thought was right."

Fin nodded slightly. "And now I'm doing what is right."

He dragged his gaze to Jessie. She straightened imperceptibly under his inspection and suddenly remembered one question she forgot to ask Fin. What to call him?

"It's a pleasure to meet you," Jessie said softly. "I'm honored and so impressed with your family…sir."

Seconds crawled by. Behind her, a crystal glass dinged against porcelain and the saxophone player melted the last few notes of his song. The elevator door opened and someone far away whispered.

But all of Jessie's focus stayed on Patrick Elliott. The man who had shaped her life when he'd decided her fate. And she waited for him to do so once again.

"Jessie," he said, his gruff voice exactly like her father's when he wanted to sound stern but couldn't. "The grandchildren call me Grandad."

She blinked at him and felt Fin stiffen.

"And what should Jessie call you?" Fin asked.

A whisper of a sigh escaped his lips. "Grandad."

The word washed over her just as Maeve stepped forward and folded Jessie into an embrace. The music started up as the room broke into a spontaneous applause. Jessie closed her eyes and inhaled the soft fragrance of Maeve Elliott, knowing that when she opened them, tears would flow. But that was all right. It was a night for tears.

But when she finally opened her eyes, her gaze landed on the man who'd just stepped out of the elevator and leaned against the wall, watching the tableau unfold.

Cade.

The thing that really got her, more than anything, were the tears in his eyes. Tears of joy for her. Tears of love.

For one moment, for one wild and dreamy moment, Jessie's world felt utterly complete.

He avoided her.

Not that Cade could manage to get anywhere near the lady in lime who was, without a doubt, the star of the Starlight Roof. She was surrounded by new friends and new family.

So Cade satisfied himself by drifting in the background, catching the occasional glance over her shoulder and satisfying himself with the knowledge that she was looking for him.

And the knowledge that he'd seen her out of that dress, out of her mind and out of control. And while that thought had its usual effect below his belt, it was the effect the memory had on his heart and head that made him reel.

His focus on Jessie, deeply involved in a conversation with Scarlet and Summer, was so intense that he didn't even notice Fin sidle up next to him.

"You know what I think, Cade McMann?"

He turned to his boss and grinned. "Usually. That's my job."

"And you're good at it," she said, raising a flute of champagne in a mock toast. "But do you know what I think about Jessie?"

His smile widened, and he used the mention of her name as an excuse to look at her again. "I think you're really happy you finally found a missing piece of yourself."

"Oh." Fin let out a little sound of disbelief. "I can't believe you said that. That is exactly how I feel. I couldn't have put it into words more accurately."

This time he raised his glass. "Told you. Knowing what you think is my job."

Fin tilted her head in acknowledgement. "I do think Jessie is a little piece of my heart that has been missing for twenty-three years. But I also think I'm not the only one in this room who's found someone to fill his empty heart."

He said nothing for a moment, his gaze shifting across the room. "Aren't we a couple of poetic publishing executives tonight?"

"Happiness does that to me." Fin laughed. "But am I right, Cade?"

Just then, Jessie laughed and he could hear the musical sound of it floating across the party toward him. "You're right, Fin."

"So what are you going to do about it?"

At the tiny bit of sharpness in her voice, he turned to Fin. "Are you asking me if I plan to make an honest woman out of her?"

Fin's expression grew serious. "I'm asking, as her mother, that you treat her with all the love and respect that she deserves."

"Fin, this isn't an affair. Jessie has asked me to be discreet. She's actually asked me to be secretive. I'm surprised you know about it."

"I've been spending a lot of time with her," Fin said. "And she's easy to read."

Jessie looked over and caught them both looking at her. Her eyes twinkled and she said something to the twins. Scarlet turned toward him, then Summer.

He held her gaze, beckoning her with his eyes. He couldn't stand being away from her much longer, but it had to be her choice to be with him publicly.

Deliberately, she set down her glass and, moving like a breeze over spring leaves, crossed the room.

"Maybe she's ready," Fin said. "Like I said, she's easy to read."

"What are you two whispering about?" Jessie asked with a gleam in her eye. "As if I didn't know."

It took everything Cade had in him to keep from reaching for her and kissing her glossy mouth. "We were just discussing poetry," he said.

Jessie looked suitably surprised and Cade laughed along with her. But Fin wasn't laughing. Instead, she was blinking back tears.

"What is it, Fin?" Cade asked, putting his hand on her arm. "What's the matter?"

She let out a short, embarrassed laugh. "I haven't cried this much in years." She glanced at Jessie. "Twenty-three, to be precise."

"What's wrong, Fin?" Jessie asked.

She looked from one to the other. "I have to tell you both something important."

They looked at her expectantly, and she took Cade's hand and then Jessie's. "Don't let other people dictate your fate. Don't…" She closed her eyes and that forced a tear down her cheek. "Don't be stubborn or stupid or worried about what people will think. Not when you're in love."

For a long moment, the three of them were silent. In the

background, the opening notes to an ancient love song began to fill the room.

"Do you understand what I'm saying?" Fin asked.

"I think so," Jessie said with a tentative smile.

Cade put his arm around her. "Then listen to your mother, Jessie, and dance with me."

Her smile widened. "I'd love to."

As he guided her toward the dance floor, he turned to wink at Fin, confident that what he was about to do would be met with the approval of Jessie's birth mother.

Jessie slipped into his arms like she'd been there forever. Like she would be there forever.

Pulling her into his chest, Cade slid his hands around her back and she looked up at him as they began to sway to the music.

"Poetry, huh?" Jessie asked with a smile. "Aren't you full of surprises?"

"Did you like the lilacs?"

"I loved the lilacs." She closed her eyes and he dipped almost close enough to kiss her, but inched to her ear to whisper, "You are the most beautiful woman here tonight."

"I thought you weren't coming," she said. "You were late."

"I had something important to do."

"What was that?"

He paused their dance, and she stilled in his arms. "I'll show you later. But I have to ask you something first."

"What is it?"

"Can I kiss you? Here, in front of everyone you know in New York?" He could feel the vibration of her heartbeat, matching his, against his chest. "I don't want to hide this, Jessie. I want everyone here to know that…"

Before he could finish, she stood on her tiptoes, tightened her grip around his neck and covered his mouth with a long, sensuous kiss that sent firecrackers through his body. And from the few gasps he heard in the crowd, a few sparklers hit the audience, too.

"You want everyone to know what, Cade?" she asked as she broke the kiss with a triumphant smile.

"That I love you," he whispered.

Her smile froze.

"I love you," he said again, a little louder.

Her eyes widened and she opened her mouth, but nothing came out.

"I love you." This time, everyone on the dance floor heard.

The music stopped, and everyone turned to look at them.

And in the one second that the room was suspended in silence, he lifted her off her feet, twirled her around and let everyone in the room know the truth. "I love you, Jessie Clayton!"

All around them, the room erupted in clapping and gasps and the "oohs" and "aaahs" from the crowd while the band started the next song, but the only sound Cade could hear was that beautiful wind chime laugh that he had grown to love.

"Come with me," he whispered in her ear. "I have one more surprise for you."

With only a quick glance back to where Fin stood watching them, Jessie slid her hand into Cade's much stronger one and let him guide her to the rotunda and down the first elevator.

"Where are we going?" she asked, her heart still battering so hard that she was breathless. And longing for the chance to tell him she loved him, too. But he didn't wait, didn't pause.

Through the lobby, onto the street, he slipped out of his tuxedo jacket and put it over her bare shoulders. "It's a little chilly, but worth it, I promise."

She curled into the silky fabric, happy for the warmth

against the cool September air, but completely bewildered. "Why are we leaving my party?"

"Because you need some wide open spaces and horses."

"Now?"

"Now."

Even at night, the street bustled with pedestrians and tourists, and taxis plowed along at well over the safe speed limit. But her attention was caught by a cluster of hansom cabs, lined up and waiting to take a lucky couple a romantic ride.

"There he is."

"Who?" she asked.

Cade flashed her a smile as they walked, pausing when they arrived at one particularly beautiful carriage painted a brilliant white and decorated with two massive bouquets of...

"Lilacs." She let out a soft laugh and curled into Cade's arm. "You're crazy, you know that?"

As they settled into the back of the fairy-tale carriage, the horse's hooves clopped steadily along the concrete and a nearly full moon peeked out from a cloud.

"This is perfect," Jessie pronounced, falling back against the cool black leather. "Everyone is going to wonder where we went, but I don't care."

"We'll tell them," he said, wrapping his arm around her. "Because this isn't secret anymore."

She looked up at him and held his gaze. "Can I please say what I've been wanting to say since that dance ended?"

"No," he responded. "Not yet."

She opened her mouth in protest. "Cade, don't you want to know that I—"

He put one hand over her mouth and reached in his pocket with the other. Frozen, all Jessie could move was her eyes, and she looked down at the black box in Cade's hand.

"All I want you to say is *yes*."

When he opened the box, the princess-cut diamond caught the light of the moon. Jessie stared at the engagement ring, too speechless and stunned to move.

Finally, she lifted her gaze to meet his.

"Jessie, this is not an affair. This is not a brief romance and this is not a secret." His gray eyes burned with the need to make her believe him. "This is real. This is love. Will you marry me?"

A little laugh, mixed with a sob, caught in her throat. "Yes," she whispered. "Yes, I will."

Cade took the ring out of the box and slid it on her finger, his own hands shaking just a bit.

"Now," he said with a half smile, "what did you want to tell me?"

She leaned her head against his shoulder and let the horse's steady trot jostle her into him.

"I'll tell you later," she said. "And every day for the rest of our lives."

* * * * *